"*Singing with the Top Down* has everything I love in a novel: a colorful cast of characters with the most appealing heroine since Scout Finch; a rollicking plot that kept me up late turning pages; and a story that's tender, heartwarming, and wise. I'm telling everyone I know: Don't miss this one!"

—Cassandra King, author of *Making Waves,*
The Sunday Wife, and *The Same Sweet Girls*

"*Singing with the Top Down* is a feast for the heart. Wise, witty, and tender, this wonderful novel brims with expertly crafted characters and sparkling dialogue. A true pleasure!"   —Karin Gillespie, author of the Bottom Dollar Girls novels

"Debrah Williamson weaves tragedy and humor into a powerful coming-of-age story. Pauly Mahoney is a shining star, and the story of her journey through a tough adolescence and the American heartland is a winner. Take the trip with Pauly, Buddy, Aunt Nora, Tyb, and Puppy—and savor the pleasures of Williamson's masterful storytelling."

—Carolyn Haines, author of *Judas Burning* and
the Mississippi Delta mystery series

"Debrah Williamson creates characters who are spunky, flawed, courageous, lovable, and above all real. With writing that sparkles, a story that shines, and a narrator who's nothing if not spunky, *Singing* is a story you can fall into and believe until the journey's end."

—Lisa Wingate, author of *Drenched in Light* and
Over the Moon at the Big Lizard Diner

continued . . .

"Pauly Mahoney, Debrah Williamson's protagonist in her wonderful novel *Singing with the Top Down*, is my favorite literary kid since Will Tweedy of Olive Ann Burns's classic *Cold Sassy Tree*. Pauly's story of finding a 'chosen' family after her parents die in a tragic carnival accident is filled with moments both laugh-out-loud funny and intensely poignant. There were lines on almost every page that I had to reread because they were so deliciously good. With Southern flair, biting wit, and charming characters, this novel is a delight."

—Dayna Dunbar, author of *Saints and Sinners of Okay County*
and *The Wings That Fly Us Home*

"This is the delightful story of the westward journey that parallels the pioneer tradition, complete with outlaws, Indians, and fellow travelers of various sorts. So put the top down on the convertible and join Pauly, Buddy, Aunt Nora, Tyb, and Puppy for high adventure. But watch out—there may be a mummy in the trunk!"

—Ann B. Ross, author of the Miss Julia series

Singing with the Top Down

Debrah Williamson

 NEW AMERICAN LIBRARY

New American Library
Published by New American Library, a division of
Penguin Group (USA) Inc., 375 Hudson Street,
New York, New York 10014, USA
Penguin Group (Canada), 90 Eglinton Avenue East, Suite 700, Toronto,
Ontario M4P 2Y3, Canada (a division of Pearson Penguin Canada Inc.)
Penguin Books Ltd., 80 Strand, London WC2R 0RL, England
Penguin Ireland, 25 St. Stephen's Green, Dublin 2,
Ireland (a division of Penguin Books Ltd.)
Penguin Group (Australia), 250 Camberwell Road, Camberwell, Victoria 3124,
Australia (a division of Pearson Australia Group Pty. Ltd.)
Penguin Books India Pvt. Ltd., 11 Community Centre, Panchsheel Park,
New Delhi - 110 017, India
Penguin Group (NZ), cnr Airborne and Rosedale Roads, Albany,
Auckland 1310, New Zealand (a division of Pearson New Zealand Ltd.)
Penguin Books (South Africa) (Pty.) Ltd., 24 Sturdee Avenue,
Rosebank, Johannesburg 2196, South Africa

Penguin Books Ltd., Registered Offices:
80 Strand, London WC2R 0RL, England

First published by New American Library,
a division of Penguin Group (USA) Inc.

First Printing, September 2006
10   9   8   7   6   5   4   3   2

 REGISTERED TRADEMARK—MARCA REGISTRADA

LIBRARY OF CONGRESS CATALOGING-IN-PUBLICATION DATA:

Williamson, Debrah.
  Singing with the top down/Debrah Williamson
       p.   cm.
    ISBN 0-451-21926-0
    I. Aunts—Fiction. I. Title.
  PS3613.07723S56 2006
  813'.6—dc22   2006000862

Set in Centaur MT
Designed by Ginger Legato

Printed in the United States of America

For Adam, Clay, and Caitlyn
—you fill up my heart

Acknowledgments

Writing may be a solitary profession, but no one can do it alone.

To everyone who provided help, inspiration, encouragement and friendship over the years, without which this book would not exist, I offer my never-ending gratitude.

To my husband: thanks will never be enough. Your faith in me is my greatest inspiration. You offer the best kind of support and have always given me plenty of room to write. You understand my writer neuroses and love me anyway. You feed me when I am on deadline and never fail to keep the coffee coming. Where would I be without you?

To my children: please don't hold all the hours I spend writing against me. You know I love you, even when my head is somewhere else.

To my mother: you taught me determination by quiet example and made me strong.

To my late father: I miss you, and your life continues to inspire me.

To my writing friends: you made me turn in pages and helped me keep my focus when the going got rough. Willie Ferguson, Diana Duncan, Cindy Munoz, Susan Gable, Tina Ferrarro, Deanna Carlyle and the Desperadas: to thank you all for everything would require a book of its own.

To the BS List: the combined generosity and brainstorming prowess of the group are amazing.

To my agent, Pamela Harty: thank you for everything. My writing goal is to live up to your expectations.

To my editor, Ellen Edwards: working with you is a joy. Thank you for loving the book of my heart and for helping me make it better.

To my students: your energy and hope and talent feed my writing passion and keep me hopeful too.

And to my readers: thank you for choosing to spend your time with a figment of my imagination.

Have Fun or Else

I had a bad feeling that hot July night. We had no business gadding off to the Fabulous Fortuno Brothers Traveling Carnival, and I did my level best to shoot down the idea. When objections based on uneasy gut feelings failed, I fell back on practical financial considerations.

My folks ignored both.

Once my father made up his mind to cut one of Mama's bad moods off at the pass, vague misgivings didn't stand a chance. Neither did plain truth and common sense. When Johnny Mahoney undertook to create a diversion, both hell *and* high water could not stop the fun.

If I had understood destiny and fateful decisions and things meant to be, I could have built a stronger case for staying home. Being a kid, I had not yet learned about such miracles. There was no way I could have known that before the night was over, our world would be turned up-side down and changed forever.

Funny thing about that. Life doesn't come with warning labels or flashing caution lights or men in safety vests waving flags to direct us out of harm's way.

Maybe it should.

The carnies had set up shop down by the Arkansas River on the edge of town. The colored lights of the Ferris wheel and Crazy Snake roller coaster spangled the dark water like dime-store jewelry spilled on black velvet. Carousel music rolled off the midway in big drowning waves and promised to make us forget our troubles for a while. Since I didn't want to be there, the hollow magic did not work on me.

Mama named me after the movie star Paulette Goddard. Pop decided Paulette was too Frenchified for our part of town and cut it down to the bone. Pauly Mahoney was not an easy name to live with. Paulywog. Pauly want a cracker. Pauly Wolly Doodle All the Day.

Since we hadn't yet wasted any of the rent money, there was still a chance reason might prevail. Prevail, meaning to triumph through strength or superiority, was a stout book word that I seldom got to use in everyday conversation. Justice prevails, as does true love. At least in novels and movies.

Pop gunned the car twice around the grassy parking area, looking for a space where he would not have to back out. The 1939 Ford's reverse gear had gone south in April, and no one had thought to get it fixed.

I raised my voice to be heard over the roar of the tee-totally shot muffler. "Maybe we need to think about this."

"*This* isn't a spelling bee, Pauly." Pop steered with one hand and ashed a smoking Camel with the other. "This is a carnival. No thinking required tonight."

"But, Pop, we can't afford to blow money at the carnival."

He cruised down the last row of cars again. "Let it go, girl. Just sit back and quit worrying so much."

Easy for him to say. The role of official Mahoney family worrier had fallen on me because nobody else could handle the job. Worrying gave Mama sick headaches and sent Pop off to the pool hall. My little brother, Buddy, wasn't qualified for anything complicated, so that left me, and I took my duties seriously. At the going rate, in next year's junior high yearbook, I would be voted Girl Most Likely to Develop an Ulcer.

"But, Pop, rent's due Friday, and we're seven short." Not the shortest we'd ever been, but short enough to work up a fret over. I kept track of our finances in a Big Chief tablet. When Pop cashed a paycheck, he gave me money to hide for the landlord, so he wouldn't forget and spend it on unthrifty things like carnivals.

Pop found a spot he liked, pulled in, and cut the engine. My aching eardrums thanked him. He peered at me in the rearview mirror, one dark brow crooked up like a question mark. "What do you mean short?"

"Short, as in don't have enough."

"Oh, yeah?" Pop had a gift for acting surprised when history repeated itself. According to Nanny Tee, only geese and Johnny Mahoney woke up in a new world every day.

"And you know what Mr. Tuttle said last time." Mr. Tuttle was not nearly as grumpy as some of our previous landlords, but having already been late with the rent twice, we were pushing our luck.

"I can handle that old gasbag." Pop ducked responsibility as he always did. With a wink and a careless wave.

Mahoneys weren't big on what's called financial planning. Bills never got paid on time, and our old car wouldn't start unless we pushed it or parked on a hill. We picked up pop bottles along the road and cashed them in for picture shows instead of groceries. We ate oatmeal for supper because oats were fulfilling and stuck to our ribs until morning. Which was fine and dandy, except on the days we had to eat oatmeal again for breakfast. Mama coveted the green glassware that came free in the box, but I was pretty sick of the rib-sticking stuff.

Mama's aunt Preet liked to say the Mahoneys didn't have a pot to piss in, but she was wrong. A pot to piss in was just about all we ever *did* have.

I had learned some in-case-of-emergency tricks. What with his leg brace and all, Buddy was good at wrenching up and looking pitiful. Sometimes I parked him on a downtown sidewalk with a tin cup in his hand. When the office workers headed out to lunch, they filled the cup with nickels and dimes, which I added to the rent tally. We were careful to dodge the beat cop, who would've run us off our corner, and I made sure Mama never found out what we were up to. She would have tanned my hide with a flyswatter and bought Buddy a Popsicle for all the trauma I put him through.

Begging was one way to look at our operation, but free enterprise sounded better. We provided a valuable community service by giving folks a chance to exercise their generosity. Everybody needed someone to think they were better than, and Buddy and I helped a lot of people that way.

Pop thought the current problem through and frowned at me over the headrest. "You sure the rent's due Friday?"

I sighed. Did he think I made this stuff up? "On the first, same as every month."

"Then I say we worry about it Friday." He tried to look serious, but when he laughed and nudged Mama, I knew serious was not going to happen. Not tonight. He was trying to josh her into a good mood by pretending everything was hunky-dory. He thought if he worked extra hard at being cheerful, he could make her cheerful too. He tried to wink the frown off my face. "Lesson for life, Pauly. Money can't buy happiness."

I plopped back against the seat and folded my arms. Maybe not. But last time I checked, money *could* buy something besides oatmeal down at Wurley's Thrifty Mart.

Buddy perched on the seat beside me, grinning like a skunk in cabbage. That boy knew squat about finances. He could barely tie his shoes. When I was eight, I could spot a bill collector a mile away. I practiced in front of a mirror until I could say, "No, sir, my parents are not home at the moment" with enough wide-eyed sincerity to make him leave. At just-turned thirteen, I knew better than to spend money we didn't have on fun we couldn't afford for reasons that didn't make a lick of sense.

Defeat wasn't something I liked to admit, so I threw my last ace on the table. "Where will we get the money *next* week? Huh?" Pop had been laid off at the luggage plant three days ago. Attaching handles to train cases had been his third job of the year.

"I'll just sign up for unemployment."

If that was his only plan, we were in deep dookey. I had accompanied him to the unemployment office on more than one occasion and was well acquainted with the stingy, steel-rimmed lady who worked there. She approved claims like she had to pay benefits out of her personal passbook savings account.

"That's nothing for sure," I pointed out as we spilled from the car. "Unemployment hardly counts as maybe."

"Stop being such a wet rag, Pauly." Mama slammed the car door with an irritated shove. "For God's sake, when somebody's trying to show you a good time, why can't you just shut your mouth and enjoy yourself for once?"

Why couldn't *they* do the right thing for once? I knew the score. No one was interested in my entertainment. We were there for one reason. Mama. If she didn't shake the blues, and fast, there was a good chance she would make the rest of us miserable too. Pop sent me a pleading look. *Don't. Don't press. Don't push. Don't argue. Don't.*

Knowing better than to talk back and risk being backhanded by Mama in public, I bit my tongue. Turning her back on me, she locked arms with Pop, and they leaned on each other as they floated away. Pop laughed, and Mama looked up at him as if to say, "Keep the fun coming. I might be persuaded."

Without another glance in my direction, my parents struck out across the parking lot and zeroed in on the bright midway like a pair of light-starved moths.

Fate Steps In

My parents lived in a bubble that was just big enough for the two of them. Pricking that bubble was the only way I could get close, but my prickliness just made them mad.

Well, Pop wasn't mad at me. Not yet. But if I kept getting in the way of him propping up Mama, he would be disappointed. I'd long since chosen sides in the battle of her versus us. Since I couldn't please my mother, no matter what, I tried never to let my father down. He didn't mean to hurt my feelings. He couldn't help it if he had to put me last.

Lesson for life. Them's the shakes.

Pop squeezed Mama close to his side. As she had often remarked, he was a handsome devil. A dead ringer for movie star Jeffrey Hunter, except Pop didn't have a dimple and his hair was curly. Mama was as light as he was dark. A strawberry blonde, she was a small June Allyson minus the friendly edges and sweet talk.

It was embarrassing the way they held hands and cuddled in public. People who got married before Pearl Harbor should not still be that lovey-dovey fourteen years later. If they hadn't messed up and had two kids, they could have gone on honeymooning forever with hardly a break in the action.

I yelled at their backs, "Let's stick together. Don't anybody go running off." I grabbed Buddy's hand and we tore out after them. Slowed down by the clunky leg brace he wore, my brother couldn't get much of a move on.

When they hit the midway, Mama made a beeline for the sucker pits. Shoddy game booths tempted passersby with promises and prizes. Ruby red compote dishes. Stuffed Mickey Mouses. Glittery chalkware statues of Snow White. To hear the oily voiced carnies tell it, walking off with the prize of your dreams was a lead-pipe cinch.

"Hey, mister! Toss the rings. Win a big prize."

"C'mon, little lady! Knock over the bottles. Win a bigger prize."

"How about you, kid? Shoot the target. Win the biggest prize of all."

Their slick talk didn't fool me. Nothing in life was easy. Everybody played an angle.

Mama squealed when we passed a dart-throwing booth. "Oh, Johnny. I always wanted a genuine German cuckoo clock. Win one for me, honey-love."

The cheap balsa-wood clocks with puny plastic birds had never been anywhere near the Black Forest. Made in Japan was more like it. "Nuh-uh. We're not playing any games," I said. I gave Pop a little nudge to steer him past the step-right-up carnie man. "They're all rigged. These guys are cheaters. Let's ride a few rides, then go home."

Like an umbrella snapping shut, Mama's smile collapsed into a frown. Saying nothing, she stood still and chill, waiting for Pop to choose. Would he stay or go? Listen to me or meet her demand? Do the smart thing or risk our uneasy security on the off chance of making her frown flip back into a smile?

"Not so fast, young lady." Pop gave me the can-do look that always came right before someone shot him down in flames. "Your mama wants a clock."

He tossed two nickels on the counter. Twirling and spinning in the twinkling light, the coins finally rocked to a stop. Milk money. Toilet paper money. Spare change. Except we couldn't spare it.

According to FDR in the seventh-grade social studies book, poor people lived at the bottom of the economic pyramid. In that case, the Mahoneys were squatters in the bargain basement. We'd never spent New Year's Day and Christmas of the same year in one house. We often moved in the middle of the night, something Pop called chasing the moon. He said landlords were too picky about the first of the month, but I didn't think those thin-lipped men in suit pants and bow ties were in the real estate business for their health.

The carnie slapped a handful of darts on the counter. The smug look he shot me said he didn't expect to fork over any cuckoo clocks tonight.

Pop flexed his dart arm, and I turned away. You can pick a rose and you can pick your nose, but you cannot pick your relatives. I loved my folks, but that didn't mean I liked what they did. When I saw a shooting star or yanked on a pulley bone, I always made the same wish:

Please let Johnny and Gracie Mahoney act more like parents in movies.

Take Judge and Mrs. Hardy, for example. A-1 parents. I didn't care if Pop wore neckties or worked at a courthouse, but it would have been nice if he at least worked *somewhere* most of the time. Movie moms played bridge and baked cookies and propped up the family with good advice. All Mama ever played was solitaire, and she snapped my head off when I pointed out missed moves. You want cookies? Bake them yourself. Need advice? Consult a fortune-teller.

I clutched Buddy's hand and tagged after Mama and Pop as they strolled from game to game, laughing and losing and strewing the rent money. Pop kept plunking down nickels, but he couldn't pop enough balloons or knock over enough bottles or hit enough bull's-eyes to take home the big prize.

The story of his life in a nutshell.

"Nobody goes away empty-handed, mister." The duck-shooting carnie man rattled a box of consolation prizes, and Pop told Mama to pick her poison. She looked over the contents like an oyster diver scouring for pearls. The box was filled with junk, but Buddy's eyes lit up when he spotted a little tin harmonica. He would have been happy with the whistle on a string too. My brother didn't make much noise and was a big fan of things that did.

"How about a big old diamond for my favorite girl?" Pop fished a toy ring out of the box and stuck it on Mama's finger.

She stared at the ring. I knew that look. She was making up her mind. Be mad or be glad. Sad was still a possibility and so was bad. To her credit, she'd been agreeable for a change, but it only took one tiny thing to spin her off in the opposite direction.

Finally, she blew on the ring, polished it on her sleeve, and held out her hand for Pop to admire. "How's the Hope Diamond look on me?"

"Like a million smackers." He kissed the back of her hand, and they wrapped their arms around each other's waists as they sauntered off.

I soaked up Buddy's disappointment and turned him away. Hope Diamond, my foot. The ugly ring would turn her finger green, and she would throw it away in the morning. Buddy could have played with that harmonica until it filled up with spit. He was that easily entertained.

I lagged behind, pouting and angry. The hot air, choky as a damp wool blanket, reeked of popcorn grease and sweat. Too many people were careless about personal hygiene. Nanny Tee said being poor didn't mean we had to look poor. Since soap and water were cheap in the big scheme of things, I took baths even when no one noticed.

Carnivals were stinky and noisy. Books and movies were better, because stories made sense. A ride on the Ferris wheel only lasted a few minutes, but a good story lasted forever. Once you read a story or watched one play out on the screen, it became part of your memories. Libraries and theaters were full of the good kind of quiet that was hard to come by at our house, especially when Mama was on a crying jag or a fit-pitching mission. When she was *too* happy, she whipped up noisy tornadoes of activity. She laughed too much and expected us to laugh too, even when we didn't get the joke.

Sometimes, she shut herself in her bedroom and didn't come out for days. Her silence flooded the house with a queasy quiet that pooled in dark corners and pressed on my chest at night and made me worry about what would happen next.

Pop had given me a driving lesson once, and I knew cars had a neutral gear where the engine idled, and the car didn't move forward or back. That's what the Mahoney family needed more of. Neutral time when nothing was happening at all.

I had come to rely on books and movies. If I couldn't rustle up a quarter for the show, I walked six blocks to the musty branch library, a place so brimming over with silence, all you could hear were creaky ceiling fans and turning pages. At the beginning of the summer, I had vowed to read every book in the adult section in alphabetical order. I had finished the *A*s and was moving through the *B*s at a fair clip when I hit the Bronte sisters. Those girls slowed me down considerably and made me realize some books were not meant to be read fast.

Mrs. Ensminger, the librarian, told me to apply for a checkout card so I could take books home, but I told her no thanks. If I did that, my folks would have to sign their permission, and then the library would stop being my secret clubhouse. Mama and Pop would know exactly where to find me when I hid out. It had been a hot summer, and I was not about to give up those ceiling fans.

Earlier in the day, when I realized Pop was hell-bent on having fun, I voted for Nickel Night at the Apache Theater. They were showing *Them!* again, and if giant mutated ants couldn't cheer up a person, what could? But no. Pop wanted us to do something special, so I was stuck at the carnival instead of sitting in the first row pretending to be Debra Paget or Susan Cabot or whatever dark-haired beauty the mutant ants were after.

I longed for a sultry glamour I would never possess, but I knew my limitations. Unlike other girls, I harbored no burning desire to be a movie star, even though I had an aunt with genuine Hollywood connections.

My goal was to sell tickets at the Apache and watch all the shows for free. If that didn't pan out, my contingency plan involved taking over when Mrs. Ensminger retired or died sitting ramrod straight behind the circulation desk. Considering how old she was, either outcome was possible. The Dewey decimal system wasn't as exciting as show business, but I could make a career out of stamping due dates and shushing people when they got too chatty. I was good at telling others what to do.

"How about we get some candy apples?" Pop stopped in front of a brightly lit concession stand. A fat woman in a yellow muumuu leaned on the counter reading a confession magazine between customers.

"I *love* candy apples." Mama gushed like Pop had offered up a steak supper with all the trimmings.

"How about it, kids?" Pop asked. "You all want a candy apple?"

Buddy's head bobbed. My brother would eat a dog turd if you put it on a stick and called it a treat.

"We ate already," I reminded everyone, including the fat lady. When Mama couldn't drag herself out of bed, I'd fixed corned beef hash and poached eggs for supper. A nice change from oatmeal. "We don't have money to waste."

Pop's smile faded. He didn't want me to say things like that where people could hear, but I didn't care. I liked the little yellow house we'd lived in for the last few months. I wasn't about to get evicted again over something as stupid as candy-coated fruit. I gave Buddy the evil eye, but dense as he was, I had to step on his toe before he got the message and shook his head.

Pop got the message too. He only ordered one apple, which he handed to Mama, saying, "Sweets for the sweet." Claiming she wanted the apple to last, she nibbled at it as we slowpoked our way across the midway.

All around us, noisy rides spun and whirled under colorful canopies. The riverbank was aglow with the fake magic of flickering lights. Carnivals were best viewed in the dark. You didn't want to look too close at the creaky machines or the scary, cigar-smoking men with hairy arms and hungry eyes who operated them.

We rode the carousel and the Tilt-A-Whirl. Wandered through the Hall of Mirrors and screamed through the Tunnel of Terror. Frightening experiences aggravated Buddy's bladder problem, so the fun house was no fun for him, but I liked it best. All that terror gave me a good excuse to scream off some steam.

By the time we reached the end of the midway, I'd taken Buddy to the john twice and had endured about all the fun I could stand. But we weren't done yet. At the edge of the river, a rickety wooden roller coaster called the Crazy Snake loomed large above the crowd lined up to ride.

"Hot damn! A roller coaster! Let's go!" Mama's bright gaze followed the train of eight open cars shuddering along narrow metal rails.

They chugged up a series of humps and rattled as they slammed down. The Crazy Snake was a small-potatoes ride with no loop-de-loos and no death-defying plunges.

"I don't know," I said. "That thing doesn't look safe to me. And the line is too long. I vote we go home."

Pop turned to Mama. "It *is* an awful long wait, Gracie. Bud's wagon is draggin'. What do you say we call it a night?"

Mama stared me down, and I allowed the hopeful expression to slide off my face. Too late.

"No," she said. "The roller coaster is the best part of a carnival. I thought we came here to have a good time."

"We did," Pop assured her with a nervous smile. "Haven't you had fun?"

"So far." She nibbled a delicate bite off the candy apple. "I'm not leaving until I ride the roller coaster."

And that was that because what Mama wanted, Mama got.

"What are we waiting for?" Pop shooed us to the end of the line. "We better grab us a spot."

Crazy Snake was what is known as a misnomer. Something wrongly named or designated. The ancient ride moved more like a spastic inchworm than a demented reptile. The line moved slowly too, and forty minutes passed before we finally closed in on the launching area. Mama told Pop to jump in the first car when it arrived because that's where all the action was.

The cars racketed to a stop. Laughing, wind-blown people climbed out the other side. Before we could take a seat in the lead car, Buddy stammered that he had to go. Really, really go. Bad. Right now. His bladder was the size of a butter bean.

"That's okay, sport, I'll take you this time." Pop stepped out of line.

Grateful to avoid another potty run, I slid into the front car.

"No." Mama latched on to Pop's arm. "I want you to ride with me, Johnny. It's no fun riding alone. Pauly can take him. You don't mind, do you, Pauly?"

Mind? Me? Would it matter if I did? She used Buddy like a weapon against me because she knew I would help him. Taking care of my brother had always been my job. I climbed out of the car. I hated her for bringing us here and for spending the rent money. Mostly I hated her for telling the world that she didn't care if I missed the ride because riding with me was the same as riding alone.

"I don't mind." I smiled around the lie, making sure my grin was cheesy enough that even Mama could read between the lines. I grabbed Buddy's hand and pushed my way back through the crowd. We took off for the toilet, a stinky slapped-up two-seater at the far end of the midway. Each hammering step pounded anger deeper into my heart.

I yanked Buddy hard the whole way and told him if Captain Midnight himself came to town giving free rides in a spaceship, he would miss out because he would be in the crapper. Buddy didn't say much. He just clutched the front of his shorts and tried to keep up. When we arrived at the john, he ducked inside. Lucky for him there was no line, because smell-wise, the toilet was no place to linger.

Someday I would sit down and calculate just how many hours of my life had been spent waiting outside toilets for my bean-bladder brother. I was thinking maybe I would need to learn algebra first, when I heard a different kind of commotion coming from the other end of the midway. The screams and shouts no longer sounded like people desperate to have fun; they just sounded desperate. Before I could sort out what was happening, a slick-haired rowdy ran by yelling that the Crazy Snake had jumped the tracks and had spewed folks all over Creation.

Having never seen a roller coaster wreck, or any other mayhem, close up, I rattled Buddy's cage until he came out, jumping up and down and trying to zip. I tightened my dragline on him, and we slipped into the mob racing down the midway. By the time we reached the Crazy Snake, we had to scrunch our way through a forest of legs to get a better look. I was not prepared for what I saw.

Up until that night, my concept of derailment involved cousin Dewayne's Lionel train set and the red caboose that flew off the track when it went around the little pond that was really Aunt Lillian's compact mirror. A toy train crash was nothing like the real thing.

Roller coaster cars had careened to earth between a corn-dog stand and a Guess Your Weight booth. Bent, broken and bloody occupants littered the ground like scattered pick-up sticks. Everywhere I looked, people were hollering. Crying. Moaning. Holding tight to Buddy's hand, I shoved to the front of the crowd. I screamed for my parents, but strangers screamed back.

"Get outta here, kid, you don't want to see this!"

"Go on, get back now!"

"Somebody get these damn kids outta here!"

Mama and Pop were surely looking for us in all the confusion. If people would stop shoving and get out of my way, I could find them. The harder I pushed against the wall of bodies, the louder I got. By the time we finally worked our way to the front of the mob, my voice was like a razor slicing the night air. People ran every which way, but I was welded to the spot with my breath knocked out like I'd hit the ground hard too.

Somebody threw a switch and bright light flooded the midway and made me blink. Poor Buddy whimpered and squeezed my hand fit to break it in two. I looked down and realized he was standing in a dark puddle of blood and rainbow Sno-Kone. A damp stain spread across the front of his shorts.

I tried to haul him away, but there were too many people. I stepped on something that rolled under my foot. I was afraid to look down, afraid not to. Finally, my gaze locked on a half-eaten candy apple, the stick still clutched in a pale white hand. Flashing lights from the roller coaster glinted off the phony diamond ring on a finger tipped with polish.

Playgirl Pink.

The color I'd brushed on the nails of Mama's right hand because her left hand had been too shaky. Like our old icebox, I felt hot on the outside and cold on the inside, but I couldn't look away. The ghostly hand was as out of place in the summer-burned grass as a water lily in the desert. I choked on the wave of hash and eggs that flooded up from my belly and gushed onto the ground. The bad feeling that had only been vague before now solidified into sharp-edged certainty.

No one had to tell me. The front car was where all the action was. It had jumped the track first and had pulled the other cars after it. Our parents weren't looking for us. They were gone, and the world would never be the same.

Surrounded by a screaming crush of people, Buddy and I were suddenly alone.

Hot tears filled my eyes, but I made no move to wipe them. The dark night sky fell down around me, smothering me, sucking me under to a place I didn't want to go. My aching lungs needed air. People bumped into me and shoved me aside. They asked if I was all right, but didn't wait for an answer. I couldn't get out of their way. I couldn't move or speak or think. Buddy shivered in the heat, and I couldn't comfort him.

In the distance, sirens screamed toward us. Everything had changed. I'd gone from being an ungrateful daughter to being an unlucky orphan in one eye-blink instant. Which was how most of life's events played out, big or little, good or bad.

In the background, carousel music, both awful and cheerful at the same time, played on as I clung to my brother, who clung to me. A roaring river of people flowed around us like water around a rock. That's what I'd become. Every vital organ had been yanked out and replaced with gravel and grit.

Policemen came and shut down the carnival and waved people away so ambulance drivers could pick up the injured. The Ferris wheel stopped turning and the carousel ponies stopped prancing.

A uniformed officer asked where our folks were. I pointed down at Mama's hand, and he pushed us toward a black-and-white cruiser. As the car drove away, I turned in the backseat and gazed through the wide window. We hadn't gone far when the carnies killed the music. They switched off the flickering ride lights, putting an end to the magic.

3

Last Rites

Earlier that summer, I had sat at a back table in the library flipping through thick, yellow *National Geographics* and reading about naked jungle people. Pictures of their droopy dangling brown parts weren't nearly as fascinating to me as the stories of how they lived. Those primitive people didn't have cars or washing machines or Wonder Bread, but they had something we did not—special rites of passage to mark the end of childhood.

We had no coming-of-age rituals on the north side of Tulsa. We didn't kill fatted calves or go on vision quests or submit to ceremonial tattooing. But I made the passage that summer and knew when childhood ended. It was over when you realized things wouldn't always be the same. When you accepted the hard fact that the only security in the world was whatever security you could create for yourself.

No matter how old you are, you quit being a child when you stop counting on other people and start counting on yourself. For some, the passage came early. For others, like my second cousin Theodore, who was born with an extra chromosome, it never came at all.

Following the accident, Buddy and I stayed with Mama's mama, Nanny Tee, while arrangements were made. It didn't take long for me to learn that arrangements required money, and there wasn't any.

My parents didn't have life insurance. They had no savings or property worth selling, except for the Ford, which Uncle Waymon bought for twenty-five dollars. Kinfolk on both sides had to chip in to cover the burial expenses. Chipping in worked no particular hardship on anyone, since we came from a big family.

A big *stingy* family. Everyone had to put in their figurative two cents' worth too. Nanny Tee warned them not to complain too much in front of poor little Pauly, but I heard things. No Teegarden or Mahoney ever passed up an opportunity to bellyache about my parents' total disregard for their convenience.

On the day of the funeral, we arrived at Corcoran's Funeral Home an hour early. Nanny Tee, whose full name was Evalee Teegarden, called it a viewing, but I didn't want to look. She made me, claiming I would be sorry later if I didn't. Since Buddy and I had a lot riding on whether or not Nanny Tee liked us enough to make room for us in her life, I couldn't let her think we were yet another cross for her to bear.

I dragged my feet across the green carpet, my eyes on the dark paneling and pastel pictures of Jesus and His Lambs. Jesus on the Mount. Jesus in the Garden. Soft organ music swelled up out of nowhere as I approached two gray coffins arranged with the heads together and a spray of pink carnations between. The flowers filled the air with a sickeningly sweet fragrance, a real-life example of too much of a good thing.

I knew Mama and Pop were lying in the coffins, but the still, waxy figures looked more like mannequins from Froug's Department Store window than my parents. Obeying Nanny Tee, I stared at them to memorize the moment so I wouldn't forget.

Mama's casket was lined with pale satin, the same pink shade as her favorite robe. She wore a new white dress, and the lace cuffs on the long sleeves concealed the stitches where the funeral man had sewn her hand back on. Her hands were crossed on her chest. I was trying to forget how I'd stepped on one of them the night of the accident, when a scary thought hit me.

If Buddy hadn't needed to go to the toilet at the Crazy Snake, there would be four coffins instead of two. If Mama hadn't made me take him, I would be lying in a satin-lined box instead of Pop. By thinking only of herself, Mama had saved me.

I should be grateful, but I was just mad. If Mama hadn't insisted on riding the stupid roller coaster, my parents would still be alive. If she hadn't cried in her room all day, Pop would never have hatched the carnival plan in the first place. Was it possible to love and hate someone at the same time? I turned away, sick and confused. It was a good thing I hadn't eaten all day, or I would have chucked up on the green carpet.

The lining in Pop's casket was also satin, ice blue. I'd never seen him dressed in a suit before, only work clothes with his name stitched over the pocket. Even when he lost the gas station, car park, janitorial, or delivery route jobs, he kept the company shirts. He was so friendly he wanted the world to know his name. I wished for a needle and white floss so I could embroider *Johnny* on the suit pocket. Then everyone in heaven would know him too.

His hands were also crossed on his chest, and when no one was looking, I touched one. Pop had never been so cold. Not even when he'd worked as a tong man at the ice plant.

Buddy's scared little squeak and pinched-up expression reminded me that I wasn't the only one hurting. His pale eyes stared, but he didn't see. He'd fallen inside himself, as shell-shocked as weary soldiers in war movies. Busy feeling sorry for myself, I had forgotten about my brother, who now had only me.

When Nanny Tee left the viewing room to whisper with another mourner in the hall, I pulled two envelopes from my pocket. To ease Buddy's fretting, I had told him that if we put our love on paper, Mama and Pop would know. I had filled two Big Chief tablet pages, but I didn't write the real truth. I didn't say I was sorry for thinking mean thoughts about them when they died.

Buddy's letters contained two pages filled with lopsided, crayoned hearts. I held him up and he slipped the envelopes into the caskets, stuffing them way down in the lining where no one would find them.

Teegarden and Mahoney kinfolk filed into the family waiting room. Some I knew, some I didn't, like Mama's younger sister who lived in California and worked in the movies. Even in her plain gray suit, Nora stood out in the crowd, a pretty, flighty parakeet perched among drab grackles. She caught my eye and winked. I looked away. Nanny Tee said it was the first time in ten years that Nora had troubled herself to come home.

Everyone stood in little groups, waiting for the service to start. Their whispered words buzzed around me like bees. Some stung like bees too.

Like the comment that Great-Uncle Waymon muttered to Great-Aunt Preet: "Ain't it just like Johnny Mahoney to go and get himself killed without a funeral plan?"

Didn't he know Pop hadn't gotten himself killed on purpose? He didn't expect to need a funeral plan for another fifty years. At thirty-two, my father hadn't figured the thought of dying in a freak carnival accident into his plans at all.

"I always said that boy was all hat and no cattle." Aunt Preet didn't bother lowering her voice. Pop always said she'd learned to talk in a sawmill. "I sure would have thought he had more ambition than going out as a greasy spot on a midway."

I pushed past them. Wearing my brand-new secondhand patent leather shoes, I *accidentally* stepped on Aunt Preet's bunions and didn't bother to say "excuse me." She squawked. "Watch where you're stepping, young lady."

My family believed children should be seen and not heard, so few even noticed me. I slipped into eavesdropping position behind Aunt Reba.

"A carnival, of all places! Now that's an unlikely place for tragedy. What in the world were Johnny and Gracie doing on a roller coaster anyway?"

Pop's cousin Myrtle poked a loose curl under her hat and gave a who-knows shrug. "Considering the usual state of their finances, they should have known better than to squander money on such as that."

Mama's double cousin Bennie Ruth agreed. "Those two never had a lick of common sense. Probably why they got along so well." She redeemed herself before I could step on her toes too. "This whole mess is just the most awful shame."

And that was the closest anyone in the family came to saying they were sorry Mom and Pop had died. My kin had never given me much reason to trust them, but as I moved around the room, lapping up their mean-spirited remarks like a dog laps antifreeze, I started not liking them in a serious way. Paying for the funeral did not give them the right to go after my parents like a flock goes after the bird with a broken wing. Pick, pick, pick until it's quivering in the dust with its eyeballs pecked out.

Their disregard made me mad enough to kick and hit and cuss them out proper, right there in the Eternity Room. I could've done it too. The unemployment office wasn't the only place Pop had taken me.

In Ernie's pool hall, the air was blue with smoke and grade-A swearing. Instead, I bit my lip. Only bad children sassed their elders, but when those elders were a bunch of raisin-hearted old poops fermenting in their own bitter juice, the urge to sass was difficult to overcome.

A fresh wave of grief and worry rolled over me, drowning my anger in silence. I moved to a corner of the room where I could be by myself. Saying nothing to nobody was situation normal for Buddy. For me, it was more like a state of shock.

Nanny Tee stood by the door talking to Aunt Preet. She dabbed her eyes with a hankie and nodded, and I hoped she wasn't agreeing with her sister-in-law's "all hat and no cattle" assessment. What had Mama and Pop done to deserve so little kindness from their blood kin?

Was there shame in being both poor *and* satisfied? Was there something wrong with expecting to get by without ever working to get ahead? Mom and Pop had never been too proud to ask for help. Maybe they hadn't felt bad enough about asking to suit the rest of the family. My future, and poor silent Buddy's, was now in the hands of our uncharitable kinfolk. A situation that could make even a sensible child develop bedwetting problems.

From somewhere down the hall, the organist hit the first note of a new hymn and everybody hushed.

"Shall we proceed into the chapel?" The stoop-shouldered funeral man stood in the doorway, quietly directing traffic.

"Pauly. Buddy. Y'all come with me." First through the door, Nanny Tee led us down a long corridor and into a special section of pews half hidden behind wine-colored curtains. Grief, a private thing, was best kept from the curious. I took a quick peek and saw that mourners only filled half the chapel's seats. The funeral man had tried to create an illusion of grandeur by artfully arranging the floral tributes. But skimpy was skimpy and hard to disguise. The coffins were closed now. Panic bubbled up inside me. I would never see my parents again. I would never have a chance to apologize for my part in what had happened.

That night at the carnival, my griping and grumbling and gritching about their irresponsible ways had been heard and acted upon. Seemed like God would have better things to do than tune in to my bellyaching, but you never know. Maybe He'd had a little time on His hands and had decided to teach me a lesson. What better way to punish a bad daughter than to take away her parents and let her see how she liked going it alone? I'd read about poetic justice, and now it had happened to me.

Poetic justice: an outcome in which vice is punished and virtue rewarded, usually in a manner peculiarly or ironically appropriate.

The thing was, God had misunderstood me. I didn't want *different* parents. I only wanted them to *act* different. More like Ozzie and Harriet. Responsible and serious, but with a sense of humor when it came to the kids.

The Baptist preacher stepped up to the pulpit, shuffled his notes, and peered at the congregation over the top of half glasses. He started out slow and quiet, building up steam as he went along. "Brothers and sisters, thank you for coming today. It is a sad day indeed! We mourn the deaths of two young people, ripped from our midst by a terrible accident. We can weep over their deaths. Or we can turn our sadness into joy by celebrating their lives!"

His fist pounded the lectern to punctuate key words. "Grace and John are no *longer* with us. They are in a *better* place. They are with our *Lord*, Jesus Christ!

"I did not know dear Grace and John as well as I would have liked. They did not find a church home in *this* world. But they were saved as *children. Baptized* in the water. Washed in the *blood* of our Savior. They will have an eternal home in heaven.

"*Yes!* Grace and John will be *missed*, brothers and sisters! Their passing leaves an aching *void* that you, my friends, can fill. How, you ask? By *cherishing* fond memories of Grace and John Mahoney."

I glanced down the family pew. Everyone was nodding and sniffling, even Aunt Preet. What memories did she cherish at that moment?

The preacher's voice softened again. "Grace and John leave behind a precious *legacy*. Their poor, orphaned children." He checked his notes. "Paulette and Jefferson."

No one called us Paulette and Jefferson. No one called our parents Grace and John either. There had been a mistake. The preacher was talking about four people I didn't know.

"God performed a *miracle* that terrible night. He kept Paulette and little Jefferson off that *fateful* roller coaster. He kept them safe for a *reason*, friends! The Lord has a *plan* for these children. A plan that mere mortals can never know."

A plan? A plan meant Mama and Pop had died for a reason. Would the preacher explain what that reason was? Had I really lived for a reason? Was it up to me to figure things out, or would the preacher tell me?

He didn't. He bowed his head and led us in prayer. Then the organist struck up another hymn. I hated to take credit away from someone as important as God, but in my heart, I knew Buddy's weak bladder had saved us. That was my first inkling of the ironic perversity of life. Maybe God wasn't punishing me for being an ungrateful daughter. Buddy and I were alive, but not because of divine intervention. We were alive because my little brother couldn't hold his water.

During the third verse of "In the Garden," one of the organ keys stuck. The white-haired organist whacked the keyboard with her shoe, detracting from the solemn occasion but perking up a couple of old folks who had nodded off.

On one side of me, Nanny Tee sniffled into a white hanky edged in black, and on the other side, Buddy sat as cold and still as the little stone boy on the fountain in the park. I closed up my face and my heart and watched from a distance so it didn't hurt so much.

People in the pews fanned themselves with the little printed program that summed up my parents' lives in two short paragraphs. I found my name in the "survived by" section, but didn't understand the significance of the word. All I knew was that our survival, mine and Buddy's, depended on Nanny Tee.

She had often declared grandmas shouldn't have to raise grandkids because they'd already served their time in the trenches. She was the logical choice even if she wasn't very grandmotherly, and I was counting on her making an exception in our case.

After the service, the funeral man's helper loaded us into a big gray car. On the way to the cemetery, somebody sniped about how Mrs. So-and-So had the nerve to show up looking like a Saturday night hussy in a pink dress and no hat. Somebody else asked if anyone noticed that the pie Mrs. Whozit had sent over was store-bought, and how even a hungry coonhound wouldn't eat Mrs. Whatchamacallit's oyster stuffing.

Aunt Nora didn't speak to anyone. She stared out the dark car window, looking as closed up for business as I felt. I leaned back against the soft upholstery and shut my eyes as we drove through the cemetery.

At the graveside, Buddy and I sat on either side of Nanny Tee under a big green tent. Aunt Nora sat beside me. She looked at me once, but I looked away. Her moist-eyed expression seemed to say it was all right to cry, but I wouldn't. Not yet.

When the poufy-haired preacher finished praying, boxes containing the only two people who had ever loved us were lowered into raw holes gouged from the red clay. It wasn't the time or place to think about myself, but I couldn't get past my parents' final act of selfish exclusion. I should have known Johnny and Gracie would take off together and leave us kids behind.

Nanny Tee urged us to our feet. She'd given us each two white carnations to drop on the caskets. I was no good at praying, but as my blooms settled on the polished lids, I silently reminded God of the few Sundays my parents had gotten up early enough for church and asked Him to please let them in. I didn't want to think of them in that other place, surrounded forever and eternal by generations of doomed tightwad Teegardens and Mahoneys.

Beside me, my brother clutched his flowers with both hands and pressed them to his bony chest. With the single-minded determination of which only a child like Buddy was capable, he wedged his chin between his doubled-up fists and held on like a bulldog. No amount of tugging and pleading could pry them from his grip, and he clung to those sad flowers all the way home.

Free to Good Home

After the funeral, the mourners converged on Nanny Tee's house to offer condolences and eat ham salad sandwiches. Buddy and I endured the head patting and tongue clucking as long as we could before escaping into Nanny Tee's bedroom to hide.

Because our grandmother liked to sleep late on weekends, she'd hung heavy, light-blocking drapes across the bay window in her room. We often played on the window seat behind the curtains, pretending to be dummies in a store window. Buddy made the best mannequin because he could go longer without talking.

Now he didn't want to play and just sat on the cushion, clutching his wilty carnations. I knew how he felt. Ever since the accident, I had been holding blindly on to something too. Hope. Hope that the preacher was right. Hope that my parents truly were in a better place. Hope that life really would go on. Hope that time might finally heal the pain.

If only the noisy relatives would leave. They'd turned the supposed-to-be-somber event into a party, and that wasn't right. I needed Nanny

Tee alone so she could explain what would happen next. How would Buddy and I fit into her life? Where would we go to school? Who would cook the oatmeal? I needed details, but no one seemed to think we were important.

I perked up when I heard grown-ups enter the room. I nudged Buddy and made the zip-lip sign, but it was an unnecessary warning. He was a naturally quiet kid who disproved the theory that still waters ran deep. Unwilling to reveal our presence, we sat frozen behind the curtains and listened.

Nanny Tee spoke first. "I can't believe poor little Gracie is gone." She honked into her hanky. "Why, just the other day she was sitting right out there at my dinette table, drinking coffee and going on about the vacation they were planning."

"Humph!" That snort came from Aunt Preet the prune. "You gotta work before you take a vacation. Those two had about as much chance of traveling as I have of being Queen for a Day."

Nanny Tee sniffled some more. "I know, but you know how Gracie liked to plan things."

"Daydream, you mean."

"Poor girl. She always had such big ideas."

Aunt Preet scoffed. "I believe what Gracie had were delusions of grandeur."

"Bless her heart, she just wanted to see a little bit of the country. She even made up a list of places to visit." Nanny Tee hated to travel. In her whole life, she'd only been in two states. Oklahoma, where she'd lived since her marriage to our long-dead grandfather Teegarden, and Arkansas. She was from a place called Hasquaw Holler, but when she said it with her Ozark twang, it came out Hog Squalor.

"What's to become of the children?" Aunt Preet asked.

That was the $64,000 question. I was suddenly all ears behind that curtain, waiting to hear Nanny Tee tell Aunt Preet how she planned to paint the back bedroom lilac so I could have a room of my own, and how nice it would be to have children in the house again so she wouldn't be alone.

"Poor little things." Nanny Tee sniffled again. "I don't know what will become of them."

She didn't know? That kind of wrong answer got *$64,000 Question* contestants buzzed off the show. How could she not know? We were her responsibility now.

"I'd like to take them in," Nanny Tee went on. "But I'm too old to raise another set of kids. My life is not set up to be a full-time granny."

Buddy was playing with a string he'd unraveled from his shirt and wasn't paying attention. But I was. Grannies in Bobbsey Twins books and Saturday afternoon matinees were energetic old ladies like Spring Byington. They wore their white hair bunned up in back, owned frilly aprons and baked pies.

Evalee Teegarden favored a curly red poodle 'do, Mamie Van Doren toreador pants, and stiletto heels. She worked for a liquor distributor and brought home sample bottles of bourbon that she mixed in milk and drank for breakfast. She didn't bake anything. In fact, I never knew her to make anything more complicated than green Jell-O with shredded carrots on top.

"For Chrissakes, Ma, you're only fifty-one. You're not exactly banging at death's door." I recognized that voice. Aunt Nora had lost her Okie accent somewhere along the way. Aunt Preet claimed she was putting on the dog, but I thought she sounded like an actress should sound. Earlier, I'd overheard some of the female relatives speculating about her, and none of it had been very nice.

Nora had arrived in the middle of the night after driving nonstop from California to Tulsa in a cream-puff 1953 Buick Skylark convertible. The boy cousins couldn't stop drooling over that convertible. A real hot machine, they said. Some of the older men drooled too, but seemed to me that it was more over Aunt Nora than the car.

I didn't know my aunt because I was only three the last time I saw her. Nobody knew much about her. After the war, she had hauled off and moved to California to be an actress. Using the stage name Nora Gardner, she'd made a career of playing bit parts. As early as I could remember, Mama had dragged me to dark theaters hoping to glimpse Aunt Nora on the silver screen.

Once, we saw her dressed as a chorus girl in a Danny Kaye musical. She didn't sing or dance, but she adjusted her stocking backstage, radiating what Mama had called star quality. In another movie, she sold a pack of smokes to a gangster played by Richard Widmark. She didn't say any lines, but her dimply smile lit up the screen.

Aunt Nora had portrayed so many nameless waitresses, maids and manicurists that Nanny Tee claimed somebody was trying to tell her something about her aptitude level. Mama had defended her younger sister, swearing that all Nora needed was a big break and she would be a brighter star than Faith Domergue or Mala Powers, either one.

My mind had wandered, and it took a moment to tune back in to the conversation on the other side of the curtain.

"Evalee's right, you know. She can't work all day and keep two kids. I guess I could take them." It was a halfhearted offer from Pop's halfhearted cousin Myrtle.

Aunt Nora laughed. "I think maybe we should get someone a little more qualified."

"Why, Nora Jean! Whatever do you mean? I have plenty of experience raising kids."

"Sorry, Myrt, but the way I hear it, your child-rearing credentials aren't exactly endorsed by Dr. Spock." Most of the family had caustic ways, but they were amateurs compared to Aunt Nora. When she insulted people, they didn't know what hit them.

"And just what do you mean by that, Nora Jean Teegarden?" In spite of her impressive size, Myrtle's voice reached a tinny shrillness unequaled in ordinary human decibels.

"I *mean*, your daughter's in a home for wayward cheerleaders and your son's serving three to five for growing wacky tabacky in a chicken house."

"That was all a misunderstanding," Myrtle blustered. "Arlen didn't know he was raising dope."

"Right. Maybe he thought those funny little plants were exotic orchids." Aunt Nora only sounded sincere. "Didn't he get suspicious when they failed to put on flowers?"

"Now, now, girls! Let's stick to the subject." Nanny Tee had grandkids to give away and needed to keep the discussion churning. The ham salad sandwich I'd eaten congealed into a rubbery rock in my stomach. I'd assumed we would be staying with our grandmother, and here we were, up for grabs like a spare peck of tomatoes or unwanted puppies.

Extra Orphans. Free to a good home.

"Jess and Lillian might take them," said Aunt Preet. "But they already have three kids and Jess lost that promotion he was counting on."

I made a face at Buddy, like Alfalfa sucking lemons. He grimaced back. No one in their right mind would want to wind up with Jess and Lillian. Their three boys were evil little humanoids about whom the best thing you could say was that they produced abundant mucus.

"What about Walt and May?" Myrtle wondered out loud.

"May's got that back problem," Aunt Preet reminded. "I doubt she'd be willing to take 'em."

"Jeez, they're not papooses." Aunt Nora paused, and I pictured her sucking hard on a cigarette. I'd watched her when she wasn't looking and knew the extent of her habit. "It's not like May would have to carry them around on her bad back."

Myrtle asked, "You think Bennie Ruth would take them?" and Aunt Preet answered, "What do you think?" and everyone laughed.

Additional ideas were tossed out and duly rejected. Quiet as a feral cat, Buddy curled up on the window seat and closed his eyes. My ear was glued to that curtain, listening to all the excuses offered on behalf of our many relatives. I'd worried about where we'd end up, and sorry to say, my concerns had been justified.

My fiction-fired imagination numbed me with visions of Oliver Twist orphanages and bowls of watery gruel. When I had considered the possibilities, it had never occurred to me that *no one* would want us. Pop may have had shortcomings as a provider, but he'd always said Buddy and I were as good as anybody. Thumb your nose at the best of them, he'd advised, and tell the rest of them to go fry an egg. He'd never provided clothes that matched or piano lessons or summer camp, but he'd given us enough love for two parents, along with the mistaken idea that love was all we needed.

As I listened to our relatives come up with creative ways to get rid of us, I realized we'd been hoodwinked. Sure as shooting. Nobody wanted us. The rest of the world did not judge merit on Johnny Mahoney's say-so.

My brother was a skinny, bucktoothed eight-year-old with stick-out ears who stuttered. He wore a leg brace because he'd caught polio when he was two, and the disease had swept through the playgrounds like a summer plague. One of the lucky ones, Buddy wasn't permanently paralyzed. He didn't have much muscle in his gimpy right leg, but he got around all right, so long as he wore the brace.

To me, who had often been accused of rattling like a two-dollar radio, Buddy's stuttering and reluctance to talk were more worrisome than his less-than-perfect leg. He listened good, his wide blue eyes taking in every detail, but he mainly only talked to me. When anyone wanted to ask him something, they had to go through me to get an answer.

I had fewer obvious defects than poor Buddy, but would win no prizes for beauty. I was thirteen but looked ten because I possessed the approximate body shape of a venetian blind slat. My curly Teegarden hair was the color of old carrots, and when I woke up in the mornings, I looked like last year's doll left too long in the bottom of the toy box.

My biggest flaw was the extra-large, economy-sized chip on my shoulder. The Prudential Insurance rock had nothing on me. A lifetime of standing on the outside looking in, of being the ungrateful recipient of other people's handouts and hand-me-downs, had made me as leery as a stray dog.

I heard someone rattling stuff around on Nanny Tee's burled oak dresser. Probably Aunt Nora looking for a place to dump her ashes. She smoked Pall Malls like they were going illegal tomorrow. Earlier, when Myrtle had warned her that smoking would cut ten years off her life, Aunt Nora had laughed and said she didn't much care since it would be the last ten. She didn't mind missing bingo and cupcake day at the rest home.

"Can we just focus on the problem here?" Nanny Tee had clearly grappled with the intricacies of the matter. "It costs money to raise children, especially sickly children with medical problems. The March of Dimes helps out with Buddy, but Johnny and Gracie didn't leave those kids a cent."

"I warned Gracie she was on the road to ruin when she married that boy." Aunt Preet sounded smug, as though she'd known all along how things would turn out. "Didn't I tell her that?"

"*Everybody* told her that." Nanny Tee sighed.

"What could she do?" Myrtle whispered. "She had a biscuit in the oven."

"Y'all let me know what you decide. I'm going to get a piece of that pecan pie before it's all gone." I heard the bedroom door open and close behind Aunt Preet, but the scent of her Pond's cold cream lingered in the air.

"Won't the kids get money from the carnival people?" Myrtle asked. "After all, it was *their* rickety old roller coaster that killed their parents."

I'd been operating on the Fiery Hand of God's Vengeance theory and hadn't considered that Mama and Pop were dead because of a loose bolt.

"They may get something in time," Nanny Tee dismissed. "The lawyer I called said it could take years. The carnival people will blame the roller coaster people, and they'll all fight it out in court. In the meantime, we still haven't solved our problem."

Being the problem, I gently parted the drapes and peeked out to size up the situation. Nanny Tee sat on the little wrought-iron bench in front of her makeup table. Every now and then she looked in the mirror, wiped her eyes, and patted her hair.

Myrtle perched on the edge of Nanny's bed, careful not to muss the rose chenille spread. She could have been Mamie Eisenhower's fat sister, in a navy blue shirtwaist with white buttons. The veil on her little hat was turned up out of her eyes and made her look like she'd been caught in a stiff wind.

Aunt Nora paced back and forth in her stocking feet, smoking like a Rambler with a bad exhaust. She was still dressed in the stylish gray suit she'd worn to the funeral, but had shucked off the white gloves and Grace Kelly hat.

Nora's hair was really red. Not the Really Red that came from the bottle under Nanny Tee's bathroom sink, but genuine flaming Rita Hayworth red. She was taller than Nanny Tee and as curvy as Marilyn Monroe. At twenty-eight she had already been married and divorced twice, a scandal in our family. She had arrived alone, and was "between men," as one of the aunts put it.

Aunt Nora stopped pacing and, as ordinary as ordering a dip of vanilla, said, "I'll take the kids."

"You?" Myrtle spluttered so hard her veil fell down.

"Why not? They're my sister's children." She jerked a few quick puffs off a fresh cigarette. "I owe it to Gracie, God rest her soul."

"Are you crazy, Nora Jean?" Nanny Tee sounded convinced of what she had only hinted at before.

"So you've told me, Ma." She glanced around the room, an actress cued for drama. "I don't see a long line of concerned relatives begging to take them in, do you? Looks like I'm it."

"Nora's right." Chubby old Myrt jumped at the chance to wiggle off the hook.

I thought Nanny Tee looked relieved too, but to her credit, she mustered a grandmotherly objection. "I don't know, Nora Jean. Children need stability, and that's never been your long suit." A polite way of saying what she had expressed to Mama many times—namely, that Aunt Nora was not only immature and irresponsible, but also totally beyond redemption.

"Stability? Good one, Ma. They spent their whole lives with Gracie and Johnny." Aunt Nora made it sound like living with Mama and Pop had been some kind of survival training.

"Nora's right," Myrt repeated, a little more firmly this time. Funny how amenable she was to fobbing us off on someone she had recently declared half a bubble off plumb.

"How are you planning to support two children?" Nanny Tee

didn't want the job herself, but at least she could work up some concern for our welfare.

"Don't worry about that." Nora waved her hand and ashes showered down from her cigarette. She flicked a smudge off her pencil-straight skirt.

"Well, Missy, it's something we need to talk about before you go packing those kids off to God only knows where." Nanny Tee to the rescue. Her tone was righteous. Almost convincing. The voice of reason. Maybe she *did* care after all.

"It's California, Ma. Not Sodom *or* Gomorrah. But if you must know, I made out all right on my last divorce. I have some money put by and an apartment at the beach."

"Do you have a job?" Nanny Tee valued steady employment almost as much as free liquor samples.

"I work when I need to."

Aunt Nora's life had long been the subject of family speculation. Like a true black sheep, she had long since cut herself loose from the Teegarden flock. Everything about her was a big secret. Other than occasional flickering moments on-screen, she appeared to have no visible means of support.

With that fancy car and her stylish clothes, she must have gotten her money somewhere. Maybe she was a gangster's moll. Ill-gotten gains would explain a lot of things.

"Well, good luck. You'll need it." Nanny Tee let go of another long-suffering harrumph. "Pauly's too big for her britches, just full of piss and vinegar. Her daddy spoiled her rotten. And that tongue of hers wags like the south end of a goose. I warn you, Nora Jean, the child can be a regular little pill.

"And poor Buddy! Why, he's so weak and woobly, it's a wonder he's lasted this long. They're not bad kids, but they are a trial. I certainly hope you can handle them."

I sent Nanny Tee an eyeball death ray through the curtain crack. She frowned in the mirror, displeased with her poodle curls. Traitor. She'd pawned us off with so little conscience I hoped her next perm turned out as frizzy as the dog it was named after.

"What's to handle?" I didn't like the look of Aunt Nora's careless shrug. "We're talking about kids, not polo ponies."

Such airy optimism betrayed a dangerous ignorance of child rearing. Someone that nonchalant probably shouldn't be in charge of kids, especially those who had, as Nanny Tee had pointed out, a number of documented problems.

Myrtle hurried out to announce they had a taker for the orphans, hallelujah, thank the Lord. When Nanny Tee and Aunt Nora started arguing about her hauling us back to California, I stopped peeking and tuned them out.

One thing for sure. It was high time to stop depending on grown-ups. Mama and Pop had let us down by dying young. Nanny Tee had let us down by not wanting the trouble of us in her life. None of our blood relatives was willing to give us a chance. Except one we didn't know.

Since no one cared, neither would I. Time to chase the moon again. I would sneak my brother out of the house in the dark of night and head for the hills. We would live like feral children in a cave, and I would teach Buddy to read by writing words in the dirt with a stick. We'd eat nuts and berries and no oatmeal until I was old enough to move back to Tulsa and find a job. We didn't need anyone. We would take care of ourselves.

One look at Buddy, curled in a knot with his bony knees drawn up to his chest, and I chucked that plan. My sickly brother could not live in a cave. Caves were too damp. We were stuck. Our only hope was a free-spirited stranger whose reasons for blithely undertaking to finish our raising were known only to herself.

We were about to be swept off to the ragged edge of nowhere, in the care of someone to whom the term "floozy" had recently been applied, and short of surrendering to the nearest orphanage, there wasn't a thing I could do about it.

When I started listening again, Aunt Nora was telling Nanny Tee how she planned to take her time driving to the West Coast. "Those kids have suffered a terrible shock. They need time to adjust. We'll take it easy and see some sights along the way."

"Say what?"

"I think they need a vacation, Ma."

I peered through the drapes again to make sure Aunt Nora was serious. She was. A vacation from grief? From guilt? A vacation from being burdensome orphans? Was it possible to take a vacation from worrying about our very existence and the fact that the last thing I had muttered under my breath to my mother as I slunk out of the roller coaster line was, "I hate you"?

Was that kind of vacation possible?

Nanny Tee frowned. "Nora Jean, what *are* you talking about?"

"National parks. Grand Canyon. Petrified Forest. Painted Desert. Cliff dwellings. Don't kids like that stuff?"

"Under normal circumstances maybe, but—"

"Ma, I want to give them the trip Gracie was planning."

"Do you think tramping around national monuments will take their minds off the fact that we just buried their folks? Poor little things." Nanny Tee's choked-back sob was more for show than sadness.

"Yes. I think a trip could be a distraction. It'll give us time to get to know each other before we set up housekeeping."

My grandmother frowned at her only surviving daughter. "You sure about that? I think you're biting off more than you can chew."

Aunt Nora drew deeply on her cigarette and puffed a series of smoke rings into the air. And Nanny Tee thought she lacked talent. "There are very few things in this world that I *am* sure of." Her tight little smile was not amused. "But one of them is that I am taking those kids out of here."

"And just how are you planning to finance this great expedition?"

"Will you stop harping about money?" Nora's flung-up hand swatted the question like a fly. "I have never asked you for a plug nickel. Not once in the ten years since I left have I *ever* asked you for a damn thing."

Nanny Tee huffed. "Motels and restaurants don't grow on trees, you know."

"Maybe we won't stay in motels or eat in restaurants." Her words sounded more like a taunt than a plan. "We can camp. The kids will get a kick out of sleeping under the stars."

Buddy sat up, his face twisted in an awful grimace. At first, I thought he was overreacting to the part about camping. Then I realized he was trying not to sneeze. I lunged across the window seat and clamped my fingers over his nose, but I was too late. He cut loose with a series of sick kitten sneezes that made his whole body jerk.

Ah-choo, choo, choo, choo, choo, choo.

Nanny Tee yanked back the blackout curtain and dragged us off the window seat by our ears. "What in blue blazes do you kids think you are doing?" Her voice was as shrill as the noon whistle down at the whiskey jobber.

I wish I could have said something suitably pill-like, such as, "Oh, just finding out how little we mean to you," but what with the depressing nature of the day's events, all I could muster was an inarticulate "Nothin'."

"Skulking around like sneak thieves! Pauly Mahoney, you know better than that! Eavesdroppers never hear anything good about themselves."

Spare the lecture. I just learned that lesson for life.

"For God's sake, Ma, give the poor kids a break." Nora sat in the dented-in space Myrtle had vacated on the bed and pulled Buddy onto her lap. I hung back. From there on out, I would live in a bubble that was just big enough for me.

"So you heard what we were talking about?" Aunt Nora asked. I nodded. When Buddy saw it was okay, he nodded too.

"So? What do you think?"

"About what?"

Aunt Nora's smile was slow to surface. "About living with me?"

"We don't know you." Someone had to point out the obvious, and Buddy wasn't saying a word.

"That's true," Aunt Nora allowed. "But I know you."

"No, you don't."

"Your mama wrote me long letters all about you. She told me when you lost a tooth and when you got an A in spelling."

"She did?" I'd never seen Mama write a grocery list with more than four items, so long letters were highly iffy.

"I know we haven't seen each other for a while, but we'll have plenty of time to get acquainted."

I waited for her to say something to cancel out the tentative promise in her words. She didn't.

This was real.

Like a condemned gangster in a prison movie, I had counted on a last-minute reprieve. I turned from the redheaded aunt stranger to Nanny Tee. *Save us. Love us. Don't send us away.* My grandmother was busy blotting fresh lipstick, no longer paying attention to the conversation.

"What do you say, kiddos?" Aunt Nora's eyes were the color of moss on river rock. Green over gray. Soft over hard. Her smile said we had a choice, but we didn't. Nanny Tee would never realize the mistake she was making by not keeping us. I could tell by the set of her thin Cabaret Coral lips that we were already past history.

"Well? How about it?" Aunt Nora wanted an answer. "Pauly? Buddy? Will you go to California with me?"

The question required mulling-over time, but life doesn't work that way. You have to think on your feet and make decisions on the fly. Nanny Tee's indifference left me no choice. Driving off into the sunset with a floozy beat eating gruel in a gothic orphans' home any day.

I nodded. I would go with this volunteer aunt, but I would not trust her. I'd obey her, but I wouldn't love her. Except for Buddy, I was done with loving.

Buddy wobbled his agreement. He had that fresh from the Tunnel of Terror look again. Scared and hanging on to nothing. His eyes filled with disappointment, like he had expected me to save us from all this. How could I? I was just another sparrow in the storm.

I would have to hurry and grow up fast, so I could take care of my brother and myself. I would scoot over and make room in my bubble for Buddy, but nobody else.

"I'm glad that's settled." With less thought than most people put into picking out a puppy at the pound, Aunt Nora had sealed our fate. Her pretty face had the Tunnel of Terror look too. Only it was the look people had *before* they went in, when they still had no idea what scary things were about to dangle from the ceiling or grab them in the dark.

She pulled us into a hug. I didn't hug back. My cynical heart was still trying to figure out her angle.

The hug went on too long, and Buddy collapsed in a coughing fit. Nanny Tee rolled her eyes. "I can't imagine what's got into you, Nora

Jean, wanting to carry that poor child off camping. I swear, he won't last as long as a paper shirt in a bear fight. He's always been spindly because of the polio. Catches every bug that comes along. Mark my words, he'll end up with double pneumonia."

Buddy was terrified of catching pneumonia. He was so sure pneumonia was out to get him that he wouldn't go barefoot until after Memorial Day or splash in rain puddles or wade in Cold Spring Creek or sleep with the windows open at night or build a snowman. No matter how parched he was, he wouldn't drink from a public fountain. His hands were often chapped and red from trying to scrub off germs he couldn't see. Maybe that's why he kept his mouth shut. To keep the pneumonia bugs out.

Aunt Nora patted my brother's back, and he finally stopped coughing. "Buddy's going to be fine." She drew a deep breath and administered another group squeeze. The tremor in her arms matched the one in her voice. Maybe her too-bright movie smile made an audience believe in make-believe, but it didn't fool me.

"He won't have to worry about catching cold," Aunt Nora said. "It's plenty warm where we're headed. Right, kiddos?"

You could say that again. We were headed for hell in a handbag.

Up a Tree

Later that week, when Buddy and I needed to hide out again, we chose the squatty old mimosa tree in Nanny Tee's backyard. I pretended to be Jane, keeping the tree house neat for Tarzan, who was gone on a lion hunt. Having perfected his monkey face, Buddy was a willing, if introverted, Cheetah.

July had been hot and dry, but that day a south wind blew up from Texas. The breeze had stirred flies on a longhorn's hide, whistled through oil derricks and skated over the Red River before heading north to shake the leaves in Tulsa.

I boosted Buddy, and he wedged his skinny butt in the crotch of the lowest limb. Wrapping his arms around the trunk, he pressed his cheek to the rough bark. Unlike the real Cheetah, he didn't like to climb but was a good clinger. I clambered past him, and the higher I went, the better the breeze felt. No wonder birds and squirrels lived in trees. Sitting up high made everything on the ground seem small and unimportant.

I longed to keep going, up and up, like Beanstalk Jack, all the way to a place in the clouds where geese laid golden eggs and parents didn't die and grandmothers didn't sell kids down the river.

Catching movement across the back fence, I watched the neighbor's nimble-footed terrier. Little Lulu was a roof walker, which is like a tightrope walker in the dog world. Lulu liked to jump up on a lawn chair, launch herself to the top of the covered rain barrel, leap over to the woodpile and scrabble onto the roof. She ran lightly back and forth along the ridgeline, turning at the end like a target at the carnival shooting booth.

Once her acrobatic urges were satisfied, she climbed down from the roof and went about her usual business, digging holes and yipping at nothing. No one understood why Lulu found the roof so fascinating. Maybe, like mountain climbers, she tackled the peak because it was there. Or maybe, like aunts, she didn't know what the heck she was doing.

Buddy thought Lulu should be on the Ed Sullivan show, but as I said, my brother was easily entertained. He always wanted a dog, but Mama said no, even when Pop asked, Why not, a boy needs a pet. Because, Mama said, dander makes Buddy cough. Dander is another interesting word, and I have been known to get my dander up a time or two.

Once the Lulu Show was over, I went back to worrying about our future. Aunt Nora had tried to talk to me a few times, but I wasn't up to holding a full-blown conversation. I had shrugged, nodded, and answered in grunts, a form of communication I learned from Buddy. As accustomed to insults as a redheaded girl with freckles and a flat chest could be, I had been driven to monosyllables by pure spitefulness after Nanny Tee's crack about my tongue wagging like a goose butt. Since the funeral, poor Buddy had just sat where I parked him. I wanted to be strong for him, but was thinking maybe I wasn't cut out for orphanhood. Guilt and grief ate at me from the inside out, slowly filling the space in my heart that had belonged to Mama and Pop. When I wanted attention, I knew how to make myself heard, but since no one currently living in the world could make me feel better, I had cried myself to sleep every night since the accident. Quietly so no one could hear.

I worried about Buddy. He didn't cry at all. Since he never talked much anyway, no one else noticed how overwhelming his silence had become. Like battle-fatigued soldiers in war movies, he would go where you led him, but his mind was someplace else.

"Are you scared?" I asked after a while.

He nodded.

"I've been thinking about California."

His fluttery sigh meant "So what?"

"Maybe it won't be so bad." I'd formed a pretty good MGM image of the place from watching picture shows. Movie magazines had filled in the gaps. "California's got year-round sunshine and palm trees and miles and miles of beaches. Hollywood has the Brown Derby and Grauman's Chinese Theater and the Walk of Fame. Movie stars are so thick around there, you can't go to the Piggly Wiggly without smacking into one."

Buddy's narrow shoulders lifted in a slight shrug, which meant he knew California was nothing like Oklahoma.

"Maybe we'll like it there."

"M-m-maybe," he whispered. After so many days of silence, that one stuttered word filled me with the kind of hope that had elated Don Ameche when he played Alexander Graham Bell making the first telephone call.

"Aunt Nora seems nice," I said.

"G-g-guess so."

"Maybe California will be a good place."

Buddy stared at me. I'd been his interpreter and only friend for as long as I could remember. Being his big sister was a full-time job. I understood what went on in his dented brainpan better than anybody. Like a crab or a turtle, Buddy pulled deep into a hard little shell when he was poked or startled.

My brother had always had a loose grip on life. From the moment he was born, three weeks early and gasping for breath, something had been trying to take him away from us. I often wondered if maybe he wasn't done rising and needed more time in heaven to bake.

I had lost my parents, but Buddy had lost more. He no longer had the cosmic carrot of hope Mama and Pop had dangled in front of him. *Eat your spinach and you'll grow strong. Do your leg exercises and you'll walk better. Be a good boy and people will like you.* They promised that he'd outgrow his childhood fears. Learn the times tables and perfect his penmanship. That he'd someday do all the things most kids took for granted and he could only dream about.

Only three people in the world had believed Buddy had something to offer, and two-thirds of them were gone. That left me to keep his dream going.

I climbed down and sat beside him on his baby limb. When I wrapped my arm around his shoulders, he leaned against me, silent and still. His thin body pressed against my sturdy one, and his bottomless pit of need pressed against my scabbed-over heart, and I knew this would be our arrangement for the rest of our lives.

A little later, Aunt Nora found us sitting in the monkey tree. Instead of hollering us down as most grown-ups would, she kicked off her loafers and shinnied up like she climbed trees every day. She settled herself on a big limb across from us, looking as perky as Debbie Reynolds in a sleeveless pink shirt and cuffed-up jeans. Her hair was tied back in a ponytail with a yellow scarf.

Her words carried Debbie's enthusiastic sincerity too. "You may not believe me, but I *do* know how bad you kids feel. I miss Gracie and Johnny too."

It wasn't the same. Aunt Nora hadn't seen my parents for ten years. She didn't know what our lives had been like. She couldn't possibly understand how we felt. I stared out into the space over Tulsa.

"Think of this trip as starting over with a brand-new life," she said. "Not everyone gets that chance, you know. We'll have fun. We'll take our show on the road and call it The Daring Adventures of Us. You'll be the stars and you'll write your names with the ink of destiny."

Debbie Reynolds better watch her back or she would lose the next Miss Perky Cheerful role to Nora Gardner.

When we didn't get caught up in her enthusiasm, she tried another tack. "Okay, what if I promise you'll see things you've never seen before? Do things you might never do again. Meet interesting people. Have the ride of your life. How about that?"

Gosh, who knew being an orphan could be so educational? I perfected my fifty-yard stare, and Buddy did his mannequin impression.

"I know I can't take your parents' place. I won't try. All I'm asking for is a chance to be your aunt. Can you give me that?"

Didn't she know? No one could give you a chance. Pop said chances were something you had to grab.

"Hey, if Mame can do it, I can too, right?" She was running on fumes. "Oh, all right. Shoot. I don't know what I was thinking. I must be out of my ever-loving mind to want to take on two children, much less drag them back to California."

There it was. She had passed her generous impulse like so much gas.

"The last thing I need is the responsibility of two kids I don't even know."

Feeling extra pill-like, I fixed her with my best glare. "I thought you said you knew all about us."

"Yeah, well, I guess letters and real life are two different things."

"I guess." When the redheaded cranky urge struck me, it was impossible to resist. "I get it. We're not as cute in person as we were on paper. Is that it?"

"No, that's not it," she began. Paused. "I just . . . I mean, I don't . . ."

"That's okay," I told her. "You can change your mind." Joan of Arc at the stake would have envied my martyred sigh. "Feel free to drop us off at the orphanage before you head home."

"Forget the orphanage. I'm not changing my mind. I really do want you to live with me." Unconvinced, we made no reply. I couldn't speak for Buddy, but I wanted her to mention, at least once, that she liked us. A little. Otherwise, what was the difference between her and Aunt Preet?

"All right. How about I lay things on the line?" She sounded earnest and nervous. "I don't know a single solitary thing about children. I don't know what you eat, or how you think, or why you do the things you do."

Who said honesty was the best policy?

"Jeez, I've never even had a cat because I thought it would be too much trouble."

"I guess cats and kids are two different things." I echoed her words with a touch of snide.

"Exactly!" She threw up her hands and almost fell out of the tree before she resituated herself. "If child-rearing experts had to pick a suitable guardian for you, I would probably cross the finish line dead last. Okay?"

If she was trying to reassure me, it wasn't working. "But if your mama and daddy had to choose someone in this family to take care of you, I think I'd top their list."

She was offering a trick choice. Would I rather have pimples or be fat? Be smart and homely or pretty and dumb? Who was a better guardian? Aunt Prune or Aunt Floozy?

One thing was true. Mama would have picked Aunt Nora. All those years they were apart, Mama had kept Nora's picture on her dresser in a shiny silver frame. She had talked about how beautiful and talented her baby sister was to anybody who would listen. When Mama was in a bad mood, she said Nora was the only smart one in the bunch because she had escaped the Teegarden loony bin and a mess of crazy relatives who could wear down the Rock of Gibraltar.

When she was sad, Mama said Nora was the only lucky one in the bunch because she was living the life that Mama herself should have had. Nora was living *Mama's* dream.

So in a way, maybe by going to California with Aunt Nora I could live some of that dream and earn Mama's forgiveness for being ungrateful and bringing down the wrath of God. Maybe I could help Buddy live his dream too.

"I guess." There was a truce in those two little words. A covenant.

"So . . ." Aunt Nora blew a lock of red hair out of her eyes and rubbed her palms on her jeans. "We all agree then. Living with me in California is better than being turned over to the child welfare people?"

Child welfare? Had things really gone that far? I'd been kidding about the state children's home. Was Nanny Tee really willing to put us in an orphanage or farm us out to strangers? My belly twisted with betrayal. All those relatives and not one of them believed that blood was thicker than water. Hot tears stung my eyes, and I blinked so Aunt Nora wouldn't see how much her words hurt.

"We want to go with you." Saying the words made the decision easier, if not true. "Don't we, Buddy?"

I had to elbow him a couple of times. "Sh-sh-shure."

"You're positive? So it really is settled?" Aunt Nora grabbed our hands as though we were a basketball team making a huddle. "Okay. How about this? I'll do the best I can. And you two won't give me too much trouble. Deal?"

We nodded. Her best was probably on a par with Buddy's inability to give trouble.

"Great." Aunt Nora let out a long breath. "Whoo! I've been so worried. This is going to be a big change in my life."

"Ours too."

"Well, sure." She patted my shoulder like I was a bed she'd just made. "Everything will work out. You'll see. We're in this together now, like the Three Musketeers. All for one and one for all. Right?"

Right.

We ran out of mourners before ham salad, and the next day Aunt Nora announced she was tired of eating funeral food. She loaded Buddy and me into her shiny movie star car and took us to the Dairy Hut for hamburgers and cherry Cokes. She started in again on how much fun we were going to have, referring to our upcoming adventure with capital letters.

The Trip.

Nanny Tee said Nora didn't know shit from Shinola about kids, but her heart was in the right place, and if I knew what was good for me, I'd better work up a little enthusiasm. All I could do was roll my eyes and sigh like Mona Freeman in *Dear Ruth*, an old movie I'd recently seen as part of a William Holden triple feature.

The story was about a teenage girl who wrote love letters to a soldier and signed her older sister's name. Everything unraveled when the soldier showed up and fell in love with the big sister, which messed up her engagement. Joan Caulfield ended up with William Holden instead of the prissy Billy De Wolfe, which gave the movie a happy ending.

I saw no such ending in our future and substituted sighs for talking. On the way home from the Dairy Hut, Aunt Nora pulled in at an army surplus store. Explaining how we had to travel light, she picked out sleeping bags and mess kits with spoons and forks that hooked together. She rifled through the dusty inventory, selecting aluminum pots, iron skillets, and a kerosene camp stove. Several trips added insect repellent, flashlights, a Swiss Army knife and a lantern to the growing pile on the counter. She selected a two-man pup tent, claiming that as small as Buddy was, all three of us would fit in just fine.

I watched the sporting goods stack up. "Have you ever actually camped out before?" I asked a reasonable question, what with her planning to drag us off into the yawning wilderness and all.

"Not exactly." She flicked dust off her full skirt and held up a net dunk bag like Girl Scouts used when washing dishes in a stream. "Think we'll need one of these?"

I shrugged. "In the movies, cowboys rub sand on their plates to clean them."

"That's a little more primitive than I care to be. We'd better get one."

When the man behind the counter totaled up the bill, Aunt Nora paid with cash peeled from a wad big enough to choke an army mule. I'd never seen so much money in one person's pocket before. Maybe she wasn't a gangster's gun moll. Maybe she was a gangster herself and printed her own money. Whether it was counterfeit or not, at least we wouldn't starve. There had to be plenty of Dairy Huts between Tulsa and Hollywood.

We loaded our purchases in the trunk of the Buick and went home to pack. Nanny Tee and the other aunts had turned out to clean the furnished rental house. Like a flock of buzzards picking all the meat from a dead carcass, they'd cleared out everything but the landlord's furniture, leaving the rooms tidy and lonesome. Nothing was left there of Mama and Pop. No dishes in the sink, no clothes in the closet, no dust bunnies in the corner.

Hot sun slanted through the bare windows in my parents' bedroom. Mama's lace curtains were gone. The baby pictures in bronzed bootie frames were gone, and so was the noisy Big Ben alarm clock that ran six minutes slow. Pop's boots no longer stood in the corner. Without so much as a stray bobby pin on the night table, it was as though my parents had never existed.

I knew their bodies were in the ground. I hoped their souls had made it into heaven. I had hoped to find their spirits in the house, but nothing remained to remind the world that Johnny and Gracie Mahoney had lived there. Having never stayed in one place long enough to belong, maybe their spirits didn't know where to go.

They were truly gone. I threw myself on the bare mattress and pressed my face into the blue-striped ticking. Someday I would die, but I didn't want to disappear. I wanted to belong somewhere. I wanted to stay in one place so long that little bits of me soaked into the furniture and the trees and the shingles on the roof. I didn't want to spend the rest of my life without a home.

Breathing hard to choke back tears, I smelled the faint scent of Old Spice and Evening in Paris. Mama and Pop *had* been here! They had lived and loved and quarreled and kissed within these walls, if only for a short time. I closed my eyes and took big, sobbing whiffs to create a memory of a fragrance I might only have imagined.

Nanny Tee called my name from the living room, and I dragged myself away from my parents' bed. Before the buzzard aunts left, they'd piled my stuff and Buddy's in the middle of the floor for us to sort. We didn't own much worth hauling west, so Nanny Tee and Aunt Nora rummaged through the pile, culling outgrown clothes and overused toys. They tossed out solitary green army men and naked dolls, puzzles with missing pieces and scribbled-up coloring books.

Some things were packed for shipping and would be waiting for us when we arrived. The books I'd received for Christmas and birthdays. My butterfly collection. My junior scientist microscope. Buddy's stuffed animals and the model airplane he got by redeeming Wheaties box tops.

When they finished, Buddy and I each ended up with a pillowcase full of faded, mismatched clothes. Nanny Tee claimed the rest for rags. I had no sentimental attachment to the discarded items, most of which had been purchased at Ye Olde Thrift Shoppe on Brown Bag Wednesday, when everything you could stuff in a sack cost fifty cents. Aunt Nora promised to buy us clothes and toys in California that had not belonged to someone else first.

Upset by the sorting and tossing, Buddy cried when Nanny Tee pitched his raggedy old stuffed dog onto the junk pile. Roscoe only had one eye and half his original stuffing, but Mama had given Buddy the toy the day he came home from the polio ward, and he had carried it everywhere for years.

Aunt Nora retrieved the brown floppy-eared pup and slipped it into his arms. "Here you go, honey," she said. "You keep this doggie close to your heart." Her sweet smile sent my hopes soaring. Maybe she *could* love Buddy. She didn't have to love me, if she would only love Buddy. Maybe she would get used to me. Maybe in time we could be a family and live in a house where we all belonged. Maybe.

Buddy couldn't form thoughts into words, but I knew he believed his life had been cast aside, because I felt that way too. Like all we owned was thrown out for trash, and all we could be had been buried with our parents.

I sifted through a shoebox of old pictures and found one of Pop and me taken when he came home from the war. He was in his uniform and held me like he'd never let me go. He hadn't seen me since I was a bald-headed baby, but that didn't matter. He loved me anyway. I slipped the picture in my pocket and kept sneaking peeks at it.

Mama always worked the camera, so there weren't many photos of her. I finally pulled out an old shot of her and Pop, taken when they were first married. That's how I wanted to remember them. When they were young and happy and still believed roller coasters were fun.

We rose early the next morning. Aunt Nora wanted to get in some driving time before the day heated up. Our departure was silent with unexpected finality. Would we ever get back to Oklahoma? In ten years? Twenty?

When I was grown all the way up, I would return and show off the prize I had won for being Librarian of the Year. I'd bring my handsome husband, who was a genius, and my clever, beautiful children. All my stingy old relatives would slobber with envy when they found out how rich we were.

Nanny Tee handed me a bag of baloney sandwiches she'd packed for the Trip, pecked our cheeks good-bye, and told us to be good for Aunt Nora. She shed no tears, and I was determined not to cry either. Even pills had pride. Still half asleep, Buddy crawled into the back-seat with his toy dog and settled on the nest of pillows we'd fluffed for him.

I slipped into the front with my knapsack. Inside were items that would enable me to keep my head down and avoid chitchat. My fa-vorite book with the pictures of Mom and Pop pressed between the pages. A coloring book and crayons. Crossword puzzles. Enough distractions to last all the way to California.

Aunt Nora slid on her sunglasses, tied a bright blue chiffon scarf over her hair, wrapped it around her neck and knotted it in the back, Lana Turner style. She folded the convertible top down and adjusted the radio and rearview mirror to her satisfaction.

"Hang on, kiddos, we're in for a bumpy ride." She got the Bette Davis line wrong, but at least she was trying. Before the Trip was over, maybe I would feel like smiling at her jokes.

Nanny Tee stood on the porch clutching her bathrobe at her throat. Her good-bye wave was happy, like we were off on a joyride around the block instead of leaving forever. Bad enough she could let us go without a second thought, but did she have to be so thrilled about it?

She would be sorry. I would become such an exceptional person that she would wish she'd kept me. When she was really old and rocking at the home with other old ladies, she would pine over me, and tell everyone how deeply she regretted her decision to exile me to California.

I had shortcomings to overcome, but I would work hard and be a model child with good manners and show extra unselfish kindness to pitiful people. I would study hard and be the teacher's pet and be the best in my class. I would outgrow my knobby-kneed scrawniness and turn into a handsome woman, because after all, my parents had been handsome, and I might have inherited good looks that had not yet come to light.

Making my grandmother feel bad might not have been a worthy goal, but my resolve gave me a sense of purpose.

"It's a grand fine morning to get our show on the road," Aunt Nora said as she backed out of the driveway. "You kids ready for the first episode of The Daring Adventures of Us?"

She didn't seem to mind that we only nodded. As we streaked down the empty streets, I looked around and realized my aunt was right. The day was brand-new and full of promise. Dew shimmered on the grass, sunlight glinted off the windshield, and for the first time since that bloody night at the carnival, a spark of hope flickered in my heart.

When Armadillos
Run Amok

The scenery unfolded in an unexciting patchwork of small towns and farms. I didn't want to play Count the Cows, and I didn't feel like talking. Except for the four times we stopped to let Buddy pee in the weeds, I pretended to sleep most of the way to Oklahoma City.

It was barely nine o'clock in the morning when Aunt Nora spotted a big red Texaco star and pulled into the station for gas. A young guy with pimples on his forehead and grease on his fingers cleaned the crusting bug guts off the windshield. He flirted with Aunt Nora, and she flirted back, winking at me on the sly to let me know she didn't mean it. She smiled and batted her eyelashes while the guy checked the oil, topped off the radiator, and let a little air out of an overinflated tire.

"Releasing a little pressure prevents unnecessary tire wear," he told her with a gulp.

"Why, thank you"—she read his name off his uniform pocket—"Leon. I know *I* always feel better when someone helps me release a little pressure." She flashed her dimpled grin and the poor guy backed into the car's side mirror, then spun around to right it.

Aunt Nora looked good, and knew it, in a blue dotted Swiss shirt-waist with a sailor collar and a white belt that cinched her tiny waist. Her feet seemed impossibly small in white ballerina flats that would have been too little for me last year. Grace Kelly goes camping. If she was planning to rough it, she had better have some dungarees and flannel shirts in her suitcase.

My aunt seemed happy despite the vagueness of our plans. Like Pop, maybe she thought if she kept smiling and joking and having fun, her enthusiasm would rub off on us, and Buddy and I would get happy too. Or maybe she was just pretending. She *was* an actress.

While she was playing goo-goo eyes with the grease monkey, I took Buddy to the restroom. He stayed in there even longer than usual. One thing about Buddy. While his number ones were frequent and urgent, his number twos were just the opposite.

When we climbed back into the car, Aunt Nora handed us each a bottle of Grapette and a brown paper bag.

"What's this?" We'd eaten a few of Nanny Tee's dry baloney sandwiches and called it breakfast, but I could stand some doughnuts. I had a wicked sweet tooth and loved jelly doughnuts almost as much as Baby Ruth candy bars.

"Oh, just a little present for you and Buddy. Go ahead, Pauly, open the sack."

Not so fast. I was willing to be won over, but couldn't be bribed with gifts. "What's it a present for?"

Aunt Nora grinned her dimply smile. "For no reason."

A present for no reason made me suspicious, but Buddy wiggled with excitement. We ripped into the bag and found two coonskin caps with big bushy tails that hung down in back.

Definitely not doughnuts.

"What's this?" I held up one by the tip of the tail. The gift of unexpected fur had left me at a loss for words.

"What do you think it is, silly?" Aunt Nora asked.

"Somebody's failed attempt at taxidermy?"

She cackled and squeezed my shoulder. "That's rich. You're an all-right kid, Pauly Mahoney. Thank God, you got a sense of humor. Makes life a whole lot easier. Go on, put them on so I can see how you look."

"D-D-Davy Crockett caps." Buddy didn't stutter much when he whispered. He nudged me in the ribs. "You know, Pauly. King of the Wild Fron-Fron-Frontier."

Aunt Nora grinned and passed us each a stick of Juicy Fruit before folding two sticks into her own mouth. This was the most Buddy had ever said in her presence. She must have been pleased with herself for making him happy enough to talk, because she broke into song right there in the car and started singing in a phony baritone about how Davy Crockett was born on a mountaintop in Tennessee.

To my amazement, when she got to the part where Davy kilt a b'ar when he was only three, Buddy chimed in and hardly stuttered a syllable. By the time she steered us back onto Route 66, the two of them had a regular hootenanny going.

"Come on, Pauly, sing with us," Aunt Nora urged.

"No, thank you." I pulled *The Yearling* out of my bag. I knew how the story ended because I'd already read it twice, and I was prepared to be sad.

"Don't you know the words?"

I gave her a guess-again smirk. Of course, I did. Everybody and his pet Chihuahua knew the lyrics to that song. It had been the number-one record in the country for five weeks and the dumb, catchy tune haunted you in your sleep. If I sang out loud, the song would be stuck in my brain all the way to California.

"Come on, sing with us."

"I can't carry a tune in a galvanized bucket."

"Who told you that?" Aunt Nora asked.

"Mama." We weren't allowed to sing in the house because the racket got on her nerves.

"Well, shoot. You don't have to sing because you're good at it. You have to sing because it feels good."

So I did. Belting out the words as we zipped down the highway felt like the best kind of freedom. I even wore the stupid cap so Aunt Nora wouldn't think I was an ungrateful pill. I don't know what kept Fess Parker from feeling like a fool in that getup, but if you're head to toe in buckskin fringe, what's a little extra fur up top?

Remembering my resolution to change myself into a paragon among orphans, I thanked Aunt Nora for the gift. "But next time, if you want to give me a present that isn't doughnuts for no reason, a new *Photoplay Magazine* would be nice."

We drove west across Oklahoma, and before long we were buzzing across the Texas panhandle toward Amarillo. Buddy played with a wad of Silly Putty in the backseat, and Aunt Nora hummed along with Tennessee Ernie Ford on the radio. After listening to "The Ballad of Davy Crockett" six times, "Sixteen Tons" was a welcome change.

"You've been awfully quiet, Pauly." Aunt Nora steered with her knee and fished another pack of Pall Malls out of the glove compartment. "Aren't you having a good time?"

"It's been okay so far." I didn't look up from my book. I was rereading the part where Penny gets snake bit, and Jody has to cut the heart out of the mama deer to save his pa. I knew all about having your heart cut out.

"Why don't you put your book away? Reading is a good habit, but you're missing all the scenery." She lit a cigarette, tilted her head back and inhaled deeply, watching me out of the corner of her eye.

Heaving another Mona Freeman sigh, I slid the book back into my bag and gazed around dutifully as miles and miles of flat, empty plains streaked by. She was right. I wouldn't want to miss all that glory of nature. Whatever would I tell my grandchildren about? Wait! Was that a rock?

"Nanny Tee says you're a real chatterbox."

Oh really? I thought she said I was a pill. When I didn't respond, Aunt Nora said, "Okay, Pauly. Why are you giving me the silent treatment?"

I wanted to tell her I was seriously worried about my uncertain future and the future of my sickly brother who was like flypaper for germs. I wanted to ask her what would happen someday when someone, somewhere realized she should not be in charge of orphan children. Then where would we be?

But I kept quiet. I could hardly admit those serious fears to a person who considered coonskin caps a good present.

"Are you mad at me about something?" she asked.

"No."

"Upset?"

"No."

"Scared?"

"No. I'm not anything. I was just thinking."

"About what?" Was she as uncomfortable with me as I was with her? If it came down to rock, paper, scissors, I would win. I actually had experience being a niece, and she was just pretending to be an aunt.

"Evolution."

Aunt Nora hooted. Her laughter was a burst of runaway hilarity that tumbled out and filled the air like the steam that rolled out when you lifted the lid on a boiling pot. Even after you clamped the lid down, it took a second for the water to evaporate. Aunt Nora's laughter lingered like that.

"Do *you* believe in evolution?" I asked in a serious scientist voice, or as serious as a scientist could be while wearing a dead mammal pelt on her head.

"Do you?"

"Sure. Evolution makes sense, scientifically speaking."

"I didn't know you were interested in science, Pauly."

"Oh?" I scraped up some sarcasm. "Didn't Mama write you a lo-o-o-o-ng letter about me winning the science fair in fifth grade?"

"Right." She kept her eyes on the road. "I must have forgotten."

That was probably it. "Ever hear of survival of the fittest? It's a famous theory."

"I think so." She spoke cautiously. "Darwin, right?"

"Right."

"What about it?" Aunt Nora's long red fingernails tapped a nervous rhythm on the steering wheel, and she streamed ashes out the window. A ciggie butt accidentally flipped into the backseat would incinerate Buddy's pillows, to say nothing of Buddy himself.

"Do you have any idea how many dead armadillos I've counted in the road since we hit Texas?" I asked.

Some had been squished, their shells cracked and leaking like raw eggs. Others were just lying there whole, with their hairy little feet sticking up to heaven. Maybe they'd keeled over of a heart attack at the thought of being plowed down by a speeding RC Cola truck.

"Armadillos?" She glanced sideways at me through her Foster Grants before turning back to the highway simmering in the afternoon sun.

"Eleven. Eleven dead armadillos in approximately one hundred miles, and those are just the ones I noticed. I was reading part of the time."

"Okeydokey."

"That's more than one for every ten miles, right?"

She did the calculations. "Right."

"Is that a lot, do you think?"

"I don't know, Pauly. I don't think anyone keeps track of dead armadillos."

"Someone should. Because it seems like a lot. Do armadillos have any natural enemies? Besides Pontiacs and Fords?"

"I don't know much about armadillos."

I narrowed my eyes the way scientists in movie labs did before announcing a disturbing discovery. "You don't think they get run over on purpose, do you?"

She laughed. "I think we can safely assume that armadillos do not commit vehicular suicide by throwing themselves in front of oncoming traffic."

"That's what I figured. Since they're probably not playing some kind of dangerous Chevrolet roulette, it's probably only the dumb ones or the slow ones that get hit and killed."

"I guess so."

"Don't you get it?"

"Get what?"

"Eventually the ones carrying genes for dumbness and slowness will become extinct, like passenger pigeons and dodo birds, and there won't be any dumb, slow armadillos around to pass those traits on to their offspring."

"That's an interesting observation." Aunt Nora's cautious tone said she thought I'd taken too much sun.

"That's the survival of the fittest theory. If all the dumb, slow ones die out, the day will come when a species of superdillos that are too smart and too fast to get hit by cars will evolve. Then there won't be any smooshed ones on the side of the road. Notice how you never see a *live* armadillo?"

"Now that you mention it."

"You still don't understand, do you? If superdillos evolve, they will multiply unchecked like jackrabbits and there will be an armadillo population explosion. Which would be a plague worse than biblical locusts. The president will have to call out the National Guard to protect the citizens, and the whole Southwest will become a bloody battleground. Humans versus armadillos. Two powerful species vying for supremacy of the land."

Aunt Nora smiled. "You've been watching way too many creature features, kiddo."

"I don't think you realize the potential horror of a nation overrun by mutated armadillos."

She peered at me over her sunglasses. "As far as I know, Pauly, armadillos do not pose any threat or danger to human beings."

There was that. "I know." I pulled *The Yearling* out again and flipped it open to another sad part. "But if they did, it could be a real scary situation."

Going My Way

We picked up the hitchhiker between Amarillo and Tucumcari. I'd heard stories about people who gave rides to strangers. They wound up in bar ditches with steak knives in their skulls, a violent end that made stopping seem like a bad idea. Then again, our hitchhiker didn't look too dangerous.

Bowlegged and scrawny, the old man was at least seventy years old and as dried out as jerky. He had white hair down to his shoulders, a big droopy mustache, and bristly white whisker stubble. He wore baggy blue jeans stuffed into run-over cowboy boots, and a sweat-stained Stetson that looked as if it had been trampled by a herd of angry longhorns.

Miles from anywhere, he stood on the side of the highway, stooped under the pack on his back, and thumbed for a ride. Based on the I-shoot-trespassers scowl on his face, he didn't expect to get one. The little black-and-white dog at his side was so feisty it levitated on every yip.

Aunt Nora shook her head. "Would you look at that old fella? He's flirting with heatstroke standing around in this sun." She braked the

Buick and leaned across me to address the stranger. "Where you headed, Gramps?"

"Anywhere but here, sister." He had a soft western drawl, like a voice overheard over a poker hand in a red velvet saloon.

"If you want a ride somewhere, our final destination is California."

"Californy'll do me jest fine." Blue eyes, as clouded as slow-frying egg yolks, gave me and Buddy the once-over. "Your kids bite?"

"Not unless they're provoked." Aunt Nora worked her dimple.

"Got room for my kit and the dog?"

"I think we can squeeze you in." She directed me to jump out and open the trunk, and the hitchhiker tossed in his pack. Buddy scooted over, and the old man settled beside him in the backseat, wary as a sinner in Sunday school. The dog, clearly glad for the ride, sat up real chipper-like between them, his pink tongue hanging out about a foot. The old man squinted at our Crockett caps. "Kill those coons yerself, sis?" he asked me.

"Yep." I matched him squint for squint. "With my bare hands."

That must have been the answer he expected, because he just nodded. His dog stunk to high heaven. I wrinkled my nose in distaste and forgot all about being a mannerly orphan. "How long since that mutt had a bath, mister?"

"A mite whiffy, ain't he?" Our new passenger's laugh was dry and rattly, like rocks rolling into a ravine. "He ain't my dog. We's jest travelin' companions."

Buddy was never one to let offensive odors or potential dander problems stand between him and new friends. He scratched the dog's head and some of the black spots jumped around.

"He's got fleas," I pointed out.

"That's why I don't 'low him in my bedroll." The old cowboy tipped his battered hat at Aunt Nora, and then stretched a hand latticed with bumpy blue veins and dotted with liver spots into the front seat. "Name's Tybalt Bisbee, ma'am. Pleased to make your acquaintance."

"Tybalt? That sounds familiar. Shakespeare, right?"

"Mebbe. My ma said she got it out of some book or t'other."

We introduced ourselves, and Buddy asked the dog's name.

"Puppy."

Buddy seemed satisfied, but I wasn't. "Puppy's not a name. Puppy's what he is."

"Suits him though, don't it?" Tybalt Bisbee was rough-looking, but so soft-spoken his words floated away on the wind. I had to pay extra attention to hear him. He didn't throw careless grins around, but once in a while his mustache twitched ever so slightly.

"Mr. Bisbee, if I might ask, what were you doing out on the highway so far from civilization?" Aunt Nora watched the road, but seemed worried about Puppy's spots getting into the leather upholstery.

"Doin' what God gave me legs fer." Like Gary Cooper in *Sergeant York*, the old man had a way of politely responding to questions without actually answering them or volunteering information.

"So, Mr. Bisbee." I was determined to keep the conversational ball bouncing. I'd grown tired of keeping quiet, and being nice was too difficult. "Are you going to visit relatives?"

"Nope. Ain't got none I care to visit."

"Where're you from?"

"Lately of Ash Lawn Manor. Fort Worth, Texas."

The name conjured up images of white columns and mint juleps and spoiled girls in fluffy dresses. "Is that a plantation?"

"Old-age home," he said with a quick spit out the window. "And a more hellish place on earth I never hope to see."

Aunt Nora's piercing look said lay off the questions, but I pretended not to notice. Kneeling on the seat, I folded my arms on the backrest and propped my chin on my arms. It took some serious prompting to keep the old man going, but by the time we'd gone fifty miles, I had most of Tybalt Bisbee's story.

He had owned a ranch outside Denton, Texas. His great-granddad had settled there after the Mexican War, and the land had passed down through the family to him. His only son didn't want to be a rancher and went to Baylor Medical School and studied to be a urologist.

"What's that?" I was ever on the lookout for new words.

"A pee-pee doctor," the old man said with a snort of derision.

Mr. Bisbee had suffered a setback when his wife passed away, and he soon began to fail. "Arthritis set in, and pretty soon, I couldn't run the ranch by myself. Couldn't set a horse all day, couldn't wrestle steers worth a damn. 'Long about that time, I started forgetting things and misplacing papers. I knew I was slipping, but I wasn't ready for the glue factory." He paused and watched the scenery stream by.

"And?" So far, Mr. Bisbee was the most interesting thing we'd run into on the Trip, and I resisted the urge to mind my own business.

"My son said I was senile and had me declared incompetent. Incompetent!" He spit another brown tobacco stream over the convertible's door. "Got hisself a court order and stuck me in a rest home. Sold the ranch right out from under me. Them low-living snake bellies got away with most of my money."

"Robbers?" I prompted.

"Worser'n that. Relatives. I went downhill fast at the home. I was in a daze all day, like somebody had spun me around a few times too many. My mind was so clabbered up, sometimes I forgot my own name. Couldn't do nuthin' 'cept sit in a corner and drool on my shirt. Figured I wasn't long for the world."

Pause.

"Then what happened?" I'd never had to work so hard for a story in my life.

"I overheard two of the aides talking one night. Turned out my son had told them I was violent and had to be see-dated for my own good. I'm a peace-lovin' man, but when I heard that, I sure as Sunday felt like stirrin' up hell with a long spoon."

Pause.

"What did you do after that?" It was exasperating how Mr. Bisbee rested on each new revelation, like he had just delivered the end of the tale. Sorry, but I had read hundreds of stories and knew the difference between a climax and a cliff hanger.

"I started squirreling away my pills, that's what. Felt better after a while. Regained my wits. Stopped drooling. When I'd missed enough doses to unscramble my brains, I decided there was only one thing to do."

Pause.

Sigh. Let me guess. Burn the place down? Call in the cavalry? Sue the bastards? "What?"

"I ran away."

Anticlimax. "You busted out of an old-age home?" Not as thrilling as Edmond Dantes's escape in *The Count of Monte Cristo*, but factor in old age and arthritis, and any form of evasive action on Mr. Bisbee's part was pretty dramatic.

"Yup. Caught me some lucky breaks and made a run for my life. That's my story, and here I am, a wild-eyed fugitive, on the lam from God's waitin' room." He turned to Aunt Nora. "Jest so's you know, ma'am, I ain't dangerous."

"I never thought you were," Aunt Nora said with a smile. "What your son did wasn't right."

"That's a fact. Ain't nuthin' meaner'n an ungrateful chile."

He looked right at me when he spoke, like he was operating on some kind of special power that told him *I* was an ungrateful child and destined to come to no good end. That arrow stuck in my heart, shutting me up good. I'd sinned on a smaller scale, but comparatively speaking, my crimes weren't so different from those of the ranch-stealing doctor and snake-bellied relatives.

I'd swiped money out of Pop's billfold to fatten up the rent fund. I'd told my parents bald-faced lies about how I got bruises at school. I'd hid out in the library when I knew they were looking for me. I'd kept the gruesome details of my life to myself so they wouldn't know how unpopular I was. I did that to keep them from finding out the truth, but I was no better than the doctor who'd drugged his father for his own good.

"Did you consider getting a lawyer, Mr. Bisbee, and taking your son to court?" Aunt Nora asked.

"Nah. Cain't trust lawyers any more'n you can trust doctors. Whole lot of 'em is in cahoots to get the little man. Now that the Rockin' B is gone, I don't want nuthin' from nobody 'cept to be left alone."

I knew just how the old man felt, having recently discovered the snake-belliness of my own relatives. Aunt Nora said she understood too.

"Well now, there is one thing I want to do," he said. "God willin', I got my mind set on pickin' an orange right off a tree."

Aunt Nora smiled in his direction. "I believe we can help God out with that one, Mr. Bisbee. But you'll have to wait a while. Oranges won't ripen in California for a few more months."

We rode along in silence while Puppy scratched out a rhythm with the Crew Cuts and Bill Haley on the radio. Mr. Bisbee didn't demonstrate much curiosity, but I couldn't let the silence be golden. I had been damming up words for days, and when the floodgate opened, our story gushed out on a wave of self-pity.

"Never heared of anybody getting killed on a rolly coaster." Mr. Bisbee shook his head. "Sorry way to go."

I agreed.

"What happened to your folks is mighty sad, little sis," he said. "Reckon you'll have a long row to hoe. Jest don't let bein' an orphan be your excuse."

"My excuse for what?"

"For anything. Remember, wrapped up in yourself, you make a mighty small package."

I nodded and mulled. Mr. Bisbee was old, and old people were wise.

He looked hard at Buddy, who hadn't said a thing so far. "Can you talk, little brother?"

"Of course he can talk," I said.

He ignored me and pressed Buddy. "I asked you a question, sonny. Can you talk?"

Buddy nodded.

"Glad to hear it. I respect a man who plays his cards close to the vest." Mr. Bisbee glanced pointedly in my direction. "Some people talk 'cause they got somethin' to say. And others talk 'cause they gotta say somethin'. Speak up and tell me why you're wearing that leg iron, pardner."

I sighed with frustration. Maybe he wasn't wise, or he'd know better than to point out a person's infirmities.

Buddy scratched Puppy's little pinhead. "P-p-polio." Transported into canine ecstasy, the dog thumped his hind leg against the upholstery in stuttered cadence.

"Cain't you walk none without it?" The old man flicked the metal bar on Buddy's brace with a long yellow talon.

"D-d-don't know."

"You never tried?"

Buddy shook his head. "D-d-doctor said n-n-no."

Having already stated his low opinion of the medical profession, Mr. Bisbee harrumphed and folded his arms across his sunken chest. His long hair fluttered in the breeze.

"He's not a cripple." I spoke up in Buddy's defense. "He wears the brace because his leg is weak."

"Don't wonder it's weak, what with him never walkin' on it. How you gonna know if a pony can run if you keep him hobbled? Doctors! They don't know everythin'."

I rolled my eyes. When it came to polio treatments, I was pretty sure physicians knew more than hitchhikers. Buddy would need a new brace soon because he'd almost outgrown the old one. Nanny Tee had made Aunt Nora promise to have him checked out when we reached California.

Mr. Bisbee was sensitive enough not to question my brother about his distressing speech impediment. We never knew what made Buddy stumble over his words. No other Teegardens or Mahoneys were so afflicted. Most of the time, Buddy just repeated sounds, but sometimes when he was nervous, his words got corked up inside him. It was painful to watch him blinking and nodding and trying to get them unstuck.

He did better when he whispered or sang songs. He could recite rhymes like "Mary Had a Little Lamb" and say the Pledge of Allegiance just fine. But put him in a face-to-face conversation with a human, and he suffered a serious handicap. Kids at school made fun of him, and I'd gotten into more than one fight on his behalf.

After one particularly heinous incident, Mrs. Pursley, the tightly girdled principal at our last school, had predicted I would wind up in a reform school. The old bat would have to change her tune when she found out I had actually wound up in Hollywood.

Mama had taken Buddy to a head-shrinking doctor once. He told her Buddy's stuttering problem was the result of a personality disorder caused by his toilet training. Since she had been the one who trained him, Mama felt bad and never took him back to see that doctor again.

There *was* something iffy about Buddy's toileting habits, but that doctor was wrong about one thing. Buddy's personality was fine, what there was of it. He was the sweetest kid you'd ever want to meet. Maybe a little shy and kind of backward, but anyone who'd spent three months in a polio hospital, locked up behind glass like a dangerous fish, would be wary.

And mixed up. Buddy had come up with the notion that if he could just get rid of the leg brace, his speech would improve. Since it slowed his walking, it had to slow his talking, too. He never got to test his theory because Mama was afraid if he went without the brace, he might suffer a setback and end up in an iron lung. He had accepted her decision, once I explained that the mouth bone was not connected to the leg bone anyway.

We rode along for a few more miles, and Aunt Nora told Mr. Bisbee how we were planning to camp out and see the sights. "We're taking our time getting to California." She glanced into the backseat. "If you're not on a tight schedule, you're welcome to tag along."

"I just go where God flings me, sister." The old man sat up straight, his hands folded in his lap. "I do have a hankerin' to see the ocean though. Ain't never seen that much water in one place. Reckon you'll be goin' anywheres near the Pacific Ocean?"

"I can drive you right to the beach."

"Mighty fine. I'll stick with ya then. Might be safer for a lady with young'uns in tow to have a man along for protection."

"I believe you are right about that, Mr. Bisbee." Aunt Nora had no problem adding another member to the crew.

"Since we'll be travelin' together, I would appreciate it if you all would just call me Tyb. I reckon I've left my Mr. Bisbee days behind."

"Glad to have you aboard, Tyb. I'll rest better knowing you're with us." Aunt Nora offered him a cigarette from her pack of Pall Malls, but he declined, saying he was a chewer, not a smoker.

He pulled a small cloth bag of tobacco from his shirt pocket, placed a pinch in his cheek, and relaxed against the seat. Puppy crawled into Buddy's lap, a joyous arrangement for boy and dog.

Aunt Nora turned up the radio and puffed on her cigarette. The ease with which my new guardian sealed friendships and took on ballast flat-out amazed me. She would feel safer with Grandpa Cowboy along?

I peered into the backseat. With his eyes closed and his mouth gaping open, Tyb looked like one of the dried-up mummies archaeologists found laid up in caves. He was so feeble a couple of Buddy's sneezes would blow him into next week. Even fortified with a steady diet of Wonder Bread and Wheaties, the old fellow wouldn't look like he could protect us from a half-crazed armadillo.

I sighed and silently prayed that no emergencies requiring his aid and assistance would arise.

8

Under the Stars

As luck would have it, Old Tyb rescued us that very night. Not from highwaymen or bears or cataclysms of nature. He saved us from having to eat cold-from-the-can Spam for supper, a fate that some people would place in the worse-than-death category.

Back at the Texaco station in Oklahoma City, Aunt Nora had spread a road map on the Buick's hood and leaned over the nervous attendant's shoulder while he drew a penciled line along Route 66, all the way from Oklahoma to the Pacific Ocean. My job was to keep my finger on the line and make sure we didn't get lost. The squiggle snaked across the map, and I was surprised to see how far we'd traveled in one day.

The scenery had changed dramatically. Whizzing southwest all afternoon, making only potty stops, we'd left the green cow fields of eastern Oklahoma, crossed the armadillo-strewn no-man's-land of the Texas panhandle, and climbed up into the highlands of New Mexico.

Just before dusk, when the sun was making a last-ditch effort to pierce the evergreen canopy, we pulled into Lone Pine Campground. I was the only one who thought the name was funny, which it was, considering how many pines there were. The ground was thick with needles, and the air was thin, like the oxygen had been skimmed off. The trees were taller than any I'd ever seen, their lowest branches starting where Oklahoma trees left off, and when the wind soughed through the boughs, it sounded like a thousand angels humming.

Buddy and I clambered out of the Buick and stood around gawking like kids who'd never been set loose in the woods before. The nippy air was too cool for July, and we pulled on sweaters. After being cooped up in the car all day, I needed to stretch the kinks out of my legs, so I ran around, trying to take everything in. Buddy limped and clanked after me. I called tag, and we raced among the massive tree trunks and hid behind boulders tumbled from ancient primeval peaks.

We didn't yell or shout. The forest was a green church with a dignified silence that should not be disturbed. I stopped and sniffed the rarefied air. It smelled piney sharp, like the brown bottle of disinfectant Mama used when she was serious about cleaning.

It saddened me to think of her, dead and buried less than a week, but I couldn't be miserable in such a wondrous place. I threw back my head and twirled around, spinning away the tears and turning the branches overhead into a kaleidoscope of swirling shapes. I was a long way from Oklahoma and people who didn't want me. The past was already a memory, and the future could be anything I could make it.

It felt good to be alive, and for the first time since the accident, I didn't feel guilty about not dying. When I plopped down on the ground and looked up into the trees, I started laughing and couldn't stop.

"Wh-wh-what's so f-f-funny, Pauly?" Buddy sat beside me.

"I just realized something."

"What?"

"We were having fun just now."

"W-w-were we?" Buddy's pale cheeks were pink with rare color.

"I didn't think we could have fun again." I still had laughter in me. Did that mean I was a bad daughter who didn't know how to grieve? Or did it mean I had a reason to live?

"Me n-n-neither." Buddy leaned close to whisper. "I'm glad we d-d-didn't stay with Nanny T-T-Tee."

"How come?"

" 'Cause sh-sh-she don't know how to have f-f-fun."

"What about Aunt Nora?"

He grinned. "Sh-sh-she knows how."

"Where do you think she got all that money?" I asked.

"She l-l-lives by the beach. Maybe sh-sh-she found a p-p-pirate's treasure."

I nodded. His explanation was as good as mine.

Other campers were scattered around, some in little silver trailers, some in tents. The smell of their suppers cooking made my mouth water. We'd finished the rest of the baloney sandwiches and ordered root beer floats from a Dairy Hut on the road, but I was starved. When we'd stopped for supplies, Aunt Nora had purchased a big steak to celebrate our first dinner al fresco. I didn't know what that meant, but I hoped it was French for grilled beef.

"So everything's okay with you?" I asked Buddy.

After a moment, he nodded. "Yep. Okay."

We helped Aunt Nora unload the car and Tyb sprinkled Puppy with the flea powder we'd bought at the store. Then the two of them disappeared in the woods to do their business. Through considerable trial and error, Buddy and I finally pitched the little tent. Once it looked like it would stay pitched, we crawled inside and spread the sleeping bags, stretching out on our stomachs for a test drive.

"C-c-can g-g-germs sneak in the tent while w-w-we're sleeping?" Buddy's scared look was back.

"Nah. Germs can't live at this altitude."

"Why n-n-not?"

"We're having trouble breathing, right?" I waited for him to agree. "Lungs on germs are really small. How could they breathe here?" He was not convinced by my explanation, so I started a tickling contest that nearly knocked down the tent.

Outside by the picnic table, Aunt Nora sang "How Much Is That Doggie in the Window?" and rattled the pots and pans. When I didn't hear the sound of steak sizzling in a skillet, I left Buddy in the tent with his stuffed doggie and joined Aunt Nora.

"What's wrong?" I heel-toed along the cold, concrete picnic bench, my arms extended like a tightrope walker's.

"Nothing." Her expression didn't match the word. Those drawn-down eyebrows definitely meant something. "Okay," she admitted, "I forgot to buy kerosene for the stove."

"Good thing there's a cooking pit." I poked in the remains of some-one else's fire with a stick. My aunt hadn't gathered any wood, and even I knew firewood was the first step to steak.

Still dressed in her blue frock, she'd tied a towel around her waist for an apron. She held a skillet in one hand and a three-and-a-half-pound porterhouse wrapped in white paper in the other. Her expression slid from worried to bumfuzzled. "It won't fit in the pan."

Small obstacle for a hungry person. "Cut it up in littler pieces," I suggested.

"Oh, good idea." Aunt Nora set the skillet down on the table. When she flopped the steak in it, the meat draped over the sides like a fat lady on a folding chair. She blew a lock of hair out of her eyes and dug around in the cook box for the Swiss Army knife. Her cherry-tinted lips pursed in concentration as she pulled out the blades, one by one. Can opener, corkscrew, toothpick, tweezers, scissors, screwdriver.

Finally . . . penknife. The little blade probably worked like gangbusters to dig dirt from under fingernails, but it was no match for the thick ring of white fat surrounding the steak.

"On second thought," Aunt Nora said with conviction, "let's have Spam for supper and save the steak for later."

"Steak doesn't shrink with age," I pointed out. "It spoils. Give me that knife." Good thing the germs had been asphyxiated, because I slapped the porterhouse down on the picnic table and commenced hacking. It was rough going, but hunger was a powerful motivator. Eventually, I sawed it into four fairly equal pieces. Puppy could eat the Spam. Camping wasn't nearly as rough as Eagle Scouts made it out to be.

"I cut, you cook," I challenged Aunt Nora.

She plopped the ragged hunks of meat into the skillet. Clearly bewildered by the whole barbecuing concept, she glanced around like she expected Betty Furness to stroll out of the woods pushing a Westinghouse range. Decked out in dotted Swiss, she even looked like Betty.

Buddy joined us and shrugged his thin shoulders. That meant he didn't understand the problem. All the grown women he knew had been capable of meal preparation, even if the sum total of their effort was often oatmeal.

"Buddy, you were in the Webelos," I said. "Show Aunt Nora how to build a campfire."

The Tunnel of Terror look came back, and he ducked his head. "We never g-g-got to make a f-f-fire."

"That's right," I recalled. "The den mother was afraid you boys would burn the house down."

"We made pencil c-c-cups with ice cream st-st-sticks."

"That's the kind of useful skill every woodsman needs to survive. In case he's lost in the wilderness with no place to keep his pencils." The airborne essence of someone's frying potatoes made me snippy. "Oh, how hard can it be? Let's get some branches and set 'em on fire. We *do* have matches, don't we?"

Aunt Nora nodded and produced a box.

"Good. That'll save Davy Crockett here from having to rub two sticks together."

"Anybody around here gettin' hungry?" Tyb called out.

We looked up to see a slow-moving pile of wood with skinny legs and cowboy boots lumber toward us. Puppy yapped around like he couldn't make up his mind which tree to hike a leg on next.

Aunt Nora looked relieved, and Buddy's face lit up as he ran to help. I, too, was considerably cheered. Of course the old man knew how to build a fire. He'd probably been on hand when combustion was first discovered.

Tyb proved to be worth his puny weight in gold, and I had to take back everything I'd thought about his potential usefulness. We had no kerosene for the stove or lantern, but he soon had a roaring fire going. He set Aunt Nora to peeling potatoes and onions. I opened cans of beans. When the fire died down to coals, Tyb threaded chunks of meat and vegetables on peeled sticks and laid them across a little tripod he'd rigged up. Juice from the meat dripped onto the hot coals and the aroma made our mouths water with anticipation.

While we waited for the food to cook, Buddy played with Puppy, and Aunt Nora talked to Tyb. I sat in the dark, just outside the fire's glow. The juicy meat smell reminded me of a happy time when we'd been a normal family. Pop had come into the bedroom in the middle of the night to shake us kids awake.

"What's wrong?" I'd asked, rubbing my eyes and blinking in the light from the hall. "Are we moving again?"

"Nah. Everything's fine. You kids come on in the kitchen. I got a surprise for you."

We woke up fast for surprises, especially when we thought the surprise would taste good. When Pop had a little extra, he splurged on special food. Jars of stuffed green olives that we ate like candy. Maraschino cherries. Day-old bakery cakes with buttercream frosting. Cans of cashews. Smoked oysters and melba toast.

Buddy and I leaped out of bed and scrambled down the short hall. It was two thirty-five by the clock on the wall by the back door. Wearing the pink robe Santa had left her, Mama sat at the chrome dinette table looking rumpled but not unhappy for someone whose sleep had been disturbed. She removed the contents of the grease-stained paper bag in the middle of the table.

Ernie burgers. Buddy and I loved the greasy pool hall hamburgers served fiercely peppered and piled with dill pickles and fried onions. Smaller than restaurant burgers, they came wrapped in waxed paper, their buns shriveled from the heat. The burgers had a special flavor. When I speculated about secret ingredients, Mama claimed the taste came from the grill not being cleaned since the Roosevelt administration.

Pop got a deal on the burgers because he was Ernie's friend, but he had to wait until two in the morning, when Ernie closed and bagged up the leftovers. The burgers were worth losing sleep over. Even on a school night.

"There's ten in there, so dig in," Pop told us. After Mama gobbled one down, she got up to put on a pot of coffee and pour milk for us children.

Ernie's snooker hall and beer joint was in a dirty brown building that squatted on a corner near Cain's Ballroom. Pop sometimes helped out around the place, sweeping up or washing dishes. Ernie was a wiry little man in a smelly white undershirt and greasy apron. He pulled beers and fried burgers and threw out drunks who got mean-mouthed.

I knew because Pop took me there when we were supposed to be collecting pop bottles. I had to promise not to tell Mama. She thought pool halls were no place for kids, but I thought it was the second-grandest place in town, after the library. I loved everything about it. The blue smoke that hung in the air like clouds on a windless day. The broken-hearted love songs that Patsy Cline and Patty Page wailed on the jukebox. The tough music of male laughter. The explosive clack of cue balls as they broke to scatter stripes and solids across green velvet. The scent of frying onions was strong enough to cover up the smell of too many men jammed in a small space.

I was usually the only female there except for the time a bleary-eyed woman in a flannel nightgown barreled in and plunked two blanket-wrapped babies on the bar in front of her startled husband. She yelled that she hadn't had a good night's sleep in two months and he could damn well come home and do his part.

After she slammed out, no one said a word. The men paused in their games, and the billiard balls stopped rolling. The daddy man paid for his beer, picked up his bawling babies like pink and blue sacks of nitroglycerin and hurried out the door and into the night.

Ernie turned to Pop and said, "Too bad they didn't draft women in forty-one. Damn war would have been over a lot sooner."

Ernie called me Carrot Top. He gave everyone what he called a special moniker, so Carrot Top meant I was part of the gang. His head was as bald as the cue ball, and he wore a patch over his left eye. Pop told me Ernie was a decorated veteran, disabled in the Pacific theater, but the bar man claimed his eye had been poked out with a pool cue when he tried to break up a fight. I never knew what really happened to his eyeball, but I wanted to believe the war story.

One-eyed or not, Ernie was an all-right guy. He let me chalk pool cues, sit on the bar, guzzle all the root beer I could hold, and scarf down ten-cent burgers on the house because I was his special guest.

There weren't many places where I was considered anything over ordinary, so I jumped at the chance to hang out with Pop in Ernie's smoky, greasy, noisy den of iniquity. In its dark recesses, I learned to play snooker and figured out that grown men and little boys were not very different.

I finished two burgers that night in Mama's kitchen before I sat back and patted my stomach. "Those really hit the spot."

Pop demolished one in three bites. "I swept up for Ernie tonight. He wanted to pay me in cash, but I said, no thanks, friend. I'll just take it home in hamburgs for my two favorite children."

"But we're your only children." Buddy and I called out the ritual response together.

"Yeah, but if I had a hundred . . ." Pop deadpanned his part of the routine.

"We'd still be your favorites," we chanted.

We sat around the table and laughed and told stories until four o'clock. Times like that, when Mama and Pop let us into their world and let me think there might be room for us too, made up for all the times they shut us out. In the morning, we missed the school bus because Mama overslept. We stayed in bed until noon and spent the rest of the day making popcorn balls and cutting paper dolls out of old Montgomery Ward catalogs. Normally, I didn't like missing school, but that day the happy feeling was so strong, I didn't want it to end.

I sat by the fire and watched Aunt Nora and Tyb and Buddy, but I couldn't stop thinking about Pop and wishing he hadn't been so impractical about midnight snacks and roller coasters.

He always said, "Don't worry about the future—just get through today and let tomorrow take care of itself."

Hard advice for a born worrier. I closed my eyes and pictured the way Pop had looked the night we sat up late acting like a real family.

Black hair shiny with Brylcreem, blue eyes full of fun. Strong and happy, with a lifetime to make good on his promises. My father would always look like that to me. His dark hair would never turn gray and his eyes would never dull with responsibility. He wouldn't grow up or grow old, and his bounce would never become a shuffle.

I took comfort in knowing age wouldn't take away his special way of looking at things, and that he died as he had lived, never taking life as seriously as folks wanted him to.

When the meal was ready, Tyb dished up the food, which went a long way toward reassuring me about our dubious adventure. Tyb moved too slowly to bring down game, but as long as Aunt Nora could hunt the grocery store aisles, his unexpected outdoor skills would come in handy.

I felt guilty about enjoying myself, but Mama and Pop wouldn't want me to be sad forever. They had been firm believers in having a good time, so wherever they were, I was pretty sure they would rather see us laughing under the stars with Aunt Nora and a prehistoric hitchhiker than crying behind Nanny Tee's blackout drapes.

After we washed the dishes, we sat around the campfire toasting marshmallows and telling ghost stories. Caught up in the chattiness, Tyb told us a tall tale about his great-granddad Bisbee, who had been captured by marauding Comanche back in Texas. Of course, he left us hanging.

"What happened?" I was getting good at prodding the rest of the story out of him.

"He got away from the Comanch by pretending to be crazy." According to Tyb, Old Granddad wallowed in buffalo dung and ate grass and poked himself with a hot stick so the Indians would think he was too loco to kill. Daring escapes seemed to run in the Bisbee family.

There wasn't much to do in the forest after nightfall, and we turned in early. Tyb and Puppy settled down next to the fire. The rest of us divided up the tent space and climbed into our sleeping bags. I fell asleep listening to the dark, eerie music of the woods and dreamed about Mama and Pop.

In my dream, they took us on a picnic in snow that looked like glitter. We climbed into a fancy Christmas-card sleigh pulled by a horse with tinkling bells on the harness. Mama wore a green velvet cloak. Pop's coat had a fur-trimmed hood like Arctic explorers in *National Geographic*. Buddy and I wore red stocking caps with fat green tassels. Most people dream in black and white, but I dreamed in Technicolor due to the Hollywood influence in my life.

Once we were deep in the woods, we sat on a red blanket in the snow and drank hot Ovaltine out of bone china cups. Bone china was the best kind, and when our ship came in, Mama said she would have a whole set imported from England. When I was little, I thought everyone had a ship at sea somewhere, loaded down with precious things to be delivered when it finally made its way into port. I've since learned better.

Mama stared into the woods, and Pop took Buddy and me to an ice cave that was warm inside, like an Eskimo's igloo. Before he left, Pop told us to rest, and we curled up on ice beds. A little while later when he hadn't come back, I ran outside.

My parents were in the sleigh, and it was being dragged over the snow by a galloping horse. Not the gentle, doe-eyed mare from before, but a big dark horse, powerful with purpose. Curls of vapor streamed from flared nostrils, and ice glittered in the billowing mane. Its black eyes were empty and wild at the same time.

I screamed for the horse to stop, but it kept running until it broke through the forest and charged out onto a vast frozen lake. Pop called to me. Before I could answer, the ice cracked like a rifle shot. A fissure opened in the ice, as wide and dark as a hole in a demon's heart. Rearing and screaming, the horse dove straight into the cold black water, pulling the Christmas-card sleigh, my parents, and my future in after it.

I tried to run, but my legs wouldn't move. I opened my mouth to call, but no sound came out. Helpless, I watched the crack in the ice slide shut like elevator doors. The lake became serene again. Winter birds chirped in the fir trees. The sun sparkled on the snow as though nothing had happened.

But everything had changed. Our parents were gone, and I hadn't saved them. I would never see them again. Never hear their voices. Never watch them hold and kiss each other and wish I could squeeze into the middle of their hug. I was left behind. Alone. This time, I hadn't gotten between them and the bad thing. I had failed.

I woke up crying, the tears hot on my face. I was scared and disoriented in the dark tent. Then I heard Buddy's wheezy snore on one side and felt Aunt Nora's warm body snuggled in her sleeping bag on the other and remembered where I was.

Feeling as dry-mouthed and hollow as I had at the viewing, I sat up and dashed away my tears. I shrugged off the remnants of the terrifying dream and lifted the tent flap.

Darkness in the city and darkness in the forest were two different shades of black. In town, lights from streetlamps and billboards and cars and houses formed an aura over the city, like the afterglow that lingers around a switched-off television set. In the forest, it was really dark. The inside of a turned-over tar bucket dark. So dark I couldn't see my hand in front of my face. I never understood claustrophobia until that moment, when I didn't know where I was in space, or if I still existed. The dream world had been terrifying, but the real world wasn't much better.

I stared up at the sky. The moon was a pale crescent, its feeble silver light swallowed whole by the grand blackness of nature. The wind made the trees sigh, and the sound of their branches swooshing overhead was like the wing beat of invisible birds. Unseen insects whirred and clicked mysterious messages in the grass. An owl called from across the void, and it was the loneliest sound I'd ever heard.

All that emptiness tightened a painful knot in my stomach because I knew what it meant to be alone in the world. My parents hadn't always been reliable, but I could count on that. I had nothing to count on now. In the faint glow of the dying campfire, I spotted the dark shape humped beside it. Old Tyb's rattly snore would have shaken the windows if there had been any windows around.

The old man lay cocooned in a threadbare old quilt that he said was one of the few things he had left of his family. His Tennessee grandma had made it before the Civil War and hauled it in an oxcart all the way to Texas, where she had married his grandfather. Tyb had managed to hang on to it when he was dispossessed and had taken it with him when he made his break from the rest home.

He called it a crazy quilt, and when he first shook it out of his pack, I thought it was the oddest blanket I'd ever seen. It was nothing like the precisely patterned quilts stitched by women in my family. The colorful pieces that made up Ohio Stars and Bear's Claws and Dresden Plates were as neat and predictable as a Sunday-school teacher.

The patches on Tyb's quilt were made of randomly cut cloth, sewn together with no apparent thought or design. Textures and colors never meant to be sewn—or seen—together. Scraps of satin, bombazine, calico, gingham, velvet, and what Tyb called linsey-woolsey, faded and worn through to the batting in places. The quilt had been embroidered with fancy stitches, which somehow created unified beauty out of all that chaos. Tyb's quilt kept him warmer than my guilt kept me.

Needing company, I made tentative kissy-kissy noises to rouse the smaller shape huddled beside Tyb. Two pointy ears perked up.

"Puppy!" I whispered as loud as I dared. A glowing log cracked in the fire, and sparks briefly illuminated his silly canine face. Bewildered, Puppy looked around as though he thought the owl was talking to him.

"Puppy! Over here! Come on, boy." He didn't belong to me, but Tyb wouldn't mind sharing, and if I had something to hug, maybe I wouldn't fly into a million pieces.

Puppy's cocked head seemed to say, "Who, me?"

"For cripes' sake, Puppy, you bonehead. Come here!" He finally got the message and stood up with a little shake and arched his skinny back. His wide yawn bared pointy teeth and a curled-up tongue. A moment later, he was beside me, but it was so dark I had to touch his warm body to make sure he was really there. He rewarded me with a moist lick.

I gathered him into my arms and buried my face in his fur, letting the tears fall. He seemed glad for the attention and whimpered his sympathy.

The fleas had jumped ship, and he didn't smell as gamey as before. He'd rolled in pine needles and the scent had mingled with smoke from the campfire. Holding him, I was comforted by the feel of his small chugging heart and the unrestrained affection of his wet tongue.

Dogs were man's best friends. Unlike people, dogs loved you when you didn't deserve to be loved. I had few friends at the moment, and Puppy seemed happy to be elected. I thought about how dogs had become pets in the first place. Probably about a million years ago, a solitary caveman had looked out at a dark world he would never understand, and maybe he had felt like me.

Maybe the thought of going it alone had made him desperate enough to make kissy noises at a wild creature slinking at the edge of the fire, because even the company of a potential predator was better than no company at all. That wild creature was probably torn between giving the caveman a lick on the face and ripping his throat out.

In the end, maybe the creature decided he could get a meal any-where, but a friend was hard to come by.

I scratched Puppy's ears, and he wriggled with sweet gratitude. He was just a hitchhiking Heinz 57 mutt, but he was warm, and he was alive, and there wasn't a chance in the world that he would die on a roller coaster or disappear into a frozen lake.

I wasn't alone in the night when the owl called the wind and the trees hummed like angels. I had something to hold on to that might maybe love me back.

9

In for a Penny

Tyb woke us before dawn the next morning and urged us to pack up and get out of the campground before all hell broke loose. Who knows where his mystical weather knowledge came from, but he was right. The storm struck with a fury just as we came down out of the mountains. Rain lashed the Buick, and tall pines swayed in the wind like masts of floundering ships. Lightning burned jaggedy patterns in the western sky, and the roll of angry thunder chased us all the way into Gallup.

Much of the drama was over by the time we pulled into town, but the storm had turned day into night and the rain drummed a steady beat on the convertible top. We'd had no time for breakfast, and Aunt Nora told us to keep our eyes peeled for a place to eat.

Gallup was what Nanny Tee would have called a wide place in the road. Plunked down between sagebrush and nowhere, most of the stucco buildings were strung out along the highway. Residents were either afraid to lose sight of civilization, or they wanted to be close to the road in case they needed to make a quick getaway. Due to bad weather and the early hour, the streets and narrow sidewalks were nearly deserted.

Across the street from the Greyhound bus terminal, I spotted a sign with the words CHUCK WAGON CAFÉ RUCKERS ELCOME spelled out in yellow lightbulbs. Aunt Nora maneuvered the Buick into a tight space between an eighteen-wheeler and a Wonder Bread delivery truck and ushered everyone but the dog inside. Afraid of the thunder, Puppy had hidden under the front seat and wouldn't come out for love or breakfast, so we didn't think he'd mind being left behind.

We ran inside the diner and a bell over the door announced our arrival. I blinked in the too-bright fluorescent light. Men in cowboy hats hunched over coffee cups at a long counter lined with salt and pepper shakers and ketchup bottles. All around the room, in booths and at tables, men sat eating, smoking, reading newspapers and talking low like boys in the back pews of church.

A tattooed man, whose five o'clock shadow had arrived nine hours early, flipped pancakes and sausage links at the sizzling grill. The smell of fried eggs and old grease made my empty stomach growl.

Buddy beelined for the toilet. Years of urinary urgency and too many accidents had given him a sixth sense in locating public facilities.

The men tracked us as Aunt Nora, Tyb, and I filed into one of the cracked vinyl booths in the back. You couldn't blame them for staring. We were an odd-looking outfit and wet as Monday's wash from our mad dash in from the parking lot: a second-rate actress who looked like Suzy Parker in strappy sandals and a bright floral skirt, a septuagenarian who looked like death on toast points, and two pitiful orphanage rejects.

The skinny waitress trudged over like her corns were killing her and flopped greasy menus down in front of us. Then, without a word, she clomped off in her turquoise uniform and white nurse shoes to refill the bottomless coffee cups of the regulars. She wound her way among the tables, laughing and teasing the men, and not trying too hard to dodge their patting hands.

Buddy returned and slid in beside me. He picked up the menu, and his face scrunched up with the effort to read it. He needed my help decoding the creatively named specials. He'd finished third grade but had missed so much school from being sick that he couldn't make out big words. Teachers had passed him from grade to grade, mainly to get him out of their classes. My brother never caused trouble, but through no fault of his own, he seemed to attract it.

Aunt Nora looked over the menu. "You kids order whatever you want. You too, Tyb." I suspected her good mood had something to do with not having to face fire-starting duty again. "Breakfast is on me this morning."

"I got some money." Indignation and pride tinged the old man's words. I imagined his "some" alongside Aunt Nora's mule-choking, counterfeited pirate treasure. Running away from the rest home as he had, Tyb had probably made his grubstake cashing in pop bottles picked up along the highway.

"Why, sure you do." Aunt Nora lobbed a little charm bomb his way. "You can treat us another time. How's that?"

"Well, I don't know," he muttered. "Don't want to be beholden."

"Now, Tyb, it's me who's beholden to you. Buying you a little old breakfast is the least I can do to repay you for fixing such a delicious supper last night. Your hair-raising stories were worth more than the price of a couple of eggs."

I rolled my eyes at Buddy, and he giggled behind his menu. Okay on the delicious supper, but hair-raising stories? Aunt Nora was a gifted actress whose footprints should be enshrined in concrete.

"It don't take much fodder to keep an old hoss like me on the trail," Tyb insisted quietly. "I'll just have a cup of Joe to warm me up."

"You folks ready to order?" The waitress was back, and her personality had not improved.

Aunt Nora ordered the Overdrive Special: a cheese omelet with hash browned potatoes, toast, and grapefruit juice. Having reevaluated his nutritional needs while the waitress was licking her pencil lead, Tyb requested the Truckers Brake-Fast: two eggs over easy, bacon, sausage, fried potatoes, biscuits, gravy, and coffee. It was anyone's guess what he ordered when he needed real sustenance.

I interpreted for Buddy, who wanted a short stack with extra syrup, a small milk, and two sausage patties to go for Puppy.

The waitress scribbled down their requests and turned to me. "How 'bout you, kid? What'll you have?"

Torn with indecision, I looked down at the menu and up at the scowling waitress. I hadn't had much practice ordering in restaurants. The Mahoneys didn't dine out very often.

"I ain't got all day, kid." The waitress was eager to get back to the rump-patting truckers.

"Do I have to order off the breakfast side?" Everyone was waiting. I should have said scrambled eggs and gone on, but something in the lunch section had caught my eye. Something I had never heard of and could scarcely comprehend.

Foot-long Chili Coney with Onions, Mustard and Cheese.

Could a weenie of such mammoth proportions really exist? A foot long. Twelve inches. One-third of a yard.

"Order anything you're big enough to eat, kid." The waitress smacked her gum and tapped her foot. She had more important things to do.

"Get whatever you want, Pauly." Aunt Nora probably thought it was a toss-up between pecan waffles and pigs in a blanket. She had no idea what kind of deviant culinary rebel she was dealing with. Pop would have understood my fascination with the foot-long hot dog. He would have tried one himself, disregarding the obvious gastrointestinal risks.

What about Aunt Nora? My future was in her hands. I couldn't have her thinking I was a troublesome child who flaunted mealtime conventions with reckless abandon, and yet I could not pass up such an opportunity. For all I knew, foot-long hot dogs had been invented in a fit of creative excess by the bewhiskered cook and might not even exist outside the CHUCK WAGON CAFÉ RUCKERS ELCOME.

"You gonna order or not?" the waitress drawled.

I swallowed hard. So what if it was eight o'clock in the morning? Convention be damned. I had to have it. "Bring me the foot-long chili cheese coney with everything on it. And an RC Cola."

The worldly waitress didn't even look up from her order pad. "You want fries or potato chips with that?"

"Fries." In for a penny, in for a pound. The waitress left, and I waited for somebody to say something.

"Pauly, it's pretty early in the morning," Aunt Nora pointed out.

"I know." Clearly I had broken some unwritten food group rule and would live to regret my rashness. Aunt Nora, Tyb, and even Buddy were staring at me like I'd just announced I was leaving for Mars on the next flying saucer.

"Are you sure you wouldn't rather have some nice French toast?" Aunt Nora asked.

"Nope." She might as well know the full extent of my strangeness.

"Okay, if that's what you want." She shrugged, blew some smoke rings, and pretended interest in the paneled walls of the diner. Some deranged ranch hand decorator had burned cattle brands into the wood in an effort to lend western flair. Other decorative touches included pieces of rusty barbed wire mounted on wooden plaques, faded pictures of cowpokes rounding up steers, and various tools of the ranching trade.

"I-I-I think a f-f-foot-long h-h-hot dog sounds g-g-good." Bless his heart, Buddy was always on my side. I folded my hands on the scratched tabletop and waited for the next adventure to begin.

Sad to say, I was disappointed by that hot dog. I didn't have a ruler handy, but it was nowhere near one-third of a yard long. More like ten inches. Tops. Still, it was as exotic as caviar to me. I looked up with a catsup-drenched fry in mid-flight and caught Aunt Nora's worried expression.

"Don't make yourself sick with that thing, kiddo."

"Don't worry, I won't." If being packed into a Buick with a chain-smoker, a leaky bladder, a spicy old man, and dog breath hadn't made me carsick, a Chuck Wagon weenie couldn't do it. I'd worked my way through about five inches of my breakfast when the bell over the door jingled again. Conversations around the room slacked off and the coffee cup clatter stilled.

A young Indian woman, her round face damp with cold rain, stood just inside the door, looking as nervous as a cat up a tree. Her blue-black hair was slicked back into an elaborately twisted bun that glistened in the diner's overhead lights. She wore a long purple skirt with a loose red blouse pulled down over her hips. A silver belt circled her ample waist and silver earrings swung from her ears.

One hand held the handles of a tattered shopping bag, and the other clutched the fist of a chubby, shivering little boy about two years old. He was dressed in a long shirt and baggy trousers, and both wore fringed, high-topped leather moccasins tied around their ankles.

Black hair, cut straight around at chin-length, framed the child's pudgy face. He sneezed and was alarmed by the outburst. He wiped his nose with the back of his hand, smearing snot across his cheek. The woman pulled him over to the counter, plopped him on a red vinyl stool, and hoisted her considerable self onto one beside it.

With hardly a glance in their direction, the cook went back to frying bacon, and the skinny waitress went on filling salt shakers.

"Hey, Ora Lee," one of the truckers called out with a snicker. "Don't you see you got yourself a couple of customers there?"

Ora Lee pretended to look all around. "I don't see anybody, Harve. Your eyes must be playing tricks on you."

The redneck slapped his thigh. "Hell, you're right. Musta been a mirage or somethin'."

After waiting patiently for several minutes, the young woman spoke quietly, her eyes downcast. "Please, ma'am. My boy is hungry. I have money."

Ora Lee rolled her eyes and flounced over to the counter, one hand on her hip. "You prob'ly can't read, but we got a sign right up there says we reserve the right to refuse service to anybody we want to."

The woman's eyes stayed down. "Not for me. For him. I'll take the food and go. I don't want no trouble."

Ora Lee turned to the truckers. "Some people just can't take a hint."

Her comment caused a round of rough laughter. My insides churned up, a sick feeling that had nothing to do with the chili dog. Mean kids at school had picked on Buddy and made him the brunt of stupid jokes. Their taunts had driven him further into silence and provoked me to fight. By the time Buddy finished first grade, I was averaging at least one black eye a month on his behalf.

There was a well-established pecking order on the playground. For reasons I never understood, Buddy and I wound up at the hard, cold bottom. I guess we were easy targets, always the new kids at school. Buddy was especially vulnerable, but together we inspired a fair amount of school-yard poetry and jump rope chants.

> *Stutter, stutter, brain like butter.*
> *Red Rover, Red Rover, let gimpy limp over.*
> *Buddy, Buddy, Fuddy Duddy, about as smart as Silly Putty.*
> *Pauly Mahoney smells like baloney.*
> *Mahoney, Mahoney, eats macaroni. Every day, every week.*
> *That is why they always stink.*

I taught Buddy not to cry in front of his tormentors, no matter how tough they were. It was better to have a good heart and a bad leg than to have good legs and mean hearts. Seemed to me the only power bullies had was the power we gave them.

The funny thing was, Buddy never hated those kids for what they did to him. Trusting and eager for any scrap of friendship, he continued to fall for their cruel tricks, way past the time he should have wised up. He always reached for the stick of gum that was just an empty wrapper, always looked into the telescope that left a black smudge around his eye. He'd gladly join their games of hide-and-seek, proud to be designated *It.* Then he'd spend the whole recess searching for the others, who had run away laughing while he laboriously counted to ten.

Longing for acceptance, and innocently expecting kindness, Buddy was surprised when they hurt him. He never got picked for real games, but he always wanted to play. When they teased him, he sat on the cellar door and I sat with him and pretended I didn't want to play either. I hated those kids, but Buddy didn't. He didn't even blame them. Unlike me, he was always willing to forgive.

Most children had cruel streaks, and the ones who thought they could get away with something were the worst of all. They'd taught me that kindness was suspect in any form. Maybe that's how I got the chip on my shoulder.

I was never invited to birthday parties and pretended not to notice when everyone else received invitations. I didn't get the pretty hearts-and-flowers valentines in my box. If I got any, they featured pictures of blushing skunks. I never had a special friend. Never slept over.

I watched other girls walk home from school with heads bent close, arms wrapped around each other's waists. Their laughter didn't include me, nor was it directed at me, and I felt the ache of exclusion that only the lonely can know. I despised them, and at the same time, I admired them. I envied their pretty clothes and television sets and doting mothers, but more than that, I envied their incredible ability to belong.

Sometimes I wondered if things would have been different had I not been Buddy Mahoney's sister. Were my own shortcomings enough to make them cast me out? Or was I guilty by my association with someone so different?

When teachers made us practice what to do in case the Russians dropped a bomb, I folded myself up under my desk and wished the Communists would blow up the whole school, vaporizing everybody but Buddy and me. If we had to be alone, we might as well have the world to ourselves.

I felt the pang of the outcast for the young Indian woman in that diner in Gallup, New Mexico. Grown-ups should know better. How could they be mean to a mother and a hungry little boy? All she wanted was to order some food.

Rude remarks were muttered around the tables. Blanket head. Squaw. Damned Injuns. Nuisance. The sad, weary look on the woman's face grew sadder and wearier. Maybe she'd heard it all before and was willing to endure the jeers in order to feed her baby.

The truckers' behavior startled me. Coming from Oklahoma, I was unaccustomed to seeing Indians treated so badly. Everyone I knew accepted them as regular citizens on account of the fact that nearly every Okie family tree had a branch or two in the Five Civilized Tribes. The name Oklahoma meant land of the red man, and some of the state's wealthiest citizens were Osages who had struck it rich in oil leases.

Which is not to say Oklahomans were immune to prejudice. They just directed their bigotry at a different race, colored people who dared to get uppity about wanting to be equal. Colored was a politer term than Negro, but I knew people who would have said "nigger" and gone on eating their eggs.

Aunt Nora slid out of the booth and approached the woman. "I'm sorry we didn't wait for you." Her words were rushed and friendly, loud enough for everyone in the room to hear. "But you know kids, they got restless, so we figured we'd go ahead and order. Hope you don't mind."

The woman pulled back, maybe thinking the redheaded lady was crazy, or even dangerous. Aunt Nora prattled on, treating the stranger like a long-lost friend. "Did you have a good trip? Boy! Isn't that storm something? A real gully washer." She took the woman's arm and gently pulled her to our table. "Scoot over, kids, and make room."

The Indian woman and I realized at about the same moment what Aunt Nora was up to. My eyes narrowed in alarm, but the mother's went soft and grateful. I slid over, and she sat down beside Buddy, holding her little boy on her lap.

The grim-faced men in the diner stared our way, sizing up the situation and mentally taking sides. I'd seen that flat-eyed look before, on the faces of playground bullies, right before they made their move. Did

Aunt Nora think she was doing a good deed? All I could smell in the greasy diner was trouble.

"Excuse me!" Ora Lee clomped over to our table and stood with a fist on her hip. "Is this Injun with you folks?"

The glare Aunt Nora leveled on the skinny waitress would have peeled paint off a barn. "That's right, Ora Lee. She's with us. Now why don't you get my *friend* a menu so she can order some breakfast?"

"You ain't from around here, are you?" The words gritted through Ora Lee's clenched teeth.

Aunt Nora smiled. "Fortunately, no."

Some of the truckers twitched. I tensed and gauged the distance to the door. If push came to shove, us against them, we were sorely out-numbered. Some guardian Aunt Nora had turned out to be. Didn't she know better than to stroll into a pen full of bulls and wave a red flag?

If looks could kill, we'd all have been maimed for life, but Ora Lee took the Indian woman's order. Milk and a scrambled egg for the little boy, and toast and coffee for the mother. She flounced off to tell the cook, and Aunt Nora reached across the table to squeeze the young woman's arm.

"Things like that shouldn't happen in this country."

"Oh, I am used to it."

"How do you ever get used to that?"

The woman smiled for the first time, shyly, like she was rusty and didn't get a chance to smile every day. "You even get used to a toothache after a while."

Ignoring the killer looks of the other diners, Aunt Nora flashed the woman a reassuring dimple. I pushed my plate away. The breakfast chili backed up and burned my chest. How could Aunt Nora act so normal when we were clearly doomed?

Buddy and I had hitched our wagon to an aunt who was totally lacking in survival instincts. She didn't understand that *we* were the out-siders here. Had she never seen a western movie? Didn't she know any-thing about lynch mobs?

Aunt Nora introduced us. In a quiet voice, the woman told us her name was Wanatela Broomcorn.

"The agent drove me in from the reservation," she said. "So I can catch the bus to Indian Wells."

"Where's that?" Aunt Nora's interest in the woman seemed genuine.

"Arizona. My mother had a heart attack. She needs me. Last night, an owl came to me in a dream and told me. I walked to the agent's of-fice to wait for the telephone call."

"What's your baby's name?" I asked her.

"I call him Root. When he was born, he was so tiny and wrinkled, his father said he looked like a little brown root."

The big-eyed child intrigued Buddy, maybe because he had finally met someone who talked even less than he did. He tried to play peeka-boo, but Root just ducked his face into his mother's ample bosom.

"Thank you for helping me," Wanatela told Aunt Nora when they finished their breakfast. "You are very kind."

"Don't mention it. I hope your mother recovers."

"I pray it will be so. I must go. The bus leaves soon." She opened a small beaded bag and tentatively placed a dollar on the table. "Will that be enough?"

"More than enough," Aunt Nora assured her.

Wanatela's head bobbed in my aunt's direction. "Thank you again." She balanced Root on one hip and scooped up the bag holding their pos-sessions. We watched them leave, but every other patron in the café, along with the cook and waitress, pretended Wanatela and Root did not exist.

Aunt Nora left Ora Lee a good tip. On a paper napkin she scrawled, *May you spend eternity with people just like yourself.*

I suggested she add *you old bat* at the end, but Aunt Nora said we had made our point.

When we stepped out onto the sidewalk, we heard the screech of hydraulic brakes as the Indian Wells bus pulled into the station across the street. The rain had stopped, and Puppy was glad to jump out of the car. He hiked his leg against the tire of a pickup truck belonging to one of the bullies guzzling coffee in the Chuck Wagon. He gobbled up the sausage patties, lapped a rainwater chaser out of a puddle, and promptly flopped onto his side under the car.

The Skylark had been a wedding present from Aunt Nora's second husband. The head-turning sportster had a big, smiling grille and wire wheels with white sidewall tires, and was equipped with power brakes, power steering, and power windows. The most intriguing thing was the foot-controlled Selectronic radio that blasted out the music of your choice with a tap of a toe.

I was climbing into the front seat when I spotted a forlorn figure standing in front of the bus terminal, staring after the departing Greyhound. "Look! Wanatela missed her bus."

Aunt Nora glanced across the street and then at Tyb. "Not hardly," she snapped. "Those yahoos wouldn't let her on the bus. Dammit, why'd they have to go and do that?"

"Some westerners still bear hard feelin's a'gin the Indians," Tyb explained. "Especially out here where the warfare was so fierce. They was enemies for a long time."

"Yeah, I know what the history books say," Aunt Nora said with a disgusted sniff. "How dare those savage Indians try to protect their families from white men who only wanted to kill them and steal their land?"

I could tell she was good and angry. Not at Tyb, but at whoever had been insensitive enough to keep a worried daughter from her sick mother.

"I just don't understand people." Aunt Nora marched across the street, her sandals slapping the wet pavement, her full cotton skirt swirling around her long, tan legs. From where I sat, it looked like she was trying to talk Wanatela into something. When the three of them headed toward us, I knew what that something was.

Aunt Nora had done it again. She'd gone and picked up two more strays.

"Wanatela and Root are going to ride with us to Indian Wells," Aunt Nora announced as she tossed their bag of clothing into the trunk and slammed the lid.

"I didn't know we were going to Indian Wells," I said.

"We are now." Aunt Nora squinted up at the sky and stretched her arms over her head. "Suppose we'll get any more rain this morning, Tyb?"

The old man looked up and scratched his brushy chin, as noncommittal as usual. "Clouds are breaking up, sun's coming out."

"Good enough for me. Let's put the top down. I like to feel the wind on my face. Wanatela, you and Root can ride in the back with the boys. Just make yourselves comfortable. Buddy, give the baby one of your pillows and don't let him put any of that Silly Putty in his mouth."

Buddy shrugged as he passed the boy a pillow. Years of reading his mind told me exactly what he was thinking. The more the merrier. To Buddy, the best part of the Trip so far was all the new friends he was making.

I sat in the front seat, shaking my head. At the rate we were taking on passengers, the Greyhound bus people would be out of business in no time.

10

You Are Here!

W̲e outran the storm in New Mexico. By the time we reached the Arizona state line, we were truly in the desert. Tyb said it was hot enough to make rattlesnakes sweat bullets, so Aunt Nora put up the Skylark's top to keep our brains from frying.

She offered to run the air-conditioning, but I wanted to crank down the windows to be closer to everything. What was the point of traveling to new places if you rode closed up inside a refrigerated box where you couldn't smell, hear, or taste what was different from the places you'd already been?

I no longer needed *The Yearling*, or crayons, or string to practice my Jacob's ladder. Those distractions were stuffed in my bag under the seat. We were less than thirty hours out of Tulsa and things had gotten interesting.

Wondering who we might run into next took my mind off my troubles and gave me something to look forward to. I didn't have much experience with sightseeing, but I found myself enjoying yet another change of scenery. Staring out the window of a fast car whipping along the highway was a good excuse to do some thinking. With time and distance between me and bad memories, I realized that Aunt Nora might have been right about the healing powers of new vistas.

Oven-baked air blew in my face. The Arizona landscape was so different from the rolling green hills of northeastern Oklahoma that we could have been on another planet. Mountainous clouds banked low on the horizon, which stretched from there all the way to forever. They scudded along in the wind, creating ever-changing patterns of sunlight and shadow on the flat face of the desert. Herds of white-tailed antelope browsed among the sagebrush. When they strayed too close to the road, Aunt Nora tooted the horn, and they sprang up like broken toys.

As an appropriate musical tribute to the moment, she suggested Buddy and I sing "Home on the Range." Even Root laughed when our loud, off-key voices spilled out the open windows and startled long-legged jackrabbits and dusty brown sage hens into mindless panic.

Then, lulled by heat and motion, Tyb, Buddy, and Root dozed off one by one. Aunt Nora tuned the radio to a rock-and-roll station that transmitted equal parts music and static, a strangely soothing combination. My curiosity about the newest members of our crew finally got the best of me and I tried to get Wanatela to talk. The closemouthed Indian woman made Tyb seem as chatty as a career politician.

"Why couldn't your husband drive you to Indian Wells?" There was nothing better than an unavoidably direct question to get a conversation going.

"He's dead." Wanatela stared out her own window as though watching for something to appear over the horizon.

"How'd he die?"

"Somebody shot him." Most people used that tone for everyday comments. *Pass the lima beans. Looks like rain. Feels hot in here.*

Somebody shot my husband.

"I'm sorry." Having lost my parents to sudden violence, I spoke from my heart and not from politeness. "Killed in the war, huh?" My father had been all over Italy in World War II, mostly driving a general around in a jeep. He hadn't been in much combat, but I'd seen the movies and knew war was hell.

"No," she replied. "In that war, people tried to shoot him, but they missed. My husband was brave and earned many medals. Would you like to see?"

"Yes, please."

She pulled a medallion on a ribbon bar from her beaded purse and passed it over the seat. "This is the biggest one."

The medal lay heavy in my hand. I showed it to Aunt Nora, who was trying to pay attention to the conversation while tuning the Selectronic to keep Doris Day's "Secret Love" from fading in and out.

"Isn't that a Silver Star?" Aunt Nora asked Wanatela.

"Yes. I think it's pretty. I'm saving it for Root, so he will know his father was a brave warrior. My husband got these in the other war, the one in Korea." She pulled out a handful of smaller but no less impressive military decorations and arrayed them for me to see.

"So, what happened to him?" I pretended not to see Aunt Nora's discouraging frowns.

"Some white man shot him."

"Why?" Tyb had taught me the importance of nudging the storyteller along.

"In an argument over a rooster." Again, her matter-of-fact tone revealed little emotion, and I wondered if her reticence was a genetic trait of her race or something she'd perfected through rough experience.

"A rooster?"

"My husband, August Broomcorn, raised fighting cocks. He was good at it, and his roosters won lots of fights. A white man wanted to buy one of his birds, but August told him the one he chose was not ready to fight. It was too young, and he did not want to sell it.

"The white man got angry. August sold him the rooster but made him promise not to let it fight until it was older." She stopped, like that was the end of the story, which it clearly was not.

"And?" I prompted.

"The man promised. But he didn't wait."

Still didn't explain a shooting. Was this how dentists felt extracting stubborn wisdom teeth? "What happened after that?"

"The rooster was killed in his first fight." She fell silent and stared out the window again.

I waited what I thought was a respectful time before prodding. So far, she'd relayed only the circumstances of the rooster's demise.

She drew a deep breath. "The white man got mad because he bet a lot of money on the fight. He said August cheated him by selling him a bad rooster."

"But your husband told him it wasn't ready to fight." Perry Mason could have settled an open-and-shut case like that in five minutes. "Did he point out that the man broke his promise?"

"Yes. But what is a promise to a white man?" Wanatela spoke sadly, as though we all knew the answer to that question, but since we were white, she hoped we wouldn't take offense. "August knew he could not win the argument, so he decided to give him back the money. I know this because others who were there have told me."

"Then what happened?" If you hoped to get to the point, you had to be relentless.

"My husband reached into his coat for the money, but the white man thought he was going for a gun. He shot August and claimed it was self-defense." Wanatela related her story quietly, as though unsure whether we would find it horrifying. "I saw that white man in Gallup once," she added in a curious postscript.

"You mean he's not in prison?" Aunt Nora switched off Doris Day in deference to Wanatela's revelations.

"He was a month in county jail, waiting for the trial. But his friend put a gun in August's hand after he was shot and the jury believed the man's story."

"What about the witnesses?" Aunt Nora asked.

"Many white men testified in court to confirm the other man's story."

"But Indians saw what really happened."

"Nobody listens to Indians."

"That's awful." Aunt Nora shook her head. "I can't believe the murderer just walked away."

"White men don't go to prison for killing Indians," Wanatela explained patiently. "They've been doing that for many years. People act like it matters. They arrest somebody. They have a trial. In the end, the white man goes home. If an Indian kills a white man, even in self-defense, he goes to the electric chair."

"That's not justice," Aunt Nora said.

"Indians don't think so," Wanatela agreed.

I had nothing to say in the face of the woman's stoic acceptance. Prejudice was the reality of her life. It was like being the sixth-grade outcast, only a hundred times worse, because Wanatela could not escape by moving to a new school or by growing up.

I glanced at the sleeping Root, his round face resting on his mother's bosom. Long, doll-like lashes brushed his pudgy brown cheeks. His black hair was damp at the temples and tiny beads of baby sweat dotted his upper lip. He was beautiful and innocent, but because a man's life wasn't deemed as important as a rooster, the little boy would never know his father, not even for a few years, as I had known mine. He would have no memories to get him through hard times and bad dreams. He'd have only the medals of a dead man, a grim reminder that dishonorable men were always willing to destroy the honorable.

Root still had his mother, so he wasn't a hundred percent orphan like me. Root was an orphan of the world. I had California, and the hope of a new life. Nowhere in the world would Root have the same chance. He looked so sweet sleeping in his mother's arms. The thought of him growing up and being beaten down by the hate and ridicule I'd witnessed in the diner made me cry on the inside.

People like Root and my brother had to be made to feel inferior so others could feel better about themselves.

I turned around, plopped down on the seat, and folded my arms across my chest. I couldn't stop thinking about August Broomcorn, a man I'd never met. I'd read books full of tragic irony, but tragedy and irony had been lost on me until now.

The more I learned about fate, and the way it slapped us mortals around, the more I realized it was pointless to worry about mine.

The Buick's radiator boiled over just east of the Petrified Forest National Park. Aunt Nora pulled into the first place we came to, a combination filling station/souvenir stand/tourist attraction called No Water Charlie's Desert Museum of Amazing Anomalies Last Gas for 150 Miles. I knew what anomalies were. Things different, abnormal, peculiar, or not easily classified.

Far less imposing than its name, the whole shebang was housed in a long, low-slung building built of oddly shaped rocks, the same color as the dust swirling around it. Aunt Nora braked alongside one of the old-timey gas pumps and backhanded a long strand of red hair out of her eyes.

So you wouldn't miss the attraction and go home with your whole vacation ruined, a huge wooden sign with a blindingly pink Gila monster and the words IT'S RIGHT HERE loomed over the empty parking lot.

Aunt Nora looked around at the empty spaces. "No Water Charlie might have been a tad optimistic about the appeal of his enterprise when he planned the number of parking places needed."

I considered the radiator's timing a lucky break. Buddy could use the toilet, Tyb could get out and stretch his creaky joints, and maybe Aunt Nora would let us all look at the desert anomalies. Ten cents for children and fifteen cents for adults.

An old man limped toward us. As grizzled and sun-baked as the desert rat in *The Treasure of the Sierra Madre*, he was dressed in clothes so faded there was no color left in them. He took a look at the Buick and several good looks at Aunt Nora.

Wearing an expression that was aggravated and worried at the same time, she stood well away from the steam rolling from under the hood. Her flower-print skirt was part of a romper set, and she'd undone some of the buttons to reveal the shorts underneath. It might have been the shorts that first attracted No Water Charlie's attention.

"You need to let that radyator cool down before you take the cap off," he advised sagely.

"I'll do that. Could you fill the tank with ethyl while we're waiting, old-timer?"

"Sure thing. If you folks is thirsty, I got cold sody pop inside."

That was the best offer we'd had all day, so we piled out of the car. Hot gravel burned through the thin soles of my Keds as I ran ahead and banged the screen door behind me. It took a minute for my eyes to adjust to the gloom inside the building, but my nose worked just fine. The air was close and musty, ideal for the olfactory systems of insects and rodents, but not up to human standards. I tried not to inhale too deeply as I looked around.

Items that No Water Charlie considered crucial to the needs of weary desert travelers were jumbled onto grocery store shelves along both sides of the room. With no thought to organization, cheap sunglasses and straw hats lined up beside blue bottles of Phillips' Milk of Magnesia and tins of Bayer aspirin. Genuine Indian crafts made in Japan mingled with road maps, yellow boxes of Kodak film, cigarette lighters, and plastic-wrapped cupcakes. Dusty cans of pork and beans and potted meat and shoestring potatoes awaited the next nomadic gourmet.

A rusty wire rack, half filled with faded postcards, revolved noisily as I reviewed the contents. In a box marked *For Rock Hounds*, I found sheets of cardboard on which small pieces of petrified wood and minerals had been glued.

The rest of the group filed in, and Aunt Nora bought pop for everyone. She let Buddy fish them out of the dented cooler because he liked to drop in the dimes and scoot the bottles along the mazelike track to the spot where he could pull them out of the ice water. It didn't take much in the way of mechanical wizardry to fascinate my brother.

"Can we go in the museum?" I spotted the entrance in the back of the room, the doorway cloaked in mystery and somebody's old shower curtain. Another garish sign enticed: DON'T MISS THE WONDERS OF THE DESERT GILA MONSTER JAVALINA PIG MOUNTAIN LION AND RATTLESNAKE ALSO NEVER BEFORE SEEN CURIOSITIES.

"Sure," said Aunt Nora. "It's about time we got down to business and had some fun on this vacation. Who wants to see the wonders of the desert world?"

Tyb's was the only dissenting vote. He felt a little short-winded and wanted to sit in a shady place and drink his pop. Charlie offered him a chair, Puppy trotted off with his unofficial master, and the rest of us paid our money and entered the museum through the rustling curtain. Except for Root, who was so little he got in for free.

It didn't take long to realize that the proprietor had used the term "museum" loosely. According to Mrs. Pipkin, a fourth-grade teacher gung-ho on field trips, a museum was "an institution devoted to the procurement, care, study, and display of objects of lasting interest or value." No Water Charlie's establishment fell somewhere short of industry standards.

Among the exhibits were the obligatory jackalope, a stuffed jackrabbit with a big set of antlers glued on his head, and a dead, leathery-looking two-headed tortoise that probably also involved creative gluing skills. In a glass tank filled with sand, busy red ants had built a universe from scratch. A long case held a collection of Indian arrowheads, pieces of broken pottery, and other genuine-looking artifacts.

Stuck slantwise on the side of a petrified log, a stuffed woodpecker was frozen in time, perpetually frustrated from trying to drill through stone. Buddy was intrigued by a hole in the floor. According to the sign, it was three feet in diameter and two feet deep and had been created when a meteor crashed through the roof in 1943. At the bottom of the hole lay a shiny black rock that could very well have rocketed in from outer space.

The museum contained a large assortment of dusty, glassy-eyed birds, rodents, and small reptiles.

"Do you think No Water Charlie is a taxidermist?" I asked.

Aunt Nora shrugged. "I don't know, but clearly he has way too much time on his hands."

We didn't find any mountain lions or wild pigs, but another sign directed us to walk out back and view live exhibits in the botanical garden.

Ready for some fresh air, everyone else went out. I stepped around a large stuffed owl to see if there was anything else worth viewing on the aisle we'd skipped. Rounding the corner, I came face-to-face with the mummy.

Inside a dusty glass case, the mummy was folded up inside a big woven basket with a cutaway side so you could look in. It was wrapped in a crumbling blanket made, according to a crudely lettered placard, of wild turkey feathers. My throat tightened against a backwash of Nehi orange. Looking gave me a strange feeling, but I couldn't tear my eyes away. The mummy was dark and shrunken up, but I could tell it was an Indian baby who had died when it was about Root's age.

Crackly skin the color of dried beef stretched over the small round skull. Patches of long black hair like Root's were still visible. The eyes were closed and sewn shut, and hands like baby claws were folded across the chest. Bony legs were drawn up in a fetal position. The slack jaw had dropped open to reveal tiny yellow teeth.

Was this how Indians buried their dead? In movies, they put them up on scaffolds so their spirits could fly away to the happy hunting ground. Back home in Oklahoma, the Indians I knew buried each other in the cemetery like everyone else. I'd never heard of anyone being folded up in a basket.

"Hey! P-P-Pauly! Come and s-s-see the mountain lion," Buddy called from the doorway.

"In a minute." I didn't want to leave the baby. It wasn't so bad to have fake jackalopes and stuffed woodpeckers on display, because everybody knew they were part of the joke. But it didn't seem right for No Water Charlie to make money by letting tourists gawk at a little dead Indian baby, even if it was over five hundred years old, as the sign proclaimed.

The mummy had once been a real live child. In view of its careful burial, its parents had loved it. They had been dead for a long time too, so that made the mummy an orphan, and it just seemed wrong for it to be in a ratty old tourist trap instead of skipping around the happy hunting ground.

"P-P-Pauly! There's wild p-p-pigs and lizards and r-r-rattlesnakes and-and-and everything. Come on!"

"All right, Buddy, I'm coming." A last look at the dead baby filled me with an emotion I couldn't name. I turned and ran out the back door, through botanical gardens consisting of a few droopy cacti and yucca plants, and into the zoo compound.

I found everyone standing around a wire cage. The decrepit mountain lion inside looked as old and toothless as No Water Charlie. A little trench had been worn into the ground around the inside of the cage. At one time, the poor creature had been optimistic enough to pace the perimeter of its world looking for a way out, a task it had long since given up as a lost cause.

In another cage a skinny coyote that Root called "goggie" trotted up and down its narrow confine. Its long tongue lolled out and bare skin showed where clumps of dirt-colored fur had fallen off the skinny flanks. Tiny black insects matted around one oozy eye. The coyote didn't look wild or dangerous to me, but Wanatela held tightly to her son's hand.

A few big rattlesnakes were curled up inside a shallow pit enclosed by a low rock wall to keep tourists from falling in. The sound of their ominous rattles on the dry, still air chilled me to the bone, a frightening summons to genetic memory.

"Look at the d-d-deadly Gila monster, P-Pauly." Buddy was determined not to miss a thing. He limped around the compound, excited by the novelty of strange sights. Everything, no matter how ordinary or low down on the food chain, was a wonder to him.

"What's the s-s-sign say?"

"It says it's poisonous to humans."

"Oooh!"

"You'd have to be stupid or paralyzed for a Gila monster to get you." I spoke with the certainty of having read the whole Book of Knowledge series in the school library.

"Why's that, Pauly?" Aunt Nora always seemed amazed by what I knew. Pop used to tell me being smart was a better deal than being popular, and I had tried like crazy to believe him.

"Because they move real slow. They don't sting or bite. They inject venom by chewing their victims. A human would have to hold still a really long time for a Gila monster to get in enough poison to do any damage."

I turned away and motioned for everyone to look into a glass case. "What can really hurt you are these." I pointed to several large scorpions scurrying around on a dead limb. "Now, those things can kill you."

"You know a lot about science, Pauly." Aunt Nora patted my shoulder.

"I like to read." I ducked away, unreasonably peeved by the note of surprise in her voice. I wasn't ready to accept her praise, if that's what it was.

Aunt Nora and Wanatela walked over to a patch of shade, where they watched Root and Buddy explore, hand in hand. Aunt Nora called out a warning to avoid the cactus stickers.

"Aunt Nora, can you come back in the museum for a minute?" I jerked my head toward the back door of the building. "I want to show you something."

"What is it?"

"You'll see." I pulled on her hand and felt a little thrill when her fingers locked into mine. Buddy started to come, but I cut him off like a collie heeling sheep and diverted his attention by pointing out the javelina pig snorting in its pen. Wanatela scooped up Root and walked back to the coyote's cage, which was just as well. I needed Aunt Nora alone for what I had in mind.

I was pretty sure that seeing the mummy baby in No Water Charlie's menagerie wouldn't sit any better with Aunt Nora than it had with me. She'd already shown good intentions by helping Wanatela and Root, so I was confident her righteous indignation would match my own.

Standing there in that broken-down museum amid dust motes and buzzing flies, I'd been caught off guard by a rush of inspiration. I had an ace-high idea, which I could not pull off on my own. I would have to convince Aunt Nora of the moral rightness of my plan, of the simplicity of its execution, and of the absolute necessity of her involvement.

How hard could that be?

11

Win Some, Lose Some

"Mr. Charlie, are you aware that it is against the law to keep human remains in your possession?"

The sight of the mummy baby languishing in its cutaway basket had outraged Aunt Nora. I'd hardly had to bring up moral rightness at all, or mention how its presence in the museum was another rank injustice to the Native American race.

In fact, with very little urging from me, she had swept through the museum's shower curtain to confront the startled proprietor behind his rusty cash register.

To his credit, the old man looked confused as he scratched his stubbly chin. "What human remains would that be, ma'am?"

Aunt Nora leaned over the counter. "You have a dead Indian in your museum."

"I do?" No Water Charlie squawked in shock at the news.

I'd become a skillful prompter. "In the exhibit?"

The expression on his leathery face revealed the exact moment understanding dawned. "Oh, you mean Sylvester?"

"Who?" It was Aunt Nora's turn to be confused.

"The mummy. I named him Sylvester because he reminded me of a midget I knew back in Lodi. Sylvester Swope was his name. That midget could drink any full-growed man under the table. Why, I remember one night when—"

"Mr. Charlie!" Aunt Nora segued into imperious, which is a kind of behavior you read about more often than witness. "May I inquire how you obtained said remains?"

"Why, I bought Sylvester back in thirty-nine off an old prospector. Gave him five bucks and a case of beans. Said he found it in a cave up in the hills."

"Well, you can't keep it."

"I cain't?"

"No, sir, you cannot. Doing so violates the law of the land and disregards social conscience."

I stood by, nodding agreement. I had just begun to develop a social conscience, but what she said sounded good.

"I dunno about that." No Water Charlie pulled off his sweaty old hat and scratched his head. "Maybe where you come from showing mummies is a'gin the law. But I ain't never heared of any such ordinance in Arizona. Why, not so long ago, a carnival sideshow was charging folks to see an old dead desperado what had been pickled in brine."

Aunt Nora leaned over the counter. "I am shocked by your callous lack of ethics."

"My calloused what?" Bewildered, Charlie looked from Aunt Nora to me.

"Mr. Charlie." Gripping his shoulders, she stared him straight in the eye. "That mummy, as you call it, was once a person. Don't you think an innocent human child deserves a proper burial befitting its native culture?"

That's when I understood the term "buffaloed." Poor old Charlie had been stampeded and didn't even know what had hit him. He didn't agree with Aunt Nora, but she must have raised doubt in his mind, because he ducked away from her to wage a defense.

"Well now, judging by the turkey feathers and all, I reckon the mummy got a good send-off way back yonder when it passed. Seems to me, it stopped being a person after the first coupla hundred years or so and is now what you might call a . . . a . . . arkalogical artafack."

"I'll give you twenty dollars," offered Aunt Nora.

Lesson for life. When appeals to social conscience fail, try a more primitive motivator.

"Nope."

"Even allowing for inflation over the last sixteen years, that's a fair profit on your five dollars and case of beans investment," she pointed out.

No Water Charlie dug in for battle. "No, ma'am, I cain't sell Sylvester. He was my first anomaly. Why, this whole place grew up around that mummy. At first, I didn't rightly know what to do with him, but then it come to me that he needed to be in a museum. I started collecting odd bits here and there. Some of them stuffed animals was road-kilt, but you'd never know it to look at 'em now. I like to preserve things."

He'd offered a noble speech. An objective bystander might even sympathize with Charlie's position.

"Then I'm sure you will want to preserve the dignity and pride of our Indian brothers," Aunt Nora insisted. "As a race, they have suffered many injustices throughout history. To keep one of their forebears on crass display for economic gain only adds insult to injury."

Charlie shook his head like an old horse dodging Aunt Nora's word-flies. "I don't reckon . . ."

"Thirty dollars."

"What in tarnation do you want with an Indian mummy, ma'am?"

"Why, to give it a proper burial, of course."

He reared back in shock. "You'd waste a perfectly good mummy thataway?"

"Forty dollars."

"Nope." The old man folded his arms across his scrawny chest. "I wouldn't sell Sylvester for all the treasure in Superstition Mountain."

"A hundred dollars, then. That's my final offer."

A hundred dollars was more money than I could imagine. Aunt Nora was willing to spend that much on scruples, which made me view her in a whole new light.

Too bad No Water Charlie had scruples, too. "No, ma'am. I ain't gonna do it. Now you jest get that idee outta your head. Sylvester's been with me a long time. He's the most educational exhibit I got."

"What about the meteor?" I put in helpfully. "That's pretty educational."

Charlie scoffed. "Nah, that's jest a piece a lava I hauled over from Sunset Crater. Sylvester's the real McCoy."

"A real human being," Aunt Nora reiterated.

Charlie wouldn't budge. He was the type of stubborn western side-kick who went down with guns blazing. "Now ain't there plenty other museums what have Indian relics and such as that? Big 'uns. Mesa Verde's got a slew of 'em, and I heared they got a mummified king of Egypt on display somewhere back East."

Point to Charlie. According to the *Weekly Reader*, the Smithsonian exhibited lots of mummies. How would Aunt Nora counter that line of logic?

"It's not the same, now, is it? That poor little baby was not an ancient king. What historical value can there be in keeping it on display?"

"Fifteen cents a head, that's what historical value it has!"

"I'm glad my friend Wanatela didn't see it." Aunt Nora's voice softened, and she employed the dimple. "Look, Mr. Charlie, I'm not trying to give you a hard time. But think how bad you'd feel if you stopped to get a soda pop somewhere and you spotted your great-great-grandpa in a glass case alongside a jackalope."

Charlie scratched his stubble again. "I don't s'pose I'd like it too much. But if your friend's an Injun, I reckon she's used to such things by now."

Uh-oh. Poor old Charlie had no way of knowing he'd just made a major strategical error. I backed out of the line of fire. Aunt Nora's left eye started twitching and a flood of furious color washed over her face.

With more outward calm than most cheesed-off redheads could have mustered, she said, "I don't think she should *have* to get used to being treated like a second-class citizen. Do you?"

"Now, ma'am, I didn't mean nuthin'. I'm just sayin' this is America, and what with free enterprise and all, I'm entitled to make whatever livin' I can so long as it's honest and don't hurt nobody."

"That's my point." Aunt Nora's palm slapped the counter, and Charlie jumped. "What you're doing *does* hurt someone."

Charlie shook his head. "I don't rightly see how."

"Displaying that mummy is an insult to Indians, who happen to be American citizens, too, you know. In case you've forgotten your history, they were here first!"

"Now, looky here, lady." The old man's voice edged toward total frustration. "More like, my exhibit is a monument to their history. How's that?"

"What you're doing is a sacrilege, and you know it."

"Nope." He shook his stubborn head. "Sylvester's the biggest draw I got."

"So, you're saying you won't relinquish my friend's ancestor?"

"Oh, corn feathers! How do you know they was even related? Your friend looks like a Navaho. For all we know, that mummy could be the last of the Mohicans or somethin'."

Aunt Nora opened her purse and fanned five crisp twenties like a poker hand. "Here's a hundred bucks. That should buy enough glue to create a whole menagerie of two-headed anomalies."

No Water Charlie stared at the money and then at Aunt Nora. Indecision wrinkled his sun-seamed face for a wavering moment. *Take the money.* I crossed my fingers and held my breath. A hundred dollars was probably more than his operation made in a year.

Take it.

"Thankee for the offer, ma'am, but I reckon I'll keep Sylvester." The old man was clearly offended by Aunt Nora's glue reference.

She started to argue, but stopped with a frustrated sigh. Maybe she felt sorry for Charlie, or maybe she recognized a hopeless cause when she saw one. She stuffed the money back in her purse. The clasp snapped like an exclamation point at the end of a sentence.

She grabbed my hand. "Come on, Pauly. Let's find the others and get out of here."

"Is that it?" I hurried to keep up with her long strides. "Are we giving up?"

She stopped and sighed. "He wouldn't take the money. There's nothing we can do."

"There must be something."

"We tried. Sometimes trying is all there is. The important thing is knowing when to try and when to let go."

"Don't you mean when to give up?" I muttered.

We found Tyb resting in a cane-bottomed chair tipped back against the front wall of the building. He looked a little sweaty but said he was feeling better. Puppy panted at his side.

Disappointed by Aunt Nora's failure to rescue the mummy, I moped around to the back of the building and spotted Buddy leaning over the rattlesnake pit. I called out, and he was so startled he nearly fell in.

"For cripes' sake, Buddy, are you trying to give me a heart attack?" I couldn't yell at Aunt Nora, so I yelled at my brother. "Get away from those snakes."

"I h-h-hate their eyes," he whispered. "They look at you so mean, like they want you to d-d-die."

I peered in the pit, and the hissing snakes stared at me with half-hooded eyes. Buddy was right. Snakes had a scary way of reminding you that you were nothing but meat. I tugged him away. "Where did Wanatela and Root go?"

"B-b-back in the mu-mu—uh . . . inside."

"Oh, great." I ran for the back door. "I hope she didn't see the mummy."

"M-m-mummy? What m-m-mummy?" Buddy was hot on my heels. "You d-d-didn't tell me there was a mummy."

I skidded to a halt when I saw Wanatela staring into the mummy case. Her hands were folded over her chest, and she had a reverent look on her face.

"This is an Ancient One," she whispered. "My people tell stories of Ancient Ones who lived long ago, when the earth was new and they were the only people. Why is this Ancient One in this bad place?"

"Because some grave robber sold it to No Water Charlie for five dollars and a case of beans." Aunt Nora joined us and didn't try to soften the blow. "I tried to buy it back. I offered the old man a hundred dollars, but he wouldn't sell. I'd hoped you could help us give it a proper burial."

Root whimpered to be held. Wanatela picked him up and continued to gaze into the case. "It must be sealed in a cave. Ancient Ones did not place their dead in the ground. There is a death chant and a prayer for the afterlife. The medicine man in my mother's village would know what to do."

"I'm sorry, Wanatela." Aunt Nora tried to tug her away. "Let's go."

The Indian woman stood firm, clutching Root, who sucked his thumb and forefinger. "We cannot leave this Ancient One behind. This is a very wrong thing."

"I know, but there's nothing we can do. Let's get back on the road. Your mother's waiting." Aunt Nora patted Wanatela's arm. Peering at me over his mother's shoulder, Root's dark eyes were old in his round baby face. I bet the mummy had looked like Root when it was alive. Leaving it behind felt like abandoning a child I knew. A lump formed in my throat, but I couldn't swallow because all my spit had dried up in the heat.

No one spoke to No Water Charlie as we filed through the front of the store, but a final statement was necessary. At the door, I turned and stuck out my tongue. Charlie responded by sticking his out at me.

I followed the two women across the parking lot, kicking up little dust storms with my sneakers. I climbed into the front seat and did a quick up-and-down bottom dance on the hot upholstery. I was breaking out in ideas like a bad rash and my latest one was the best yet. Putting my plan into action would involve the cover of darkness and breaking at least one Commandment, to say nothing of regular laws.

Somehow I had to convince Aunt Nora that confiscating sacred Indian relics to right the wrongs perpetrated on an entire race of people was not the same as stealing.

Not technically anyhow.

*　*　*

We drove across the Painted Desert, which wasn't nearly as colorful as I had expected. The landscape was mostly rusty pink, with some brown and red thrown in. We left the main highway and took a side trip to the Petrified Forest National Park. I had assumed the trees would be upright, as the term "forest" implies. Once I realized the "forest" was just a bunch of logs lying around on the ground, it was hard to get excited by whatever geologic events had transformed them into fossils.

A young park service ranger in a Smokey Bear hat stood around looking helpful. When I suggested the government consider renaming the place the Petrified Firewood National Park, the ranger winked at Aunt Nora and said he'd take it up with the Secretary of the Interior.

Aunt Nora asked about camping, and he directed us to an area nearby. We could have gone on to Indian Wells that day, but Tyb was pale and wheezy in the backseat and didn't look up to more traveling. We discussed spending the night with Wanatela, and she agreed to the delay. She said she would know if her mother's condition had worsened and had received no such message.

Stopping for the night gave me a chance to implement my plan, but I had to pick the right moment to unveil the particulars. That's the thing about plans. Many a good one has failed due to poor timing.

After stretching out on his quilt for a while, Tyb rallied and got his second wind. He built a fire in the concrete camp grate, and we roasted hot dogs on sticks. Buddy and I set up the tent and gave Wanatela one of the sleeping bags. She and Root didn't mind sleeping outside under the stars.

Tyb and Wanatela watched Buddy and Root play chase around the picnic table, and I talked Aunt Nora into taking a walk. I had to get her away from the others to outline my proposal for restoring dignity to the Native American race.

To her credit, she heard me out before she refused. "I know your heart's in the right place, kiddo, but we can't heist that mummy out from under No Water Charlie's nose."

"Why not?"

"Because it wouldn't be right."

"I thought you said it was against the law to keep human remains."

"I was bluffing. I have no idea if it's legal to keep archaeological artifacts or not."

"There *should* be a law against keeping mummies." Something about that lonely little bundle of bones and feathers made me want to fight city hall.

"Yes, there should be. Maybe someday the government will become enlightened enough to do something."

"Do we have to wait 'til then?"

"I'm afraid so. We may not agree with Charlie's philosophy, but we can't break into his place of business and take something that belongs to him because we think he's wrong. That would be stealing."

"But we wouldn't really be stealing Sylvester," I insisted. "We'd be rescuing him."

A carefully plucked eyebrow arched. "From what?"

"From being like a two-headed turtle . . . a . . ."

"An anomaly?"

"Exactly. You saw Wanatela's face when she looked at that Ancient One."

"Yes."

"She sure was sad."

Aunt Nora considered. "You're right, she was upset. But she didn't say anything else about it."

"Wanatela doesn't say much about anything."

"True."

"Seeing that Indian baby mummy made me feel funny."

She smiled. "You're lucky, Pauly. You're just a kid and you already know something some adults never learn."

"What?"

"That being a member of the majority doesn't give you the right to hurt people born outside the club. In truth, we have a responsibility to protect them."

The notion intrigued me, and I thought of how I'd tried to protect Buddy, who would never be in anybody's club. I'd protected Mama and Pop from finding out that their children were social pariahs, which is what members of the lowest caste were called in India. I never divulged the daily pain or sought their comfort. I was pretty sure that my need for consolation would hurt them more than the childish taunts hurt me.

I wanted them to think they were doing a good job raising us. If they had known what failures Buddy and I had been, they would have felt like failures too, and everyone would have been miserable. Pop had enough trouble keeping Mama happy as it was.

Our parents had made us the best they knew how. I couldn't let them know they'd done a bad job. They were fragile in a way I didn't understand. I was the tough one. I could take whatever the world and the meanest sixth-grade bully dished out so long as I didn't disappoint Johnny and Gracie.

Sometimes I wondered how I'd managed to pull it off. Maybe I'd inherited Aunt Nora's acting ability. Did Mama and Pop really believe those black eyes and skinned knuckles were the result of spirited games of Red Rover and tag? Didn't they ever suspect I was at the library all those afternoons when I said I was playing with nonexistent friends? Were they so preoccupied with each other that they failed to notice what was right under their noses? Or had they only pretended not to see?

"You know what really burns me up?" Aunt Nora plucked a fuzzy seed head from a weed alongside the path.

"What?"

"If Sylvester had been a white baby, No Water Charlie wouldn't dream of putting him out on display like that."

"Nope, he sure wouldn't." Solidarity was the way to go. Not only was Aunt Nora listening, she agreed with me. Maybe my plan had a chance. "You know what's worst of all?"

She looked at me curiously. "What?"

"I bet those truckers down at the Chuck Wagon Café wouldn't think it was wrong to keep an Ancient One in a sideshow." Aunt Nora did another slow burn. With a little effort, I could take this home. "They'd probably think the whole thing was a big joke and laugh their dumb heads off."

"I'm sure they would," she said quietly.

I hoped she was recalling how the men in the diner had taunted Wanatela. Empathy would help my cause. "Poor Wanatela." I worked a dramatic tremor into my voice. "First a white man shoots her husband over a chicken, then a skinny white waitress won't sell her any food, then a white bus driver kicks her off the bus. If that weren't enough to make her give up on the world, she has to go and find one of her ancestors on display like a stuffed woodpecker."

I sniffed and peered at Aunt Nora from the corner of one eye to see if my terse summary of the young woman's woes was having the desired effect.

"The injustice is staggering," she said.

"Makes you ashamed to be white, doesn't it?"

She stopped in her tracks, knelt down and clasped my shoulders, looking me right in the eye. "As much as we might care, we can't make up for all the prejudice in the world, Pauly."

I was encouraged by her look, her touch. A warm connection kindled between us. "But we could make up for *some* of the injustice," I suggested hopefully. "Couldn't we?"

Common sense and social conscience battled in her mind. Finally, her slow grin gave me hope. I'd kept my fingers crossed behind my back and the magic had worked. "So we can do it?"

"I must be crazy, but why not? Tonight, when everyone else is asleep, you and I are going to pay an unauthorized visit to No Water Charlie's. Are you game?"

"You're darned tootin'."

And so, fate plunged us down another unexpected path. For once, I had seized the opportunity to help the less fortunate, as opposed to *being* the less fortunate. The notion of righting a wrong had an exhilarating effect on me. I was about to join the ranks of Robin Hood, Batman, the Shadow, and other heroes who were forced to work outside the law for the good of mankind.

Something amazing happened on that warm Arizona night when Aunt Nora decided right may be right and wrong may be wrong, but sometimes doing the wrong thing was the right thing to do.

The shared plotting of a subversive act gave me a sense of belonging that I'd never felt before. I wasn't just a piece of flotsam in the flash flood of life, swept along by events beyond my control. I could influence others. I was capable of idealistic thought and deed. I wasn't alone anymore. I had a compatriot, a kindred spirit.

A partner in crime.

Grand Theft Mummy

Using a strategy lifted from an Abbott and Costello matinee, Aunt Nora and I scheduled our covert rescue of the Ancient One, popularly known as Sylvester the Mummy, for the crack of midnight. When the others were deep asleep and sufficient darkness had fallen, we dressed in dark clothes like art thieves in a Charles Boyer movie and snuck out of camp. I steered the Buick, and Aunt Nora pushed it far enough away to avoid waking the others. We switched places and she started the engine.

We planned to drive up to No Water Charlie's with the headlights off, park around back, purloin said mummy, and make a clean getaway. We had no idea where the old man slept but were pretty sure he didn't bunk in the museum. As Aunt Nora pointed out with a shiver, "Who could rest with a room full of little glass eyes staring at you?"

Younger, faster, and keener on the enterprise, I was the first one out of the car when we arrived. I crept through the botanical garden with all senses on red alert. The musk of animals stirring in their cages hung heavy on the cool desert air. I was going for stealth, but the crunch of my tennis shoes on the gravel sounded as loud as a freight train on a trestle. Aunt Nora followed, tiptoeing and shushing me every step of the way.

I rattled the knob on the back door. "It's locked." I whispered in case someone was awake and listening.

"Figures. Old Charlie's got a valuable collection to protect." Aunt Nora was grimly resigned to unlawful entry. "Give me the knife."

I slapped the Swiss Army knife, our all-purpose kitchen utensil and burglary tool, into her outstretched palm.

She fingered the knife's various components in the dark. "Maybe this will work." She stuck the metal toothpick into the lock experimentally. Nothing happened. Not on the first, second, or third round of jiggle, jimmy, jiggle, shake, cuss. "Oh, shoot!"

Nanny Tee said "shoot" was just shit with glasses on, but now didn't seem like a good time to mention it.

"We might as well try yelling open sesame." Aunt Nora blew a strand of hair out of her eyes.

"I don't think yelling is the way to go. Keep trying." I scanned the grounds, which were much scarier in the dark than in broad daylight. From a pit a few feet away, the vibration of deadly rattles reminded me that a tangle of venomous snakes was wide-awake and probably hoping one of us would fall in during our escape. "Poke harder."

She did, and the metal made a racket like thunder on the still night air. "Shoot! Even with the moon shining, it's darker than the back lot of hell out here."

"If it wasn't dark," I pointed out, "Charlie might see us."

She looked up with a sheepish grin. "Oh, right."

"Want me to hold the flashlight?"

"You brought a flashlight?" She seemed as surprised by my unexpected resourcefulness as I was by her lack of it.

I pulled the Eveready out of my hip pocket and aimed the narrow beam on the doorknob. "Does that help?"

She nodded in grudging respect. "Do I need to worry about you, Pauly? You seem to have an aptitude for this kind of work."

"Pop always said I would be good at whatever I set my mind to." It had probably never occurred to him that I might take up cat burglary.

Turning back to her task, Aunt Nora gave the toothpick another hard jiggle. Incredibly, the knob turned. She let out an incredulous little squeak and spun around on her toes, her eyes bright in the moonlight. "Holy cow. I can't believe it actually worked. Let's grab that thing and get out of here before someone catches us and hauls us off to an adobe jail."

Escaping undetected was definitely part of my plan, modified from Lou Costello's in that regard. My heart pounded with excitement as I followed Aunt Nora through the open door. This was how Robin Hood and his Merry Men must have felt before relieving oppressors of ill-gotten gains.

It took a moment for my eyes to adjust. Inside, the museum was dark and creepy, filled with nooks and crannies where ravenous wolf men and bloodthirsty monsters could hide. I gulped at the thought of all those zombie birds and jackalopes coming to life in the shadows. After being on display for so long, they would be hungry, and we were the only food in sight.

With the flashlight's beam flickering before us, we picked our way down the aisles of desert wonders. Careful not to bump into stuffed woodpeckers or two-headed tortoises, we finally located poor Sylvester's glass case.

Aunt Nora stopped suddenly, and I bumped into her. She yelped again. "For Pete's sake, Pauly," she whispered. "You scared the bejeezus out of me."

"Sorry." Could I help it if I was new at breaking and entering?

She stood in front of the display, one hand holding the flashlight, the other on her hip. "So what do we do? Break Sylvester out? Or hijack him, case and all?"

She wanted my opinion. We truly were partners, bonded in our commitment to make a preemptive strike for native peoples. "Take the case. If we shake the mummy around too much, it might crumble up into dust or something."

I had a sudden vivid image of the little black pellets Pop had bought on Independence Day. He didn't like the sound of firecrackers, said he'd heard enough of that during the war, so all we ever got were sparklers and snakes. We lit those little black pellets with our punks, and they fizzled and hissed into spirals of ash. When they stopped growing, Buddy and I took turns stomping on them, leaving nothing but a gritty black spot on the sidewalk.

The same thing might happen to Sylvester if we jostled him too much. Wanatela and the other members of her tribe wouldn't be impressed with an offering of mummy dust and turkey feathers, no matter how good our intentions.

"Let's grab it and get out of here," Aunt Nora said. "This place gives me the heebie-jeebies."

The glass case weighed a ton. We heaved it up between us and realized too late that we'd overlooked a cardinal rule of professional banditry. In any cooperative transporting effort, it's a good idea to plan who will walk backward *before* you grab the goods.

We fumbled around, trying to get a grip in the dark. I worried that any minute No Water Charlie would flip on the overhead lights with a raspy "Aha!" and there we'd be, caught like two roaches trying to make off with a crumb.

Somehow, despite our clumsy efforts at plundering, we managed to

sidle our way to the back door with Sylvester in one piece. I was beginning to think we might actually get away with our crime.

Then the coyote howled. Aunt Nora was so startled she yelled shoot
without glasses. Her outburst scared me so much I nearly wet my pants.
Then we realized it wasn't Lon Chaney on a werewolf rampage, only
Charlie's mangy old exhibit baying at the moon.

"What if the coyote wakes up Charlie?" I asked. "He might come
running with a shotgun or something."

It was a reasonable concern, but Aunt Nora laughed so hard we
nearly dropped Sylvester again.

"What's so funny?" I hissed under my breath.

"I just got a mental picture of No Water Charlie in his long johns,
chasing us at gunpoint."

"What's funny about that?"

"Everything." We baby-stepped our way past the animal cages to
the car. "I cannot believe I'm doing this." The moonlight sparked in her
hair and her eyes implored heaven. "A couple of weeks ago, my life was
almost normal. Now here I am with a mastermind kid criminal in West
Jesus Nowhere, pinching a five-hundred-year-old mummy in the name
of liberty and justice for all. And the whole escapade is set to a score
thoughtfully provided by a coyote."

"You're not gonna chicken out, are you?"

"Of course not," she huffed as we wrapped the case in a sleeping
bag and hefted it into the car's trunk. "I was just commenting on the
absurdity of the situation is all."

"I was afraid you might have changed your mind."

"There's no turning back now." She shooed me into the front seat.
The car's top was up, affording some protection from the night. Without a word, we turned simultaneously in paranoid panic and slapped

down the door locks, forgetting for a moment that we were the only social deviants around.

"We're doing the right thing," I insisted.

"Sure we are. You know it and I know it, and maybe even the
mummy knows it. But try convincing a judge if we get caught. You can
bet I'm going to let him know this whole crime spree was your idea, Ma
Barker."

We rode along in silence for about a mile before Aunt Nora yelped
again and slammed on the brakes. I spun around in alarm, expecting to
see the whirling red lights of a sheriff's car behind us. The desert was
calm and dark for miles in every direction. "What's the matter?"

"Shoot! I was in such a hurry to get out of there, I forgot to leave
the money."

"What money?"

She slapped both hands against the steering wheel. "I meant to
leave the hundred dollars for the old man."

"What?"

"The hundred dollars. For the mummy."

"Are you crazy? Just keep driving," I pleaded. "If we turn back now,
we're sure to get caught, and besides, if Charlie finds a hundred dollars
where Sylvester used to be, he'll know we took him."

"I think he'll figure that out anyway. I doubt Arizona is overrun
with mummy snatchers."

I took the rational approach. "He'd know it was us and call the law.
How long before they track us down? This car sticks out like a cello in
a cheese factory. So step on it. Please." Incarceration had never been
part of my plan.

She gripped the steering wheel. "You have a point. But if I leave the
money, it won't seem so much like stealing."

I glanced nervously back the way we'd come. Maybe I had a twinge of guilty conscience, but I was sure I would see that flashing red light at any moment. "That's why you're going to *mail* No Water Charlie the money."

"Mail it?"

"In a month or two when we're in California and the heat is off, you can send Charlie a money order and a nice letter with no return address telling him all about Sylvester's farewell party."

"Mail it, huh? That might work."

"Of course it will. Charlie gets his money, Sylvester gets to the happy hunting ground, and we don't get arrested."

Aunt Nora grinned. "You know, Pauly, you think of all the angles. You'd make a darned good crook."

I must have looked flattered because she added in a raspy Edward G. Robinson growl, "But don't get any ideas, toots. After this job, we're going straight, see?"

The long stretch of desert road unwound before us like my uncertain future. We really had passed the point of no return. There was no going back. Not this night. Not ever. Whatever we were in for, we were in it together. I liked the sound of that. "So will you just drive already?"

Aunt Nora hooted and pressed her foot hard on the accelerator. The car purred into high gear.

After a few more minutes with no cops on our tail, I leaned out the window and yelled into the quiet night, "We did it! We really did it!"

"Cheer, why don't you? I've only been your guardian for a few days, and I've already turned you into a felon."

"I'm a vindicator!" My arm pumped up in victory. "A crusader for mankind. A defender of justice, a champion of the underdog." I felt like one of the famous heroines featured in the true-blue biographies from the library, famous women who challenged society and changed the world. Clara Barton. Florence Nightingale. Dorothea Dix.

"Call it whatever you want"—Aunt Nora looked my way and laughed—"but I'm pretty sure what we just did falls somewhere between a misdemeanor and a felony."

I didn't care. For the first time, someone wasn't laughing *at* me. Aunt Nora was laughing *with* me. We were sharing a joke, and I wasn't the punch line. This time I wasn't on the outside looking in. I was in. I was *way* in.

"I thought we were goners when that coyote howled," she croaked.

I grinned. "You should have seen your face."

"*My* face? You looked like the Creature from the Black Lagoon had just invited you for a midnight swim."

"I guess I was a little worried."

"*You* were a little worried? I was scared spitless." She giggled, and I giggled with her. My heart expanded in my chest. Was this what it felt like to have a friend? To share an experience? To make a memory? I'd never known real friendship, but I'd read enough books to recognize the feeling when it bowled me over. Tom and Huck. Betsy and Tacy. The Five Little Peppers.

Happiness was a warm blanket against the chill of isolation. Oh, it was true, all right. I *had* passed the point of no return. One intoxicating taste of acceptance, and I could never go back to toughing it out alone. It took too much energy to pretend not to care.

With amazing clarity, I realized that I had a chance for a do-over in California. No one there knew anything about me. Baloney Mahoney existed only in my heart. I would abandon that unhappy girl along the way. Dump her like a cigarette butt in a ditch, and write my own story. The knowledge filled me with quiet pleasure and unholy dread.

Aunt Nora concentrated on the road, humming, "If I Knew You Were Coming, I'd've Baked a Cake." She had unknowingly offered me a chance to get it right.

I settled back into the seat, my eyes on the distant moon-washed horizon. Anything seemed possible as we sped through the sage-scented desert like desperados, trailing dust and high hopes behind us.

Everyone was sawing logs when we returned to camp. My recent brush with lawbreaking had heightened my awareness of illicit doings, and I realized how easy it would be for someone with bad intentions to sneak up on us. Aunt Nora advised me to get some sleep, but I was so excited that I lay awake in the backseat of the car and stared out the window at the stars. There were a gajillion of them, so many more than we had in Oklahoma. They were brighter too and close enough to touch.

I thought about Pop and wondered what he would make of the night's adventure. He was so honest, he'd once driven all the way back to the grocery store to return an extra dime he'd received in change. He quit a good job at a service station because the owner wanted him to sell oil to lady drivers who didn't need it. He even complained to the Better Business Bureau about the produce man who kept his thumb on the scales when he waited on old folks. Despite his ramshackle finances, Johnny Mahoney had been an honest man. Right is right was the simple creed he'd lived by.

I figured Pop would agree that taking Sylvester wasn't thievery but reparation. Another word I didn't get to use very often. It meant making amends or giving satisfaction for a wrong or injury, and that's what Aunt Nora and I had done. Pop might even have been proud of me.

Mama was a different story. It was harder to win her approval. She rarely expressed opinions of her own, declaring, "Whatever you say, Johnny, is fine with me." If I wanted something, she waved me away and told me to ask Pop. Didn't matter if it was something big like a pony, or little like a cookie, Mama didn't like to make decisions.

She didn't like a lot of things. I never knew exactly what brought on her bad spells, but moodiness was part of her, like not worrying about bill collectors was part of Pop. Sometimes when we came home from school, she would still be in bed, with the covers over her head. When I asked if she was sick, she said no, just down in the dumps. Her get-up-and-go had got up and went.

She'd tell me to take Buddy out to play, so she could pull herself together. Sometimes, she managed to fix a meal, but sometimes the steps necessary to put food on the table were too complicated, and I had to do the cooking.

Pop could usually cheer her up when she was down-spirited, but Buddy and I knew better than to try. If we came home and found her sitting at the kitchen table with a big ashtray full of butts and her hair not even combed, we knew to lay low until Pop got home. She didn't scream or hit us when she got that twitchy look, but if we plagued her, she would start bawling, and when that happened she couldn't seem to stop. Buddy and I hovered out of sight, helpless and confused in the face of such uncontrolled sorrow.

Pop was the only one who could make her feel better. He called her Gloomy Gus or Moody Mama and teased her until she smiled. Sometimes he pulled her up and twirled her through a jitterbug routine they'd perfected years before. Other times he loaded us into the car and we went for ice cream. Two scoops of banana nut could turn her around.

Mama's good spells made up for the bad ones, but they could be scary. Like the little girl in the nursery rhyme, when she was good, she was very, very good. Hair rolled up in tight pin curls under her favorite scarf was a good sign and meant she wanted to look pretty for Pop. She wore her nice blouse and Evening in Paris perfume. On happy nights, we had chicken or pork chops for supper and apple Betty for dessert.

We sat at the table and laughed at Pop's stories and everyone pitched in to wash the dishes, like a real family. If it was still light out, Pop would play catch with us in the backyard while Mama sat on the stoop and smoked. If it was too dark to play ball, we'd dump a jigsaw puzzle on the table, and Pop would help us fit the pieces together. Sometimes, Mama helped too, but she couldn't sit still for long.

When she was in one of her going moods, she cleaned the house like she was fighting fire. She had so much extra energy that she washed windows and turned mattresses and made jam and fried doughnuts. One time she sewed us clown costumes to wear trick-or-treating, using a needle and thread, a striped bedsheet and no pattern. That's how relentless she was. She hardly slept at all and would get up and wax the kitchen floor at two in the morning.

Sometimes I felt like I had two different mothers. The trick to getting along was knowing how to act around whichever one she was at the moment. When she was sad, we learned to be quiet so we wouldn't bother her with our foolishness. When she was hopping like a bug on a griddle, we had to keep up with her or suffer the consequences. We tiptoed around her, afraid to light her fuse because we never knew if she would blow up in tears or anger.

As confusing as life with Mama could be, I knew I could count on Pop. He was like the mailman: rain or shine, sleet or snow, nothing ever bothered him. Or maybe he just didn't want to do anything to make Mama sad. If he lost his job, he didn't worry because he said someone always needed a good hand. If we ran out of money and the rent was due, he talked about pennies from heaven and how lucky we were. He said after what he'd seen in Italy, he was just glad to be alive. There were plenty of boys who weren't.

Now Mama and Pop and their confusing ways were gone, and I could finally think about them without filling up with tears. Maybe that's what folks meant when they said life goes on.

The next morning, we left the campground at sunrise. Aunt Nora wanted to be out of shotgun range before No Water Charlie realized his most educational exhibit had flown the coop. Once on the road, she recounted our nocturnal adventure and explained our plans to the others.

Tyb scratched his chin. "I don't hold with stealin'."

"It's not stealing," I assured him. "Stealing was taking Sylvester out of the cave in the first place. We're just putting him back where he belongs." I explained how we were doing our bit to make up for all the dirty rotten things white men had done to Indians over the years.

"Well, put thataway, I reckon it don't sound so bad," Tyb allowed.

"We plan to send No Water Charlie a hundred dollars to cover any financial loss he might incur."

"Well, what you done might not be strictly legal, but mebbe it was for the best," Tyb speculated.

"How c-c-come I always g-g-get left out of the f-f-fun?" Buddy complained.

"We didn't do it for fun." I didn't think he'd understand something as complicated as moral conscience.

Wanatela didn't say much, but she seemed pleased that the Ancient One would be restored to its rightful place in the spirit world. "The People will know what to do."

So far, things were working out just fine. I had one good deed under my belt and a new admiration for Aunt Nora. Not only was she proving more dependable than Nanny Tee had claimed, she was a better survivor than I had given her credit for. Worn out from the excitement and loss of sleep, I leaned back on the front seat, closed my eyes and slept all the way to Indian Wells.

* * *

Wanatela's mother's hogan was located on the outskirts of town. The round house was small and dark and appeared to list to one side. A couple of skinny dogs lay panting in the dust by the door. Other hogans clustered along the dirt road, and a few dark-eyed children darted into them when our car approached.

Wanatela invited us into the single room, which was about twenty-five feet in diameter. Herbs and dried foods and articles of clothing were suspended from nails pounded into the beams. We stood quietly while she and her mother exchanged greetings in their language. The old woman sat propped up on a pallet in the corner, covered with a brightly patterned blanket despite the heat. Her dark eyes were sunken in their sockets, and her hair was more white than black. Her skin was the color of walnuts, and deep furrows etched her mouth and eyes.

A wizened old man in baggy clothes and a black hat sat cross-legged on the dirt floor, surrounded by a haze of fragrant smoke.

Wanatela introduced us. "This is my mother, Nezlina Begay." The old woman nodded but said nothing. "And our medicine man is Nasdi Tsosie. He chanted a curing ceremony, and my mother has recovered from the pains that hurt her heart."

Wanatela turned to the elderly Navahos. "These friends have helped me." She slipped back into rapid-fire Navaho to explain, I guessed, about Sylvester. "It is a good sign that Nasdi Tsosie is here. He knows what to do with the Ancient One."

Mr. Tsosie asked questions, which Wanatela answered. When he requested to see the Ancient One, everyone except Mrs. Begay trooped outside. Aunt Nora opened the trunk and unwrapped the mummy case.

Chanting in Navaho, the old man made signs over the case with feathers he removed from a small leather pouch hanging from his belt.

"Nasdi Tsosie says you have done a good thing by bringing this Ancient One to him," Wanatela informed us. He spoke again, and Wanatela interpreted. "To honor what you have done, and for helping me, he will bless your journey and bid you safely to your home."

"Please thank him for us," said Aunt Nora.

"He thanks *you*," Wanatela said. "You are good friends to the People."

The old man nodded and smiled, baring toothless gums. He closed his eyes, waved the feathers again and chanted quietly. When he finished, he spoke to Wanatela.

"What is it?" Aunt Nora asked.

"He says you have lost much but will find more. The road home will be long and treacherous, but stay on the westward path and do not turn from the setting sun."

"Oh." Aunt Nora smiled, but I could see that the medicine man's words had confused her. "Thank him for letting us know."

Wanatela turned to me. "He says you, the girl with wise eyes, must not worry."

Girl with wise eyes? Was that my Indian name? I liked it better than girl with chip on her shoulder. Girl with no parents. Girl with bad luck. "But what . . ."

Before I could ask my question, the old man stretched his skinny arms around the heavy glass case and waddled it over to a battered pickup truck. He loaded it in the front seat and returned to speak to Wanatela once more before climbing behind the wheel. Ignoring the road, he drove off toward a distant red rock mesa.

"The People's ways must be followed," Wanatela said. "No white people can witness sacred rites."

"Of course." Aunt Nora hugged Wanatela. "I hope your mother gets well soon. It was a pleasure to meet you. Thank you for sharing our journey for a little while."

"Good luck and great happiness." Wanatela stood outside her mother's hogan with Root riding one hip.

"What will happen to the mummy now?" I tried to give Root a kiss, but he hid his face in his mother's shoulder. He had good reason to distrust the affection of strangers.

"The Ancient One belongs to the People," Wanatela told me. "Nasdi Tsosie will see that it is reburied properly."

And that was the last we saw of Sylvester the Ancient One, late of No Water Charlie's Desert Museum of Curious Anomalies.

Watching the mummy disappear in a cloud of dust without so much as a heigh-ho Silver put what is called an anticlimactic spin on our little adventure.

Which is a real lesson for life. Sometimes you anticipate an event with a sense of impending wonder, elevating it to a near spiritual experience. Then when the great day finally dawns, whatever it was that you thought would be so special turns out to be ho-hum. On the other hand, the most unexpected events can nip in out of nowhere and change your whole life.

"Are the folks in California as mad at Indians as they are here?" I asked as Aunt Nora steered the Skylark onto the bumpy road.

"I don't think so. Why?"

"I just wondered." We drove away, and the Broomcorns grew smaller and smaller until I could no longer see them. A hawk swooped over a mesa, flying high and free. We should have invited Wanatela and Root to go with us. California was a starting-over place. Maybe they could start over too.

Even as the wish formed in my heart, I knew it could not come true. Wanatela wouldn't leave the People. The empty desert belonged to her, as much as she belonged to it. She would endure injustice, just as her sacred land had endured centuries of wind and rain and burning sun. Wood might turn to rock, but prejudice could not erode Wanatela's quiet spirit, or the strength that came from knowing where she fit into the world. Even if the only place left to her was the sharp, rusty edge of no-man's-land.

Confused, I swallowed a salty tear. Which decision would be harder to make? Staying and knowing what you had to face?

Or going, and having no idea?

Horse on a Rock

We stopped in the settlement to restock supplies. Few people were around in the heat of the day, but children with round, brown faces peered out from the doorways of unpainted houses. Screen doors flapped on loose hinges, and the windows had no screens at all. The place was strangely quiet, a ghost town whose spirits were busy elsewhere.

Junk littered the hard-packed dirt between the houses and the road. Deep in scraggly, colorless weeds, insects droned, and their buzzing vibrated inside my skull. Hungry-looking dogs soaked up the sparse shade of scattered cottonwoods. Fuzz from the trees floated like albino space spiders in air that was thick with heat and dust. There was no color. No flowers, no shrubs. Nothing green except wicked-looking cactus.

"All this time, I thought we were poor." I stared out the window, and the desolation stared back.

"If this is the government's idea of helping people, I'd hate to see what they would come up with for punishment." Aunt Nora choked on the dust blowing in the open convertible.

"Reservations usually end up on land nobody else wants," Tyb put in. "Indians always get the hind teat."

I thought of the succession of rental houses we'd lived in, some for a few weeks, others for a little longer. Small and in disrepair, they'd been mansions compared to the tumbledown huts we passed. A few times, Mama had gotten antsy enough to plant four o'clocks around the door, but she always forgot to water the seeds. I'd made sure they survived by irrigating them with water from a peanut butter jar filled at the kitchen sink. I fertilized those plants with hope and coffee grounds, praying we'd stick around long enough to see them bloom. I cut the grass with an old push mower because Pop never remembered that you had to mow it down regular to keep the landlord happy.

Pop had teased me about my efforts and accused me of being house-proud. Houses weren't something he could own or take pride in. To him a house was just walls and a roof. A temporary stop where we sorted laundry before moving on. His vagabond view did not jibe with my image of home. A house could never inspire anyone to flights of sentiment. But a home could.

I knew from reading books and listening to music that people longed for home, wrote songs about it. There's no place like home. My old Kentucky home. Back home again in Indiana. Home on the range. Home was embedded deep in the language. Hearth and home. Home is where the heart is. Home sweet home.

I wanted to be a Homebody with a capital *H*. Home was a warm place where you could always find shelter from the cold. The shacks on the reservation looked more like places to run away from than to go home to. How hopeless would a person have to be to stay there day after day?

Aunt Nora parked in front of the trading post. "I'll run in and buy bread and cold cuts. Everybody want pop? We can find a picnic spot on our way back to the highway."

Tyb unfolded himself from the backseat and leaned against the car to catch his breath. Buddy and Puppy, both in dire need of relieving themselves, took off around back. I walked across the road and approached two dark-haired children playing in the dirt. The little boy ran away when he saw me, but the girl eyed me curiously.

"My name's Pauly. What's yours?" She didn't answer, and I wondered if she spoke English. I didn't know Navaho, so I patted my chest like Tarzan. "Me Pauly."

She giggled. "My name's Mary. Why do you come here?" She sat in the dirt and invited me to do likewise.

"We brought someone home to see her mother." I folded my legs in the Indian fashion. "Wanatela Broomcorn. She has a baby named Root. Do you know her?"

Mary nodded. "Where do you come from?"

"Oklahoma. But we're on our way to California."

"The old man is your grandfather?"

I looked over at Tyb, who was wiping his face with a grungy handkerchief. "No. He's a hitchhiker we picked up in New Mexico." That wasn't right. Tyb was more than that now, but I didn't know how to explain him.

Mary handed me a flat rock on which she'd drawn a picture with a piece of charred wood.

I admired the design she'd created with the makeshift materials. "That's a pretty good horse."

"Thank you."

"Do you have a horse?"

"Only dogs and sheep around here."

"Do you go to school?"

"When they can find a teacher. Mostly no. Teachers don't want to live here."

I could believe that. "How did you learn to draw?"

"No learning. Just doing."

"Wait here." I dusted the seat of my shorts as I raced back to the car. Aunt Nora had finished shopping and was stowing a brown bag of groceries in the front seat.

"We're ready to go, Pauly," she said.

"I'll be right back. I want to give Mary something."

"Who's M-M-M-Mary?" Buddy climbed into the backseat, and Puppy bounced in after him.

"Somebody I met." I retrieved the box of crayons and the *Day at the Zoo* coloring book from my bag. When I returned, Mary was still sitting in the dirt.

"Here." I held out my gifts.

She handled them like something with a short fuse. "Why do you give me these things?"

"You're a good artist. You need colors." Her world was composed of endless shades of brown, but her imagination could put the other twenty-three crayons to good use.

Her shy eyes lit up as she flipped through the coloring book. "Okay."

Aunt Nora tooted the horn. "I have to go now. It was nice meeting you."

Mary didn't say anything. She hugged the crayons and coloring book to her heart. At the car, I looked back. The little boy had returned. He peered eagerly over Mary's shoulder as she opened the box and shook the crayons into her hand. I smiled when she locked straight onto the pink one.

We were well down the road before Aunt Nora spoke. "That was an unselfish thing you did, Pauly, giving that little girl your crayons."

"She needed them more than me."

"I think you brightened her day."

"It made me feel good."

"Doing a good deed usually does."

"Is that why people do good deeds? So *they* can feel better?"

"I like to think we do good things because it makes *other* people feel better."

"What about bad people?"

She looked over her sunglasses. "What about them?"

"Do they do bad things because it makes them feel good, or because they want other people to feel bad?"

"That's pretty deep. We may be discussing philosophy here."

"So what do you think?"

"That you just asked the sixty-four-thousand-dollar question," she said with a grin. "Sorry, you want a serious answer? I think bad people don't know how to feel good, so they settle for hurting others."

"Because they're evil or just deep down sad?"

"I don't like to think people are evil," she said. "Maybe they feel so bad about themselves that they can't let any goodness in their lives."

Had Mama felt bad about herself? Was that why she had needed cheering up so often? I glanced in the backseat. Tyb was already snoozing. Buddy was playing with Puppy and not paying attention to our conversation. "Like the kids who made fun of Buddy?"

"Kids made fun of Buddy?" Aunt Nora whispered in alarm.

"Sometimes."

"Just sometimes?"

"Lots of times."

"How'd you feel about that?"

"Mad as a doused cat. Like when those truckers were mean to Wanatela. I wanted to chew nails and spit tacks."

"I wanted to spit a few thumbtacks myself."

"There's something you should know about me." I needed to confess. Somewhere between yesterday and today, a soft thing had unfurled inside me where my aunt was concerned. What had once been cold and hard had sprouted into hopeful new feelings, as tender as pale green leaves reaching for the light. I had to know if she could feel that way about me.

"What's that, kiddo?" She snapped her gum and grinned.

"I have a bad temper and it gets me into trouble."

"Is that so?"

"And fights. Buddy and I aren't what you might call popular."

"Oh?"

"We never fit into the right crowd."

"Did you want to?"

"Well, gee, yes!"

"Would you have acted like the other kids, if that had made you more popular?"

Another trick question. "You mean like teasing simples and cripples and people who can't help being what they are?"

She nodded. "That's part of it. Would you do things you didn't want to do if it made people like you more?"

Aunt Nora's question was nothing new. I had thought about that many times. I almost said yes but decided there would be no joy in having other people like me if I didn't like myself. "I guess not."

"You probably could have been chums with those kids if you'd been willing to join in their meanness. Kids can put a lot of pressure on each other. It takes strength of character to stand up to them."

"That's me," I said. "A leper with strong character."

"How do you know about lepers?"

"*Weekly Reader.* There are sanitariums in Louisiana where lepers live. They can't leave. I used to worry that I'd catch leprosy and get shipped off to the swamp."

She laughed. "You worry too much."

"That's what Mama said. Sometimes I *wanted* to be exiled to a leper colony. I least I would have fit in."

"Things couldn't have been as bad as all that."

What did she know? She didn't stutter or limp or have frizzy hair. She wasn't as plain as a mud fence. I suspected she hadn't just been part of the right crowd, she'd probably been the president. A nice girl who didn't join in the taunting because she never noticed the kids on the receiving end.

"Ever hear of the untouchables?" I asked. "It's the lowest caste system in India."

"*Weekly Reader* again?"

"Geography book."

"What about them, Pauly?" Aunt Nora asked gently.

"Nothing. I just didn't want you to think it only happened in India. There are untouchables everywhere."

She gave me a long, measuring look. "How about you keep your eyes open for a place to eat lunch?"

I stared out the window, pretending to scout for picnic spots, but I couldn't think about food. Talking about good people and bad people, and the relative merits of each, made me remember another picnic. I'd been eleven the day we'd driven out to the lake with a bunch of Mahoneys to celebrate the Fourth of July.

There were kids of all ages, and I was playing in the shallow water with my cousin Linda when two big boys we didn't know came up and started splashing us. It was fun at first, and we splashed them back. Pretty soon, they let us ride on their shoulders so Linda and I could try to knock each other off.

We horsed around until Linda got a cramp and went back to the bank. The boy whose shoulders I was riding walked farther out into the deep part, away from the picnic area. I got scared and told him to take me back, but he said not to worry, he wouldn't let me drown. He took me off his shoulders and held me in front of him.

I tried to squirm away, but I couldn't touch bottom and wasn't much of a swimmer then. Deep water scared me, so I wrapped my arm around the boy's neck. We bobbed around in the water for a few minutes, and I scanned the bank for a sign of Pop, or any grown-up to save me. The strange boy was acting stranger, and I had a bad feeling about him.

On shore the little kids hollered and splashed and waded along the edge. I asked the boy to please take me back, and he said he would. In a minute. But first, he wanted to show me something. He touched my stomach, and the next thing I knew his hand was inside my bathing suit bottom, rubbing between my legs and poking me with his finger. I told him to stop and pushed away from him. He let me go, and I sunk under the water. I thought I would drown before he pulled me up, coughing and spitting.

He told me in a mean voice that he would let me sink if I didn't behave. I would drown and no one would find my body until it was puffed up and blue and nibbled on by catfish and turtles. Did I want to die? Did I want to make my mommy and daddy cry? I didn't know him, and I was afraid he really meant it. I was in deep water, and no one knew where I was.

He grabbed my hand and pushed it into his swim trunks. I felt his private parts and wiry hair and jerked my hand away. I'd rather reach into a nest of snakes. He pushed my head under the water and held it down, then yanked me up and told me I'd better do what he said or else. He forced my hand back down, telling me to touch it. Pet it. It won't bite. Wasn't it soft as silk? It grew in my hand, and I felt sick. I started to holler and the boy let me slip under the water again. That time he didn't pull me up until I had nearly choked to death.

Behave, he said. Cooperate. Be a good girl. But I knew what we were doing was bad. Panicked, I scanned the bank and saw Buddy sitting in the shallows, filling up a pop bottle with water and letting it run out. Buddy was safe.

Pull on it, the boy whispered. Gently. Faster. Squeeze a little bit. Then he jerked and something warm squirted into my hand. The boy had his eyes closed, and I thought he might drop me, so I clung to his neck, but I didn't like touching him.

When he came back to life, he told me I was good. Only I didn't feel good. I'd done something so terrible that if anyone found out, they would think I was a wicked person. The boy said if I told, the stuff that had squirted out would make my hand turn black and everyone would know I was a nasty girl.

I knew right there in the cold water that I wouldn't tell. Black hand or not. Come hell or high water. This was an ugly secret, and I would keep it.

The boy paddled back to the bank and sat me down by the other kids like nothing out of the ordinary had happened. He ran off to find his friend, and I never saw him again. I couldn't even say what he looked like. He was just a big boy with bumps on his face and long, white arms and legs. That's all I remember.

The rest of the day, I kept to myself, checking my hand periodically to make sure it was still pink. When it was time to eat, I told Mama I wasn't hungry. I couldn't hold a fried chicken leg in that hand. It felt as numb and useless as Great-Granny Mahoney's stroke hand. I curled up on a blanket under a tree and closed my eyes. The sound of talking and laughing and firecrackers rose up around me. Uncles joking, aunts gossiping, cousins giggling, babies crying. Life sounded far away like the down deep buzzing of bees in a clover patch over the hill.

I pretended to be asleep and nobody bothered me. All afternoon, I lay there with my hand in a tight fist inside Pop's shirt that I'd slipped on over my bathing suit. I'd felt bad before, when kids teased me or pretended to pass along the cooties they caught by getting too close to me. But those times I'd felt angry bad. Smack somebody bad. Spit in an eye bad. Not dry up and blow away bad. Not sick enough to die bad. That day was the first time I felt so awful about something I'd done that my stomach knotted up in a big, hard rock of sorrow.

We spent the whole day at the lake. I finally fell asleep, and when I woke up I needed to pee, but I stayed where I was. My bursting bladder was my punishment, but it was insignificant in the face of my misery. When dusk settled and it was time for the fireworks to start, Pop came over and knelt beside me. He put my head in his lap, stroked my hair, and felt my forehead for a fever.

"You okay, sport?"

"Uh-huh."

"You don't act okay."

"Just tired."

"You got too much sun."

"Probably."

"You ready to get up and watch the fireworks?"

"Nah. I don't want to."

"But you love fireworks. We never miss 'em."

"You go on, Pop."

While Buddy and the cousins swung sparklers around, I stayed curled up on that blanket, wondering if all men did what the big boy had done. Did my uncles? Did Pop? Was that what Mama and Pop did in their room when they closed the door and told us to play outside?

I never told my parents what happened. After a while, I stopped checking my hand for telltale signs of decomposition and went on about my eleven-year-old business. I pushed the memory so far down in the cracks of my brain that pretty soon it seemed more like something I'd read about in a book. Something that had happened to someone else. Vivid but unreal.

Maybe someday I would tell Aunt Nora.

I'd always wanted someone to tell.

Say Good Night, Gracie

Just outside Flagstaff, Arizona, Aunt Nora announced we would find a motel and stay a few days. "Everybody okay with that plan?"

We were.

"We need time to rest," she said. "To do laundry and buy supplies before we head on to the Grand Canyon. We might as well sleep between sheets while we have the chance. And it won't hurt us to take baths, since we'll be roughing it for real soon enough. Besides, we're on a vacation and in no big hurry, right?"

Right.

"Pauly, check the map and find some sights for us to see while we're here."

I put my finger on Flagstaff and looked for national monuments in the area. "There's an extinct volcano called Sunset Crater, Indian ruins at Walnut Canyon, and Humphreys Peak. That's the highest point in Arizona. Elevation over twelve thousand feet."

"Sounds good. Won't it be fun to visit those places?"

We agreed it would.

"I wouldn't mind seeing a volcano up close," Tyb said.

"Wh-what's a v-v-volcano?" Buddy wanted to know.

"You tell him, Pauly," Aunt Nora said. "You're the scientist in the group."

By the time I was finished, we'd driven into town. I read from the brochure we'd picked up at a gas stop. "Flagstaff is surrounded by Co-conino National Forest, the world's largest contiguous ponderosa pine forest."

"I understand what a ponderosa pine tree is," Tyb said. "But what in tarnation is contiguous?"

I knew the answer. "Contiguous just means the forest is continuous and uninterrupted."

"Hmph," snorted Tyb. "Why didn't they jest say so?"

Flagstaff provided yet another change of scenery from the desert. The air was cool and smelled green, and tall pines made that soft tree music in the wind. Aunt Nora said we should pick a motel with a swimming pool and pulled into the Blue Spruce Motor Court. Ten log cabins nestled among the pines. The VACANCY sign beckoned, and in front of the office, a kidney-shaped pool sparkled in the afternoon sun like a blue cement jewel.

The manager gave Aunt Nora the key to cabin number five, and she parked the Buick in front so we could unload our stuff. A small porch with two metal lawn chairs gave Tyb a nice place to sit out in the cool shade. He never complained, but too much heat made him look peaked and clammy.

I'd never been in a motel room and was impressed by the spacious-ness. Besides a bathroom with a shower, the main room contained a small table with four chairs, a large dresser, a double bed and a studio couch, both with brown spreads. A lamp made from a section of tree trunk pooled dim light on a pine nightstand between the beds, and a rollaway cot stood in a corner. A picture of a mountain and lake hung on one knotty pine wall, and Indian rugs covered the wood floor. The curtains on the picture window featured scenes of cowboys lassoing cows.

"Tyb, you take the couch." Aunt Nora looked around. "Buddy can have the rollaway, and Pauly and I can share the double."

"Ain't no need for you to put me up, Miss Nora," Tyb objected. "I can sleep in the car."

"You'll do no such thing." Aunt Nora didn't have to twist his arm. The thought of resting his creaky old bones on a mattress after so many nights on the road must have proved tempting, because he gave in easily enough.

"Can we swim now?" I asked once we had unpacked.

"Sure, why not?" Aunt Nora checked the bedside clock. "You have time to play for an hour or so, then you need to shower and clean up for dinner."

She and Tyb relaxed in the lawn chairs while Buddy and I changed. We grabbed towels from the bathroom and headed for the pool.

I found a faded orange life vest hanging on the fence and made Buddy put it on before helping him remove the leg brace. His arms and legs were like sticks and his ribs could have belonged to a half-starved dog.

"Can I g-g-get in now, Pauly?"

"Bombs away!"

Instead of jumping in, Buddy tiptoed down the concrete steps into the baby end of the pool.

"W-w-watch what I can d-d-do, Pauly!" He dipped his face toward the surface, but as soon as his nose touched the water, he jerked it back.

I clapped because he liked applause. "That's good, Buddy. Before long, you'll be swimming like Johnny Weissmuller."

I dove into the deep end, swam to the side of the pool and watched my brother bob around. His spirit was tougher than his frail body; otherwise, how would he have battled polio and the long quarantine that kept him away from us for so long?

I was seven when he got sick, old enough to wish that the polio had taken me, a tough girl who would have had a fighting chance, instead of Mama's precious baby boy.

Once a week, I had accompanied my parents to St. John's Hospital to visit him. It wasn't a real visit. We could only gaze at Buddy through a plate-glass window, like he was a platter of nut fudge in a candy store display. I don't think he even knew we were there.

The nursing sisters moved with quiet purpose among the cribs of damaged babies, dark habits floating just above the floor, heavy crosses swinging from their waists. It was a religious place, that hospital, with stained-glass windows and pictures of Jesus and Mother Mary. An anteroom to heaven where sick babies waited to be called back.

The ones who died were the littlest angels, and the sisters tacked their pictures on a bulletin board in the hall. It was sad to arrive for a visit and find their iron cribs empty, crisp white sheets folded and tucked with nunlike precision to await the next unfortunate occupant. I worried that Buddy would die too. Then I worried he would live and be crumpled and bent forever. I worried he would be confined to an iron lung, a machine like an ironing mangle that pressed air into lungs instead of wrinkles out of clothes.

Once while Buddy was in the hospital, a storm blew through town. The next morning I found a tattered nest that had fallen from an oak tree. Lying on the sidewalk among the ruin of twigs and leaves and bits of dog fur were three blind, naked baby birds, their small dead bodies broken and blue. Bare wings for tiny arms and red beaks for little lips.

They weren't birds but polio babies, and I couldn't stop crying over them. I couldn't eat lunch. I couldn't explain what was wrong. I couldn't forget how they had looked when they were dead with no mother to keep them warm.

As little and weak as he was, Buddy survived the hospital and struggled through a painful recovery at a special children's convalescent home, enduring daily sessions in a big swimming pool. A famous Australian nurse named Sister Kenny figured out water therapy was the best way to help polio kids walk again. When we visited him there, I sat on the side of the pool and watched the attendants move Buddy's bony bird legs back and forth, back and forth. Buddy cried for Mama the whole time.

Maybe the therapy hurt him, or maybe he just didn't want to get his face wet. He looked about as substantial as a water bug, like one hard pinch could squeeze the life right out of him. I didn't think any human could be that pitiful and live.

But he did. When he finally came home, Mama tried to wrap him up in cotton batting like the Christmas bulbs, but she couldn't protect him. He was attacked in turn by whooping cough, measles, mumps, chicken pox, and just about every childhood illness known to medical science. He caught mysterious fevers and developed alien rashes that disappeared as suddenly as they appeared. He was allergic to medicines that would have made him feel better.

When he got older, he didn't do well in school because he was absent so much. All he had to do was sniff a big snot wad and Mama would keep him home, because everyone knew public school was a seething hotbed of germs. It took Buddy longer than most kids to learn new things. Reading was work, writing a chore. He just couldn't get the hang of pencil holding, couldn't crack the alphabet code. He couldn't run fast or play baseball or grasp the intricacies of blindman's bluff. As far as anyone could tell, Buddy possessed all the intellectual and athletic gifts of a hubcap, but that didn't make me love him any less.

When Buddy had finally come home, caring for him had been about all Mama could do. Sometimes he was too much, and she had to lie down with him when he napped. She fussed and fretted over him day and night, because she knew how easy it was for a sick child to pass through the waiting room doors and never come back. When I complained, she told me I was healthy and didn't need her the way Buddy did. I was a big, strong girl and could take care of myself. I could get my own glass of water and fix my own sandwich. She told me to play quietly so Buddy could sleep. Don't bang the door. Don't sing in the house. Don't laugh too loud. Don't ask for anything.

"Dammit, Pauly, can't you see I'm busy?"

I wanted to get sick too, so I could lie in her lap all day, petted like a Pekingese puppy. But I never even caught a bad cold. When the stomach flu leveled my third-grade class, I had my favorite teacher, Mrs. Wilhite, all to myself for two days. Mama said I was full of vinegar, and bugs couldn't live in an acid environment. I felt bad about bouncing all the germs back onto Buddy.

Despite all the time he'd spent in the therapy pool at the convalescent center, Buddy couldn't swim a lick. But the kapok Mae West allowed him to paddle around instead of sinking to the bottom like a rock.

I was a good swimmer now. After that horrible Fourth of July, I vowed never to be afraid of deep water again. Had I known how to swim that day, I could have kicked that mean boy in the juggernauts and made my escape. I had begged to take lessons at the public pool, and even though I never told him why, Pop could see how important the lessons were to me and agreed.

I was a fast learner, and before long I could dive, do the breaststroke, and the dead man's float. Since we would be living right on the beach in California, I figured my aquatic skills would come in handy.

After a few laps, I joined my brother in the shallow end. We hadn't had much time alone to talk. He clung to the side of the pool and kicked up a churning froth of water.

I edged close enough to speak without getting splashed in the face. "What do you think so far?"

"About wh-wh-what?" He stopped kicking and scissored his legs quietly beneath the surface.

"About Aunt Nora."

"Sh-sh-she's nice."

"What do you think about the Trip?"

"It's okay, but I miss Ma-Ma-Mama and Pop."

"Me, too." We held hands and floated on our backs for a moment. I couldn't talk to Buddy about our parents' deaths. Or tell him how guilty I felt. Would he understand? Or forgive me if he did?

I couldn't admit that there were times when I had hated our mother. The thought jelled in my mind before I could unthink it. No. I didn't hate her. I loved her. I just hadn't tried hard enough to understand her. All those nights when I covered my head with my pillow and whispered, "I hate you, I hate you, I hate you" into the mattress, I didn't mean it. What I should have said was, "I don't understand you. I don't understand you. I don't understand you."

Nanny Tee had called Mama "high-strung," but what did that mean? High-strung like a clock wound too tight? Like a nervous horse? A snappy dog? A colicky baby? Like a yo-yo that rolled out and snapped back, easy as you please, then tangled into a hopeless knot for no reason?

I couldn't talk to Buddy about any of that. "I think this is what Mom and Pop would want us to do."

"I guess s-s-s-so."

"Do you miss Nanny Tee or any of them?"

"No." His eyes narrowed into slits as he squinted in the sun.

"Me neither." Tulsa was no longer home. If my life was a book, that chapter was finished. California wasn't home yet, but in time, it might be. I couldn't stop thinking about starting over. In the whole big state, not one person knew me. No one would base expectations of me on past performance. I could rewrite my life story, and my only limitation was my own imagination.

My mind spun with possibilities. Maybe Aunt Nora would help me do something with my hair. If I mimicked the way she talked, I could lose my Okie accent. I could even toss some of the big words I knew into everyday conversation and see what happened.

Next to me, Buddy was busy treading water. He could start over too. Beginning now. "Race you to the other side!" I waited for him to push off and paced myself to let him win.

"I b-b-beat you!" He sputtered and wiped water off his face with both hands.

"You sure did. I think you're getting stronger."

"R-r-really? You d-d-do?"

"Yep. The mountain air must be good for you."

He beamed. "I f-f-feel stronger, Pauly. And bigger. I th-th-think I'm growing."

After our swim, we returned to the cabin and cleaned up. Buddy went first, and when I came out of the shower, he was asleep, curled in a ball on the cot with his hands under his cheek. Wet hair plastered his skull and his bird legs poked out of his baggy shorts. The leg brace stood in the corner where we'd left it. Was it possible? Could he cast the steel and leather aside and walk without support? Had the doctors been wrong? Maybe he really was growing stronger. I pulled the bedspread over him and went outside.

Aunt Nora had showered while we were in the pool. Her damp hair was pulled back in a ponytail, and she had changed into white pedal pushers with a red-and-white sailor top. She'd made up her face and looked like a model in a magazine ad for lipstick.

I held out my hairbrush and a rubber band. "Will you put my hair in a ponytail?"

"Sure, sit down." She gave up her chair and stood behind me, drawing the brush gently through my tangled hair. "Pauly, you are so lucky."

Lucky was an adjective I had never used to describe myself, especially where hair was concerned. "Why?"

"With all that natural curl, you'll never have to pay for a permanent."

"I hate my hair." The clownish color, the wiry texture, the every-which-way-but-tame attitude.

"I know starlets who would kill for this hair. When we get home, I'll show you how to roll it on curlers to relax some of the wave."

"I'd like that." *When we get home.* The words sent a shivery chill down my spine.

"There you go." She returned my brush, and I returned her chair. "Where's Buddy?"

"Asleep."

"Is he all right?" Such questions revealed how little she knew about children.

"Sure." I tossed my head, reveling in the playful swing of the ponytail. "He likes to take a nap in the afternoon."

"You know, we don't have to go out to eat," she said. "Tyb, do you mind staying with Buddy while Pauly and I do some shopping? I need to pick up a few things, including tennis shoes if I plan to do any hiking."

"Nosiree, I don't mind one bit." Tyb held Puppy in his lap and scratched the dog's belly. "I like settin' here breathing fresh air. Don't worry about the boy none."

"What do you say, Pauly?"

Leave Buddy? With Tyb? That did not seem like a good idea. "I don't know . . ."

"Don't you like to shop?"

I didn't know about that either. I had no experience. "Yes, but . . ."

"Don't you worry about Buddy," Tyb assured me. "I won't let him out of my sight."

"Great." Aunt Nora jumped up. "We'll bring back supper. We passed the House of Wong when we drove in. Everyone likes Chinese, right?"

Tyb and I exchanged glances. "Chinese what?" I asked.

"Food, silly. Chow mein, chop suey, egg rolls."

"Never had it," Tyb stated.

"Me neither," I said.

Aunt Nora laughed. "It's time to expand your culinary horizons. Man cannot live by burgers alone, you know."

"What's an egg roll?" Tyb asked when she'd gone inside for her purse.

"Beats me. Maybe Chinese people roll eggs up in a ball or something."

He scratched his chin. "Don't reckon I'd like that."

"Let's try it, for her sake. She'll be disappointed if we don't."

"I reckon."

Aunt Nora and I found a variety store and combed the aisles for treasure. She found a pair of red sneakers in size six and a straw hat with a wide brim to keep the sun off her face. She bought two new short sets for me and Buddy, underwear and new socks. She let me pick out two pairs of plastic sunglasses, purple for me and green for Buddy.

"Maybe we should get a postcard for Nanny Tee," she suggested. "You can write and tell her you're fine."

"Okay, as long as I don't have to say wish you were here."

"Let's get Tyb a surprise." Aunt Nora held up a shirt bright with flowers and parrots. "How about this?"

I shook my head. "Tyb is more the western shirt with snaps type."

"Of course. What was I thinking?" We looked around and found a nice blue-checked shirt with white piping on the yoke. Very Roy Rogers. Then we picked out a pair of black high-top tennis shoes so the old man wouldn't have to hike around in cowboy boots.

We took our selections to the checkout counter. "We didn't get Puppy anything," I pointed out.

She stopped in mock alarm. "We can't forget our mascot. What do you have in mind?"

"A collar and leash so he can walk around with us? You know how he likes to run off."

"Roger that. Anything else?"

"I saw some chew toys. He might like one of those."

"And a bag of dog food? He can't keep eating sausage patties and baloney." She whispered behind her hand, "That's why he farts so much."

We stowed our purchases in the Skylark, and Aunt Nora suggested we get a root beer at the drugstore across the street. We walked between aisles of Alka-Seltzer and aspirin to the soda fountain at the back of the store and sat at a little round table to sip our drinks.

"This place reminds me of the Walgreens where Gracie was working when she met your father."

"She was a counter girl, right?" Pop had told me how he met Mama, but I wanted to hear Aunt Nora's version, which was sure to have more details.

"That's right. It was a summer job. 1941. She was just sixteen and looked so cute in her pink uniform. I was only thirteen and too young to get a job. Boy, was I jealous."

Aunt Nora told me the whole story because she was on hand when most of it happened. Until she explained what Mama and Pop had overcome to be together, I'd had no idea how hard life could be for teenagers in love.

Mama had been busy serving doughnuts and coffee and tuna salad and limeades at the Walgreens lunch counter when Pop came in and ordered a ham and cheese on white with a glass of milk. She thought he was the cutest boy she'd ever seen. He was eighteen years old and parked cars in the downtown Auto Hotel around the corner. He wore jeans and a red shirt with his name embroidered over the pocket. He had the bluest eyes and black hair combed back in a pompadour.

He asked Mama how come he'd never seen her before, and she explained she'd only been working a week. He leaned on the counter and flirted between customers. He ordered a piece of coconut cream pie and another glass of milk, but when the druggist started giving Mama dirty looks, she told Pop he'd better go. He returned every day that week to eat lunch at her counter. On Friday, he asked her to go out with him.

Mama had never been on a date because that was against her father's rules. Grandfather Teegarden didn't allow his daughters to wear shorts or smoke or cut their hair short. They couldn't get their ears pierced or wear any makeup besides pink lipstick, and not too much of that. They couldn't dance or listen to Benny Goodman or watch gangster movies.

Mama figured if she was old enough to work, she could make her own decisions. She told Pop she'd love to go to a movie with him and they set up a date.

When Mama got home, Nanny Tee said she couldn't go without her father's permission. Of course, he refused. Mama pitched a ring-tailed hissy fit, but that did not change his mind, and he sent her to her room.

Mama didn't know how to contact Pop to cancel the date, and when he showed up at the appointed time on Friday, Grandfather Teegarden refused to let him in the house. He declared no daughter of his was going off with a punk in a car and slammed the door in Pop's face. Mama stood at the upstairs window with her heart breaking and watched Pop's old Ford pull away from the curb.

After Pop left, Grandfather Teegarden stomped up the stairs and threw open the door. He forbade Mama to ever see Pop again. He'd never amount to anything because he had dropped out of school and played pool all day. He and his brothers had run wild since their mother died, and their stumblebum father was nothing but a boozehound.

Mama yelled back that he had a job parking cars. She got away with more because she was their daddy's favorite, but she didn't get anywhere that night.

Grandfather Teegarden reminded her that one of Pop's brothers was in the pen for *stealing* cars, and he'd probably take up the family trade eventually. According to him, the Mahoneys were shanty trash and not worth the lead it would take to shoot 'em.

Mama spouted off some awful things to her father, and that's when he yanked off his belt and gave Mama three good lashes on her bare legs for being so disrespectful. Then he put his belt back on and told her in a calm voice, with his finger in her face, that she'd better mind him and stay away from that Mahoney kid or he'd give her something to really cry about.

After he stomped out of the room, Mama wailed like a banshee having her wisdom teeth out. Aunt Nora tried to comfort her, but Mama was past the calming-down point. She swore she'd make their daddy sorry he'd ever hit her.

Aunt Nora reminded her about their plans to move to Hollywood and break into the movies after Nora graduated from high school, but

Mama said four years would seem like forever. She didn't know if she could wait that long to get away from their father.

The next day was Saturday, and Pop surprised Mama by showing up at her lunch counter. When she apologized for breaking their date, he told her not to worry, it wasn't her fault. Fathers were supposed to protect their little girls.

Pop's gentle words and sweet smile swept Mama off her feet and into a sea of love. If she didn't go out with him, she would just die. Mama told Pop she could get out of the house next Friday night if she told her father she was going to the show with a girlfriend. They agreed to meet at the movie theater.

Pop told Mama he didn't want to get her in Dutch with her old man, but Mama laughed and said what the old man didn't know wouldn't hurt him.

So they had their date. Pop stopped by Walgreens every day to eat, and they continued to go out whenever Mama could sneak or lie her way out of the house. When school started in September, she quit her job at the lunch counter, and Pop quit his job too, because parking cars wasn't any fun if he couldn't see Gracie on his break.

In December they eloped.

When Frank Teegarden found out, he was fit to be tied. Nanny Tee tried to make him see reason, but he would not be defied. If his daughter wanted to sneak off and marry a shantytown hood, then she was no daughter of his. In a rage, he tossed Mama's clothes into the yard and threw away all her pictures. He told Nora she couldn't talk to her own sister, who was nothing but a liar and a sneak and other names Aunt Nora preferred not to repeat.

"In July when you were born," Aunt Nora said, "Ma begged Daddy to let her see you and Gracie. He said over my dead body so often and so loudly, I guess somebody upstairs finally heard him. Four months later he *was* dead."

"What happened?" I asked.

"An aortic aneurysm ruptured while he was raking leaves. Forty-three years old, and he dropped like a brain-shot bull in the front yard."

"Heart attack."

Aunt Nora nodded. "A few weeks later, Johnny got his draft notice and climbed on a bus for Fort Hood. Gracie moved in with Ma and me for the duration. She was so upset about your daddy going in the army that she wouldn't eat, and she had such nightmares about the war that she couldn't sleep. Her milk dried up, and we had to feed you with a bottle.

"Ma took care of you. Gracie spent most of her time writing letters to Johnny and waiting for the mailman. She got pneumonia that winter because she ran barefoot through the snow to the mailbox.

"I liked having my sister home again, but Gracie just wasn't the same. She was distant and sullen and tearful. She couldn't take care of you at all. I raced home from school every day to play with you. Why, I carried you around like a doll and changed your clothes to see how you looked in different outfits. Ma and I took turns getting up for feedings until you started sleeping through the night.

"Then things got really bad. Gracie locked herself in her room for three days when Johnny shipped overseas. I don't know which was worse, the weeping or the silence. When she was quiet, we worried she'd hang herself with a bedsheet. Ma called in the family doctor, who diagnosed a nervous disorder and gave Gracie medicine to calm her down.

"That was the beginning of Gracie's moodiness. In those days, it didn't take much to make her happy. An airmail letter from overseas carried her for two or three days. It took even less to send her reeling into despair. Bad news from the European front made her take to her bed, and when she listened to President Roosevelt's speeches on the radio, her hands shook so bad she couldn't hold a coffee cup.

"We did our best to reassure Gracie that Johnny would come home when the war was over, but she said she wouldn't believe it until she saw him walk in the door."

We sipped our soft drinks in the quiet drugstore. Aunt Nora said, "Most of the family sympathized with Gracie, but Aunt Preet blamed Daddy's death on the elopement. She was convinced her poor brother had died of a broken heart, and Gracie was the one who'd broken it."

"Did you think so, Aunt Nora?" Maybe being responsible for a parent's death was a curse on our family. Had history repeated itself? Was I fated to follow my mother to an unhappy end?

"Of course not. Daddy's bum artery was a time bomb waiting to go off. No one was to blame for his death."

"Why did he hate Pop so much?"

"Daddy didn't like the Irish, and Harry Mahoney was only second generation from the old country. Daddy was wrong, but he thought the Irish drank too much and lived on the dole. He was stubborn and prejudiced, that's all."

"So what happened to Harry Mahoney?"

"He died too, a few months after Daddy. He was walking home one night and passed out on the train track."

"Was he drunk?"

"I suppose so."

"So Grandfather Teegarden was right?"

"Not about Johnny. Your daddy was on the level. He went out of his way to be honest, probably to prove something to the Teegardens. I know he took care of your mama, and we both know she was not easy to live with. I think she felt guilty about what happened to Daddy."

I knew all about guilt. My mother and I were more alike than I had ever dreamed. "Was that why she had sad spells?"

"Could be." Aunt Nora stirred the ice in her glass with a straw.

I finished my root beer. Mama hadn't told me about Aunt Nora playing with me when I was a baby. Maybe she had more aunt experience than I'd given her credit for. I tried to imagine her changing diapers and heating milk bottles, but the image wouldn't come. Still, it was comforting to know she'd taken care of me when Mama couldn't.

"Did Mama blame me for what happened?" She'd never let me get close. It was like she lived on one side of a thorn fence and I lived on the other. We could see each other and talk over the top of it, but there was always something big and prickly between us.

"Blame you? No. Why would you think that?"

"She didn't want to take care of me when I was a helpless baby. She couldn't have liked me very much."

"Oh, honey, it wasn't that Gracie didn't *want* to take care of you. She *couldn't*. She wasn't equipped to be a mother. She was too worried about your daddy to think of anything else. She wasn't very nurturing to you, but understand, your mama was the one who needed nurturing."

I thought about that, but the facts didn't add up. Mothers were supposed to put their children first. Protect them. Hug and kiss and cuddle them and tell them they were the best kid in the whole world. Like she did Buddy. Maybe she'd gotten into the habit of setting me aside when Pop was in the army and just never switched back to full-mother gear when he came home. Maybe Pop tried to spend extra time with me to make up for Mama.

"She didn't have any trouble mothering Buddy," I pointed out.

"Think about that, Pauly. Did she mother him? Or did she smother him?"

"Was she mad because Pop loved me?" I'd always been torn between loving my father and making my mother happy.

"I'm sure she was grateful you two were close. She knew she had failed you." Aunt Nora reached across the little table and held my hand. "Remember those letters she wrote me?" When I nodded, she went on. "She told me she didn't know what to do with you. You were so bright you scared her. She knew you would turn out just fine, but she worried about Buddy. She depended on you. That's why she let you take on more of his care. She could count on you to do the right thing."

The right thing? I wanted to love my mother but was afraid I hated her. What was right about that? Heartbroken by what Aunt Nora told me, I didn't know what to say. All I ever wanted was to understand why Mama acted the way she did. Now I had no way to fit that understanding into my memories of her.

I looked up. "What about Pop?"

"What about him?"

"I wasn't premature, was I? Mama got in trouble, like Myrtle's daughter. Did Pop marry her because he had to?"

"He loved your mama with all his heart. He thought she hung the moon. They eloped because they were afraid Daddy would make Gracie give you away."

So I'd come close to being passed on like an extra bag of squash once before. "How do you know what Pop felt?"

"He told me." She stared into her glass as she sucked up the last of her root beer. "When he came back from the war, we talked. About Gracie. She'd changed, and I knew her better than anyone."

Pop didn't understand Mama either. I felt a little better. "And you're sure she loved him?"

"I'm sure. Your daddy was an easy man to love." Aunt Nora choked on her drink and coughed until her eyes filled with tears. "He was afraid that by loving her, he had stolen her dream of being in the movies. He promised to spend the rest of his life making it up to her."

He had kept his promise. He had stood by his wife, even when she was difficult. He'd provided for his children the best he knew how. "All that time, when things were rough? He could have left us."

"No." Aunt Nora's tears spilled down her cheeks. "He could never do that. Not ever."

15

Shave and a Haircut

It was nearly four o'clock when we returned to the Blue Spruce, loaded down with presents and Chinese food. Eager to show Tyb and Buddy what we'd purchased, I opened the door and looked around, but the room was empty. The drapes were tightly drawn, the bedspreads straight and smooth. The swamp cooler in the window rumbled, making the air as damp and musty as the inside of a rubber boot. Buddy wasn't where he was supposed to be. The good feeling I'd had since my chat with Aunt Nora was replaced by dread.

I dashed outside to look around and reported back in a pant. "They're not anywhere."

Aunt Nora unpacked the little white cartons of food and set them on the table. "I'm sure they're around somewhere. Don't be such a worrywart."

Didn't she know by now that I'd gotten that wart from worrying about Buddy? "Where could they be?"

"I don't know. Calm down, you're making me nervous. Here, fold these new clothes. Maybe that will keep you busy."

A few minutes later, I heard Tyb and Buddy laughing outside. My heart slipped down from my throat and settled back in my chest where it belonged. The door opened, and Puppy ran in first, doing his yip and jump dance. Running over to the table, the dog stood on his hind legs and tried to sniff the cartons.

"Here, Puppy," I called to him. "How about some nice dog food?" I shook dry kibble into one of the plastic bowls we'd bought. Puppy dismissed my offering with an apathetic sniff and gave me a look that said, "You're kidding, right?" He spun around and reclaimed a spot by the table.

"Oh, my goodness, what *do* we have here?" Aunt Nora's tone made me look up as Tyb and Buddy walked through the door. "Where have you two been? Visiting a magician?"

"Nope. Just down to the barbershop." Tyb danced his own limpy jig. He looked so different I almost didn't recognize him. Clean-shaven, his cheeks looked as soft as my own. His long hair had been neatly cut and combed, his wild eyebrows and droopy mustache tamed into neat obedience. He no longer looked like a hobo. Instead, he resembled my favorite movie grandpa, Charlie Ruggles.

Seeing the real Tyb for the first time made me back up against the bed and sit down hard. When Aunt May's dog went too long between trips to the groomer, she started looking like a mutt off the street instead of an elegant cocker spaniel.

That's how Tyb looked. Elegant.

And Buddy! The barber had given him a crew cut. His brown hair was so short and wispy that his pale scalp showed through and his ears stuck out more than ever.

"H-h-how do I l-look?" he asked.

Like a different boy. Aunt Nora couldn't stop smiling, and Tyb beamed with pride. What had he done to my brother?

"You should have asked me first," I told Tyb a little too sharply. "You're not in charge of Buddy. You're not even related."

The old man's smile faded. "I'm sorry, I meant no harm. The boy wanted his hair cut and—"

"It's not up to him," I insisted.

"Is too!" Buddy stepped between his friend and me. "I'm eight! Big enough to be the boss of my hair. I don't have to ask you, Pauly!"

We were all stunned by the outburst, not one syllable of which had been stuttered. Buddy looked as shocked as the rest of us.

Aunt Nora gave him a hug and threw me a disappointed expression. "You look just wonderful. Like a brand-new boy."

"R-r-really? That's wh-wh-what I want to be. A new b-b-boy."

I didn't know what to say. I had wanted Buddy to be different, and now he was. I should have been happy.

"You are one cool cat," Aunt Nora assured him.

"I truly am sorry, Miss Nora." Tyb rolled the brim of his old hat in both hands. "Pauly's right. I ain't part of the family. I jest got ahead of myself, I reckon. I only wanted to get myself spiffed up a mite, but the boy had his heart set on getting sheared. I meant no harm."

"Don't you worry, Tyb. If Buddy likes his new haircut, we like it too." Aunt Nora turned to me. "Don't we, Pauly? I believe you owe Tyb an apology."

"I'm sorry." Making the old man feel bad was probably one of the meanest things I'd ever done.

"I understand. Seeing Buddy with his fleece shorn off was just a shock, that's all." Tyb pulled away from the group, as I had done on the school ground when kids wouldn't let me play.

"Can I touch your hair, Buddy?"

"Sure." All smiles again, my brother ducked his head in my direction, and I stroked his scalp lightly with my palm. His hair, which had been too long and prone to fall in his eyes, was feathery and soft, like the baby brush I'd used to tame his flyaway hair when he was tiny.

Determined to clear the air, Aunt Nora revealed our purchases. "This is your lucky day, gentlemen. How about new clothes to go with your new looks?"

Tyb teared up when she gave him the Roy Rogers shirt and shoes. "That's mighty nice of you, Miss Nora, but I cain't be lettin' you buy me clothes and such."

"Why not?"

"It ain't seemly. I don't want to be beholden."

"We've enjoyed your company and your help on this trip, Tyb. Surely, you'll allow me to repay your kindness with a few little things you need."

"I can pay you back." He reached in his back pocket and pulled out a tattered billfold that was held together with a rubber band. It looked thin and hungry.

"Put that away." Aunt Nora smiled. "You paid for Buddy's haircut. That's enough for now. Come on, let's eat before the food gets cold."

We sat at the table and passed around the little white cartons. Aunt Nora tried to teach us how to use chopsticks. Buddy wasn't exactly handy with regular utensils, but he didn't hesitate when it came to learning a new way of eating. As he concentrated on mastering the new skill, I realized he really wasn't the same boy he'd been a week ago. He not only looked different, he *was* different.

In his quiet way, my brother was braver than me, because he didn't mind going along to get along. Faced with a difficult task, he had jumped in with uncharacteristic gameness. Maybe all the miles we'd traveled had let him outrun the fear that had paralyzed him at home.

"How do Chinese people do this?" I couldn't get the hang of chopsticks and resorted to spearing chunks of meat with the pointy ends. "I would starve to death."

Aunt Nora manipulated the sticks like a native. "The Chinese learn when they're small, just as we learn to use utensils. It's natural for them."

"Well, it ain't natural for me." Tyb dug around in his pack until he found a fork. "I'm willing to eat Chinaman food, but I'll do it with American tools, thankee very much!"

We spent the next morning sightseeing around Flagstaff. We drove up to Sunset Crater, so named because the volcano's dormant cone glowed a pinkish red from a distance. Aunt Nora parked the car, and we walked around lava beds that spread out from the peak for what seemed like miles in every direction. The black rock landscape was how I imagined a distant planet would look. Mercury or Pluto.

Tyb seemed to have forgiven my harsh remarks. Light-footed in his new sneakers, he exclaimed he'd never seen the likes of such a place in all his days. He scratched his newly shorn head in wonder that a river turned to stone could exist without him ever hearing about it. He and Buddy made good walking partners. Neither one could move very fast.

Buddy had to carry Puppy because the hot rock burned his pink paw pads. The little dog adapted easily to the collar and leash, and hadn't objected to the shower we'd given him the night before. After we'd dried him off, he had flopped on Buddy's bed and gnawed his rubber T-bone like he'd always belonged with us. That was another good thing about dogs. They attached themselves to new people without a worry. They never looked back or thought ahead. Dogs just found an empty place in somebody's life and filled it. Easy peasy. If that place didn't work out, they found a different spot. Stray dogs didn't stay strays for long.

Neither would stray people, if Aunt Nora had her way.

Later in the car, she said Sunset Crater was really something, and she was glad we'd had the chance to see it. She'd once worn a black wig to play a native girl in a South Seas volcano movie, but thought the only real ones were in places like Hawaii and Fiji. Like Tyb, she'd had no idea Arizona had a volcano that had been extinct for millions of years.

We didn't drive to the top of Mt. Humphreys after all, since no road went that high. We stopped at a scenic turnout and stared up at the highest peak in the state. The snow on top made it resemble a picture puzzle I had put together once.

We visited the Indian ruins in Walnut Canyon, hiking a narrow trail that wound up and down the forested canyon. Peering into little houses carved in the sides of the canyon like caves, we could see holes in the floor where the Ancient Ones had stored corn, and ceilings streaked with black soot from fires. Quarters were cramped, and even Buddy and I had to duck to fit through the doorways. We decided the Ancient Ones must have been a race of very short people.

I wondered if the mummy baby had lived in such a home all those hundreds of years ago. I hoped Nasdi Tsosie had given little Sylvester a good send-off. I would enjoy the Trip more if I could believe the mummy had finally reached the happy after-place and would spend forever with his parents.

Someday, I hoped to meet up with Mama and Pop again. There were so many things I wanted to say. I wanted to tell them I wasn't angry now about them dying together and leaving me and Buddy alone. I could take care of the future. Mainly I wanted them to know I no longer blamed them for not letting me all the way into their lives. It was okay that they needed each other more than they needed me.

In the afternoon, the temperature climbed, but our cabin was dark and cool, and the cowboy curtains fluttered in the breeze. The sun had burned Buddy's face and scalp pink, and he curled up on his bed to rest.

Tyb unlaced his new sneakers and pulled them off before stretching out on the studio couch. "Boy has the right idea, all righty."

Aunt Nora gathered our dirty clothes and stuffed them into a pillowcase. "Pauly, do you want to go with me to get the clothes washed or stay here and rest?"

I'd felt queasy all day, and my skin was stretched tightly over bones that were suddenly a size too big. Figuring I'd had too much sun and grape soda, I decided to go. "I don't think I could sleep unless somebody slipped me a Mickey."

"I don't mind staying with Buddy," Tyb said quietly. "If that's okay with you, Pauly."

I nodded. If he wanted another chance to get babysitting right, I would give it to him.

Aunt Nora and I hopped in the car and drove a couple of blocks to a grocery store. She bought detergent and movie magazines to read while we waited.

We turned our clothes over to the laundry attendant to wash in old-fashioned wringer Maytags. It was early afternoon, and there weren't many customers in the place. We settled on folding chairs lined up against the wall, and Aunt Nora held up the magazines, *Photoplay* and *Screenland*.

"Do you want to read about Clark Gable getting married? Or about Debbie Reynolds and Eddie Fisher, out on the town?"

"Debbie and Eddie." All the magazines said it was just a matter of time until the young couple tied the knot.

Aunt Nora had also bought Cokes and bags of peanuts. We made funnels of our hands and poured the nuts in the bottles. The soda fizzed. Aunt Nora said, "Peanuts and Cokes are a little like life, salty and sweet at the same time."

I flipped through my magazine, looking for pictures of Debbie. Maybe I would try to fix my hair like hers. "Aunt Nora, do you know any movie stars?"

"You mean personally? As in, why don't you come over and we'll paint our toenails together?"

"Yeah."

"Nope." She folded back the cover of her magazine.

"Have you ever met any?"

"Sure. I met actors and actresses on sets where I worked. Jennifer Jones. Barbara Stanwyck. Dan Dailey. I once ate lunch at the same commissary table as Farley Granger."

"What was the last movie you were in?"

"I was an extra on an MGM musical. *Seven Brides for Seven Brothers.* Did you see it?"

"Yes! Mama said you were in it, but we didn't see you. Did you get to dance?"

"No, I just stood on the sidelines in a long dress and watched other people dance." She grinned. "Not a bad job. I could look at Howard Keel all day."

"What about Russ Tamblyn? He's the brother I liked best."

"He's cute too. And very nice."

"So you know those people?"

"Let's just say we once breathed the same air."

"How many movies have you been in?"

She thought about it. "I've had parts in fifteen, no, sixteen pictures. Sixteen jobs in ten years. Not exactly a résumé to write home about."

"I think that's good." She had just confirmed my suspicion that the big roll of money had come from another source. Maybe she owned racehorses. Or just bet on them.

"Well, they were small parts. Some were walk-ons or extras. You know, strolling down a street or eating in a restaurant. I was a murdered showgirl in a mystery once."

"Was it hard to play dead?"

She laughed. "Nope. Even dogs can do that. The trick is lying still and holding your breath so you look fully expired."

Sixteen minor parts in ten years really wasn't much work, but I had no idea how much actors got paid. It must be a lot, because all the stars in *Popular Screen* and *Hollywood Secrets* lived in big houses. They wore fancy clothes and drove flashy cars. I hadn't seen Aunt Nora's house, but her clothes and car were definitely movie-star quality.

"Mama used to talk about how you and her had planned to go to Hollywood together."

"That's right. Then she got married and that was the end of that idea."

"How come you decided to go alone?"

"It was time." She seemed to think it over. "I graduated, the war ended, and Johnny came marching home. After a few weeks, he moved you and Gracie out of the house, which left me alone with Ma."

"How did you know you could be an actress?"

"I played Lady Macbeth in the junior-senior play and based my vocational decisions on Lenny Krupnik's review in the school paper. I saved my money until I couldn't stand living with Ma one minute longer. Then I bought a bus ticket and headed west."

A big step for a girl from Tulsa. There was a lot of empty country out there to get lost in. "Weren't you scared going all that way by yourself?"

"I was too dumb to be scared. I thought all I had to do was wear a tight sweater and sit on a stool in a drugstore until I was discovered, like Lana Turner. I'd read way too many movie magazines," she confided as she flipped the pages of one.

"You're pretty enough to be a star." She had the tall glamour of Suzy Parker and the exotic sultriness of Rita Hayworth.

"Well, looks and a dime will buy you a cup of coffee in Hollywood." She laughed. "Seriously, being pretty is no big advantage in a town that has more gorgeous women per square foot than any place in the world."

How would I ever fit in with all that beauty? "Mama took us to see most of your movies."

"Oh, yeah?" She looked pleased. "Which ones?"

"We saw you in a Danny Kaye musical once, and one with Richard Widmark when he was a bad guy."

"Those were pretty good parts. At least I could breathe."

Her bubbling laughter burst over me and I ached inside. I wanted that laughter in my life. "Was your husband an actor too?"

She laughed. "Which husband?"

"Either one."

"My first husband was Teddy. He thought he was an actor, but the casting directors in town had a different opinion." She sighed. "What he lacked in talent, he made up for in looks. The man was a living doll. Like Rock Hudson, only shorter. Too bad he never could memorize lines."

"Why did you get divorced?"

She laughed again. "We had a little disagreement. I thought he was married and he didn't."

"What about your other husband?"

"You're just full of questions, aren't you?"

"I'm sorry." I stared at the toes of my sneakers. Mama said curiosity killed the cat. Things were going pretty well, and I didn't want to get crossways with Aunt Nora.

"Hey, kiddo, it's all right. I guess you have a right to know what you're getting into. Chick, my second husband, was a director. He made westerns with singing cowboys."

"Like Roy Rogers and Gene Autry?"

"Yep. Movies where cowboys kiss their horses at the end of the reel and ride off into the sunset alone."

"I love those movies."

"So does Chick. He's a lot older than me, but we got along pretty good for a while. Then later, well, it just stopped working. We're still friends though. I'll introduce you to him sometime, and you two can discuss your favorite sagebrush heroes."

I swished the peanuts around in my Coke bottle. Aunt Nora was pretty and fun to be with. There were probably lots of men who wanted to be with her. When Pop was around, Mama never had eyes or time for us kids. What if Aunt Nora got wrapped up in a man? Where would that leave us? She might decide she didn't want two orphans weighing her down.

Why hadn't I thought of that before? I was afraid of her answer, but it was a question I just had to ask.

"Aunt Nora? Do you have a boyfriend?"

16

Aunt Flo, Go Away

Aunt Nora winked and flipped magazine pages. "Let's just say I have friends who happen to be men."

"Do you think there's a chance you'll get married any time soon?" It was too much to hope I could be important in my aunt's life, but I'd played second fiddle all my life. When it came to finding out where you stood, sooner was better than later.

"I'm in no hurry, if that's what you're worried about. I wouldn't get married again unless I was sure he was a keeper."

"How can you tell?" I'd read about romance in novels and watched movie stars fall in love on-screen. My only firsthand knowledge came from observing my parents' relationship. Their brand of love was all-consuming and fatal. Nothing I cared to aspire to.

"I just will. I'll listen to my heart and not my head or . . . any other parts. Especially the other parts." She closed her magazine and turned to me. "This might be a little over your head, but you're a bright girl, so what the heck? The first time I married, I had passion without love. The second time, I had love without passion."

"There's a difference?"

"I'll say. A big one. Maybe you're too young to appreciate the fine points, but marriage works best and lasts longest when you have both. Love *and* passion, in equal doses. I've settled for less in the past, but I won't settle again."

Love and passion. I thought maybe my parents had both, and that hadn't worked out so great. Our silence grew companionable, and sunshine slanted through the laundry's plate-glass window. I thought of Buddy. What would happen to him when I grew up and found someone to love with passion? Would he ever find someone? His nap would be over by now, and I worried about what he'd think when he found me gone.

Then I remembered how he'd paired off with Tyb. He followed that old man around like a lost pup. My brother might not even notice I was gone.

Aunt Nora checked on the wash. The lady had put a load in the dryer, so it wouldn't be much longer. Once we left the warm, moist laundry cocoon, I might not have another chance to talk to her like this, and there was one more question I was aching to ask.

"Aunt Nora, how come you never had kids?"

A few seconds ticked by before she spoke. "Just so you know for future reference, Pauly, that's considered a very personal question. However, since you asked nicely, I'll answer it. I had two babies."

I sucked in a surprised breath. Mama had never mentioned babies. "What happened to them?"

She stared at the dingy ceiling. "I lost them, before they could be born. Now I can't have children. Ever. I used to be sad about that, but you and Buddy make me feel better."

No one had ever told me that before. Mostly I had been a tribulation. "Is that why you agreed to take us?"

"Maybe. Is it selfish not to want to be alone?"

"No."

"I couldn't imagine you growing up with Evalee."

"Why not?"

"*I* grew up with Evalee."

"Nanny Tee's not so bad." Feeling generous for a change, I defended her, even though she'd never gone out on a limb for me.

"You're right, she's not so bad. Something snapped inside her when Daddy died. All of a sudden, she started doing things she never would have done when he was alive."

"Like work in a whiskey shop?"

"That's one." Aunt Nora listed Nanny Tee's indiscretions on her fingers. "She cuts her hair and dyes it red. She wears outrageous clothes. Drinks beer. Goes out with men named Bubba."

That was the Nanny Tee I knew. I tried to imagine her as a mother, raising two little girls, but I couldn't. She didn't seem interested enough. "Was she really going to turn us over to the welfare people?"

"That was mostly talk, to up the ante. Ma likes drama, almost more than me." She squeezed my shoulder. "I couldn't let you go. When I found out you and Buddy were alone, I dropped everything and headed for Oklahoma."

"I thought you came for the funeral."

"I did. But I mostly came for you and Buddy."

"Why?"

"Because all I ever wanted was a family, and I'd just about given up on ever having one. Because I loved your mother and father, and I can see them in you. You may look like a Teegarden, Pauly, but you are a Mahoney in your heart. Buddy is a special little boy. How could I not love you? Both of you."

She loved me? Us? My queasy stomach flipped over, and my heart creaked open like a rusty vault. "That's what I want, too."

"What do you want, Pauly? What do you need?"

"A family. A home we don't have to pick up and leave."

"I can give you that."

The words I'd reined in so long knocked down my inhibition in a wild stampede. Once I started talking, I couldn't stop. I dropped my longing and pain at her feet.

"Mama and Pop are dead because of me. I was mad that night at the carnival. At Mama. I wanted to ride the roller coaster with her, but she didn't want me. I said I hated her, but I didn't. Not really. I never meant for them to die. I didn't know God would hear me. Or that he would punish me for being selfish by taking them away."

"Don't cry, honey." She pulled me into her arms and hugged me close. I smelled her sweet perfume and felt her heart pounding in her chest. "God, Pauly, whatever gave you that idea? Gracie and Johnny were killed in an accident. You had nothing to do with what happened."

"But how do you *know*?"

"The police investigated. Before we left Tulsa, they told Nanny Tee the roller coaster car derailed because another passenger's purse had fallen out of one of the cars and landed on the track."

I eased away from her, and she wiped tears from my cheeks. "So what happened really *was* an accident?"

"Yes." She pulled me close again. "Oh, yes, Pauly. They were simply in the wrong place at the wrong moment."

"Bad luck?"

"The police ruled it a misadventure."

A misadventure. Not divine punishment. The news should have made me happy, but I felt sick. My stomach contents shifted like cargo in a storm-tossed ship.

Aunt Nora held my face between her hands. "Pauly, what happened to your parents was a terrible, senseless thing. But you can give meaning to their deaths."

I swallowed hard. "How?"

"By being happy and living a fulfilled life. You can honor their memory by being a good sister to Buddy and by finding your destiny."

Destiny sounded good. I could do that. If I knew where to look. "I've been thinking."

She grinned. "That's a good way to spend your spare time, Pauly. Don't ever stop thinking."

"You and Tyb and Buddy and I are all alone, but we don't have to be lonely. We can stay together."

She sniffed and smiled. "You *do* have good ideas. So you think we should just take matters into our own hands and make a family for ourselves?"

"That's what I was thinking." By saying the magic words, Aunt Nora had opened the door to our future. I wouldn't have to carry the burden of Buddy by myself. Aunt Nora loved us, and I loved her too. I could trust her to take care of us. Home was getting closer all the time. I could almost see the light in the window.

We sat side by side. She pulled me into her bubble, and it was a warm place to be. After a few minutes, I clutched my stomach as my insides twisted in rolling waves of pain. How could I feel so bad when I was happier than I'd been in days? My bellyache was like nothing I'd ever felt. I excused myself and bolted for the restroom.

I had no idea what was wrong, but I soon figured out the problem when I found a dark red smear in my underwear. I wasn't sick. And I was not prepared. I'd only had one period, and that had been more than three months ago. I had been in trouble with Mama about something else at the time, so I'd taken a sanitary napkin from the box she kept under the sink and secured it to my underwear with safety pins.

If not for the pamphlets the teacher had passed out to girls in health class, I would have been totally in the dark. Scared and worried, I faked the stomach flu and stayed in bed for three days until it was all over. Mama must have missed the pads, but she never said anything, and I didn't dare approach her.

A week later, when I came home from school, I found a box of Kotex and a sanitary belt on my dresser. If it was possible, Mama was even more distant after that. I had so many questions, but I hid the feminine supplies in a drawer and never asked her.

I was trying to fold toilet paper to make protection when someone knocked on the bathroom door.

"Pauly, are you all right? You've been in there fifteen minutes."

Aunt Nora. If I told her my problem, would she get mad at me too? Things had been going so well, I didn't want to ruin our new friendship by being a pest. "I, uh, have a little problem."

"What kind of problem?"

"You know. A girl problem."

She was quiet for a moment. "Oh. Right. Stay here with the door closed, and I'll be right back."

In a few minutes, she returned with a change of clothes, still warm from the dryer, and a sack from the grocery store. I looked inside and found a blue box of pads and a Junior Miss sanitary belt.

"You need any help?" She smiled encouragingly, and I shook my head. "Okay, I'll wait outside."

I dried my tears and read the directions on the package. The belt was a better deal than safety pins, but not much more comfortable. I probably couldn't stay in bed until this one was over. I stepped out of the restroom, and Aunt Nora walked me back to our seats to wait for the rest of the laundry.

"Everything all right?"

I nodded. "I'm sorry. I've only had one, uh, other time, and I didn't know when it would come back."

"You can figure on every twenty-eight days or so. Didn't your mother tell you that?"

"She must have forgot."

"But she did tell you the basics, right?"

"She probably would have, if she'd felt better."

Now Aunt Nora did the prompting. "Don't be shy or embarrassed, Pauly. Menstruation is perfectly normal. If you have any questions, just ask."

I could trust her with my fear. She wouldn't turn away or make me feel guilty for being normal. "How long do periods last?"

"Three to five days usually. Sometimes longer."

"Every month?"

"Once you become regular. Then when you hit the change of life, it all goes away."

"That's a relief."

"Except you go a little crazy. I think that's what happened to Nanny Tee."

"But it does stop?"

"Yes, when you're fifty or so."

"Fifty!" I lowered my voice. "Are you serious? I have to go through this every month 'til I'm fifty years old?"

Aunt Nora started laughing, but she wasn't laughing at me. She was laughing with me. The Trip had taught me the difference.

"That's right, toots. Hell of a deal, huh?" She wrapped her arm around my shoulder and gave me a hug. "We don't call it the curse for nothing."

"I'll say." Thirty-seven years of pads and belts and cramps and blood. What a mess.

"Your mama and I used to say Aunt Flo was visiting when we got our periods. We called pads vanilla wafers, as in 'Do you have a vanilla wafer I can borrow?' It was a code so people wouldn't know what we were talking about."

"There's a *code*?" I was bewildered and a little angry. Mama should have told me this. I thought about the three days I'd stayed in bed, afraid I was dying. She could have made it easier. She could have cared.

Aunt Nora eyed me speculatively. "Won't be long until you'll need an over-the-shoulder-boulder-holder too."

I sighed, half in shock, half in frustration. Being a kid was hard, but being a woman was turning out to be mind-boggling.

When the laundry was done, Aunt Nora stashed the clean clothes in the backseat and slid into the front beside me. "Feeling any better?"

"A little."

"Still worried?"

"A little." The unfamiliar bulk between my legs felt awkward and burdensome. Surely, anyone who looked at me would see it, or notice me walking funny.

"We'll stop and get you some Midol to help with the cramps. And the crankiness."

"Thank you, Aunt Nora. For everything."

"Do you know what menstruation means?" Aunt Nora asked softly.

"My horseback riding days are over?"

She laughed. "Oh, honey. Do you know where babies come from?"

"Kind of." I knew easy girls could "get in trouble," but the stork was still mixed up in the equation, so clarification was in order. "Not really."

"Your mother never told you about boys and girls or any he/she stuff either?"

"I guess she forgot that too." The truth was, Mama never talked to me about much of anything. She never asked about my day when I came home after school. She never shared her childhood stories. It was as though she hadn't started living until she met Johnny Mahoney. In between crying jags and happy spells, she was mostly just there, waiting for Pop to come home, like you wait for the lights to go down at the movies. Excited and knowing that for a little while you won't have to think about the real world.

When I was really little, maybe three or four, my parents let me lie between them on their bed while Mama read Zane Grey novels out loud. Pop loved those books, and even though I didn't understand the words, I liked falling asleep with my head on his shoulder and her lulling voice in the background.

When I awoke in my own little bed, I knew Pop had tucked me in and maybe even kissed my cheek. Mama thought I was too big to crawl in their bed, but Pop always said, "What's the harm? I missed the first three years of her life. Let her stay."

Once Buddy came, he used up all of Mama's limited resources. I was five when they brought him home from the hospital. Nanny Tee had stayed with me while Mama was gone. She was about to make me a jelly sandwich when Pop burst in the kitchen carrying Mama's suitcase. Mama followed with a tiny blue-wrapped bundle. She went straight to her room and put him down in the bassinet.

Nanny Tee couldn't stop gushing about how their precious boy had a full head of hair, unlike bald-headed Pauly, who didn't sprout fuzz until she was two. What big blue eyes he has, Nanny Tee said. Doesn't he look like a wise little man? Oh, Johnny, you must be so proud to finally have a son.

Like daughters didn't count.

I had sat at the kitchen table waiting for my sandwich, but no one even noticed. When I got up to pour myself a glass of milk, the bottle slipped and broke on the linoleum. I finally got some attention, but not the kind I wanted. Nanny Tee rushed in yelling, "What in the world is going on in here?" When she saw the milk on the floor, she grabbed my arm and swatted me hard. Why couldn't I be a good girl? Did I have to ruin Mama's first day home? Jefferson Daniel wouldn't grow up to be so naughty.

She sent me to my room hungry. I didn't get a good look at my brother until Pop said I could hold him if I sat in a corner of the sofa. Mama delivered him into my arms. Pop looked on and smiled. "Our boy's the luckiest baby in the world," he said. "Because he has you for a big sister. Watch out for him, Pauly. Treat him right."

I have always tried to follow Pop's instructions.

It didn't take long for my brother's puniness to appear, and it seemed he was always sick with something. Even though I was healthy as a wood rat, Mama accused me of spreading the germs that little Jefferson caught. I'm the one who started calling him Buddy, because Jefferson was a name for a president, not for a baby who leaked milk out his nose. Soon, everyone called him Buddy, and he was situated firmly in the middle of our universe. As far as everyone but Pop was concerned, I orbited somewhere on the remote edge, very near Pluto.

Except in the beginning when I didn't know better, I was never jealous of Buddy. With all his problems, it didn't seem right to stir a hateful sister into the pot.

Aunt Nora was staring at me with a little frown on her face. She snapped her fingers in front of me. "Pauly? Did you tumble down a rabbit hole? What's wrong?"

"I'm sorry. I was thinking. What did you say?"

"Now that you're becoming a woman, maybe we need to have a heart-to-heart talk."

And that's how I learned about the birds and bees. Sitting in a 1953 Skylark convertible in front of a washhouse in Flagstaff, Arizona, Aunt Nora told me everything I needed to know about men and women and the respective roles each played in the propagation of the species. She educated me about male parts and female parts and how they were de-signed to perform particular functions. I went on record as saying those functions were not something I ever wanted to personally partic-ipate in. In addition to code words, she taught me real names for things like I was studying for a doctor test. I was overwhelmed, to say the least.

Menstruation, embryos, boulder-holders. Penises, vaginas, vanilla wafers. Sex. To think it had been going on all around me for years. Peo-ple I knew had probably engaged in it, and I had been dumb as a bump on a log. Knowing the ins and outs, so to speak, put a whole new slant on things.

I don't know what possessed me, but before I could even consider what I was doing, I hauled off and told Aunt Nora about the boy at the lake. I was desperate to know how that episode fit into the whole man-woman scheme of things. When I got to the end of the story, I was cry-ing, and Aunt Nora was crying too.

She gave me a big hug and pressed me against her bosom. "Oh, baby, that's not the way it's supposed to be. What that boy did was wrong. You were just a little girl. It wasn't your fault. He did an ugly thing. But it won't be ugly when you fall in love with the right man. It will be beautiful. Without love . . ." She bit her lip and stared through the windshield at the laundry's OPEN FROM 8 TO 8 sign.

"Without love it's a rock in your heart?"

"Yes. That's exactly what it is."

She hugged me again and told me to try and put the episode out of my mind. Maybe I could now. Nasty, dark things shrivel up in the bright light of sharing. Aunt Nora said not to be scared of my body or the changes taking place. I could talk to her anytime about anything. She asked me if I had any questions, and I didn't. I was quizzed out.

Life, she said, would be confusing the next few years, but it would also be wonderful. Good and bad. Up and down. Dark and light.

She gave me another hug and assured me that whatever happened, I would not be alone. She promised to be there to help me every step of the way.

She *promised*. No one had ever promised to stick around just for me before.

The $64,000 question was: would she keep that promise?

17

Lost and Not Found

Tyb and Buddy were sitting on the porch when we parked in front of our cabin at the Blue Spruce. My brother jumped up, dressed in his swim trunks and dragging a towel. "Pauly, I-I-I was waiting for you to swim with m-m-me."

Swimming was out of the question. I was operating under a new set of restrictions, imposed on me by womanhood. "Sorry, Buddy, I can't."

His face fell. "B-b-but why not? I w-w-waited."

Aunt Nora winked over the laundry. "Pauly's tired, kiddo. You had a nap. It's her turn to rest. Tell you what, help me put these clothes away, and I'll swim with you."

He perked up again. Swimming with Aunt Nora was better.

After they left for the pool, Tyb went outside to sit on the porch. I swallowed two of the Midols Aunt Nora had bought, curled up on my side on the studio couch and pressed a pillow into my achy stomach. I pulled Tyb's quilt over me and traced the pieces with one finger.

Most quilt pieces were laid out in a geometric pattern, repeated over and over. Predictable. Tyb's quilt was called crazy for good reason.

But the more I studied it, the more sense the design made. Like life, nothing in the quilt was expected. The colorful fabric contained surprise after surprise. Fancy embroidery stitches outlined pieces like silken frames, lending weight and importance to each oddly cut shape. I began to see a plan in all that randomness.

I turned my face into the musty folds and breathed deeply until I could smell every person who had ever slept under its weight. Tyb's long-lost family had left their scents behind. Mothballs and licorice and lavender sachet. Tobacco and cedar. Baby powder. Bread dough. Wood smoke. Sunshine from the clothesline. Rain from being left out after a picnic. I sorted out Tyb's unique old-man smell. Campho-Phenique and chewing tobacco and sweat.

Scent memories told stories if you listened with your nose. The threadbare coverlet had passed through many hands and revealed the people caught in its folds. Old, sickly, newborn, a ranch hand tired after a hard day's work. It showed me all the places it had been, starting in Tennessee as a dream pulled from a young bride's scrap box. Traveling to Texas in an oxcart. Tucked in a cedar chest on a cattle ranch and spread over a temporary bed in an Arizona motor court.

What would happen to the quilt when Tyb was gone? Would it end up in a secondhand store where someone would buy it for a dollar to cushion a bureau he was moving? Would newlyweds, poor in cash but rich with passion and love, buy it to cover the bed they shared? Maybe, a lady who collected quilts would recognize its worth and buy it to hang on the wall like art. I hoped the quilt of many colors wouldn't go to someone deaf to its history and the people who had treasured it.

Tyb was lucky to have a solid link to his past, a reminder of who he was and where he came from. Except for a few pictures, I had nothing of my family to pass on to future children. No heirlooms lovingly crafted by someone connected to me by blood and love. No charm against the dark. My relatives showed little attachment to their flesh and blood, much less objects. The Teegardens and Mahoneys were about as sentimental as turtles that buried their eggs in the sand before hightailing it to deep water, every man for himself.

I pressed my face into the quilt, imprinting on my heart the feel and smell of something that did not belong to me. I would make my own heirlooms. Create my own treasures. I would find my place in the world and build something that would live longer than me. Something that would touch people who didn't know me, so they wouldn't forget my name.

I awoke a couple of hours later. I felt better and went outside. Tyb wasn't in his usual spot on the porch. I walked down to the pool, but Buddy wasn't paddling around in his life vest. I spotted Aunt Nora dozing on a towel with her big sun hat over her face.

"Where's Buddy?" Old panic flooded back to turn my question into an accusation. "You were supposed to watch him."

"What?" She startled awake, put on her sunglasses, and glanced around. "Don't blow a gasket, Pauly. Buddy got tired of swimming and walked to the park with Tyb."

"In his trunks?"

"No. Didn't you hear him changing in the bathroom?"

The Midol must have knocked me out. "How long ago did they leave?"

"Not long. Don't worry. Tyb will take good care of Buddy." She clamped her hat on her head and stretched out her hand. "Pull me up." She collected her lotion and towel, and we walked back to the cabin.

"How about I change clothes and go pick up a bag of burgers for dinner," she suggested. "The boys'll probably be here when I get back."

They weren't. Another hour passed, and still no sign of them. Aunt Nora encouraged me to eat a burger, but my taste buds had been worried out of commission, and it tasted like dust off the saw-mill floor. "Maybe we should walk down to the office. The desk clerk might have seen them."

"Pauly, there's no need for that...."

I was already out the door. The sun was setting and shadows had drifted onto the porch. Darkness fell hard in Arizona, and Buddy was scared of the dark. Aunt Nora stepped outside and called after me, but I ignored her summons and ran to the office. The lady behind the desk said she hadn't seen Tyb or Buddy since coming on duty at three. I slammed out the door and into the wavering heat.

Buddy was my job. I never should have left him alone or trusted his care to Aunt Nora. Overcome by female problems, I had ignored my responsibility. What if I couldn't menstruate and function at the same time? I ran back to the room.

"They're gone." My gut was a seething knot of sharp-fanged snakes. I felt weak, like my life was running out of me.

"They'll be back." Aunt Nora was reading *Photoplay*, calm as pud-ding. For an actress, she had a rotten sense of the dramatic.

Irritation crashed into the rear end of anxiety. "I think we should go look for them."

"Sit down, Pauly, you're going to have a stroke."

I gulped up some oxygen. What was the worst that could happen? Buddy couldn't get any more hair trimmed off. "I didn't give Tyb per-mission to take Buddy anywhere."

"I did. And I'm the guardian, remember?"

I wasn't the official grown-up in charge, but I was the most experi-enced Buddy-watcher in the group. "It's getting late. If they went to the park, they would have been back by now."

"They're probably on their way."

A wheezy old man and a limpy kid with a leg brace. That could explain the delay. "I don't like it."

"Don't you trust me?"

Of course I did. Didn't I? Like Nanny Tee, I'd been plenty happy to pass the torch and wriggle out of my duty. "Yes, but Tyb is old, and Buddy can be a handful."

"I think it's nice Buddy gets along so well with Tyb. Aren't you happy he made a new friend?"

"Buddy has no friend-making experience," I pointed out. In fact, my brother wouldn't know a friend if he tripped over one in the dark. "And I doubt Tyb has much practice babysitting. He might do okay watching Buddy sleep, but when it comes to keeping up with him . . ."

"I know Tyb doesn't move very fast. But neither does Buddy." She tossed the burger wrappers in the trash, and refolded the bag to keep the extras warm.

"So you're okay with some stranger just taking off with my brother?" Aunt Nora had been nonchalant about us all along. The closeness we'd shared earlier had made me forget, temporarily, that I didn't really know her at all. The mind-altering properties of the curse had made me let my guard down.

Aunt Nora took her time responding. "Tyb isn't some stranger. He's the sweetest old man I ever met. He would never hurt Buddy. I think you know that."

There she went again. Being rational. "Maybe not on purpose. Didn't Nanny Tee tell you how much trouble Buddy can get into without even trying?"

She laughed. "I never take what Nanny Tee says seriously. You worry too much."

For good reason. I knew my brother. Mama had accused me of

stirring up worry storms, just to watch the fur fly. She often asked what she had done to deserve such an overwrought child. I wanted to believe Aunt Nora was nothing like Mama. That she understood me. But they _were_ sisters. Genetic disposition couldn't be ruled out.

"Buddy's not like normal kids. You have to watch him as close as divinity. I'm just saying I don't think a hundred-year-old cowboy is up to the job."

"Are you jealous, Pauly?" Aunt Nora sat on the double bed and rubbed lotion on her arms. "Is that what this is all about?"

"Jealous?" I scoffed at the notion and flopped down on the studio couch to show her how _un_jealous I was. "Of Tyb? Why on earth would I be jealous of that old rawhider?"

I didn't care that Tyb liked Buddy more than me. I didn't even care that Buddy had begun to depend more on the old man than he did on me. That's what I had asked for all along. To have some of the Buddy burden lifted.

She offered me the lotion, and I shook my head. "You've been a good sister, but Buddy is getting older. It's time to let him make decisions on his own."

I rolled my eyes at the ceiling. Like a decision was something my brother could make. At least Mama and Pop had grasped the situation. They had said they wanted Buddy to be strong, but they knew better than to cut him loose and let him try. "Buddy is too trusting. Not everyone in the world is on the level, you know."

"And not everyone isn't. Holy heck, Pauly, how did you get to be such a cynic?"

Cynic. One who believes human conduct is motivated wholly by self-interest. What was wrong with that? Besides, it wasn't cynicism that motivated me, more like a healthy dose of self-preservation. "I wasn't born yesterday."

She opened the door. "I'm going to wait on the porch. Care to join me?"

"I can't sit around. I'll walk down to the park and see what's keeping them."

"If that'll make you feel better." Aunt Nora settled into one of the porch chairs.

I ran at first, but halfway to the park, I had to slow down and hold my side. When I got there, I did a 360° submarine scan of the swings and teeter-totters, but my brother wasn't there. Dusk had settled, and it was almost dark. Greasy panic rolled up my throat. Where *were* they?

I ran back to the Blue Spruce, hoping to find Buddy and Tyb laughing over their hamburgers, but Aunt Nora was alone. She'd finally started to fret.

"Something's going on," she admitted. "Tyb wouldn't keep Buddy out this late without letting me know. Maybe something happened to Tyb. He's been a little shaky the last few days."

"Maybe they were kidnapped." I could barely say the word.

"By who?"

"I don't know. Kidnappers."

"That's unlikely."

"Bad things happen to children who go missing." I thought of all the kidnapping stories I'd ever heard. Then I thought of what the boy at the lake had done to me. I knew what it felt like to be helpless and over-powered.

"Stop it, Pauly! Don't even think like that."

Now that the idea was firmly planted in my mind, I couldn't think of anything else. "So where are they?"

"I don't know, but let's not jump to dangerous conclusions. I trust Tyb. They probably started walking around town and forgot the time. They'll turn up."

From the way Aunt Nora paced and checked the clock, she must have done some dangerous conclusion-jumping herself. I thought of poor murdered Bobby Greenlease, the little boy from Kansas City who had been kidnapped in broad daylight from his first-grade class in a high-toned private school. Aunt Nora must have heard of that case. The story had been all over the news. The gruesome details hadn't been reported, but I didn't need details. My imagination filled in the blanks.

I was a wreck by the time darkness finally shrouded the cabin. My hand shook when I reached to switch on the log lamp by the bed. The click echoed like a gunshot, and Aunt Nora jumped to her feet.

She grabbed her purse. "Stay put in case they show up. I'm going to the police station."

I needed to swallow my fear, but I couldn't. I could barely speak. "To do what?"

"To report Tyb and Buddy missing."

18

A Stranger in the Night

The hour spent alone in the cabin waiting for word of my brother was one of the worst I'd ever lived through, and I had been through some bad times. My imagination tortured me with all manner of numbing scenarios until Aunt Nora walked through the door. Frantic for word of Buddy, I jumped up, but when I saw she was alone, my knees nearly gave out.

"Well?"

"I found Tyb." She sunk onto the edge of the bed and cradled her head in her hands. "He's in the hospital."

What about Buddy? Was he dead like our parents? Could fate really be that merciless? I couldn't go on without my brother. What reason would I have to live?

"Is Buddy in the hospital too?"

"No." Before I could sort out that ominous two-letter word, she took my hand and pulled me down beside her. "Pauly, I'm sorry. Buddy is lost."

"What?" Good thing I was sitting down, because the bottom

dropped out of the room. Impossible. Buddy was afraid of the dark. He wasn't allowed to cross the street alone. He was gullible and trusted everyone, even bad people. My brother could not be lost. That only happened in my nightmares, not in real life.

"According to the desk sergeant at the police station, Tyb showed up around sundown asking for help. He told them Buddy and Puppy were playing in the sandbox, and he was watching from a bench. He thinks he dozed off for a few minutes, because when he woke up, they were gone. He said he looked everywhere, but—" A choking sob swallowed the rest of her words.

Tyb had fallen asleep and let Buddy wander off. Anger boiled up inside me. "I told you! You never should have left Buddy with that old man."

She looked up at me, her eyes sad and bereft. "That old man? The one who is in the hospital this very minute? Don't you even care what happened to Tyb?"

Shame and guilt pushed anger aside. "Is he all right?"

"For now." She wiped away tears. "He's in trouble. His son reported him missing when he escaped from the nursing home in Texas. When the police figured out who he was, they took him into custody. He put up such a fight they had to lock him in a holding cell until they reached his son."

"The same son who stuck him in the old-folks home in the first place?"

She nodded. "His name is Anson Bisbee, by the way. When the police finally spoke to him, he told them Tyb is delusional and needs medication. That's why they sent him to the hospital."

"So they could give him the stuff that scrambles his brains and makes him drool?"

"I'm afraid so." Tears filled her eyes and spilled onto her cheeks. "I went to see him. Visiting hours were almost over, so I didn't have much time. He tried to talk to me, but he was too sedated to make much sense."

"Did he tell you anything about Buddy?"

"No, he couldn't. They're holding him at the hospital until his son drives in from Texas to get him."

Tyb wasn't a hundred percent safe, but we knew where he was, and he was alive. We could worry about him later. "So the police would rather lock up a harmless old man than look for a little lost boy?"

"They're looking, Pauly. Flagstaff isn't a big place, and they put out an all-points bulletin. Officers are searching for him right now."

"We need to look." I tried to get up, but she held my arm.

"They told me to stay here, so they can contact us when they have news."

"I don't like to sit around and do nothing." I crossed the room and looked out the window. *Where are you, Buddy?*

"I don't like it either, but we have to let the police do their job. They're hopeful he just wandered off and hasn't been . . ."

"Snatched?" Run over by a car? Trapped in a well? Dragged off by timber wolves? I flung myself back on the bed. "Is that why we have to stay here? In case we get a ransom note?"

"Pauly. It's not likely that Buddy will be held for ransom. No one knows us here."

"So if it's not a ransom situation, then—"

"Don't." She sobbed again.

How could I not think the worst? Bad things happened to children who fell into the wrong hands. "What if someone hurts him? Someone even bigger and meaner than the boy at the lake? Buddy can't take care of himself like I can. What if—"

"Pauly, please." Aunt Nora had given up all pretense of being brave for my benefit. She couldn't stop crying.

"This is all my fault," I admitted. "I was feeling sorry for myself this afternoon. I was selfish and chose a nap over Buddy."

Aunt Nora stroked my hair. "Honey, you weren't feeling well. You didn't do anything wrong. It's no one's fault, but if you have to blame someone, blame me. I'm the one who gave Buddy permission to go with Tyb."

I rolled away from her. I didn't want to feel her hand on my hair. I didn't want to feel better. She *was* to blame. I'd trusted her, and she'd let me down. How quickly I'd forgotten my resolve not to depend on grown-ups. I'd been wrong to place my life, and that of my brother, in her hands. I had given her power, and she had abdicated that power to an old man she barely knew.

"But Buddy isn't your brother." My words were firm, hard pellets that I threw at her. I wouldn't cry. Crying was weakness. "Pop trusted *me* to take care of him, not you."

Aunt Nora's shoulders heaved. "Was I wrong to think I could raise children? What do I know? I'm not used to thinking about anyone but myself. I let Buddy down, and I let you down, Pauly. I'm so sorry. Will you forgive me?"

The hardest, coldest part of me took pleasure in her pain. She was to blame, and losing Buddy wasn't my fault.

When I finally fell into a restless sleep, I dreamed I was back in the hall of mirrors. Buddy called my name, but I couldn't find him. I saw a hundred Buddy reflections, but when I reached for him, he wasn't there.

In the still, gray hours before dawn, I was dragged from the dream by the sound of someone banging on the cabin door. I sat up and switched on the lamp.

Aunt Nora, red-eyed and still dressed in street clothes, ran to answer the knock, and I stumbled after her. She threw open the door and there stood Buddy, looking like an answered prayer. A wish come true. The nightmare was over, and I would never let him out of my sight again.

He held a wriggling Puppy, and grinned as though he'd just stepped out of the room for a moment, instead of disappearing from our lives for nearly twelve hours. His face was streaked with dirt and what looked like cherry lollipop.

"Buddy!" We fell on him like starving rats on a bread crust and hugged him so hard, Puppy wriggled from his arms. The dog skittered across the floor to lap water from his dish.

"I f-f-found Puppy." Pride widened Buddy's grin and puffed out his chest.

"What?" I asked.

"Puppy r-r-ran away in the park. Tyb was sleeping, and I found h-h-him. All by m-m-myself!"

"You got lost because you chased that stupid dog?" I'd been so happy, and now I was furious. Like my mother, my mood had changed in an instant. Was I angry because Buddy hadn't asked me to solve his problem?

"P-P-Puppy is *not* a stupid d-d-dog! He's my pet and I f-f-found him."

"You should have come after me." I didn't mean to yell, but once I started, I couldn't stop. "Why didn't you tell me? I would have found him for you. What were you thinking? You're just a little kid."

"I'm eight!" Buddy's defiance shocked me into silence. "I didn't have to ask y-y-you. I found him myself!"

"Pauly, take it easy." Aunt Nora held my brother close. "He's all right."

"But—"

"I said that's enough. Buddy is okay."

Buddy's display of independence scared me, but not nearly as much as my own reaction. Had I made my brother as dependent on me as Mama had been on Pop?

We realized Buddy was not alone when a tall man stepped out of the shadows. He wore grimy pants, a wrinkled shirt and scuffed boots. A dusty green duffel bag rested on one shoulder. He didn't look like a policeman.

"I take it this is your kid?" He had a voice that was soft and powerful at the same time. It belonged in a pulpit or on a stage or shouting orders on a battlefield and seemed out of place on the porch of cabin number five at the Blue Spruce Motor Court at four in the morning.

Aunt Nora pulled Buddy into her bubble and wrapped her arms protectively around his shoulders. "Yes. Buddy is my nephew. Who are you?"

"A Good Samaritan."

He didn't look like a good anything, but I knew from Buddy's wide Howdy Doody grin that the stranger hadn't hurt him. He knelt on one knee and spoke to my brother, man to man.

"This where you want to be, pal?" Buddy nodded and hugged Aunt Nora's waist. The man rose and stepped off the porch. "Good enough for me. Don't take any wooden nickels, kid."

"Wait!" Aunt Nora stood in a puddle of porch light. "I'm Nora Teegarden. I haven't thanked you."

"No need." The man turned away. He was tall, too thin. His dark hair was shaggy, like he'd gone too long between haircuts. He'd gone too long between showers too.

"Mister!" I called out. "Aren't you going to tell us what happened?"

He stopped and slowly turned. "Why?"

"So we'll know." I couldn't create a story or make a memory without all the facts.

"Come back!" Buddy limped to the stranger's side and clasped his hand.

The man hesitated before accepting the porch chair Aunt Nora offered. "Simple situation," he said quietly. "I spotted the boy wandering the street and returned him. End of story."

Buddy piped up. "I t-t-told him I was losted. But I found Puppy. Puppy wasn't l-l-losted."

"He looked too young to be on his own, so I asked him where his folks were. He said you were traveling and staying at a motel. Didn't know which one."

"I forgot. Now I k-k-know. It's the Bl-Bl-Blue Spruce."

"Now you tell me." The man scrubbed Buddy's sheared head lightly. "All he could remember was that the place had a pool and cowboy curtains. We must have visited every motel in Flagstaff before we found this one."

"Why didn't you just take him to the police station?" Aunt Nora asked. "We filed a missing-person report."

The man's dark-eyed gaze held steady. "Didn't seem like a matter for the police." He stood and hoisted his bag. "Now that you've heard all about it, I need to be on my way."

"I'd like to give you something for your trouble," Aunt Nora said. "A reward."

He shook his head. "Don't want a reward. Boy was lost and now he's home. Everybody can get on with living happily ever after."

"At least let me give you money for a hot meal."

He'd walked a few steps, but turned around at Aunt Nora's words. "For the record, lady, I'm on my way to Los Angeles 'cause I got a job waiting for me. I'm no bum."

"I never thought you were," she said. "I'm grateful to have Buddy back and would like to repay you somehow."

"Try keeping a tighter rein on your kid from now on."

"What's your name?" I asked.

"Hatton. Joe Hatton."

"J-J-Joe's hitchhiking," Buddy put in.

"And if I want a ride, I gotta get on the road." Without another word, he strode out of the yellow light and across the dark parking lot. Since we were all headed for the same general destination, I waited for Aunt Nora to offer Buddy's rescuer a ride. She'd been open and trusting of people so far on the Trip, and I expected her to make room in the Skylark for Joe Hatton.

She didn't.

"J-J-Joe! Wait!" Buddy stepped off the porch. "I want you to m-m-meet my friend." He looked around and called for Tyb before turning to Aunt Nora. "Where *is* he?"

"He's not here. He had to go to the hospital."

Buddy's face crumbled. "He's sick?"

"No, no. He's fine. Don't worry. I'll tell you all about it later."

When Buddy turned around, Joe Hatton had disappeared around the corner. Another disappointment. "I w-w-wanted Joe to wait."

"He's a man in a hurry." Aunt Nora stared after the stranger for a few moments, as though willing him back. The whole episode seemed unreal, and I knew exactly how the town folks felt at the end of the Lone Ranger shows.

Who *was* that masked man?

With Aunt Nora between us clutching both our hands, we walked down to the all-night motel office and phoned the police to let them know they could call off the manhunt. We'd found Buddy. Or rather, Buddy had found us.

"Wh-wh-what about Tyb?" Back at the cabin, Aunt Nora helped Buddy into his pajamas. "Can I go see him?"

"Not tonight. He's resting." She glanced at me, giving me a look that begged, "Please, spare the details."

"T-t-tomorrow? I have to tell him I f-f-found Puppy, so he won't worry."

"I'm sure he knows you'll take good care of Puppy." She kissed his cheek and pulled the sheet up to his chin. "Go to sleep. We'll sort everything out in the morning."

Aunt Nora soothed his worries, and before long Buddy was snoring peacefully, unaware that he had just scared ten years off my life and given Aunt Nora a coronary.

Happy to be back in the bosom of his accidental family, Puppy curled up beside Buddy and rested his head on my brother's thin hip. The little dog's flighty ways had landed us in a difficult situation, but he suffered no guilt. Dogs were lucky. They didn't have to deal with feelings like worry and regret.

Half our problem had been solved when Joe Hatton returned Buddy. Tyb presented a more serious dilemma. There wasn't much night left, but I changed into pajamas and sat cross-legged on the bed.

"So how are we going to help Tyb?"

Aunt Nora's face was the saddest I'd seen it since the funeral. "What do you mean?"

"We can't go on to the Grand Canyon and leave him here. His son will drag him back to the rest home. We have to do something."

"What *can* we do, Pauly?" She brushed out her hair. "According to the police, his son is his legal guardian. A court of law declared Tyb incompetent."

I knew what that meant. *Unable to function properly.* "Tyb's not incompetent!"

"I know that. But the law is on his son's side." After kicking off her shoes and slipping into pajamas, Aunt Nora climbed under the covers and leaned back against the headboard. Buddy's disappearance had etched tired lines in her face. "Turn out the light, Pauly, and go to sleep."

Go to sleep? While there was still so much undone and unsaid? Not hardly. Now that my brother was snoring peacefully, we had to work on the Tyb problem. Aunt Nora had been game to rescue a mummy. Why not a friend?

"How can you sleep knowing what's going to happen to Tyb?" I asked. "We need a plan."

"I can't form a thought right now, Pauly, much less a plan. Go to sleep."

"Tyb's son will take him back to Ash Lawn Manor. You know he doesn't like that place. That's why he ran away."

"I know. It broke my heart to see him doped up in that hospital bed. I hated leaving him there. I feel bad about what happened, Pauly, but my hands are tied."

"There must be something we can do." Talking the talk was one thing, but walking the walk was what mattered.

"I don't know what. We can't shanghai him out of the hospital ward. The doctor said Tyb is medically stable and ready to be discharged, and they have orders to hand him over to his son when he arrives."

"Why don't we take him instead?" Less plan, more germ of an idea. If Aunt Nora wasn't willing to follow through where Tyb was concerned, how could I depend on her to follow through for me and Buddy?

She snorted. "Right."

"We can't just sit around and expect everything to work out." We had waited for the police to find Buddy, but they hadn't. If not for Joe Hatton, a random stranger, my brother would not be safe in his cot.

"Pauly. Can we please talk about this tomorrow?"

"We could steal him, like we stole Sylvester. If we hide him until he wakes up from the medicine and can think for himself, he can decide whether he wants to go back to Texas with his son or to California with us."

Aunt Nora started to laugh, but when she saw I was serious, her face folded into a frown. "Pauly, be realistic. We cannot hijack a semi-conscious old man. We can't just waltz in there and take him either. The police and the hospital staff have seen me. They will never let me leave with him."

Such minor problems could be solved by devious minds. I flung myself back on the bed and thought hard. There had to be an answer.

"Pauly, I know you want to help Tyb, but you need to get that idea out of your head."

"I thought we were going to be a family together? What about that?"

"That was before the cops got involved. I like Tyb, but—"

"You're not willing to go to jail for him?" Would she always bail when the going got tough?

"If I thought landing in jail would do that old man any good, I would lock myself up. But what useful purpose would be served by me getting arrested for kidnapping? You and Buddy would end up in an Arizona foster home. Is that what you want?"

I was thinking. The solution was there, just out of my mind's reach.

"Besides, remember how you said Tyb didn't have any rights when it came to cutting Buddy's hair?"

"I said I was sorry. I didn't mean that."

"Well, when push comes to shove, we don't have any rights where Tyb is concerned. I'm sure his son is looking out for his best interests."

My turn to scoff. "I'm *sure* Dr. Son had him shot full of loony juice and warehoused him in a rest home for his own good."

"That's not for us to say, is it?" She stared at the ceiling for a moment. "I guess we could wait until Anson Bisbee arrives and try to reason with him."

I rolled my eyes. "When Tyb was telling us about his lower-than-a-snake's-belly son, was there a point where the man sounded like the reasonable sort?"

"It's the only idea I can think of." She reached to switch off the lamp, but I stopped her.

"Wait! I've got it!" The answer was simple. Why hadn't I thought of it right off? "What if his son checks him out?"

"What?" She shook her head in confusion. "As far as I know, that's the plan."

"No, no, no. Listen. This will work. Here's what we can do. We find that Joe Hatton guy and pay him to *pretend* to be Tyb's son."

This time she did laugh. "He may be a Good Samaritan, but I doubt we can sweet-talk him into turning kidnapper."

"Hear me out. Joe needs to get to Los Angeles, right?"

"That's what he said."

"Think cynical. If he's looking out for number one, he might agree to help us if you offer to buy him a bus ticket."

"What makes you think so?"

"A ticket would get him to California a lot faster than his thumb. Just because he wouldn't take a reward doesn't mean he can't be bribed."

She heaved a weary sigh. "And what do you know about bribes, Little Miss Criminal Mastermind?"

"All Joe needs is a suit and tie and a shave and haircut. He could pass for a doctor. He's grumpy enough. What do you say?"

"I say *you* are the one who's been taking loony juice." She gently pushed me down on the bed and pulled the covers over me. "Good night!"

"But—"

"Forget it, Pauly. No. You are not sucking me into another crazy scheme. Absolutely not."

"At least say you'll think about it." I gave her the quavery smile I used on Pop to get my way. "Please?"

"Pauly . . ."

"How about this? It'll be morning in a few hours. When the sun comes up, we'll go look for Joe. If he's already caught a ride and is singing 'California, Here I Come,' maybe it's meant to be. We'll go on to the Grand Canyon and leave Tyb behind. We'll forget about him and let him drool out his days in Ash Lawn Manor. A place, if you recall, that he declared the most hellish spot on earth."

She turned off the lamp, and the room went dark. "Pauly . . ."

"Aunt Nora . . ."

"No."

"But if we find him . . ."

"Oh, for heck's sake." She flounced over and turned her back to me. "Girl, if we find Joe Hatton, then we have a real problem."

19

Putting Out Hell with One Bucket of Water

Buddy woke up hollering for Tyb, but strenuous good deeds like finding lost dogs worked up a man's appetite, and we were able to distract him with the promise of pancakes. We would discuss our next move over breakfast at Mo's Sunnyside Diner. It was only half a mile down the road from the Blue Spruce, but we piled into the Skylark anyway. Aunt Nora's motto was *Why Walk When You Can Drive?*

We had yet to formulate a rock-solid plan for saving Tyb from his own fate worse than death, but Aunt Nora had slept on my stand-in doctor idea and had finally agreed to consider it. That is, *if* we could locate Joe Hatton in time. *If* we could persuade him to stick his neck out for us. *If* we could beat the evil Dr. Anson Bisbee to the punch.

Attaching that many ifs to the enterprise decreased our chances of success from slim to none. Tracking down a hobo on the move was the biggest *if* of all, so when I spotted a familiar shaggy head bent over a newspaper in Mo's back booth, I knew we were on the right track. Saving Tyb was meant to be.

"Aunt Nora, look! There he is! There's Joe." I yanked her sleeve. "Can you believe it? Hallelujah, glory in the morning. We don't have to hunt him down. He's right over there."

Her exasperated sigh was not the reaction I expected. "Well, what do you know? This must be our lucky day."

"Come on, let's go talk to him." Pumped up by such an incredible long-shot coincidence, I was already pulling her to the other side of the diner.

Aunt Nora was leery of the plan, but I had no doubts. I could tell by the way Joe Hatton held himself that he was as strong and fortifying as the coffee he was drinking. Ordinary, everyday Joe. His rough-around-the-edges appearance inspired little confidence, but who was I to judge a book by its cover? This convenient stranger was someone we could count on when the chips were down.

"Mr. Hatton? Remember us?" The wattage of Aunt Nora's silver-screen smile would dazzle anyone.

Unable to tear himself away from the news, Joe was slow to look up from the paper. Then his dark eyes met my aunt's, and suddenly they weren't dark at all. They were filled with light.

I knew in that moment that Joe was yet another random piece that would someday fit into the crazy pattern of my life. With nothing scientific on which to base my unlikely assumption, I believed we had found this stranger for a reason.

"How could I forget?" He winked at Buddy. "You 'losted' again, pal?"

"Nope!" Buddy's grin was wide with hope and expectation. He had faith in his new friend. My brother rarely asked questions, but that morning he had grilled us about Tyb and wouldn't give up until we'd explained the plan, which he heartily endorsed.

"What can I do for you?" Joe wasn't one to wow you with friendly patter, but I knew all about reserving judgment. Unlike Aunt Nora, I'd never been quick to jump into new relationships, and had no idea why I felt so good about Joe. But I did.

Aunt Nora had agreed to include him in the plan because he was our only choice. I wanted to include him because he was the *best* choice. The smoky hint of underlying danger surrounding him didn't frighten me. When it came to handing off risky missions, the smart money was on the man who could handle himself in tight places.

"I guess you didn't get a ride, huh?" I asked.

"Nobody heading my way. Yet." He leaned forward and gave us the wild-eyed look that overcame Lon Chaney Jr. right before he sprouted werewolf fur. "Or maybe I scared them off."

Despite the whisker stubble darkening his jaw, I didn't think Joe looked scary. Just down on his luck, which we could do something about. I nudged Aunt Nora, who seemed to have forgotten why we were there.

"Mind if we join you for breakfast, Mr. Hatton?" she asked.

"I'm just having coffee, and I enjoy peace and quiet when I read the paper."

Hint, hint. Too bad. I snapped my head at Buddy, and he slid into the booth next to Joe. I slipped in across from him, and Aunt Nora sat down beside me. He swallowed hard and went back to reading his newspaper.

The waitress came, and when we'd finished telling her what we wanted, Aunt Nora said, "And bring the gentleman here a deluxe breakfast platter, please."

This time, Joe didn't look up at all. "I'm not one of your kids, lady. If I want bacon and eggs, I know how to order them." He spoke slowly, like John Wayne when he said, "Drop that gun if you know what's good for you, pilgrim."

Aunt Nora gave him the once-over and seemed to like what she saw. "Well, you don't look like you're watching your figure, so I assumed you didn't order because you lacked ready cash."

"You assumed right." He folded the paper when the waitress returned to refill his cup. Seemed to me it was Aunt Nora's figure he was watching. "Dough ran out in Albuquerque."

"So you're not planning to eat between here and L.A.?" Aunt Nora unfolded a napkin and placed it in her lap.

"I can go a long time between meals."

I believed that. He had the lean, narrow look of a caged wolf on a hunger strike. When the food came, he didn't say no. He ate like a wolf that had decided there was no percentage in hunger strikes, riveting wordless attention on his plate until every bit of runny egg yolk had been sopped up with toast and devoured.

"Okay." He leaned back in the booth. "The score's been settled. I returned your lost kid, and you bought me some eggs. Order is officially restored to the universe."

Aunt Nora had fallen into a bemused trance. With her head tipped to one side, she stared at Joe like he was a puzzle she could unravel if she concentrated hard enough. I nudged her in the side, and she cleared her throat before getting down to business. "We have a proposition for you, Mr. Hatton."

"That so? Don't be fooled by my present unsavory condition. I am not willing to kill anyone for you."

"That's good," I whispered across the table. "Because kidnapping is our game."

Aunt Nora explained what we wanted him to do, and as expected, he flatly refused. Said he wasn't currently living a life of crime, which could have meant he *had* lived one in the past.

"In exchange for an hour of your time," Aunt Nora pitched like a vitamin salesman, "I'll give you a hundred dollars in cash, buy you a new suit of clothes *and* a bus ticket to Los Angeles. I don't know what kind of job you have lined up out there, but you can't beat those wages."

Joe frowned. I could tell by his squinty eye that he was less disinterested than before. "What's this old guy to you anyway?"

"We picked Tyb up hitchhiking," I said. "But he's like family now. He wants to see the ocean and pick oranges, but his son wants to keep him under lock and key in an old-age home and dose him with medicine that scrambles his brain."

"And you know what's better for him than his own son?"

Aunt Nora faltered, leaving me to trot out the "there's nuthin' meaner'n an ungrateful chile" story. I told Joe how Dr. Anson Bisbee had stolen Tyb's ranch, and how Tyb had been forced to escape captivity and go on the lam after being declared incompetent.

"*Is* he incompetent?" Joe asked. "Is the old geezer out of his head? Loco? Crazy as a bedbug?"

"No." Aunt Nora was adamant. "Tybalt Bisbee is a perfectly rational man."

"So what did he do to get himself in such a fix?"

"His main crime was getting old." Aunt Nora explained how the police had detained Tyb when he went to the station to report Buddy missing. Tyb was locked up because he had cared enough to help us, and we cared enough to help him.

She pled a pretty moving case, but clearly, it wasn't budging Joe Hatton. I'd taken him for a man with heart, like Pop, but maybe I'd been wrong. Maybe he was like most grown-ups and couldn't be relied on.

I could plead moving cases too and wasn't about to take no for an answer. "Tyb will die if he has to stay in that horrible place."

"Sounds like a dicey proposition to me." Joe sat back in the booth and swigged hot coffee.

"Please, J-J-Joe." Buddy's simple plea shocked the rest of us into silence. He spoke slowly, confidently. "You helped me when I was l-l-lost. You said I was your p-p-pal. Help me help Tyb, 'cause he's m-m-my pal, and I don't want him to be l-l-lost too."

For once in my life, I had nothing to add. Buddy had pled the most moving case of all. Where had this new strength come from? Had he found himself when he was lost?

By acting on his own initiative to rescue Puppy and asking Joe for help, Buddy had taken the first steps toward fulfilling our parents' dream for him. For the first time since that long-ago day when my father had placed Buddy's tiny blanket-wrapped body in my arms and told me to treat him right, I saw him for what he was.

A brother. Not a burden.

Diner sounds rose and fell around us as we waited for Joe's answer. Cups clinked in saucers, forks scraped dishes. The plate-up bell dinged in the service window. Patrons chattered. The cashier rung up sales at the register.

Joe's eyes shuttered down in thought, and he was quiet for long moments. Finally, he focused on Aunt Nora. "You're on the up-and-up, right? This isn't some kind of swindle, is it?"

Did we look like bunco queens? "Everything we've told you is God's honest truth," I assured him.

Aunt Nora leaned forward, pretty and hopeful, dimples in full array. How could a man say no to that face? "What do you say, Joe? Will you help us?"

Joe leaned forward too, his arms folded on the table between them. "I gotta have the money in advance."

"No problem."

"You trust me that much?"

Their gazes locked across the table, and I wondered who would blink first. Aunt Nora sighed. "Truth is, we have no choice. You're our only hope."

"Lord, lady, don't say that. I don't want to be anybody's only hope. . . ."

"But you'll help us?" I prompted.

Joe gulped the last of his coffee. "All right. I need to get to L.A. by Friday because that job is *my* only hope."

"Really?" I was afraid to believe. "Does that mean yes?"

"It means why the hell not?" Joe stared out the window. "I know a thing or two about being held against your will. There's nothing worse for a man than losing his freedom. Lock up a man, and he might as well be dead. If you're sure busting out of the hospital is what the old fella wants, I'm in."

He smiled at Aunt Nora and shook his head as though already regretting his decision. "Busting out is getting to be a habit with me."

We walked to the nearest clothing store, and Aunt Nora outfitted Joe from the skin out. He insisted on picking out his own underwear, but she enjoyed making the other selections. She settled on a charcoal gray suit, a white shirt, striped red tie, dark socks and shiny black shoes.

Outside the store, she peeled five twenty-dollar bills off the wad, which had not melted much during the Trip. Maybe she'd won a big jackpot in Vegas, but wherever the money had come from, I was glad she had it.

"Go get a shave and haircut," she told Joe. "And a shower wouldn't hurt. You're supposed to be a successful urologist, so try to look the part."

He shifted the shopping bag. "What's a urologist?"

"Don't ask," I said.

Aunt Nora used a pay phone to call the hospital. The nurse reported that Tyb was resting quietly, which could only mean one thing. They were still pumping him full of sedatives. Tyb would not be "resting quietly" if he were in full control of his mind and body. Aunt Nora inquired about his discharge, and the nurse reported Dr. Bisbee was expected to arrive from Dallas tomorrow afternoon.

"Timing is crucial," Aunt Nora told us later. "Joe, if you show up too early, they'll know you couldn't possibly be Bisbee. Too late is not an option. Go get yourself cleaned up, and meet us at the cabin in the morning to go over the rest of the plan."

We said good-bye, and Joe strode away. After a few steps, he turned around and walked backward as a slow grin creased his face. I waved, but he didn't even notice me.

"Don't you disappoint me, Joe Hatton," Aunt Nora said softly as she watched him disappear around the corner.

Even though she'd rejected my plan at first, the inequities of Tyb's situation had changed her mind. She had proven herself a worthy champion of underdogs. Now that I'd finally realized what my brother meant to me, I had a better idea of what we meant to Aunt Nora. She had little experience taking care of others, but she'd survived on her own in California for years. And I was convinced that her heart really was in the right place.

Last night, I'd selfishly ignored her pain, which had been as deep as my own. But we had both suffered over Buddy, and we really were in this together.

All for one, and one for all.

We hung around the Blue Spruce all afternoon, feeling antsy and working out details. Since the hospital staff would recognize Aunt Nora, I convinced her to let me go with Joe. Otherwise, poor Tyb would think he was being kidnapped by a well-dressed stranger and would kick up another stink. The mission had a better chance of succeeding if the old man knew it was friends abducting him. She reluctantly agreed.

Morning arrived and Joe didn't, which threw Aunt Nora into a room-pacing panic. "We might never see that guy again, you know. He probably took our hundred dollars and bought his own bus ticket. He could be halfway to L.A. by now, for all we know. Talk about a swindle."

"He'll be here." I was packing in anticipation of a quick getaway. I'd never trusted anyone, not even my parents. Time after time, I'd been tricked by life. Busy concentrating on the perversity of fate, I'd never looked for meaning. I knew better now. Things *did* happen for a reason. There really *was* a plan. Faith meant trusting what you had no reason to believe in.

"I don't know what I was thinking." Aunt Nora lit another Pall Mall off the stub of her last. "I swore I'd never be blinded by good looks again."

My ears perked up. "Do you think Joe is good-looking?"

"Don't you?"

"Well, he's not pretty-handsome like Rock Hudson. Joe's face has more character and angles, like Gregory Peck's."

Aunt Nora ignored me and puffed and paced and puffed some more. "I never should have trusted him."

"Don't worry. Joe won't let us down." I finished packing my clothes and started folding Buddy's.

"Famous last words. What makes you so sure?"

"I don't know. Just a feeling." I had a lot of strong feelings where Joe Hatton was concerned. Feelings I couldn't explain. I'd seen the way he stared at Aunt Nora over breakfast, as though her face was a poem he had to memorize. The way he'd smiled at her on the sidewalk before we parted told me he'd be back, and the longing in Aunt Nora's whispered warning convinced me he wouldn't disappoint her.

Getting to a good place with my aunt had not been easy. One of my biggest worries was having her latch on to some man and losing interest in Buddy and me. I hated the idea of sharing her with anyone else, but I wouldn't mind sharing her with Joe. He needed her as much as she needed him, as much as I needed both of them.

The Trip had taught me a lot about fate and destiny and inevitable things you couldn't change. I felt a deep calm in my center knowing the hungry-eyed stranger had come into our lives for a purpose and might stay to fulfill a plan.

We both jumped when someone knocked on the door an hour later. Puppy yipped in a circle, and Buddy ran to answer. Joe walked in and set two paper bakery bags on the table. If pressed to come up with an appropriate adjective to describe how I felt when I saw him, "dumbstruck" could not be improved upon.

No doubt about it. The barbers of Flagstaff had mastered the art of amazing transformations. One had taken Tyb from roadkill to Charlie Ruggles. The barber's touch had the opposite effect on Buddy, as it had on poor Victor Mature when he played Samson. It had given him strength.

Now a barber had changed Joe from a shaggy hobo into a wellgroomed and potentially believable doctor. Freshly washed, dressed in his sharply pressed suit with his stubble shaved and his hair neatly trimmed, our last hope cut a very dashing figure.

Our jaw-drop reaction wasn't lost on Joe. He pivoted in a circle with his arms widespread. "Think I'll fool anyone into believing I'm rich?"

Hubba hubba. Paging Dr. Bisbee. I let out a low whistle of appreciation and glanced over at Aunt Nora, who had been impressed into speechlessness.

We reviewed the plan over the donuts and coffee Joe had supplied. It was agreed that I would pretend to be his daughter and wear my hair in pigtails to look younger. Since no one at the hospital had seen Nora's car, Joe would drive the Skylark and hope no one noticed the California license plate.

Once we had pulled Tyb off the meat hook, our plan was to return to the cabin for Buddy and Puppy and Aunt Nora, who had already settled the bill by paying for the cabin through the next day. We would drop Joe at the bus station and duck out of town before anyone could stop us.

One last chance to chase the moon.

We didn't know if the real Dr. Bisbee would sic the police on us, but we figured it would be smart to avoid the highway for a while. When we reached the Grand Canyon, we'd lay low for a week or so until our trail went cold, banking on the fact that the authorities wouldn't think to look for desperate runaways in a national park campground.

While waiting to leave for the hospital, I tried out my story-dredging skills on Joe. As usual, I opened with a hard-to-evade question. "So, Joe, did you just break out of prison or what?"

"Pauly!" Aunt Nora shot him an apologetic look.

"Are you always so nosy?" he asked.

"I'm curious. Nobody ever got anywhere by sitting in the shade. And you're the one who said busting out was getting to be a habit. Remember?"

He chuckled, and I knew he was on the up-and-up. A real jail-breaking criminal would not have been amused. I would never forget the first time I heard him laugh. I was piling up memories right and left. *I made Joe laugh in the Blue Spruce Motor Court in Flagstaff, Arizona.*

"What gave you that idea?" he asked.

I shrugged. "Reading between the lines."

"You're a smart kid. I *was* in prison."

Aunt Nora's head snapped around in alarm. "You were?"

Her obvious shock made me deadpan my next question. "Alcatraz or Sing Sing?"

"Neither."

"What then?" Persistence had paid off in the past, and I wasn't about to be left hanging on *that* cliff.

"Prisoner-of-war camp. I was a navy fighter pilot and was shot down in fifty-one. Spent a hundred and forty-seven days as a guest of the North Korean army. Can't say I cared much for their hospitality."

"You escaped?"

"Me and another prisoner. He's the buddy who lined up the job for me."

Aunt Nora stepped back into the conversation. "What kind of work are you planning to do in California?"

The fateful fact that Joe's final destination was mere miles from our own was not lost on me, or on her, I hoped.

"If things work out, I'm going to fly airliners for TWA." With prompts on my part, and encouraging looks from Aunt Nora, Joe went on to tell us how he'd been slow to readjust to civilian life. After the war, he left his native Chicago and took to the open road, moving west but unable to lock in on a purpose. He worked oil rigs and cattle ranches and hop harvests, but never stayed in one place for long.

"I carried my buddy's phone number in my pocket for over a year. I couldn't make myself call him. I guess I wasn't ready to start living again."

"What changed your mind?" Aunt Nora asked softly.

"I don't know. A week ago, I woke up one morning knowing it was time to get to L.A. I called my navy buddy, and he said the offer was still good. And here I am."

I looked at Joe and then at Aunt Nora. Smart as they were, they still didn't get it. But I did. A week ago, *we* had headed west. His out-of-nowhere decision had set him firmly in our path.

"Well, you will certainly look successful for your interview." Aunt Nora's eyes had softened as he told his story. "I hope things go well for you."

"I have a feeling life is going to turn out swell. Do you believe in fate?"

"I do!" I was laboring under the misconception that I was part of the conversation.

Joe ignored my happy exclamation without bothering to look my way. "How about you, Nora Teegarden? Do *you* believe in fate?" He couldn't take his eyes off her, and I felt the air crackle between them. I knew as much about love and passion as a goose knew about scripture, but I figured such powerful feelings had to start somewhere.

Maybe love and passion were tangled vines that grew from seeds planted in a single, shared glance. Maybe the seeds sprouted when one person looked into the eyes of another and saw a hint of the future.

"I never did before," Aunt Nora admitted after a long moment of soul gazing. "But I may have to adjust my thinking."

20

Cavalry to the Rescue

Making off with Tyb turned out to be easier than stealing the mummy, because this time we had broad daylight on our side. Playing the part of shy young granddaughter, I was careful not to say anything that would expose us as fakes winging a rescue. Watching Joe Hatton act like a barky, get-out-of-my-way doctor was more entertaining than a Cary Grant double feature.

"Where do I sign?" Joe bellowed at the charge nurse. "Hurry up! You're wasting my time. I want to get my father out of this one-horse hellhole and back to civilization."

Right. Like Dallas was the center of the cultural universe. His brazen tactics paid off. Having already gotten an earful from Tyb about what a blankety-blank martinet his son was, the nurse fell all over herself shoving paperwork in Joe's scowling face. A martinet, another word I hadn't gotten to use before the Trip, was someone who stressed rigid adherence to details of form and method. In other words, a pain in the keister.

"You'll need to go down to accounting to pay the bill, sir."

A storm cloud darkened Joe's face. I had to hand it to him. He was good. "Haven't you heard of professional courtesy, young woman?"

"Yes, sir." She gulped.

"You have my address. Send me the bill."

"Of course, Dr. Bisbee. I'll get a wheelchair."

"You do that." He snapped the pen down on the counter and spun on his heel. We had to get to Tyb's room and warn him what was happening before she returned.

"Tyb!" The old man was dressed and sitting on the edge of the bed. His head hung down, but he looked up when he heard me. Medication dulled his cloudy eyes and slurred his voice. He moved like a film running in slow motion.

"Pauly?"

"Don't worry, Tyb. We're going to get you out of here." The nurse's rubber soles squeaked in the hall. "This is our friend Joe. He's pretending to be your son, so play along."

A ghost smile teased Tyb's chapped lips. He squeezed my hand. "You're a lifesaver, girl." When the nurse came in, he powered up as much indignation as he could. "It'll be a hard fight with a short stick to make me go back to Texas."

"Now, now, Dad." Joe's sonorous reassurance would have soothed any real objections the old man might have had. "I know we had a little misunderstanding, but things will be different. If you won't come home for me, won't you come for poor little Pauly? She cried her eyes out every night you were gone."

I sniffled for effect, thinking maybe I might have a future in Hollywood. "Please, Grandpa. Don't leave me again."

The nurse helped Tyb into the chair, where he collapsed with a loud whuff. "Well, all right, then. I reckon I can come home for *you*, honey."

I hugged his neck, and Joe grabbed the wheelchair handles and started for the door.

"Sir," objected the nurse. "I'm supposed to do that. Sir. Sir!"

Halfway down the hall Joe called over his shoulder, "Don't I look like I know how to push a damn wheelchair, woman?"

"Yes, sir," she whimpered. "You do."

Back at the Blue Spruce, Buddy and I climbed into the backseat with Tyb between us. He gave my brother a special hug. "I don't know how to thank you folks."

"Just get to feeling better," I told him. "That's thanks enough."

Buddy fluffed up a pillow for his head. "Do you n-n-need anything?"

When Tyb said, "I got all I need right here," and patted Buddy's head, my brother's face beamed with love. No matter what happened from here on out, Buddy would be all right.

Joe helped Aunt Nora throw our belongings in the trunk. We had to blow out of Flagstaff. The police knew where we were staying, and when the real Anson Bisbee showed up to report our double-cross, it would be easy to find us. Aunt Nora called the bus station from the motel office and reported that a Greyhound was scheduled to depart for Los Angeles at 3:17 p.m.

"How are you feeling, Tyb?" I held the old man's hand, and it hardly trembled at all.

"A mite swoggled, but I reckon I'll sleep it off."

Aunt Nora settled behind the wheel, then turned to look into the backseat. "It's not too late, Tyb. You sure you want to go to California instead of waiting for your son?"

Despite being dazed on loony juice, Tyb nodded firmly. "I'll ride to the edge of the world with ye, Miss Nora. Jest don't let 'em drag my tired old rump back to Texas."

There weren't many people at the bus station in the middle of a weekday afternoon, which was good because the fewer witnesses, the better.

Aunt Nora and Buddy and I stood outside the car with Joe, while Tyb rested in the backseat.

"Good luck with the job," she said.

Joe's lips turned up in another slow smile. The emptiness I'd glimpsed in his eyes that first night had been filled with the kind of optimism that had once kept Pop afloat. I recognized hope when I saw it. "I have a hunch things are going to be aces from here on out."

"I hope so. Thank you again for your help."

"Glad to do it. Have a safe trip."

"Say." Aunt Nora feigned nonchalance, but I suspected she had been waiting for the right moment. "Why don't I give you my address and phone number? If you get a chance, you can call and let us know how things turned out."

"I'd like that." He stood close to her while she wrote the information on the back of a grocery store receipt, and then slipped the paper in the pocket over his heart.

"Bye, Joe!" Buddy grinned up at his new hero. Maybe I imagined it, but my brother seemed taller than he had back in Tulsa. He didn't stutter at all when he added, "Don't take any wooden nickels!"

Joe brushed a palm over Buddy's crew cut. "Take care of the ladies, pal."

"I will."

Joe turned to me. "So long, Pauly."

"I can't tell you good-bye," I said.

"I thought we were friends."

"I don't like good-byes. I've said too many." Dale Evans had the right idea when she composed "Happy Trails" on the back of an envelope. I stood on tiptoe to hug Joe and whispered in his ear, "Until we meet again."

When I saw Aunt Nora reflected in his eyes, I knew we would.

He whispered back, "Keep smilin' until then."

"Pauly, stay with Buddy and Tyb while I go inside to the ticket window with Joe."

He slung the duffel over his shoulder, and as they walked away, I thought what a nice-looking couple they made. I didn't see what happened when they parted company inside the station, but I had a clear picture in my mind's eye, thanks to all the romantic movies I'd seen.

I want to believe that they gazed lingeringly at each other until the loudspeaker announced, "Greyhound to Los Angeles, leaving in five minutes." I think those words prompted an impulsive hug that led to a brief, yearning kiss that startled them into making a rash promise to meet at the Brown Derby in thirty days to see what fate had in store for them.

At least that's how the scene would have played out, had their good-bye been made into a feature called *Bus Station Serenade* starring Sal Mineo and Natalie Wood.

When Aunt Nora returned, she and I leaned against the Skylark and watched Joe's bus pull out of the station.

"Do you think Joe's a keeper?" I asked. "What are you going to do about him?"

The Greyhound turned west and headed into the sunset. Aunt Nora smiled. "I'm going to listen to my heart for a change."

We weren't prepared for our first glimpse of the Grand Canyon. Aunt Nora parked in a scenic overlook, and we stood by the railing and gawked. The setting sun played across the canyon walls, painting them with color. I'd never seen anything half that grand, and looking down into the giant chasm reminded me that I was no more than the little end of nothing. The earth would go on forever, but all the problems of all the humans who ever lived on it would last no more than a blink of time's eye.

We found a campground nestled among piñon pines on the South Rim and chose our spot for its proximity to toilets and showers and a nearby playground. Each site came with a water spigot, a picnic table, and a grill for cooking, making an extended stay moderately comfortable. It was late July, but the air was cool under the trees. Sheltered by their branches, I fell asleep that night listening to the familiar rustling of the wind.

The first couple of days, we stayed in camp so Tyb could recover from the effects of the medication. When he had regained his strength, we stuck to tour bus rides and easy walks, and avoided anything strenuous. We viewed the canyon from different points, and at different times of day.

At sunset, we watched the gorge fill with a flood of liquid gold. At dawn, the rising sun revealed the immense formation bit by lavender bit. We observed distant thunderstorms so high in the clouds that raindrops evaporated before reaching the canyon floor, where the Colorado River snaked like a silver ribbon. We dropped dimes in big binoculars and watched a plodding mule train pick its way down a rocky path carrying swaying tourists in the saddles.

With Tyb's patient instruction, Aunt Nora finally got the hang of campfire cooking and learned to flip pancakes like nobody's business. In the evenings, we walked down shady, needle-strewn paths to a pavilion, where we sat in a circle on benches carved out of logs and listened to nature talks by park rangers.

I had an ear for facts and had no trouble memorizing numbers. The

Canyon was two hundred seventy-seven miles long, ten miles across, and one mile deep. I developed an interest in geology when I learned how it all started two billion years ago and how it took millions and millions of years for advancing and retreating oceans, volcanic activity, and erosion to form such a spectacle.

Rangers told us about the park's plants and animals. Tiny hummingbirds that mistook the red lights on trucks for flowers. Frogs and lizards and snakes. Rare squirrels and chipmunks and prairie dogs. Cougars and mule deer.

When we visited the souvenir shop, I picked out another postcard to send Nanny Tee. The lump of hard feelings caused by her betrayal had finally broken apart, leaving a dry layer of grit on the bottom of my heart. Choosing a card with a close-up picture of a mule showing big yellow teeth, I struggled to compose an appropriate greeting from a cast-off grandchild.

We are fine, how are you?

I signed Buddy's name and mine, but left off the love and kisses. I wasn't completely over the betrayal.

Aunt Nora bought Buddy a genuine plastic tomahawk, and when pressed to pick out a souvenir for myself, I chose a little bag containing a miraculous dormant desert plant that would grow into something amazing when sprinkled with water. I'd seen many hopeless moments take a turn for the better, and the idea of transforming a lifeless twig into a thing of beauty no longer seemed impossible.

Buddy became Tyb's shadow, tagging after him on short jaunts around the campground. The first time the two wanted to take off alone, I had a hard time letting go. Then I remembered what Joe had said about a man needing his freedom. Aunt Nora reminded me that I couldn't keep Buddy in a box like Mama had. Or protect him to death like Tyb's son tried to do with him.

Tyb liked to chew the fat with other campers. Having never before been more than a hundred miles from his birthplace, he was amazed to learn the distances others had traveled.

"Can you believe those folks come all the way from Ioway?"

"That couple from Florida has a kitchen in their trailer and a bed they make out of the table."

"Met a fella from New Jersey who is going all the way to Yellowstone."

He and Buddy would be gone exploring for hours at a time. Aunt Nora thought Tyb was becoming the grandfather Buddy never had. Puppy trotted after Buddy, legally secured on his leash at all times as the signs required. Buddy had taken over much of the dog's care, putting out fresh water and food. He gave Puppy baths. The traitor dog even slept in the tent, curled up in Buddy's sleeping bag. If Tyb felt rejected by the transfer of affections, he didn't let on.

One day while the guys were off rambling, I persuaded Aunt Nora to tell me another story from her life with my mother. Snapshot glimpses of Mama as a child made her seem close and normal, two things she had never been when alive.

Aunt Nora told me about the time she and Gracie were told to clean up the kitchen after supper and ended up having a food fight, pelting each other with balled-up pieces of leftover biscuits. They didn't clean up the mess they'd made, and the next morning when they came down to breakfast, they found dirty brown bits of dough piled on their plates. Frank Teegarden, opposed to wastefulness in any form, didn't say a word as he ladled gravy over those nasty biscuit bullets and told them to eat up.

Aunt Nora agreed they had learned a lesson for life: always cover your tracks. The experience spoiled her from ever enjoying Fig Newtons because the tiny seeds felt like dirt between her teeth.

"Mama wouldn't eat Fig Newtons either," I said. "She never explained why." I'd learned more about my mother since she died than I ever had while she was alive.

"Well, now you know."

Aunt Nora eventually ran out of stories, and to keep the conversation going, I said, "Joe's probably in Los Angeles by now."

"I'm sure he is." She scanned a movie magazine she probably knew by heart, keeping her eyes on the page, more interested in Kim Novak's romantic escapades than her own.

"Joe seems like a great guy."

"Hard to tell on such brief acquaintance, Pauly. Get to know someone before you make judgments like that."

"I hope he calls us when we get home." I loved saying that word. *Home*. I liked the word "us" even more.

"Don't hold your breath. If there's one thing you need to learn about men, it's that they don't always keep their word."

"Joe will."

"I hope you're right. For your sake. Okay. For mine, too." She tossed the magazine aside. "I think I'll take a beauty nap. Will you be all right alone?"

Funny question, but I didn't bother to explain why I laughed. I lounged on my sleeping bag reading *The Yearling*. I was in the middle of the part where Penny gets so mad at Old Slewfoot that he oils up his bear gun and takes after him through the swamp. It was hard to stay interested in the Baxter family's problems when my own had worked out so well.

Chipmunks scurried over rocks and came right up to camp. Signs warned visitors not to feed the wildlife, but I snuck them Post Toasties on the sly. They looked funny standing on their hind legs, nibbling on cornflakes held between tiny paws.

I wished young Ranger Rob would stop by on his rounds, as he often did that time of day, to answer my questions about geologic formations and flirt shyly with Aunt Nora. Ranger Rob had seemed disappointed when she told him we'd be leaving soon, though it was beyond me why he thought a woman as sophisticated as my aunt would camp for the rest of her life.

Aunt Nora and I were starting supper when Tyb and Buddy returned to announce they had a surprise for us. Tyb directed us to sit at the picnic table with our eyes closed, no peeking allowed. I heard a flurry of movement and whispering, then Tyb said, "You can open your eyes now."

I didn't see anything that qualified in the surprise category until Buddy crawled out of the tent and started walking toward us. It was a moment before I realized what was different about him.

He wasn't wearing his brace!

"Look, P-Pauly, I don't need it anymore."

Aunt Nora gave them a nervous smile. "Are you sure it's okay for him to leave off the brace, Tyb?"

"The boy's doing jest fine. We been practicin' a little ever' day when we were off visitin'. He's come along nice."

I started to object, but Aunt Nora shushed me with a look, forcing me to deal with my confusing feelings in unnatural silence. Tyb had no right to take that part of Buddy's care upon himself, and yet, I'd never seen my brother's grin so wide. He looked proud as he paced around in a slow circle, demonstrating his new skill, like he'd invented the concept of upright mobility.

"Are you s-s-s-surprised, Pauly?" he asked.

To put it mildly. How could I tell Buddy that Tyb was wrong to remove the brace, when he thought everything was a-okay? "What made you think of it?"

"I didn't. Tyb a-a-asked me did I want to t-try exercising my leg, and I said y-y-y-yes."

Tyb beamed. "First we left off the brace so Buddy could work his knee joint. Then he started standin' without it. Just standin', nothin' fancy. Finally, he felt like he could take a few steps on his own, and by cracky, he did."

"When did all this start?" Aunt Nora's concern dissipated as mine mounted. How long had they been pulling the wool over our eyes?

"Back at the Blue Spruce when you and Pauly was out shoppin' and such."

Aunt Nora held out her arms, and Buddy walked into them. "How big and strong you look without the brace weighing you down. Only a very brave boy would take such a risk. I'm proud of you."

Buddy reveled in her embrace, but the look on my face made his smile fade. "What's the m-m-matter, Pauly? Aren't you glad I can walk?"

Of course I was. But I should have been the one to give him such a gift. "I just don't know if all-or-nothing is the way to go. The doctor back in Tulsa said you needed the brace."

"But I d-d-don't." Where had his new confidence come from?

"Mama and Pop thought you did. Seems wrong to throw it away without a doctor's say-so."

"I figure we can give the boy some time out of the contraption ever' day. To build up his strength." Tyb was proud too. "Just like breaking a colt to saddle. After a while, he won't need it at all."

Aunt Nora nodded. What did she know about polio? What did she know about isolation wards and empty cribs and dead baby birds? "Sounds reasonable, doesn't it, Pauly?"

"No. It doesn't." I kicked at an anthill near my feet and sent the tiny insects scurrying. "Doctors who specialize in polio kids know more about what Buddy needs than a hitchhiker we picked up on the side of the road."

I regretted the hateful words as soon as they spewed out. They sucked all the joy out of Buddy's surprise, and the crushed look in Aunt Nora's eyes let me know that I'd disappointed her too. And Tyb? I couldn't even look at him.

What was wrong with me? What mean spark made me lash out and hurt members of a brand-new, made-from-scratch family?

Nanny Tee was wrong. I wasn't a pill. I was much worse. Buddy was the only one who'd learned anything on the Trip.

Freedom from the leg brace that shackled him and the stutter that tied his tongue was nothing to be angry about. That was cause for celebration.

Tyb let loose a sad little sigh. "I didn't mean any harm. Seems like I'm always steppin' in it. After all you folks did for me, I jest wanted to do somethin' for the boy. I'm powerful sorry if I was wrong."

"Pauly? What do you want to say to Tyb?" Aunt Nora expected me to do the right thing.

I sat at the picnic table staring down at the ants I'd kicked into chaos. They were already busy rebuilding their house of sand. Maybe it was a temple for ant worship, or a university for really smart ants, or a monument to a famous fallen ant leader. I had no idea what was important to ants.

But I knew what was important to Buddy.

"I'm sorry, Tyb. I didn't mean to sound like I wasn't glad. I'm happy you figured out a way to help Buddy." I finally looked up and met the old man's watery gaze. "You're right."

"Don't fret none about it." He swallowed hard. "Buddy was so het up over walking on his own, I got carried away."

"It was for *you*, Pauly!" Buddy spoke without hesitation and slipped away from Aunt Nora to stand before me. "I want to be strong l-l-like you. I don't want you to be a-a-ashamed of me anymore."

"I'm not ashamed of you, Buddy."

"Yes, you are. You st-st-stand up for me when other k-kids aren't nice, and they hurt you. I don't want you to feel b-b-bad because of me."

He wrapped his skinny arms around my neck, and his tears dripped on my shoulder. Only a shriveled-up raisin heart would be jealous of what Tyb had given Buddy. I had to let go, even if letting go made me as useless as spit curls on a frog.

"I love you, Pauly. You're my favoritest s-s-sister."

"I'm your *only* sister."

"I know. But if I had a hundred . . ." He pronounced his part slowly and perfectly, pausing for me to insert my line.

"I'd still be your favorite." I hugged him too hard, and he started coughing.

"Will you w-walk to the playground with me, Pauly? And push me on the swing?"

"Sure." I took his hand, and we struck out in that direction. For the first time ever, Buddy did a game job of keeping up.

When I heard Aunt Nora speak to Tyb, I slowed down, unable to break the eavesdropping habit.

"You've come to mean a lot to Buddy," she told the old man. "In fact, you're important to all of us."

"Thankee, Miss Nora. You and them young'uns are the moon and the stars to this old hoss."

"Would you consider staying on with us in California?"

"I'd be right proud to do that."

"Thank you, Tyb, for giving Buddy the most valuable gift a little boy could have. He'll be a better person because you had faith in him when everyone else had given up."

Buddy and I walked toward the swings, and I finished Aunt Nora's sentence in my head.

Including his own sister.

Snakes in the Grass

The next afternoon while Buddy and Tyb were off on a jaunt and Aunt Nora was talking to Ranger Rob, I grabbed a handful of Post Toasties and slipped away to feed the chipmunks. I found a lonesome spot at the canyon's edge and sat on the retaining wall. Overhead, the skies threatened rain, and for once there weren't many tourists around to report my criminal activity to the wildlife police.

The curse had lasted three days, and I was relieved to be done with it, at least for another month. I had a feeling I would not enjoy being a woman.

Nearly three weeks had passed since the accident that had killed Mama and Pop, and I thought about how much my life had changed. Would change more, once we hit California. If we'd stayed with Nanny Tee, I would have gone on being Baloney Mahoney, Girl Outsider, with a skin thick enough to hold in the pain. It was crazy to turn sentimental over something I'd fought so long, but there had been comfort in that role.

I had known my lines. I had acted according to a script that others gave me. Mad at the world and I don't care. The prospect of leaving my old self behind like a dry locust husk was scary. What if I couldn't grow a new skin?

Baloney Mahoney had known what to do. Her place in the family was clear. She'd been the voice of reason. The one who bailed the canoe when it was up the creek without a paddle. At school, she'd been the defiant one. The one who told the world to go suck an egg.

All that had to change. Aunt Nora didn't need me to manage the details of her life. Pretty soon Buddy wouldn't need me to fight his daily battles. I had to create a whole new role for myself.

I nibbled a cornflake and looked up to find a bright-eyed chipmunk staring at me reproachfully.

"Yeah, these were supposed to be for you." I tossed it a treat and hugged my knees.

"Hey, kid. What are you doing out here by yourself?"

The chipmunk scurried away, and I turned around to see who owned the voice, expecting a ranger ready to confiscate the contraband cornflakes. I was wrong. The skinny man's dirty blond hair was greased back and his face was pocked with pimple scars. He smelled like an ashtray with B.O. I didn't think anything could make him look more cheapjack until I saw the tattoo on his forearm. A snarling wolf with dripping fangs.

"I asked you a question, girly. What are you doing here by yourself?"

He was too dense to take a hint. "Minding my own business. You should try it sometime."

"Think you're pretty smart, do you?"

"I *know* I'm smart. Do you know how annoying *you* are?" I tossed the rest of the cornflakes on the ground. If he wouldn't buzz off, I would.

Tattoo clamped his hand on my shoulder and pushed me down on the rock wall. "Where you going, Red?"

Where had this shit-heel come from? He didn't look like the visitors we'd seen crowding the rim. I glanced around, trying not to act nervous. Normally, the place would be crawling with tourists, but the clouds had kept them away. There was never a sightseer around when you needed one.

I glared at the hand squeezing my shoulder. His nails were dark with grime. Memories of that day at the lake rolled over me, and the queasy feeling in my stomach was divided between disgust and fear. "Get your filthy hands off me." I copied Joe's voice, trying to sound like John Wayne. "Now."

"You're a little spitfire, ain't you?" He withdrew his hand. "That's what I like about redheads."

"There's nothing I like about you." I stood up, and this time Tattoo didn't stop me.

"Why are you so scared? I ain't gonna hurt you."

"I'm not scared." I was, but he'd never know it.

"I just want to teach you some tricks." He reached out and lifted one of my braids. "Can't we be friendly?"

Not even when hell froze over. I stepped away from him. I was rattled by my newly acquired knowledge of men and the potential misuse of certain anatomical components. My previous bad experience with a too-friendly boy didn't help matters.

"Can't we just talk?" The corners of his mouth turned up, more leer than smile.

A crack of thunder sounded nearby, and a moment later the clouds flung down a drizzling rain.

"I'd rather eat worms and sip a pond scum chaser." With that, I broke and ran, not really knowing where I was going as long as it was out of Tattoo's grubby clutches.

I ran into a family stuffing kids into a station wagon and stopped to catch my breath. I didn't see my would-be "friend" anywhere. By the time I made it back to camp, the drizzle had become a downpour and everyone was sitting out the storm in the Skylark. I jumped in the front seat and slammed the door.

It wasn't cold, but I shivered hard enough to make my teeth rattle. Aunt Nora, Tyb, Buddy, and even Puppy stared at me.

"What?" I asked.

"Where were you?" Aunt Nora handed me a towel.

"Watching chipmunks out at the rim."

She let out a slow breath. "We were scared to death."

"I thought y-y-you fell o-o-over the edge," Buddy said with a sniffle.

"You shouldn't wander off without tellin' us where you're goin', Pauly." That was Tyb's pot calling my kettle black.

"Why are you shaking?" Aunt Nora wanted to know. "What happened?"

"Some jerk tried to bother me, but I'm fine. Holy cow, don't you all have anything better to do than worry about me?" It felt odd being the worriee instead of the worrier for a change.

"What jerk?"

"Some guy gave me a hard time. I handled it."

"What kinda hard time?" Tyb demanded. "He hurt you? Do I need to find him and knock the slobber out of him?"

"Forget it, okay?" I'd like to see Tyb put up a fight, even against someone as gangle-shanked as Tattoo. I scrubbed my wet arms with the towel.

"We should report the incident to the ranger station." Aunt Nora was determined to do something.

"Forget it." Lesson for life: Pick your battles. Smart talk and insults might work with sixth graders, but not grown men.

The rain pelted the car and lightning streaked the sky. Then as unexpectedly as it had hit, the storm blew away and the sun came out. Buddy was first out of the car.

"L-l-look, everybody! A rainbow!"

The colorful bridge of color spanning the canyon almost made me forget my run-in with Tattoo.

"Rainbows mean good luck," Aunt Nora said.

We could use it. "I heard there's a pot of gold at the end of a rainbow."

Tyb nodded. "I reckon if you was to find a pot of gold, you could make your own luck."

Later that evening, Aunt Nora and I walked to the village to pick up potatoes and toilet paper before the store closed. She'd discussed Zion National Park with Ranger Rob, who explained that if we took a northern loop, Utah wouldn't be too much out of our way.

I was thinking I'd seen enough natural wonders for one trip, when I noticed two men following us. They tried to be sneaky but couldn't fool me. They wore cowboy hats but they weren't cowboys. Nothing about them indicated that they'd ever heard of the code of the west. The tall one eased around the end of the aisle, and I noticed the thick, puckery scar on his cheek.

Aunt Nora told me to stop staring, but I was trying to get a look at the short guy. His head was turned away from me, but there was something familiar about the set of those bony shoulders. When he reached for a tall bottle of beer, I saw the dripping fangs on his arm. Tattoo!

Part of me wanted to point my finger and yell bloody murder until the rangers came and dragged him away. A more sensible part suggested I get out of there before Aunt Nora caught on and got her red up.

The men paid for beer and cigarettes before walking out the door. We checked out and stepped outside. It was nearly dark. The air was cool and shadows crowded under the trees. I carried the toilet paper and Aunt Nora carried a five-pound sack of potatoes. I recognized the two men loitering out front, and my heart squeezed up my gullet.

"Hey, ladies." Scar tipped his cowboy hat.

"Hello." Aunt Nora didn't slow down or glance in their direction. She kept walking and I stuck to her like a tick.

The men didn't have the guts to try anything with Aunt Nora and climbed into a rusty old pickup truck.

"Shoot," she muttered under her breath when they pulled up alongside us on the road.

"You ladies need a ride?" Tattoo leaned out the window, his watery blue eyes silently daring me to mention our first meeting.

"No, thank you." Aunt Nora looked straight ahead.

"It's a shame two pretty gals like you have to walk. We can squeeze over and make room for you. Be real cozy-like. Why don't you hop in?" Scar suggested.

"Why don't you take a flying leap?" I pointed. "I believe the canyon's that way."

"Ain't you the feisty one?" Scar laughed, but Tattoo glared at me.

Aunt Nora whispered for me to be quiet. I didn't see why. They were the ones causing all the trouble.

The driver eased a little farther down the road, then turned the pickup and blocked our way, making it impossible for Aunt Nora to ignore them.

"We're just trying to be nice to you ladies. Why you playing so hard to get?" Reeking of sweat and smoke and beer, they climbed out of the truck and leaned against it to light up.

"Leave us alone." Aunt Nora's tone was low and strong, a quality she shared with Joe.

"We ain't done nothing wrong," said Scar. "Yet." He poked Tattoo in the side, and they laughed.

The sound of their oily laughter gave me the jimjams.

"You two sisters?" asked Tattoo. "No way could you be her mama."

"None of your business." Aunt Nora took my hand and led me off the road, but the two of them just kept jumping in front of us, trying to engage us in an evil game of dodge 'em.

"You hear that?" Scar asked Tattoo. "It's none of our business."

Tattoo feigned a lightbulb moment. "Why don't we *make* it our business?"

Aunt Nora didn't feign anything. She was dead serious. "Get in your truck and beat it right now, or you will be very sorry." Pilgrim. John Wayne had nothing on her. She shifted the sack of potatoes, and I wondered if they could be used as a weapon.

Scar must have wondered too. "What are you gonna do, girlie? Whack me with that sack of spuds?" He cowered in mock terror. Like the rattlesnakes back at No Water Charlie's, Tattoo looked at us like we were meat.

Before Aunt Nora had a chance to fire a deadly spud missile, a horn honked and everybody jumped at the sight of a ranger truck. Aunt Nora and I were relieved, the two men angry.

"Hey, you two move this vehicle out of the road. Are these men bothering you, Miss Gardner?" Just like in the movies. Ranger Rob to the rescue.

"As a matter of fact, they *are* bothering us," she said.

"They tried to make us get in their stinky old truck," I put in before Aunt Nora could stop me. "Like we'd have anything to do with a couple of pissants like them."

"Okay, fellas, move on." Ranger Rob threw some of his park service weight around. "You don't want to get run out of here, do you?"

The men slunk away from his authority like cur dogs from a raised boot.

"We didn't mean anything," said Tattoo.

"Yeah, we were just having some fun," agreed Scar.

"Go on, now. If you cause any more trouble, I'll personally escort you to the exit."

I heard Tattoo mumble, "You and what army?" as they got in their truck and took off.

"Thank you, Ranger." Aunt Nora settled the bag of potatoes on her hip like a squirmy baby.

"My pleasure. Do you need assistance back to your campsite?"

Ranger Rob was pretty cute, not to mention gallant. I would have gladly jumped in his truck, but Aunt Nora held me at her side.

"It's not far. We'll walk. Thank you anyway, Rob." Aunt Nora worked her dimple to good advantage.

"Will I see you at the nature talk tonight?" More plea than question. "I'll be speaking on Major John Wesley Powell's early exploration of the canyon."

"Sounds interesting, doesn't it, Pauly? We'll try to make it."

"I hope to see you there."

"Bye-bye." She gave him a little wave.

"Good-bye." Ranger Rob tipped his Smokey Bear hat and nearly walked into a tall pine as he watched Aunt Nora stroll past. He flushed red and backed toward his truck.

Aunt Nora attracted men like Buddy attracted dirt. Without even trying. How did she know which ones were okay to flirt with and which ones to avoid? Seemed to me, a woman had to be careful not to attract rough men like Tattoo and Scar. You couldn't base character on the number of days since the last bath, because Joe Hatton had disproved that theory. So what was the tip-off?

I decided it was all in the eyes. Safe men looked at you with warmth and curiosity. Dangerous men looked at you with a snake's yellow glint. Things had been much easier when boys just threw spitballs at me. Back then I'd never lost sleep over my looks and was resigned to what I had to work with. Wild hair, freckles, and no figure.

My plan had always been to be the plain, smart girl who was more interested in getting somewhere in life than going on dates. My goals had shifted. Deep down, I wanted to be the kind of woman who made nice men walk into trees.

22

Cat Looks Big till Dog Shows Up

Aunt Nora said there was no reason to mention the incident on the road to Tyb and Buddy. I agreed because everyone knew the more you stirred a cow patty, the more it stunk. The quicker we forgot about Scar and Tattoo, the better.

That night, Tyb didn't feel strong enough to trek down to the nature talk, but he encouraged us to go without him. I learned more than I ever wanted to know about Major John Wesley Powell, a one-armed Civil War veteran who had been the first white man to explore the canyon. I scanned the audience, relieved not to see Scar and Tattoo lurking around.

Later, lying in my sleeping bag, I thought about how far I'd come. Not just in miles, but in my thinking too. When Mama and Pop first died, I figured I would go on feeling sick and miserable forever, but that wasn't how things worked. Life was like a book, and every time you turned a page, something new appeared to take your mind off the old. The mind wasn't able to cling to pain, because if it were, no one would ever open the book in the first place.

I couldn't sleep and thought about subjects that a mere month ago had just been words in the dictionary. Predestination, for example. I'd read how some believed a person's life is all planned out from the moment of birth and nothing they do can change it. It was an interesting idea to mull over. If Mama and Pop had known that roller coaster had their name on it, would they have done anything differently?

I didn't know what to believe. I didn't want to think my parents' lives had ended early so I could find my destiny. But it was harder to believe they had died for no reason. Being a kid was easier than growing up. A kid only had to believe in real-life things that spit in your eye.

Thinking about ends and beginnings, and everything in between, wore out my mind, so I tried to concentrate on tomorrow. Aunt Nora thought it was safe to get back on the road. We were pulling out early for Zion National Park. Seemed to me if you'd seen one major geologic formation, you'd seen them all, but Ranger Rob had sold Aunt Nora on Utah. She said camping was more anonymous than staying in motels, which meant she was still concerned about Anson Bisbee catching up with us and stealing Tyb back.

I was about camped out. Sleeping bags were not a comfortable place to park your carcass, regardless of what Boy Scouts would have you believe. No matter how carefully I picked over the ground before spreading out, I always missed one pointy little pebble that poked me in the hip all night.

Rain was no fun because it made everything damp and mildewy, and pretty soon even fellow travelers who weren't dogs started smelling like them. Twiddling your thumbs in a car while water pelted down or drizzled or sprinkled was nothing to write home about. Luckily, we'd only experienced bad weather a few times, which was plenty, thank you very much.

As far as camp food went, I hoped never to eat another pork and bean. The only thing good about them was the little hunk of greasy fat, which I had learned to flip off a spoon for Puppy to catch in midair.

Don't get the idea that I wasn't having fun, because I was. But I was itching to light someplace and stash my belongings in furniture instead of lugging them around like a hobo. That's why most vacations only last two weeks. There's only so much fun a person can stand before it begins to wear on the nerves.

I wanted to get to California and find out where we'd be living. Aunt Nora had an apartment at the beach and we could swim whenever we wanted. She lived in a place called Venice, like the town in Italy, and said the streets were lined with palm trees and flowers.

I would have my own room because a woman needed her privacy. I didn't feel like a woman, even if, as Aunt Nora had pointed out during our talk at the washhouse, I could now bear children and attract unwanted male attention. I had a long way to go before I would even consider such things as what she said men and women in love did in the throes of passion.

The summer had been full of loss and filled with discovery, all at the same time. I wished I could stay a kid a little longer and envied Buddy for being eight and having many years of childhood still ahead of him.

I peeked out the tent flap and saw Tyb humped up by the carefully banked fire. Even if he was too old to take my side in a fight, knowing he was nearby made me feel safe. When I'd asked him why he didn't sleep in the car, he said bunking on the ground reminded him of his youth, when he'd worked cattle on his pappy's ranch and slept out in all kinds of weather with other cowboys.

I tried to imagine what Tyb's life had been like, starting as it had in the year 1883, which was a whole different century from the one we lived in. I wasn't as keen on history as I was on science, so most of what

I knew about the old days came from westerns like *High Noon*, *Broken Arrow*, and *Shane*. Boiled down to the essence, good guys always came out on top and bad guys, who were often named Kincaid, always met a violent end.

In Hollywood westerns, problems of a troublesome nature were solved in a hail of bullets, but I couldn't feature Tyb striding down the street to square off with a guy in a black hat. I couldn't see him in a rest home either, parked in a chair like an abandoned car, out of his head on nerve pills.

I thought of him strolling along the beach in the high-topped tennis shoes that made him walk flat-footed like a duck.

If an old man like Tyb could adjust to all the changes he'd been through in his long life, I could handle whatever came my way.

I turned over in my sleeping bag, but couldn't get comfortable. I needed to visit the public toilet, which I could see from our tent, but I'd never gone alone at night. I peeked out the tent flap at the quiet campground. Fires had burned low and lanterns had been snuffed out. If I listened carefully, I could almost hear people snoring.

I slipped on my sneakers and pulled a red sweatshirt over my nightie. I wasn't afraid of the dark, but I fished around for the flashlight, so I wouldn't trip over a rock or snake. I was crawling through the flap when a voice startled me. I dropped the flashlight, and the fright didn't do my bladder any good either.

"Can't you sleep?" Aunt Nora whispered.

"I gotta go to the bathroom."

"Wait a minute and I'll go with you."

"You don't have to."

"I need to take care of business, too." She put on her sandals, changed into shorts, and tucked her pajama top into the waistband.

The night sky glittered with stars. We cat-footed our way to the public facilities, the flashlight's yellow beam leading the way. Pine needles cushioned our footsteps, and for once even the birds were silent. During the day, the park was full of big black ravens that perched high in the trees, cawing hoarsely and dive-bombing trash cans for scraps.

We were washing our hands when we heard voices on the men's side of the restroom. Aunt Nora said we should wait until they left. Our experience on the road that day had taught me that there were people in the world you didn't want to bump into in the dark.

A few minutes later, we stepped out of the building and were greeted by an unpleasantly familiar voice.

"Well, well, will you looky who's here?"

Scar stuffed his shirttail into his jeans. Tattoo was having a smoke. Their truck was parked next to the building with the engine running.

"If it ain't Potato Gal and her smart-ass kid." Tattoo took a final drag and flipped the butt onto the ground.

Aunt Nora pushed me around behind her. "What are you doing here?"

"Same thing as you, baby doll. Only we do it standing up," said Scar.

"This can't be a coincidence. My luck isn't that bad."

"Oh, shit, she's on to us." Scar's transparent dismay was phony. "Truth is, we just happened to be up having a beer when we saw you headed this way. Thought you might want to join the party."

"Come on, Pauly, let's get out of here." Aunt Nora urged me along.

"Think you're too good for us, don't you, Miss High and Mighty?" Scar stopped faking a friendly tone.

Aunt Nora didn't respond. She tried to walk away and pulled me with her.

"You're not going anywhere." Tattoo grabbed my arm.

"Leave her alone, you son of a bitch." Aunt Nora yanked me the other way, like a pulley bone at Sunday dinner.

Scar slunk around behind us. When Aunt Nora opened up to yell for help, he clamped his hand over her mouth. She kicked and fought like a badger in a trap, but he twisted her arm up behind her until she cried out in pain.

"Keep squirreling around, lady, and I'll break it," he warned.

I ducked my head and charged for him, but Tattoo got one arm around my neck and plastered his other hand over my mouth. He clamped down on me so tightly I felt the calluses on his hands and smelled the beer on his breath. I stomped hard on his foot, but my sneakers did little damage. No matter how hard I wriggled and squirmed, I couldn't get loose. I was good and stuck.

They dragged us into the men's room, so anybody stirring around a nearby campsite couldn't see what they were up to. I glanced over at Aunt Nora, who was still struggling, but outrage had been overcome by fear. Her eyes were open wide, and her chest heaved from the effort she put into the fight. Her pajama top had worked out of her shorts, baring the smooth, white skin of her belly.

"Listen, dammit, we don't want to hurt you," Scar spit in her ear. "I'll let you go if you promise to shut the hell up."

She nodded, but as soon as he loosened his grip, Aunt Nora rammed a knee between his legs and screamed like a starlet warning the world of a giant ant attack.

"Bitch!" Moaning from the pain she'd inflicted, Scar hauled off and landed a John Garfield punch to her face.

Shocked numb by the violence that seemed so much worse in real life than in the movies, I felt the fight drain out of me. I was paralyzed like a bug on a pin. These men wanted to hurt us. They were too drunk to listen to reason, and Ranger Rob wouldn't show up this time to save us. We were on our own.

"That one's liable to be more trouble than she's worth." Tattoo jerked his head in Aunt Nora's direction. "Let's ditch her and take the kid. I got nothing against jailbait."

His suggestion made Aunt Nora renew her fight, and she twisted her head away from the hand that gagged her. "Leave her alone, you filthy bastard. Lay a hand on her, and I'll cut off your balls."

I'd never heard her use that cold, brittle voice before. Scar better believe her, because I sure did.

He twisted her arms behind her. "How you gonna do that when you're bound and gagged and stuffed in the shower? Nobody will find you 'til morning, and by that time we'll be long gone. With a little party girl to keep us company on the road."

He pulled a length of rope out of his back pocket and twisted it around Aunt Nora's wrists, knotting it tight enough to make her wince. He yanked a bandanna out of his pocket, but before he could gag her, Aunt Nora started to cry.

Her tears scared me more than anything the men had said or done. In a voice as limp as I felt, she said, "She's just a little girl. You're not the kind of men who would hurt a child. You're angry and you've had too much to drink, that's all. Why don't you get in your truck and leave before you do something you'll regret?"

"Shut up!" Scar finished tying her up and kicked her leg for good measure.

I hung in Tattoo's grasp, devoid of gizzard or guts. If Aunt Nora couldn't fight them, how could I? I wanted to let go with an ear-piercing scream, but the vocal cords in my tight throat had stopped working. Even if I could holler, who would find us before Scar and Tattoo tossed me in their pickup and sped away?

"Aunt . . . Nora." I sobbed because sobbing was all I could do.

"Leave her," Aunt Nora said desperately. "I'll go."

"What the hell are you talking about?" asked Scar.

"Leave her alone, and I'll go with you." Her voice dripped ice like a roof in winter.

Scar didn't buy it. "And she goes running for help before we're even out of sight."

"You can tie *her* up." Aunt Nora was wild with pleading. "Gag her. Stuff her in the shower. By the time someone finds her, you'll be long gone, remember?"

Scar turned to Tattoo. "What do you think?"

"I think she's a goddamn liar. Ain't no way she'll go easy."

Scar considered. "Maybe for the kid she will."

"Yes, anything," she put in. "Leave her here, and I'll go wherever you want. You can let me go when you're . . . finished."

"No!" I finally found my voice. I wouldn't let Aunt Nora bargain to save me. "Don't do it." Fear had short-circuited my brain, and I only had a vague idea about what they would do, but I knew they would hurt her.

"I think this one'll be easier." Tattoo shook me like a dog with a rat. "Look how scrawny she is. She won't put up much of a fight."

Scar was thinking. "I prefer grown women. Here, gag the kid." He tossed the bandanna, which Tattoo secured around my mouth.

Scar ordered Tattoo to bind me, hand and foot. He pushed me down on the cold cement floor of a shower stall. I couldn't believe this was happening. What if they didn't let her go when they were . . . done? What if I never saw her again? The thought of losing her ripped open the raw wound of my parents' deaths.

My beautiful aunt smiled through her tears. "I'll be all right, kiddo."

The kidnappers' smugness over the way hostage negotiations had worked out was short-lived.

"Let her go, you low-life sonsabitches." Looking like a geriatric

Gary Cooper, John Wayne, and Randolph Scott all rolled into one, Tyb loomed in the doorway pointing a huge pistol at Scar's belly.

"Who the hell are you?" Scar demanded.

"A knight in shining armor," Aunt Nora breathed.

Old as he was, Tyb cut an intimidating figure with that big peacemaker in his hand. Aunt Nora looked so relieved I couldn't help feeling better myself, even if I was trussed up like a goose gone to market.

"You." Tyb swung the gun in Tattoo's direction. "Untie the girl and no funny business. I'm old and my hands shake. This blame thing is liable to go off and blow a hole in you wide enough to drive goats through."

Sobered up by the sudden reversal of power, Tattoo scrambled to get the gag and rope off me. Without having to be told, he backed up to the wall and put his hands up like an obedient bad guy.

"You wouldn't shoot me, old man," Scar sneered, more confident than he had a right to be.

"You willin' to bet your life on that? Sure hope you're a lucky man."

"That old pistol probably doesn't even work."

Tyb aimed for Scar's face this time and I noticed, as I was sure Scar did, that his hand wasn't really that shaky. "I reckon I could try 'er out, if you want to find out fer sure."

"You're crazy, you old coot." Whatever courage the beer had given Scar had evaporated in the face of Tyb's determination.

"That I am. Crazy as a spring steer on jimson weed." He waved the gun menacingly. "I'm so crazy I'd just as soon shoot you both as spit in your eye. Now git down there on the floor, both of you. Move or even think about somethin' I wouldn't like, and I'll plug you. Good riddance."

Scar fell to his knees. Tattoo had dropped like a stone at the first recommendation.

"You can't get us both, old man." Scar pushed his luck.

"No, I can't," Tyb said amiably enough. "Do you really want to find out which one I'll go for?"

"Dammit, shut up, you fool," Tattoo snapped from his belly-down position on the floor. "I didn't get in this to have my brains blown out."

Having recovered sufficiently to take action, Aunt Nora used Tyb's pocketknife to cut the rope in half and bound up the would-be kidnappers. She and I shoved them into the shower stall.

"If you two varmints know what's good for you, you'll grab a little nap." Tyb continued to point the gun at them. "I reckon the ranger will be by directly."

Visibly shaken, Aunt Nora yanked the plastic curtain shut and put her arm around me. We all hurried outside. Tyb reached into the pickup, removed the key from the ignition and flung it as far as he could into the darkness. Even if Scar and Tattoo got loose, they wouldn't get far on foot.

23

Getting Out of Dodge

Back in camp, Aunt Nora woke Buddy and ordered us to start packing. Her voice shook as badly as her body.

"What about them two yahoos?" Tyb nodded in the direction of the restroom.

"May they rot in hell."

"That's a good plan for later, but oughten we to stop at the ranger station and report 'em for what they done?" Tyb said reasonably.

"No." Aunt Nora rolled up sleeping bags like she was killing snakes. "Remember what happened last time we asked for help? I won't risk having you picked up again, Tyb. Let's just get as far away from here as we can."

"The law needs to know what those idjits was up to, Miss Nora."

"They made some threats. They scared us. You stopped them before anything worse could happen, and I thank you."

"What if they try something like that with another girl?" I definitely placed Scar and Tattoo in the dangerous men category.

"Right." Aunt Nora thought hard. "Okay. I'll call the ranger station from a pay phone as soon as we're out of range. I don't want to stay here another minute. I want to go home."

"What about Utah?" I asked.

"Utah?" She frowned like the word was a new one on her.

"You've been saying how we're going to Zion National Park next," I reminded.

"No. Not anymore. Forget it. I want to go home. I want all of us to go home. Can't we just go?" She collapsed on the picnic table bench and bawled, head in her hands, shoulders shaking.

The sight of her froze me in place. I'd seen my mother succumb to tears and despair. Was that happening to Aunt Nora? Would she snap out of whatever mood she was in, or was this how things would be from here on out? Like Mama, maybe my aunt had two sides, and we were finally seeing what happened when the bad side took over. The idea that Aunt Nora might suffer the same moods as my mother scared the bejeebers out of me.

I wanted to throw myself into her arms and tell her everything would be all right, but I couldn't move. I wanted to tell her not to cry, but I couldn't speak. Buddy stood by the tent, clutching Puppy, his eyes wide with questions he didn't have the words to ask.

Tyb patted Aunt Nora on the shoulder. "Whatever you say, Miss Nora. We'll skedaddle out of here right now if that's what we need to do. You kids take that tent down. Get to loadin' up. No lollygagging now. Shake a leg."

I was relieved to have something to do, and someone to tell me to do it. Though she'd come through for me in the restroom, Aunt Nora's meltdown raised a question regarding her reliability. Buddy and I went to work, and fifteen minutes later everything was loaded. It was not the first time we had scrammed in the middle of the night.

"You up to drivin', Miss Nora?" Tyb asked.

She swiped the back of her hand across her nose. "Yeah, yeah, sure. I can drive. That's all I *can* do."

"Then let's hit the trail." Tyb tossed his pack into the trunk and slammed the lid.

We took our accustomed places and lit out like we'd robbed a bank. I kept looking over at Aunt Nora, whose only purpose in life seemed to be keeping the car on the road. I had a million questions to ask, but every time I opened my mouth, she said, "Please, Pauly, not now. I don't feel like talking."

By the time we reached the highway, Buddy was asleep. That was another thing I envied about little kids. They could sleep through hailstorms. Sleep was the ultimate form of escape, but I wouldn't be dozing off anytime soon. I was wound tight as a cheap toy and might snap any minute.

Tyb was breathing hard in the backseat. I figured he was awake and keeping quiet. Aunt Nora's reaction had probably startled him as much as it had me. I watched her closely in the green glow from the dashboard, looking for signs that she was cracking up. She never looked my way. She kept her eyes on the night road, staring at the blacktop and driving like hell was out for noon. She puffed one cigarette after another, her hands shaking so bad when she lit up that I had to take over the job.

I waited for her to come back to earth, to say something, anything, but she just gripped the steering wheel and ignored everything else, including speed limits. I couldn't stand all the quiet, so I turned around in the seat and asked Tyb the question any reasonable person would want answered.

"Where'd you get the gun?"

"Recollect me tellin' you how my quilt was one of the only things I had left of my family?"

"Yeah."

"Well, that old Colt was t'other thing. It belonged to my grand-pappy. It's over a hundred years old."

"Does it work?"

"Nah. The firin' pin's been busted for years. I keep it out of senti-ment."

I looked over at Aunt Nora to see how she had received that bit of news. Didn't she appreciate the humor? A wobbly old man had bluffed his way out of a tight spot with a piece-a-junk pistol. Aunt Nora was intent on driving and smoking and acted like she hadn't even heard.

Tyb was wheezing again. I asked him if he was all right.

"Don't worry about me none. I jest got ahead of my breath."

I must have slept after a while, because when I woke up the sun was streaking pink across the horizon and we had parked at a roadside rest stop. The air was cool, and birds chirped morning songs in the trees. For a moment, I thought I had dreamed the whole Scar and Tattoo in-cident. I hoped it was the scariest nightmare I would ever have.

Then I saw Aunt Nora sitting in the middle of a picnic table with her arms wrapped around her drawn-up legs. She held Puppy's leash and he sniffed the ground looking for a place to pee.

The terror came crashing back. Last night had really happened. Scar and Tattoo had tried to kidnap me, and Aunt Nora had begged them to take her instead, and now she was in a bubble by herself. This time I couldn't make everything right. I couldn't be the voice of reason because I didn't know what reason was.

Tyb snored in the backseat, and Buddy slept soundly beside him. I had no idea how far we'd gone, but at least we were closer to California. It was early and there weren't many cars on the road, but every once in a while a big truck rumbled by on its way to deliver canned goods or flammable liquids.

Aunt Nora stared far away at nothing. Why was she still so upset? We were okay. We would never see Scar or Tattoo again. As terrible as the night had been, it was over. The sun was almost up. I couldn't stand it if Aunt Nora never laughed or joked around again. What if she'd slipped into a pit of unhappiness like those that had consumed my mother? This time, there was no determined Johnny around to drag her back to the world of the living.

The car's ashtray was running over with smelly butts. I dumped them in the yellow trash can. Aunt Nora looked up when she heard the car door shut, and I winced. A bruise had blossomed on her left cheek like a blood rose. Her eye was swollen, too, narrowed into a slit. Scar had hurt her. Maybe that's why she was so sad, why she'd cried so much.

"Aunt Nora?"

"Yes, Pauly?" Her voice scratched with every one of the cigarettes she had smoked.

"Are you okay?"

"I will be."

"Does your face hurt?"

"Not too much."

"Where are we?" I looked around at the tall grass and scattered junipers and the blue mountain in the distance.

"I have no idea."

"Are we still in Arizona?"

"Nevada, maybe?"

"Is that the road to California?"

"I hope so." She stared down the road, never looking at me at all.

"When will we get there?"

"I don't know."

"You must be awful tired."

"I am."

She sounded distant and hollow, like she was sitting at the bottom of a well. She didn't smile and her eyes were red. I sat on the table beside her, and hoped the warmth of my body would draw the chill from her heart.

"Everything's all right now, Aunt Nora. None of the bad men can find us."

She made a croaking sound, a laugh choked by a sob. "You shouldn't be comforting me. I'm supposed to be the official designated guardian."

"It's okay."

"I promised to take care of you and look what happened!"

"You *did* take care of me," I insisted. "You fought Scar and Tattoo."

"Who?" She squinted, one eyebrow cocked in question.

"The bad guys. Scar and Tattoo."

She shook her head and a tear squeezed out of her puffy eye. "I'm sorry, Pauly. I don't deserve you."

"You would have gone in my place. You would have saved me if Tyb hadn't showed up."

"I was so scared." Her words released a freshet of pain. "As soon as I saw those creeps standing there, I knew something terrible would happen and there wasn't a damn thing I could do."

"It wasn't your fault," I assured her.

"I've never been in a mess like that. I've always been able to handle myself. I would have kicked and run, but there you were, looking to me for help, expecting me to do something. It was my job to protect you."

"You *did* protect me." She had just described how I'd felt when Mama and Pop died and Buddy had become my responsibility. Being in charge wasn't always fun.

"I've never had anyone who depended on me before. Now I have you and Buddy, and I don't know if I can do it."

I panicked. Had she changed her mind? Like Nanny Tee, had she decided we would be too much trouble?

"I'll look after Buddy." I tried to take the pressure off. "I always have. Most times I can take care of myself too. I froze back there, but only because those men were so scary. I've stood up to plenty of kids bigger than me. I promise we won't cause any more problems."

She gripped my shoulders. "Oh, Pauly! Do you think I'm worried about *you* causing *me* trouble?"

"Aren't you?"

"God, no. I'm afraid I'm not good enough for you and Buddy. I'm afraid I'm not cut out to be a parent."

"You took care of me when I was a baby. You changed my diapers and held my bottle in the middle of the night."

"That was kid stuff, playing house. It wasn't real. This is forever. What if something else happens? What if next time Tyb isn't there to bail me out? What if I fail and something bad hurts you or Buddy?"

"You don't have to do everything right all the time," I told her. "Just do *some* things right, *part* of the time."

"I don't think I can handle the responsibility. God, I'm such a coward."

I'd never heard a grown-up admit that before. Warming her up wasn't working. She still felt cold. "Remember what you told me that day at the washhouse about growing up? About how there would be changes, but I shouldn't be afraid of them?"

"Yes."

"Maybe you shouldn't be afraid either. You said we could get through things if we stuck together."

"I remember."

"I've been holding on to that."

"You have?"

I nodded. "Things aren't so hard when you can share them. I counted on us being together, a fam...a team." Maybe the idea of family was too much for her. "One for all and all for one. Remember?"

She wrapped her arms around me and hugged me so tight I felt the ice inside her start to break up like a spring thaw. Drawing a deep breath, she wiped away her tears. "I always knew you were a smart girl, Pauly, but I had no idea what a joy you would be. Johnny and Gracie would be very proud of you."

"So . . . are we a team?"

"You're sure you still want me?"

I pressed my face against her shoulder. "One hundred percent positive."

"You're the best part of Johnny and Gracie, Pauly. I love you," she whispered.

I love you was so easy to say. Why hadn't I said those three words to Mama and Pop? Why hadn't they said them to me? Why had Nanny Tee held back when we left? Going would have been easier if she'd said those three words.

When push came to shove, love was the only thing we could give each other. I would never withhold love. From here on out, anyone I loved would know it.

"I love you, too, Aunt Nora." My eyes watered from relief and happiness. "I love Buddy, and I love Tyb."

"So do I."

I grinned. "I even love Puppy." I made kissy noises and the little dog perked up at the end of his tether, his head cocked to one side as if he had followed the whole conversation. He responded with an "I love you" yip that made us laugh.

Aunt Nora drew me into her bubble and held me there. "You know what? So do I. Puppy was part of the posse. While you were asleep, Tyb told me Puppy woke him up last night to let him know we were gone. That's why Tyb came looking for us."

"Puppy, you're my hero." I laughed when the dog stood on his hind legs and danced in a circle like a ballerina.

Everything was all right. Aunt Nora hadn't changed her mind. She had derailed temporarily, but she was back on track. We'd gone through one of those rituals of fire that I'd read about in *National Geographic*, coming out of it older and wiser on the other side. I wasn't sure how things would work out, but I finally believed they would.

In time.

Time was all we had. Days and weeks and years to be together. Time to understand and care and rebuild our lives. Time to create something worth passing on to the next generation. A legacy of love that would outlast us.

Aunt Nora needed me as much as I needed her. Fate had set us on a path we would travel together. Because alone just wasn't any fun. Side by side, we sat at a rest stop in the middle of nowhere and watched the sun come up on a new day.

Heart to Heart

A few hours later, we pulled into a truck stop near Needles, California. Aunt Nora announced she needed coffee bad and did anyone want anything to eat? She hadn't had a wink of sleep and her eyes were red-rimmed and dry behind her sunglasses. Before going inside, she dug out her makeup kit and dabbed pancake foundation over the bruise on her cheekbone.

We crowded into a booth, and it occurred to me how much of the Trip had been spent in diners. Even in the middle of a life-and-death situation, people had to eat. Tyb was breathing hard, like he'd been hiking a hilly trail instead of riding in the backseat. His hand was swollen when he reached for his water glass, his fingers as puffy as sausages.

He claimed his only problem was sitting still so long and he'd be fine once he was up and moving around. Aunt Nora chain-smoked Pall Malls and gulped coffee, signaling the waitress for refills before she hit bottom. She stirred around the food on her plate but didn't eat much.

"Are we going to U-U-Utah?" Buddy was slow on the uptake.

"No," Aunt Nora said.

"Where *are* we going?"

"Home."

"Why d-did we l-l-leave in such a hurry last night?"

"Because we did, that's why." I kicked him under the table.

"Wh-wh-what happened?"

"Nothing you need to know about." Aunt Nora and I had agreed not to discuss our own brush with a fate worse than death. Buddy didn't need to have scars and tattoos added to the list of things he was scared of.

Tyb had hardly touched his plate of pancakes. He was still breathing hard.

"Are you all right?" I asked him. "You don't look so good."

"I always was an ugly old cuss. I'll be right as rain. Just a little tuckered out is all."

His face was pale and shiny with sweat, even though the café's air conditioner was running full blast.

"Everybody ready to go?" Aunt Nora stood and picked up the check. "I'd like to get back on the road so we can make L.A. today."

"Is the v-v-vacation over?" Buddy asked.

She nodded. "It's over. I think what we all need is to get home."

Home.

I was ready. Our talk at the rest stop had convinced me that three generations of strangers could make a life together.

There was no question of using the air conditioner on this final leg of our journey. The midday sun in the Mojave Desert was relentless. The radio played popular songs as we streaked across the desert landscape, but no one felt like singing along.

"I . . . see . . . some . . . sand," Buddy said slowly to no one in particular. "I . . . see . . . the . . . sky."

"What in the name of sweet Jesus are you doing?" I asked after several minutes of his verbal accounting.

"I'm p-p-practicing. Tyb . . . said . . . if . . . I . . . talk slow . . . I can . . . get . . . the . . . words . . . right. See! It . . . works!"

"Great, Buddy. But . . . talk . . . ing . . . real . . . slow . . . sounds . . . pretty . . . weird."

"I k-know. That's . . . why . . . I'm . . . practicing." He went back to announcing what he saw out the window, tending to repeat himself due to the emptiness of the terrain. After a while, I noticed that he spoke with shorter pauses between words. Maybe Tyb's strange brand of speech therapy was working.

The old man still didn't look so good. His breath was wheezy, his hands still swollen. Even his eyelids were puffy. In general, he resembled an overinflated pool floatie. His head was tipped back on the seat, and he appeared to be sleeping.

"Aunt Nora? There's something wrong with Tyb."

She took her eyes off the road to glance my way. "What do you mean?"

"Have you looked at him lately? He's puffed up. And breathing funny, too."

She checked the rearview mirror. What she saw must have alarmed her, because she pulled over on the side of the road. She climbed out, tipped her seat forward and leaned in. "Tyb." She shook his shoulder, gently at first and then more forcefully. "Tyb, wake up."

"What is it, Miss Nora?" His voice was ragged with effort, and his eyes didn't open all the way.

"How do you feel?"

"Like the dogs has had me under the house, I fear."

His lips were dry and I asked if he needed a drink of water. His answer was a spasm of coughing and more rattling breaths. Aunt Nora looked worried when I passed her the blue water jug.

"We need to get you to a doctor, Tyb." She held the container so he could take a sip.

"No, ma'am. I don't want no more doctors," he rasped. "They'll send me back to Texas."

"But you're sick. Something is wrong and you need medical attention."

"I'll be all right. Don't worry about me none."

"You're having trouble breathing," she said. "And your hands are swollen."

"It'll pass directly," he assured her.

"Has this happened before?"

"A few times. Don't usually last this long, though." He shivered and his whole body shook.

Aunt Nora felt his head. "You're burning up with fever. You need a doctor."

He would have protested if he could have rallied the strength to do so.

"Pauly, get Tyb's quilt out of the trunk and help me cover him up."

After we tucked the quilt around him, Aunt Nora climbed behind the wheel and turned down the air conditioner. We had passed Barstow a while back and she estimated that if she floored it, we would be in Los Angeles in a couple of hours.

I looked at Tyb huddled in the backseat. "What's wrong with him?"

"I don't know." Her knuckles were white on the steering wheel.

"Will he be all right?"

"I don't know. I'm not a nurse."

"Is he going to die?"

"Dammit, Pauly! I told you I don't know. I don't know anything.

Okay? I can't even take care of myself and now I have three people depending on me. I don't know what to do."

"I've been thinking. Maybe we should give the hospital a fake name for Tyb. That way, they can't call his son."

"Good idea. What name did you have in mind?"

"Maybe Joe wouldn't mind if we used his."

"Probably not, but he may need to use it himself someday."

Right. If he came back into our lives, it wouldn't do to have two Joe Hattons in the same family. "Remember when Tyb saved us from Scar and Tattoo?"

"I'll never forget."

"He was as brave as Duke Wayne *and* Gary Cooper."

She smiled. "He was, wasn't he?"

"How about we call him Duke Cooper?"

"That has a nice ring to it. Duke Cooper it is." She pressed her lips in a grim line and drove to race the devil. I kept my fingers crossed. It wouldn't pay to run into a state trooper as we flew across the desert.

Buddy stopped practicing slow talk and thumbed through a picture book with Puppy curled beside him, his head in Buddy's lap. It was lucky neither of them had expressed a need to stop and pee, because the way Aunt Nora was going hell-bent for election, it was doubtful she would have slowed down for number two.

"How's he doing?" she asked from time to time.

"About the same." I explained his new identity to him, and he seemed to understand.

I wasn't big on praying. Coming from a family of heathens, we only said grace over our food at Christmas, Thanksgiving, and Easter. I had very little experience asking God for anything. In fact, since the Crazy Snake, I'd been pretty disappointed with Him in general. Still, I prayed for Tyb. God might not think I deserved an answer, but I didn't want the old man to die. The way he looked and sounded, death seemed like the next thing on the program.

I closed my eyes and folded my hands in my lap and silently beseeched God to look down from heaven and help Tyb hold on until we got him to a hospital. I didn't think I should hope for a miracle cure, in case He thought that was asking too much. I'd only known Tyb a short time, but he was part of my life, even more than Nanny Tee, who I'd known since I was born. That page was turned now, and Nanny Tee lived in the past. Tyb lived in the future.

As far as we knew, the old man didn't have anyone except the ungrateful son who had put him away. His family home was lost to him and all he had to show for seventy-two years on earth was an old quilt, a froze-up pistol, and a dog that had thrown him over for a younger, more energetic master. Seeing as how Tyb had so little, maybe fate had provided Aunt Nora to drive him to the help he needed.

And me to pray we wouldn't be too late.

The Skylark screeched up to the emergency entrance and Aunt Nora leaped out hollering, "Get a stretcher out here fast!" Two men in white and a nurse lifted Tyb out of the car and onto a gurney. The nurse handed me the quilt, and they wheeled him away down a long corridor.

Aunt Nora admitted him under the name Duke Cooper and told the woman at the front desk that she would be responsible for the bill. We sat on green plastic chairs, doing what the area was designed for, waiting. At dusk the streetlights flickered on, and for the first time I noticed we were in Los Angeles.

I'd been so worried about Tyb, who was gasping and looking blue around the lips, that I hadn't paid attention to my surroundings. I can't say much about my first impression except that the hospital was clean and modern and seemed to be staffed with people ready to help. Outside were more cars and people than I'd ever seen.

We sat in the waiting room so long Buddy had to go to the bathroom three times. Aunt Nora found a snack bar and bought us pimento cheese sandwiches for supper. When she asked the lady at the front desk to check on Tyb, the lady told her the doctor would be out to talk to us when he had something to report.

The walking wounded came and went down the hall, people in various stages of disrepair. Some bloodied and broken, some who had to be carried, and some who could move under their own steam. I had never witnessed so much crying and moaning and praying. Next time you find yourself wallowing in self-pity, try sitting in a hospital emergency room for a while. If that won't snap you out of it, nothing will.

There weren't many others around, so Buddy and I shared a couch, wrapped in Tyb's quilt. Aunt Nora paced the floor, puffing on Pall Malls like she had in Nanny Tee's bedroom the day of the funeral. Pacing and puffing was what she did when she was worried or thinking hard about something. Every now and then, she'd glare at the desk lady, who shuffled papers and ignored her.

"Aunt Nora?" I caught her on one of her circuits around the room. "Why don't you sit down? You must be awful tired from driving." What would we do if she collapsed?

She sank onto a chair without a word, lighting another coffin nail off the butt of the one she had going. For a moment, she had a cigarette in each hand.

"Aunt Nora? Don't you want to put that one out?"

"What?"

I nodded pointedly at her hands, and she shook her head absently before stubbing the butt out.

"What do you think is happening?" I asked.

"I don't know."

"Tyb's been in there a long time. Is that a good sign, do you think?"

"It must be. I'm sure the doctors are doing everything they can to help him."

I asked the question we'd all been dreading. "What if he dies?"

"He's not going to die."

I didn't know where she got her information, but I wanted to believe it. I stroked a velvet piece on the quilt and traced the faded red embroidery with my finger. Since God had been good enough to answer my previous prayer, I thought I'd take a stab at beseeching him to save Tyb so the old fellow could see the ocean and pick an orange, which was the reason he'd headed for California in the first place.

A short, thin man in a white coat appeared in the door of the waiting room. He wore a stethoscope around his neck.

"Cooper?" he asked the room.

Aunt Nora jumped to her feet. "Yes?"

"Are you with Mr. Cooper?"

"Yes, we are."

The doctor introduced himself. He was a cardiologist. I didn't know what that was, but it sounded important. The doctor pinched the spot between his eyes. "He's resting comfortably now."

"What happened?" Aunt Nora asked.

"With no history to go on, it's hard to say just how long he's had a heart condition, but I'd guess it's been some time."

"So it was his heart?"

"Atherosclerosis. Hardening of the coronary arteries."

"What caused it?"

"Age mostly. I'd say Mr. Cooper has been suffering from chronic congestive failure for a while now. In some patients it can be a slow, insidious process."

Aunt Nora swallowed hard. "What brought on the attack?"

"Could have been any number of things. Has he been under any emotional or physical stress recently?"

Aunt Nora and I exchanged glances. Rescuing us from would-be rapist-kidnappers surely qualified in the stress department. Aunt Nora's voice was soft. "Yes, he has."

"Well, that could have caused it. Good news is, I don't think his heart disease is intractable. With treatment, he should recover."

"Thank God." I hadn't said much so far, but I figured He deserved my appreciation.

"What kind of treatment?" Aunt Nora asked.

"I've put him on medication to reduce the edema. His extremities were swollen due to fluid retention. I've also given him something to lower his blood pressure. Pneumonia is always a concern, but his chest X-ray was clear."

"What about the fever?" she asked.

"Temp's normal now. Once Mr. Cooper is up and around, a program of mild exercise, such as walking, will increase his strength and stamina."

"Thank you, Doctor. How long will he need to stay?"

"A week or so. Afterward, I want to see him in my office regularly. We need to keep an eye on him to try and prevent future problems."

"Yes, sir."

The doctor smiled. "I gather Mr. Cooper doesn't have the highest regard for those of us in the medical profession."

"He can be pretty stubborn," Aunt Nora admitted.

"He'll need someone to make sure he takes his medication and complies with orders."

"We can do that," Aunt Nora assured him.

"When he's ready to go home, I'll discharge him to your care."

"Can we see him?"

"He's on his way to the second floor. Go on up and ask at the nurses' station."

"Thank you again, Doctor."

The head nurse on the second floor was a middle-aged woman with dyed black hair tucked up in a bun under a starched white cap. Her name tag said she was Mrs. Ramsey. Guarding her Patients, with a capital *P*, like a mother wolverine, she questioned our intentions and assured us that Mr. Cooper needed peace and quiet.

"We just want to see him for a moment," Aunt Nora explained. "To let him know we're here and that everything will be all right."

Aunt Nora's charm didn't seem to work as well on women as it did on men. "No children under twelve allowed in Patient rooms," she said firmly.

"I'm thirteen," I informed her.

"If you're thirteen, I'm twenty-one. No kids allowed. Rules are rules."

"We want to give him this." I held out the quilt.

"You can't leave that with the Patient." She made a face like she'd just smelled a dog fart. "It's not sanitary."

"Please, Nurse," Aunt Nora said. "He's an old man and he's scared to death. We just want to go in for a few minutes to reassure him."

"I don't suppose *he's* over twelve?" The nurse leveled an accusing finger at Buddy.

Buddy stood up straight and tall. "Twelve last week."

"We're small for our age," I put in. "Hereditary anomaly."

"The doctor said it was all right," Aunt Nora tried.

"Only immediate family gets in to see heart Patients. Are you family?"

The three of us spoke simultaneously. "Yes."

Stepping aside, Nurse Ramsey fired a final warning. "Do not upset my Patient, or I will run you out of here."

Tyb was laid up in a big bed with machines all around. An IV line ran from a bag of clear liquid into his arm via a needle taped in the crook of his elbow. He was still pale, but his lips were pink again and he was breathing easier.

"You come to bail the Duke out of this place?" he asked with a weak grin.

"Not yet," Aunt Nora answered. "You need to stay here for a few days."

"I druther not."

Aunt Nora held his hand. "You have to stay until the doctor says you're ready to go home."

"Pshaw! Fool doctors! What do they know—"

"Dr. Martin is a heart specialist. He knows what he's doing. Calm down. It's not good for you to get worked up."

"Specialist? I can't afford no specialist."

"Don't worry about the bill."

"I won't have you payin' my debts, Miss Nora. It was a nice thing you did, picking me up off the road and all, but you can't be taking me to raise."

She smiled. "I can't afford not to. Do you think these two would let me do otherwise?"

I sidled up to the bed. "Get well, Tyb, so we can go see the ocean together."

"Yeah, Tyb." Buddy laid his hand on the blanket. "Get well."

Tears welled up in his eyes. "I got lucky the day y'all drove into my life."

"We all did," Aunt Nora said gently.

"I brought your quilt to you," I said. "But that mean old nurse said I can't leave it 'cause it's not sanitary."

Tyb's chuckle was as dry and crackly as the pages of a family Bible. "She may be right about that. You keep it for me, Pauly. I trust you to take good care of my quilt until I bust out of here."

"Yes, sir, I'd be honored."

"Buddy?"

"Yes, Tyb?"

"I'm counting on you to mind Puppy for me. He's a spry rascal and liable to get into a spate of mischief if you don't keep a firm hand."

"I will, Tyb."

"And Buddy? You're doing good, pardner. Keep up those exercises."

"I've been . . . walking without my brace . . . all day."

"Good for you. Both of you mind your aunt Nora and be a credit to your folks."

We promised to make Nan and Bert Bobbsey look like juvenile delinquents.

"Miss Nora, everything I was savin' for my old age was tied up in that ranch, and you know the story on that."

"Please, Tyb, don't worry about a thing. We'll figure out something."

He cleared his throat. "I'm willing to go to a rest home. That no-good son of mine can pay for it, I reckon."

"Don't even think about that," Aunt Nora scolded gently. "Nobody in this family is going to a rest home."

And I knew none of us would ever be alone again. We *were* a family. Made, not born. You couldn't pick your relatives. They were assigned to you at birth whether they liked the idea or not. Whether they liked *you* or not.

But a family was different. You *could* pick who you lived with, who you counted on, who you loved. Family was not the people connected to you by marriage and blood. Family was the door that never closed. The light that never went out. Family rescued you in your darkest hour.

My Mahoney and Teegarden relatives didn't want to be part of our lives. Aunt Nora, Tyb, Buddy and I had chosen to be together. We shared a heart tie that could not be broken.

Maybe Tyb understood the connection too, because his thin shoulders shook and fat tears dropped down on Nurse Ramsey's starched white sheets. "Y'all been good to me. Better'n my own people. And you don't hardly know me from Adam."

"We know you, Tyb," I insisted. "We're saving you a place."

"Just get well," Aunt Nora said. "Everything else will work itself out."

The door opened on Nurse Ramsey's disapproving face. She fussed with the IV and shooed us out. "Time's up, folks."

I squeezed Tyb's hand. "As soon as you get out of here, we'll go for that walk on the beach. And when the oranges get ripe, we'll find some to pick. Won't we, Aunt Nora?"

"We sure will." She smiled at Tyb. "What do you say? Is it a date?"

"Been a long time since I had myself a date." Tyb's gnarly fingers worried the blanket that covered him. "Ain't no way I'm gonna miss that one."

"Everybody out. Now!" Looking impatient, Nurse Ramsey held the door.

"Bye, Tyb. We'll see you real soon," I called back to him.

"I hope so. Oh, I surely hope so."

No Place like Home

"This is your new home. Living room, of course, and the kitchen is through there." Aunt Nora gave Buddy and me a tour of her apartment, which took up the whole ground floor of Palm Canyon Villa. The pink Spanish-style stucco with iron balconies and arched windows was grander than anything my imagination could have dreamed up.

"There are four bedrooms," she said, "so you can each have your own room, and we can fix one up for Tyb."

"This place is bigger than our last three houses put together," I marveled. What did she do with all this space?

"When Chick and I bought the building, we knocked down walls and made one apartment out of four. There are four small apartments upstairs, all leased. You'll meet our neighbors later."

Buddy and I walked around the sun-filled rooms, gawking like we were in a museum. The ceilings were twelve feet high and the wood floors shined like mirrors. Colorful paintings of birds and flowers hung on the white walls. The modern furniture was nicer than anything I'd ever seen, even in catalogs, and the sectional sofa had built-in end tables. Tall front windows looked out on a quiet tree-lined street, where old people watered flower beds and young mothers in short shorts pushed babies in strollers. At the back of the apartment, the ocean was visible through the dining room's glass-paned doors.

"You own the whole building?" I asked.

She nodded and led us down the hall. "And a few others too. My second husband got me interested in buying and selling property. There was a real estate boom after the war. We figured when the soldiers came home, they'd get busy raising children and would need places to live."

I gasped. "That makes you a landlord."

"Right." She opened a door and we stepped into a pretty yellow bedroom. The furniture was white and gold. A ruffled spread covered the full-size bed. "What do you think, Pauly? This will be your room."

"It's beautiful." And it was. There were shelves for books, and a small desk by the window where I could sit and watch the ocean.

"Come on, I'll show you Buddy's room." Aunt Nora opened a door across the hall. "The twin beds will come in handy when you have friends sleep over," she told him. She sounded so sure he would make friends and made me believe it too.

I grappled with the bombshell she'd just dropped. "Wait a minute. How can you be a landlord? Landlords are mean."

She laughed. "Where did you get that idea?"

"Well, personal experience for one thing."

Aunt Nora showed us the room that would be Tyb's. She used it for storage, but said we would have time to fix it up while he was in the hospital. "There's no furniture in here, so you kids will have to help me pick some out."

When we reached the big kitchen with its bright tiles and fancy appliances, she poured Coca-Cola over ice and gave us each a glass.

"Let me get this straight." I took an appreciative sip of my refreshment. "So are you saying you're mostly a landlord? Is that where your money comes from?"

"You didn't think I bought this place on a bit player's salary, did you?" She took a drink of her cola. "I started with one old apartment house eight years ago. Cleaned it up, slapped some paint on it, and made enough from rentals to pay off the mortgage in a couple of years.

"I figured I could save money on real estate commissions if I got a license and handled the sales myself. Now a lot of my business comes from contacts I made in the movie business."

So *that's* what she was. Real estate agent to the stars.

I caught Buddy's eye, and we started laughing. We'd speculated long and hard about the source of Aunt Nora's money, and we hadn't even been warm. No racehorses. No gangsters. No counterfeit operation. No buried treasure on the beach.

She'd made her money the old-fashioned way. Through hard work. Getting in on the ground floor of a boom proved she had acumen, which is shrewdness in practical matters.

"Okay, I give up," she said. "What's so funny, you two?"

"Nothing," we said together. We laughed again, and pretty soon, Aunt Nora was laughing too. I never wanted the laughter to stop.

Lesson for life. Never underestimate a pretty face.

We cleaned out Tyb's room and the furniture store delivered the furniture we picked out. A twin bed, a brown easy chair with matching ottoman, and a small bureau. We hung his clothes in the closet and spread his granny's quilt on the bed.

"Think he'll like it?" Aunt Nora smoothed the new curtains and stepped back to admire our handiwork.

"I know he will." I straightened the painting we'd purchased from an artist peddling his work on the street. As soon as I saw it, I knew we had to have it, because the picture of a cowboy on a horse herding cattle would remind Tyb of the Rockin' B ranch.

Later that night, after Aunt Nora made good on her promise to send No Water Charlie money for Sylvester, she sat on the edge of my bed. She'd already tucked in Buddy, who was snoring like a baby buzz saw across the hall.

"Get to sleep. We have a busy day tomorrow." She stroked my hair as she had every night since we'd arrived. She leaned over and kissed my cheek. "Sleep tight. Don't let the bedbugs bite."

"Good night, Aunt Nora."

She slipped out and closed the door. Moonlight spilled through the open window, and I sat up and looked around one more time to make sure I wasn't dreaming. We'd stopped by the bus station to pick up the belongings Aunt Nora had shipped from Oklahoma. My junior microscope sat on the desk, and my butterfly collection hung on the wall over it. The books I had rescued from our house in Tulsa stood lined up on the shelves, like old friends waiting for me to visit again.

I'd placed the pictures of Mama and Pop in small frames, which stood on the nightstand beside my bed. It was too dark to see their faces, but knowing they were there made me smile. They were gone, and yet they were still with me. Would always be with me. Like my new life, this new room felt familiar because it was home.

Lesson for life: even when everything changes, some things stay the same. I was a stronger version of the girl I'd been in Oklahoma, but I was still me. Buddy was fast becoming the boy our parents had hoped he could be, but he was still my brother. I missed Mama and Pop, but I no longer cried when I thought about them. Now I could smile. Just as the preacher had promised, they were together in a better place.

And so was I. So were we all.

Beyond my window, the restless ocean rolled onto the beach in never-ending waves. I grew drowsy. Listening to the hypnotic sounds of the surf was like falling asleep with a seashell pressed to my ear. I laid my head on the pillow and closed my eyes. My room was real. It was my life that was a dream.

The morning we were to pick up Tyb, Aunt Nora and I worked in her cheery kitchen, trying to make a German chocolate cake for his welcome home party. She wasn't much better at cooking indoors than she was over a campfire, but together we got the cake in the oven. I perched on the counter, licking the batter spoon and watching her every move.

"Aunt Nora?"

"Hmmm?"

"How come you never told anybody in the family what you were doing out here?"

"I told your mama."

"You did?"

"Sure. Gracie and Johnny knew the score."

"Nobody else?"

"Nope."

"How come?"

"I guess you're old enough to hear the hard truth." Her expression was serious as she set a bowl of coconut pecan frosting on the table. Finally. She was about to reveal the secret that would explain why the Teegardens were so rough on their kin. I leaned forward expectantly.

"Pauly," she said gravely, "you come from a long line of sourpusses."

I sighed my frustration. "Tell me something I don't know."

She laughed. "If those tin-hearted Teegardens had found out I was anything but broke and hopeless, it would have ruined their day."

We talked about that, and I told her what they'd said about her being half a bubble off plumb and how some of the female relatives had called her a floozy.

That really made her laugh. "I think I'll take that as a compliment, since I am just about the unflooziest woman in Hollywood."

"They had everything wrong, didn't they?" They'd been wrong about Mama and Pop too. Wrong about Buddy and me.

"Pauly, some people in this world just love having someone to down-trod. Makes them feel better. I was happy to oblige, but that was the *only* thing I was willing to do for them."

Later, as she removed the cake pans from the oven, I told her what I'd overheard before the funeral and how upset I'd been over the family's mean-spirited comments.

"Johnny and Gracie were close at hand," she said. "They had to take a lot of guff over the years."

"So that's why you stayed out here all that time?"

She nodded and spread frosting on the first warm layer.

"Aunt Nora? Did you send us money? When Pop was out of work, I mean?"

"What makes you ask?"

"I just think you did, that's all."

She concentrated on stacking the layers together. "Well, none of that matters now, does it? What's done is done."

The back door banged open and Buddy and Puppy dashed into the kitchen.

"Thirsty!" Buddy gulped down an aluminum tumbler of water from the tap and ran out again. He'd made two friends in the neighborhood, and I loved those little California boys for treating my brother like he was one of the gang. Buddy's face was dirty, and he hadn't fretted over germs at all. Hadn't worn the leg brace either. Wouldn't even let us unpack it from the Skylark. Out of sight meant out of mind, and Buddy said if he couldn't see the brace, he didn't have to worry about it. As long as it remained locked in the trunk, his leg would continue to get stronger. He practiced his exercises every day so he could walk tall for Tyb.

Now that Buddy was in an interesting place with lots of things to look at, he practiced the "I see" drills every day. He could say whole sentences without a stumble. He was bolder in conversation too, and I figured at the rate he was going, by the time school started, the only thing different about his speech would be his Okie accent.

We brought Tyb home from the hospital that afternoon, and the first thing we did was show him the place we'd saved for him. We couldn't show him the place he had in our hearts, so the little bedroom would have to do. He stepped inside and leaned against the bureau. We watched from the doorway.

"All this for me?" He stared at the cowboy painting and swiped the back of his hand across his eyes.

"Do you like it, Tyb?" Buddy asked.

"It's the finest room I ever saw. Fit for a king."

"Or a Duke!" My comment made everyone laugh, and the warmth of belonging filled me to bursting. Tyb had decided to hang on to his alias for a while. He had said maybe someday he would write his son and let him know he was still alive and kicking.

"See, here's your bureau and here's a chair where you can put up your feet." I ran around the room pointing out the obvious. "We put your quilt on the bed, and your pistol in the drawer."

He shuffled across the polished wood floor and bounced the mattress a few times. "You fixed me up a right comfortable bunk. Nobody ever did anything half this nice for me before."

His gaze lit on the big bowl filled with oranges that we'd placed on the bedside table.

"It's too early to pick oranges around here," Aunt Nora explained. "These imported ones will have to do until the fall harvest."

He picked up an orange with his wrinkly brown hand and held it close to his nose. He inhaled deeply. "Know what that smells like to me?"

"What?" Buddy asked.

"Smells like home."

I pulled his hand. "Come on, Tyb. Let's take a walk on the beach. You still haven't seen the ocean."

By the time we got there, the sun was starting to slip toward the horizon, dripping sparkles on the water and turning the waves silver. I'd been to the beach every day, and while it was still plenty wondrous, this time I saw it through Tyb's eyes.

"Sure is big, ain't it?" Tyb gazed in awe at the horizon, where the sea met the sky. "I never seen so much water in one place. What a sight to behold."

Down the beach, men fished off the side of a long pier that stretched out over the water. Squawking gulls wheeled overhead, then dove down to scavenge from a forgotten picnic. Tourists crowded the snack stands and bait shops and strolled along the boardwalk. Handsome brown lifeguards sat atop tall stands watching swimmers splash in the surf. Nearby, three young men worked on building a giant sand castle, but they couldn't seem to keep their eyes off the girls stretched out on beach blankets in polka-dot bikinis.

"What's that feller doin' out there on that ironing board?" Tyb shaded his eyes and stared out to sea.

"That's a surfer," Aunt Nora explained. "He's riding the waves."

"Well, I'll be. And I thought ridin' a bucking bronc was hard."

"You have to take your shoes off, Tyb, to get the whole experience." I kicked off my sandals, and the others followed suit.

Tyb wiggled his pale, bony feet in the sand, and a wide smile spread across his face. "Now that is just about the best thing these old dogs have ever felt."

Buddy took Tyb's hand and led him down to the edge of the water, where the waves rolled over their feet. Wanting to show off a trick they'd been working on, Buddy tossed a stick of driftwood into the surf, and Puppy splashed after it. Tyb cheered their efforts.

After a while, he rejoined Aunt Nora and me, and we sat in the sand and watched Buddy and Puppy play tag with the waves.

"I'm glad you decided to stay with us." Aunt Nora patted Tyb's shoulder.

"I'm proud you offered," he said. "I never had me a daughter, Miss Nora, but you've been all that and more. I wouldn't be alive if it weren't for you."

"It was nothing compared to what you did for us."

No one spoke of that night at the Grand Canyon. We couldn't discuss the events that bound us together. Some memories were best forgotten.

"I have a favor to ask you, Tyb," said Aunt Nora.

"Say the word. I'll do anything I can for you."

"I have an opportunity to buy some property in the foothills up in the San Fernando Valley. Problem is, I don't want to get in over my head. I need someone with experience to help me manage the spread."

The old man scratched his stubbled jaw. "I'd like to help, but I don't know nothin' about the landlording business."

"This isn't a rental. It's an investment. The property is about an hour from here, mostly pastureland. The current owner runs a few head of cattle, and I thought it might be fun to try my hand at ranching. Small-scale, of course."

"Small-scale, you say?"

"The house is an old hacienda called Rancho Naranja."

Tyb smiled. "That's Spanish. Means orange."

"There's a small grove too. No real commercial value, but the owner claims the trees yield enough fruit to sell at the farmers' market. I'd appreciate it if you would consider being my ramrod on this venture."

Aunt Nora and Buddy and I had already visited the rancho. The papers were ready to sign. She'd found a part-time hired hand to do the heavy chores, and his wife had agreed to cook and clean in exchange for their room and board. Tyb's beloved Rockin' B was lost forever, but a new place to tend might start to fill up the empty space in his heart.

Tyb's lips trembled, and several long moments passed before they firmed up enough for him to speak. "I'd be right honored to help you, Miss Nora."

She held out her hand. "Let's shake on it, then we'll walk over to the pier and see if we can buy some fish for supper."

After we cleared the table that night, Aunt Nora cut the cake to celebrate our reunion. While she passed the dessert plates, I tapped my fork against my glass to get everyone's attention. "Lady and gentleman, Buddy has worked up a special surprise for your entertainment. Ready, maestro?"

"Ready!" Buddy stood up and cleared his throat, did a round of mi-mi-mi-mi to loosen up his throat. Then he belted out "For He's a Jolly Good Fellow" in a high, clear voice.

"Bravo!" Aunt Nora called when he was finished. Everyone applauded, and Buddy bowed like a tenor at Carnegie Hall.

That song led to others, and Buddy insisted we sing "Davy Crockett" for old times' sake. Everyone joined in on the chorus, even Puppy, who sat up on his hind legs and howled.

While we sang and laughed, talked, and ate cake, I soaked up the happiness my crazy quilt family had given me. Someday, when Joe Hatton called, we would open our circle and make room for him too. Like odd, random patches cut from different fabrics, we didn't match, but we fit together just fine. Love was the silken thread that would embroider our lives and give them meaning.

About the Author

Debrah Williamson has written professionally for twenty years and is the author or coauthor of nearly thirty novels. A native Oklahoman, she lives in Norman and teaches professional writing at the University of Oklahoma. Visit her on the Web at www.debrah williamson.com.

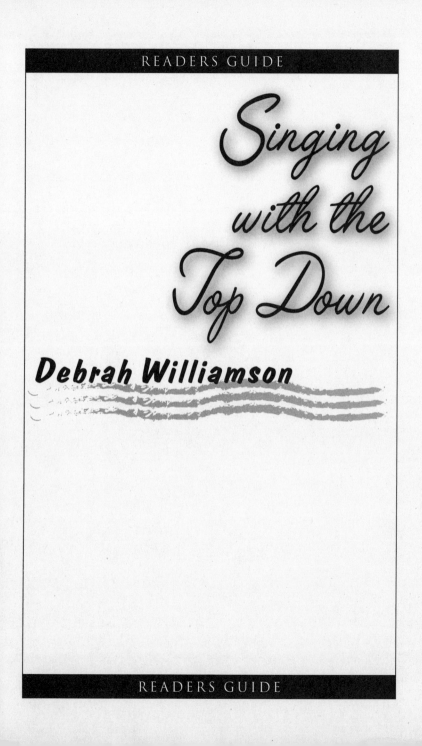

Singing with the Top Down

Debrah Williamson

A CONVERSATION WITH
DEBRAH WILLIAMSON

Q. How did you come to write Singing with the Top Down*?*
A. I rarely choose to write a story. More often, the story chooses me.
With this one, the character of Pauly came to me first. I know it
sounds strange, but she just started talking to me in a voice that was
unlike any I'd heard before. Yes, I confess. I am one of those writers
who claim to hear voices. So far, the situation has worked out quite
well for me.

I first started communing with Pauly more than twenty years
ago. She'd stop by for a chat, usually when I was busy or involved
with life or another project. I'd take enough notes to satisfy her, and
she'd go away for a while, always with the admonition: "Don't you
forget me!"

I couldn't. The time finally came when I thought I was ready to
undertake her story. I'd collaborated on more than twenty published
romance novels, so I felt I'd developed the writing skills to tackle a
bigger story. I finished the book, but Pauly wasn't happy with it, and
neither was I. Something was missing, but I couldn't figure out how
to fix the problem. I put the manuscript away, knowing I hadn't done
the character justice, but hoping the day would come when I could
try again.

I wrote five more solo romance novels, continued to study, and honed my writing skills. When Pauly visited me again, she threw a hissy fit. She stamped her foot and declared she wasn't leaving until I rewrote her book the way it was supposed to be. When I took another look at the manuscript, I realized I had gained the knowledge I needed and knew what I had to do. I rewrote the story again, and the rest, as Pauly likes to say, is history.

Q. *So is Pauly the character you identify with the most? Is she your alter ego?*
A. I probably do identify with her, but she is not me. We do have things in common, of course. As a child I also preferred escaping into books and movies. And I spent many summer hours in the backseat of the family station wagon on long car trips to national parks. But very little in Pauly's actual life experience is based on my own. She just is. Like a force of nature.

Q. *Pauly has been compared to the character of Scout Finch in* To Kill a Mockingbird. *Do you think there are similarities between the characters?*
A. Since *To Kill a Mockingbird* is one of my favorite books of all time, I am delighted by the comparison. So yes, I would like to think the two girls have something in common. Like Scout, Pauly is a keen observer of her world. She has a questing nature and is never content to accept without understanding. She always wants to know why.

That makes her a difficult child to live with, but sets the stage for her to become an enlightened adult. And like Scout, I think Pauly is equal parts spunk and heart.

Q. What other books have you loved? What authors have influenced or inspired you?
A. In general, I love Southern novels, starting with *Gone with the Wind*, which I read in the ninth grade. I also enjoy reading books with young narrators like *Ellen Foster* by Kaye Gibbons, *Peace like a River* by Leif Enger, and *Summer of the Redeemers* by Carolyn Haines. Seeing the world afresh through young eyes always renews my writing spirit.

Q. Your novel explores the complicated issue of mother-daughter relationships. Is that a theme you find yourself turning to again and again?
A. I don't choose themes in a conscious way, but I think writers tend to deal with similar issues and ideas, over and over. In several of the novels I've written, female characters do not have mothers. Or they have mothers who are emotionally distant or unsupportive.

This has never been a problem in my real life. I'm close to my mother, and I have a strong bond with my daughter. Perhaps because I do have good mother-daughter relationships, I feel compelled to work through this issue in my writing. One of the most frightening things I can imagine is maternal absence or abandonment.

Q. You incorporate themes of inevitability in the story. How have fate and destiny influenced your own life?
A. I believe there is a plan in place for everyone. The secret of life is becoming aware enough—dare I say enlightened enough—to pick up on the sometimes subtle directions we receive from the higher power. Believe me, I came late to this philosophy. When I was younger, I thought I was in the world alone, and it was up to me to steer my own ship. Thank goodness, I have since wised up.

Q. So there is a reason why Pauly's parents are killed in that freak roller-coaster accident?

A. Of course. There is always a reason for everything. And everything happens for a reason. Gracie and Johnny could have died in a car accident, but where is the surprise in that? For me, irony is an important element in fiction. So when an event intended to bring fun and relief into the characters' lives inexplicably turns into tragedy and ends those lives—well, that raises a question and makes us think.

Q. Do you plan to write a sequel to Singing with the Top Down?

A. I haven't actually planned to, but Pauly's been visiting again. She's twenty-three now and claims to have another story to tell. Maybe I'll see what she has to say.

Q. One more question. Why do you write?

A. There is no easy answer for that one. In fact, I could write an essay, or maybe even a whole book on the subject. To quote Franz Kafka: "I am a writer even when I don't write . . . and a nonwriting writer is, in fact, a monster courting insanity."

I guess I have to write. I already hear voices and can't really afford to tempt fate.

QUESTIONS
FOR DISCUSSION

1. The primary characters in the novel range in age from an eight-year-old boy to a man in his seventies. With which character do you most closely identify, and why?

2. Following the death of their parents, Pauly and Buddy's grandmother has no trouble letting them go with their aunt Nora, even though it is clear she will have little future contact with them. What do you think of Evalee's decision? Should grandparents always be responsible for their children's children, or do they have a right *not* to make the sacrifice in order to live their own lives? Why, or why not?

3. Much of Pauly's personal journey involves coming to terms with the relationship she had—or more specifically, did not have—with her deceased mother. What kind of mother-daughter relationships have you experienced or observed? Why do you think so many mother-daughter relationships are fraught with conflict?

4. The underlying catalyst that sets the story into motion is Gracie's undiagnosed and untreated mental illness. Do you know anyone who

has had to deal with a family member's illness? What impact did the illness have on others?

5. Johnny is very protective of Gracie. How is his behavior supportive? In what ways is it enabling? How could he have handled his wife's illness better?

6. A theme of rescue runs throughout the novel. Can you think of times in your own life when you rescued someone or were rescued by another? How did the act of rescuing affect your relationship with the other person?

7. Pauly is a capable, parental child. A survivor. In what way does gaining too much wisdom too soon prevent her from living a normal childhood? Were you, or was someone you know, forced by circumstances to grow up at an early age? If so, what impact did that have later in life?

8. Pauly and Buddy consider themselves outcasts. Tyb is an outcast too. And in her own way, Aunt Nora has cast herself out of her family. Do you believe these outcasts will overcome past experiences and form a happy family group? How can the taint of isolation and exclusion influence lifelong behavior?

9. How relevant do you think the time period is to the story? Could the events portrayed have taken place today? Why or why not? In what ways do the characters behave in a manner consistent with

the social atmosphere of the mid-1950s? What elements of the story are timeless and could happen in any setting or time?

10. Can you imagine a life for the characters beyond the end of the book? Where do you think they will be in five years? Ten years? Twenty years?

11. What aspect of the novel most appeals to you? What's the funniest part? The saddest? The most moving? What aspects seem most true to life? Not true?

12. Did the story end in a satisfying way? Would you like to see Joe reenter their lives? Why? What purpose does Joe fulfill within the context of the story? How could he play an important role later on?

13. Pauly believes in fate and in the power of destiny. In what ways have you seen fate at work in your own life? Do you believe in coincidence? Or, as Pauly thinks, does everything happen for a reason?